Pushing the Envelope

By Kim Dare

Pushing the Envelope
ISBN # 978-1-910081-20-4

Copyright © Kim Dare 2011

Published by Kim Dare
Edited by Christine Allen-Riley and Shannon Leeper
Cover Art by Kris Norris
Author Logo by Catherine Dair of catherinedair.com

First Edition – August 2011
Second Edition – September 2016

Dedication

To all those readers who read one of my short stories and wanted to know what happens next.

Here is Scott and Joe's story – complete with the "next".

Table of Contents

Part One: For the Attention Of

Joe Stuart pulled a crumpled envelope out of his jacket pocket and stared at the neat line of block, capital letters written across the front of it. That was definitely his name.

He glanced up at the dilapidated house he'd just driven to. It was set several yards back from the pavement, and those bits of the building that hadn't been completely consumed by ivy hinted that it had once been a magnificent old place. A fancy sign attached to the rusting, wrought iron gates proudly labelled the house, *21 Tudor Avenue*. A lopsided addition had been fastened just beneath it. *Student accommodation, very reasonable rates.*

Taking the letter out of the envelope, Joe ran his eyes over the contents once again, just in case it had changed since the previous night, when he'd found the note shoved into his locker at one of the clubs where he tended bar.

He was certainly at the right address, but the spark of recognition he'd expected to strike him was conspicuously absent. He shrugged and strode up the path anyway. The front door was propped open, so he went straight in.

Joe barely noticed the messy jumble of belongings that littered the hallway. The instructions in the letter were very specific. *Room nine. Upstairs, last door on the left.* Jogging briskly up the stairs, he headed straight to the designated room. The door marked number nine was closed. He rapped his knuckles firmly against the faded woodwork, idly wondering if he'd recognise the man who lived there.

No one immediately answered his summons. Joe frowned. He had the horrible feeling that someone was winding him up. He looked over his shoulder and down the line of doors that flanked the corridor, trying to work out what the punchline might be. Whoever had conned him out of his nice warm bed to investigate the mysterious note, they'd better hope it turned out to be bloody funny.

He knocked again.

Nothing.

No one answered his knock, no one jumped out and shouted "surprise". Not a single damn thing happened. Joe sighed. That was what he got for letting his curiosity get the better of his common sense.

Shaking his head at himself, he stepped away from the door, wondering if it was worth going home to bed or if he should try to find some other way to amuse himself until he started his next shift at the club.

Halfway along the corridor, Joe paused. For some reason, he found himself retracing his steps and trying the door handle, just on the off chance. It turned easily within his grasp. The door swung open.

Joe stared silently into the room for several seconds. The central ceiling light was on, highlighting every detail of the man lying face down on the double bed opposite the door. The guy was completely naked but for the leather cuffs wrapped around his wrists and ankles, and he was stunning.

Lean lines of pale muscle called to Joe, just

begging him to grab a whip and paint pretty lines across the pristine canvas. At the same time, a spark of possessiveness crackled through Joe. Stepping forward, he closed the door behind him and turned the key in the lock for good measure. This canvas was his. No other guys were going to be allowed to play on it until he was done.

A combination of floppy blond hair and an awkward angle obscured the bound man's face. Joe still didn't have a clue who he was about to screw. He took several steps forward. He was only three paces away from the bed when the lightning bolt of recognition finally hit him.

Scott!

The name circled around and around in Joe's head as he ran his eyes over Scott's body. Gradually, more words were added to the exclamation.

Scott.

Scott—naked.

Scott—naked and tied up.

Scott—naked, tied up, and apparently waiting for Joe to screw him.

Joe's mind came to a stop then. He wasn't sure how that scenario could get any better. Every element of his favourite fantasy was already there.

Frowning slightly, Joe tore his gaze away from Scott and looked around the room. There had to be a hidden camera somewhere. Things like this didn't happen in real life. They happened in wet-dreams and solo jack-off sessions. They happened when he failed to hook up with anyone at the club and went home alone, his mind inevitably crammed full of fantasies involving the quiet guy who lurked on the edge of his group of friends.

To hell with it. If someone was filming them, that was fine with Joe. If nothing else, it might prove to be a hellishly good souvenir of the occasion.

Joe placed his fingertips against the inside of Scott's ankle, just above the leather cuff. Scott jerked. The chains connecting his bondage to the bed-frame rattled. Joe waited, his fingers resting lightly on Scott's skin. No actual protest arrived. Joe gave Scott a few extra moments, just in case he wanted to speak up and tell him what the hell was going on.

Nothing.

It seemed that Joe had free rein. He smiled to himself as he shrugged off his leather jacket and tossed it onto a chair in the far corner of the room. That was when he saw them.

He'd been wrong to think there was nothing anyone could have added to the scenario to make it even better. Joe strode across to the chest of drawers and stared down at the row of toys some thoughtful person had laid out on top of it.

Joe glanced over his shoulder. Scott's eyes were still closed. Whatever private fantasy he was playing out, it didn't seem to include seeing the man who'd be screwing him just yet.

Joe hummed cheerfully to himself as he considered his options. Floggers, and butt-plugs, and whips, oh my! He picked up a thick wooden paddle and tested the weight of it in his hand. It was heavy — far too substantial to be used on a guy who wasn't used to getting his arse spanked very hard and on a very regular basis.

Joe studied Scott's naked form once more. Scott

had an amazing arse. His buttocks were rounded and well developed, with just a little bit of extra padding. His skin was pale—as if he'd hidden it away from the sun for years.

It was hard to believe anything had ever landed against the lean lines of muscle that decorated Scott's body. He was so perfect, so untouched—virgin territory. And, for a little while at least, he was Joe's to do with as he pleased. Damn, but the world was a bloody brilliant place on occasion.

Joe set aside the paddle and picked up a small leather flogger. The strands were soft. The impact would be light. In the hands of someone who knew what he was doing, it would be perfect.

Joe turned toward the bed.

Scott's forehead was furrowed with concentration, as if he was struggling to work out where Joe was, and what Joe was doing, without opening his eyes.

Joe flicked the leather lightly against the back of Scott's calf, right above the patch of skin he'd caressed with his fingertips. Scott lurched against his restraints. He opened his eyes.

"I was starting to think you'd fallen asleep on me," Joe teased.

So much worry flickered in Scott's eyes, Joe forgot about all the fun he'd planned to have with the flogger. He sat down on the bed next to Scott and pushed a lock of blond hair back from Scott's face.

"Second thoughts?" Joe asked, careful not to let any annoyance seep into the question.

Scott shook his head, rubbing his face against his pillow in the process. He closed his eyes once more.

Joe tightened his grip on Scott's hair and tugged until Scott opened his eyes.

"You've never struck me as a guy who makes a habit of tying himself up and offering his arse to a stranger."

Scott jerked his shoulders, as if he was so new to bondage he'd yet to work out that a man couldn't shrug properly while bound that way.

"Cat got your tongue?" Joe prompted.

A blush spread across Scott's cheeks. "That's — that's, kind of...I m-mean, that's the whole p-point."

Joe stared down at him, trying to work out what the hell that jumble of words was supposed to mean.

"You're not the easiest guy to talk to." Scott pronounced each syllable very slowly, very carefully, as if he had to focus really hard to get them out properly.

Joe didn't often find himself speechless, but for several seconds he couldn't think of a damn thing to say. Finally, he asked, "I'm not?"

Scott turned mute again. He shook his head, tugging at Joe's hold on his hair.

"I don't remember you ever..." Joe smiled. He couldn't remember Scott uttering a single word to him in all the time they'd been regulars at the same club and shared the same group of friends.

He did, however, recall Scott blushing a lot. Now that he thought about it, he recalled catching Scott staring at him more than a few times too. All the pieces clicked together inside Joe's head. "This is one hell of a way to get a man's attention, darling!"

Scott stared down at the bed sheet, uncertainty shining brightly in big blue eyes.

"Bloody effective way too," Joe admitted.

Scott glanced up for a moment. Their gazes met.

"It's safe to say I'm completely fascinated," Joe said.

Scott offered him a tentative smile.

Standing up, Joe adjusted his grip on the flogger. The toy stopped being something that just rested idly in the palm of his hand and once more became something to be used.

So, Scott had a crush on him and was too shy to just hit on him in the usual way. Joe wasn't about to complain. "Your safe word is unicorn. Understand?"

"Y-yes."

"Good." Joe managed to catch Scott's eye just before he brought the flogger down lightly against Scott's leg, an inch above where it had last landed.

Scott gasped, but there was no trace of fear in his expression. No mythical creature rushed to his lips.

Joe brought the flogger down on Scott's other ankle and set about working his way up each of his legs with perfect symmetry. He kept the touch of the leather light, more a tease than anything else. It was barely a hint towards what Scott might receive from him in the future, but it was the most he could risk. Scott was obviously a novice, and Joe didn't have that much time before he was due at work. If he was going to whip and run, he had to be careful.

Damn, but Scott really was gorgeous. His arse

clenched each time the leather fell against his skin. It was so easy for Joe to imagine being buried inside him to the hilt. He could practically feel Scott's muscles working around his shaft, trying to milk the orgasm from his cock.

A pale pink hue spread across Scott's skin as Joe drove the scene forward. It almost looked as if Scott's buttocks were embarrassed at being flogged. Or, perhaps, embarrassed at how much he liked it. A steady stream of gasps and groans filled the air between the gentle thwaps of leather against skin.

Moving up the bed, Joe aimed the flogger at Scott's arms. Keeping the strokes extra-light in deference to the thinness of the muscles there, Joe deftly spread that pretty pale blush all the way to Scott's wrists.

An especially loud moan of pleasure left Scott's lips when Joe turned his attention to Scott's back, and began to bring the flogger down just a little more heavily. No words. No stuttering. Scott arched off the mattress in a completely instinctive offering. He was begging for more, even if he wasn't conscious of it.

Joe tilted his head to one side and studied Scott's profile. There was no hint of worry there now. Scott was lost in pleasure and obviously loving every moment of it. Little by little, Joe coated Scott's back with rhythmic kisses from the flogger.

The leather strands danced across Scott's skin, keeping perfect time. The rhythm was addictive; so was the sight of Scott moving to meet each lash. Joe's pulse fell in time with his strokes. Every heartbeat sent more blood rushing to his cock. His shaft ached behind his fly, desperate to be allowed in on all the fun.

Joe rubbed the heel of his hand against his crotch as he finally set the flogger aside. As he watched, Scott's expression slowly morphed into one of complete and utter horror.

More than ready for what would come next, Joe folded his arms across his chest and waited. Several seconds passed before Scott blinked and opened his eyes.

"You—you s-stopped!" No accusation of murder could have been laced with more condemnation.

"Don't I have that right?" Joe shot back.

Scott opened his mouth, only to hesitate and close it without saying anything.

"Don't I have the right to do whatever I want with you?" Joe pushed.

With his lips pressed tightly together, as if he was struggling to hold back an argument, Scott nodded.

"Good," Joe murmured. As he ran his eyes over Scott's body, Joe absentmindedly toyed with his fly. He couldn't remember the last time such a mild scene had him so close to coming in his jeans. He didn't even realise he was massaging his cock through his clothing until he saw the way Scott was staring at his groin.

Joe stepped forward, not in the least inclined to stop playing with his cock. It felt too good to quit. It made far more sense to make the muted sensations stronger.

Scott's eyes followed Joe's every move as he undid his jeans and pushed the denim aside. There was no other fabric to get in the way, no need to get rid of boxers he hadn't bothered to put on. From the look on his face, Scott couldn't have been more surprised if he'd discovered his "date" was wearing a lacy pink thong, rather than simply going commando.

"How long have you been imagining how it will feel when I screw you?" Joe asked, keeping his tone of voice light and almost conversational.

Scott whimpered. No real words happened.

The guy had a stutter — Joe was fine with that. But not even trying to answer? "That's not good enough."

Scott looked up and met Joe's eyes for a moment, before turning his attention back to Joe's cock.

"I want a verbal answer."

Scott's Adam's apple bobbed rapidly. Joe barely held back a groan as he imagined how it would feel if Scott were deep throating him while he did that.

"For — forever," Scott finally managed to stutter out. "I've been i-i-imagining it f-f-forever."

Joe tightened his grip around his cock as pre-cum leaked from its tip and smeared along its length. "Have you ever done this before?" he asked.

Scott jerked his gaze up to Joe's face. "I'm n-not a — I mean of c-c-course I've — "

Joe grinned. Scott was cute when he blushed. "So you've been screwed before, have you?" he translated helpfully. "You're not a virgin?"

Scott gave up on words and simply shook his head. His fringe fell into his eyes.

"But have you ever subbed to another guy,

ever been tied up?" Joe asked.

Another shake of his head.

"You've never been owned by a dominant, never promised to do as someone else said or accept the consequences?"

Scott stared longingly at Joe's cock, but made no attempt to answer, not even with a gesture.

Definitely not good enough. Joe turned his back on him.

Chains rattled, letting Joe know that Scott was pulling hard at his bonds. It was so easy for Joe to imagine Scott trying to peer around his body so he could continue to watch the show, but Joe didn't look over his shoulder to check, no matter how tempted he was.

"N—never," Scott said.

Joe didn't even try to hide his pleasure with that admission as he turned back to face Scott once more. "Perfect."

Hope shone in Scott's gaze as their eyes met. *Yes*, Joe repeated silently to himself, *completely perfect*. "You know what that means, don't you?" he asked, as he stepped closer to the bed to stare directly down at Scott.

* * * * *

Scott Evans knew he had to answer Joe if he wanted Joe to remain facing him, but it wasn't easy. He opened his mouth, but he was so nervous, all he managed to do was croak out something unintelligible. Whimpering his annoyance with himself, he shook his head and prayed that would suffice.

It might not have been a verbal answer, but it was honest. The longer he spent tied up in Joe's presence the more certain Scott was that he didn't know a damn thing about anything.

Joe was still jacking his cock, his movements slow and lazy, as if he had all the time in the world, and fully intended to spend it doing a million and one erotic things. Scott helplessly watched Joe's hand move up and down around his erection, again and again.

There was nothing half-hearted about Joe's actions now. His grip tightened. Each stroke covered his cock all the way from root to tip. Joe's jeans slid down a little as he worked his shaft, revealing large, low hanging balls covered with a dense coating of short dark hairs.

Scott licked his lips, desperate to taste Joe, to be allowed to wrap his mouth around Joe's cock and show him that he wasn't a complete novice.

Joe stepped closer to the edge of the bed. "That means," he said, leaning down until his lips almost caressed Scott's ear, "that a part of you will always belong to me. I will always be the first man you submitted to — I will always own that."

Scott turned his head, straining his neck in an effort to face Joe properly. Joe remained leaning over him. His lips were just an inch away from Scott's mouth. Maybe if Scott could twist his neck around just a little further then —

Joe pulled away just a moment too soon. A frustrated moan hit the air, and Scott knew the noise had to have come from him. Joe's grin just grew wider when he heard it. He didn't relent in the slightest. There would be no kiss.

Scott slumped back against the mattress, letting himself fall face first into the pillow as he struggled to hide his disappointment. Every inch of skin on his back still tingled from Joe's touch. It was hard for Scott to believe the flogger wasn't still dancing over his body as he closed his eyes and made a concerted effort to accept Joe's refusal to kiss him with something like good grace.

Tugging at the leather around his wrists and ankles, Scott squirmed and rubbed his erection against the mattress. His cock was so hard. He needed to come so badly. Not being kissed was the least of his troubles, really.

The sheet covering the mattress teased his shaft as he squirmed, but it wasn't enough. Scott needed more. He needed Joe's cock buried deep inside him. He needed Joe's hand wrapped around his hard-on. He needed—

A sudden flash of lightening earthed itself in Scott's right buttock. He gasped. Twisting against the mattress, he desperately tried to look over his shoulder. He was just in time to see Joe's hand leave his arse. A faint palm print was already blossoming in its wake, a darker patch of pink against the lighter blush the flogger had already painted on him.

"That's enough of that."

Scott dragged his gaze up until he reached Joe's face. Joe didn't look angry. That was good. He actually seemed amused.

Joe moved to kneel on the bed between Scott's spread legs. His jeans were bunched up around his hips. He still had his T-shirt on, though the thin material did little to hide Joe's glorious build.

Craning his neck, ignoring the way the muscles cramped across his shoulders as the cuffs pulled at his wrists, Scott watched in silence while Joe spread a generous coating of lube over his fingers.

When Joe moved his hand out of Scott's line of sight, Scott lowered his head back onto the pillow. The first slick touch against his arse made him tense. Joe made no complaint about that as he circled Scott's hole with one fingertip.

The single digit caressed the tight ring of muscle again and again. Spirals of pleasure grew inside Scott, and each twirling rope of sensation only increased the tension inside him.

"Relax for me."

It was the worst thing Joe could have said. Scott's muscles instantly knotted until each one ached from the strain. Scott doubted he'd been that tight when he'd been a virgin.

Scott closed his eyes, knowing he was screwing up his one chance with Joe, but not able to do a damn thing about it.

"That was an order, Scott. Not a suggestion."

The pressure behind Joe's fingers remained light. There was no anger in his words. They were just statements of fact, and they slipped past all of Scott's defences.

Bypassing his brain completely, the command rushed to his cock. If it was possible, he got even harder. From there, letter by letter, the words danced up and down his spine. Slowly, his body began to obey Joe's order.

Scott felt himself relaxing, one set of muscles at a time, until his hole finally welcomed Joe's finger inside him. It took Joe less than a second to find Scott's prostate. He rubbed against that sensitive little spot as if in praise for Scott following the order so well.

It was impossible to remain still and silent while Joe toyed with him that way. Scott turned his face into the pillow in an effort to disguise his moans as Joe slid a second finger inside him alongside the first.

Scott bit down on his pillow. His hips bucked. Any control he might have had over his body deserted him. Sucking in gasps of air around his pillow case, Scott helplessly tried to ride Joe's fingers.

Without warning, the pillow disappeared from beneath Scott's head. Cotton rasped against his lips as it was jerked away from him. Scott gawped in confusion as the pillow flew through the air and landed in the far corner of the room.

"I'm the only one who's allowed to gag you from now on," Joe growled. "And if I don't gag you, it's because I want to hear you."

Joe's hands came to rest on the sheet to either side of Scott's body as he leaned over him. Denim rubbed against the inside of Scott's thighs; Joe's T-shirt teased the lightly flogged skin on his back. The mattress dipped, causing the cuffs to tighten around Scott's wrists and ankles. Those sensations all became irrelevant when slicked latex brushed against Scott's hole.

"Please." Scott arched his back and pushed out his arse.

Joe's whole body pressed down against him as Joe bent his arms. Suddenly, he nipped at Scott's neck. It wasn't a kiss. Joe's lips didn't touch Scott's skin. It was nothing but a display of primitive dominance, and Scott tipped his head to one side in eager acceptance of it.

Solid muscle pinned Scott to the bed, holding him in place just as effectively as any leather bondage. Joe rubbed his cock against Scott's arse, but Scott seemed to be the only one who was in a rush to have it inside him.

"Tell me how much you want this," Joe ordered.

Panic raced through Scott's veins at the prospect of admitting any such thing, but there was no way he could have disobeyed any command from Joe while there was a chance that compliance might lead to Joe screwing him.

"N-need it," he blurted out. "Need your c-cock. N-need it in me. Now!"

Joe rocked his hips, pressing the tip of his erection more firmly against Scott's hole, teasing him without actually entering him. "Is that all you want from me?"

Scott shook his head. Another nip to his neck killed that gesture in its tracks.

Gestures weren't going to be enough to get him what he wanted. Scott needed words.

Words. *Orders. Sex. Suck. Leather. Control. Cum. Lick. Chains. Paddles. Hurt. Please. Need. Please!*

Scott offered Joe everything he could think of and, when he ran out of those things, he offered all the things he hadn't even fully admitted to himself that he wanted.

Words tumbled from Scott's tongue, but he had no idea if Joe could understand the breathless, stuttering syllables. He only paused when he ran out of air, and even then, he only intended to stop for long enough to gasp.

Joe thrust into him, lodging his cock deep inside Scott with one rough movement. Words became unnecessary. Scott screamed. The sound tore through the air, full of pleasure and relief. There were no attempts at syllables to mar the raw truth in it. If it hadn't been for the soreness in Scott's throat, he'd never have believed that he'd been the one to make the wild noise.

"Is that what you need, sweetheart?" Joe snarled into his ear.

Scott whimpered. He barely had enough free brain cells left to understand the question, let alone nod his agreement. Every other part of his mind was completely absorbed with processing the waves of ecstasy rushing through his body.

It wasn't just a hard cock and a tight hole — not all the bliss racing around his veins was coming from his cock, or even his prostate. Far more than Scott would have ever believed possible poured out from that same part of his mind that had first prompted him to surf websites that sold the kind of toys Joe had a reputation for playing with.

As Joe pulled back and thrust into Scott again, every movement was rough and unyielding. It was obvious to Scott that Joe wasn't just screwing him; he was taking possession of him.

This part of you will always belong to me…

Scott closed his eyes very tightly. His hands formed into fists above his cuffs. Some of his more intimate muscles clenched around Joe's cock. Fear swirled through Scott, mixing in with his pleasure and making his head spin. In spite of all logic, it made his cock throb, too.

The possibility of Joe simply walking away the moment he zipped up his fly, of his ownership of Scott ending before it had even started, scared the hell out of him. But Scott couldn't deny that Joe having all the power over him was as hot as any underworld could be.

Scott scraped the headboard with his fingertips as he scrambled for any sort of hold on the world. He gasped for breath as another hard thrust forced him down into the mattress. His shaft slid against the sheet each time Joe pounded into him. It was almost enough.

Joe's thrusts sped up. His hips smacked into Scott's freshly flogged arse with each deep thrust. The cuffs around Scott's ankles bit into his skin as Joe pushed him further up the bed.

"Come!" Joe lifted himself a little higher on his hands. His angle changed. Suddenly, it was enough.

Scott wasn't the only one who obeyed Joe's demand. There was less than a second between their orgasms. As Joe yelled out his pleasure above him, Scott's breath lodged in his throat, and rendered him completely mute. Pumping against the mattress as much as his restraints would allow, Scott made the most of every strand of cotton beneath him and tapped into each bit of friction to prolong his orgasm.

Wave after wave of scorching perfection raced

through Scott's body as his cum spilled between him and the mattress. His mind shut down. There was nothing in the world other than bliss. But, instead of floating through pleasure the way he so often had in the past, Scott now found himself trapped in a web of it. This time, his orgasm didn't take him gently by the hand — it grabbed him by the balls and twisted.

Scott whimpered gently as he slowly made his way back through a maze of sensations and reality reasserted itself around him.

Joe's body was still covering his, pressing down on him, making it difficult for him to take a deep breath. It was impossible for him to move, and more perfect than he'd ever known reality could be.

Every breath Joe took reverberated through Scott's torso. Scott helplessly murmured his pleasure. He was in bed with Joe. He'd just been screwed by Joe Stuart. Part of him belonged to the hottest man he'd ever set eyes on. Life was good.

Scott had no idea how many lifetimes passed before Joe began to pull away from him. All he knew was that, as their bodies separated, he'd never felt so alone or so empty in his life. He kept his eyes closed as he heard Joe moving about the room, no doubt dispensing with his condom and straightening up all those clothes he'd never got around to fully removing.

The sounds of the door to the tiny en-suite bathroom opening and closing floated across the bedroom to Scott. A moment later, something warm and wet brushed across his arse.

"What the — ?" Scott jerked away from it, as far as he was able — which wasn't very far. His cuffs rattled, but held strong.

Joe smiled as Scott peered over his shoulder at him. He moved the wet flannel over Scott's skin once more, deftly cleaning away the excess lube that had been drying against the cleft of his buttocks.

"You d-don't have to..." Scott mumbled. "I can—"

"I thought we had a deal," Joe cut in.

Scott could only blink at him in confusion. He automatically tried to turn around, but his limbs reminded him, very sternly, that there were still four pairs of cuffs keeping him firmly in place. He slumped back against the mattress.

"And the deal is that I can do whatever I want with you, and you can't do a damn thing about it." Joe sounded so bloody calm.

Scott tried to think of a response and failed. It was difficult to argue against facts he loved. He remained silent as Joe finished his self-assigned task and tossed the washcloth back into the bathroom.

There was no reason for Joe to hang around any longer. Scott knew that. He wasn't going to make a fool of himself by asking for things to be any different than they were. He closed his eyes. They'd hooked up. He'd had fun. If Joe had enjoyed it even a fraction as much as him, then maybe, just maybe, he'd want to screw again sometime?

"I'm going to go out on a limb here and guess that you're single." The mattress shifted beneath Scott's body as Joe sat down next to him and casually rested his hand on his backside.

Scott frowned. "I..." The way Joe palmed his arse made it so damn difficult to think. Scott swallowed rapidly and tried to make words happen, any words.

"Do you have a boyfriend? A friend with benefits? Is there anyone who comes into contact with your arse, your cock, or your mouth on a regular basis?" Joe prompted.

Scott shook his head.

Joe slid his fingers down between Scott's arse cheeks and stroked his hole. He was sore. Even the slightest touch was enough to send a jolt of pleasure through him after the pounding he'd just taken.

"You're sure?" Joe pushed. "I won't be pleased if I find out that you lied to me about this."

"Yeah, I'm s-sure," Scott managed to say.

"Good."

Scott wanted to lift his head and look over his shoulder, but he just didn't have the energy anymore. It was far easier to just lie there limply and let Joe play with his body in whatever way he liked. "G-good?" he echoed.

Without any warning, Joe's hand disappeared from Scott's backside.

Scott nibbled on his bottom lip. Did that mean that he wasn't good anymore? "Joe?"

Joe didn't answer him, but that didn't matter, because his hand had already returned to Scott's world. Joe's fingers brushed against Scott's left wrist.

Scott looked up and watched Joe deftly undo the buckle to free him.

Scott shook his head. He didn't want to be free. But explaining that there was no reason for Joe to untie him, that he could easily undo the safety releases on the cuffs after Joe left, involved far too many words that would make him stutter.

Long before Scott managed to get a word out, Joe had undone the cuff attached to Scott's right ankle as well. A second later, Scott's left ankle had been released from the rail at the bottom of his bed too.

"Roll over."

When Scott didn't immediately do as he was told, Joe nudged him pointedly in the ribs. As desperate to please Joe as ever, Scott managed to make his limbs work, after a fashion. He twisted around until he was finally on his back. His left wrist was still fastened to the head-board and he wasn't sure if he was allowed to release it himself.

Not ready to look Joe in the eye. Scott found himself staring at his own body. His cum had dried on his stomach. His cock had softened. Scott automatically moved his free hand to cover himself.

"No, you don't." Joe caught hold of Scott's wrist and pinned it to the bed. There was no way Scott could keep his gaze lowered then.

* * * * *

Joe slowly dragged his eyes up Scott's body until he finally reached Scott's face. He'd never seen anything so perfect. It wasn't just that Scott's body was hot, or even that Scott looked so much more debauched than Joe would have believed possible before that night.

Joe had never seen a man so happy or relieved to be submitting to another guy — to be submitting to him. The complete contentment on Scott's face raced to Joe's cock, trying to make him harden long before it

22

was physically possible.

Scott tugged slightly at Joe's hold on his wrist. Joe automatically tightened his grip. His fingertip met his thumb as he encircled Scott's wrist. Apparently, that was all Scott had wanted him to do. He instantly stopped struggling and lay back on the bed, relaxed and perfect — and single.

As his lips twisted into a smile, Joe ran his free hand down Scott's chest, tracing the centre line of his rib cage. Joe lowered his hand further, until he reached the little happy trail of light blond hairs that led to Scott's cock.

Scott's pubes were neatly trimmed around his cock and balls. Joe wondered if Scott had tidied himself up especially for their date. He also wondered how shocked Scott would look if Joe ordered him to shave himself completely bare. What about if he was tied down, legs spread wide apart, and he saw Joe approaching him with a razor?

There were so many firsts left in Scott, and Joe wanted to be the one to introduce Scott to each and every thing that he had yet to try. Joe was going to own every one of those memories.

"Did you buy all those toys especially for this occasion?" Joe asked, glancing toward those still neatly arranged on top of the chest of drawers.

Scott nodded. Colour rushed to his cheeks at the admission, making Joe grin.

"Did you get them all on line?"

Another nod.

Joe hummed to himself, already planning Scott's first trip to a real sex shop. Standing up, Joe made his way to the chest of drawers in order to inspect the selection of toys once more. He'd noticed earlier that everything that usually rested on the chest had been pushed aside in order to make room for the toys. Now, he took a moment to check over those things too.

Joe jerked as every muscle in his body tensed. Amid the jumble of loose coins and almost empty tubes of hair gel, were two packets of envelopes – the same kind of envelopes that Scott had put his note to Joe in.

Joe snatched up the envelopes and counted them. He let out a breath he hadn't realised he'd been holding, as he calculated that only one envelope had been taken from either of the packs.

No one else had been invited to Scott's room – yet.

"How many letters are you intending to write?" Joe demanded, spinning around to face Scott.

Scott peered across the room at him, as if he didn't have a clue what Joe was talking about.

Joe held up the packets of envelopes with all the flair of a legal prodigy displaying the ultimate piece of damning evidence.

There was no dramatic intake of breath, no scrambling to prove himself innocent. Scott merely stared at the envelopes for several long seconds. He shook his head then, as if to clear his senses. Finally, he spoke. "They w-were buy one, g-get one free."

Joe closed his eyes and stayed very still. It was the only way he could stop himself bursting into laughter. When Joe opened his eyes, Scott was watching him in obvious confusion, but that didn't matter. Relief sang through Joe's mind. He grinned as he tossed the envelopes back onto the chest of drawers.

There would be no more invitations issued, no mysterious little notes left for any other men. About to turn back to Scott, Joe stopped himself short. If Scott was ready to start to explore his kinky side in earnest then, even if he hadn't bought the envelopes with the intention of sending them to other men, leaving them there would still be tempting fate.

After a little bit of searching through the debris on top of the chest of drawers, Joe unearthed a pen and a spiral notebook. With his back still to Scott, he tore a piece of paper from the notebook. Several seconds slipped by before Joe decided what to write. But, once he knew what needed to be said, it only took a moment for him to scrawl his orders across the sheet.

Sealing the piece of paper into one of the envelopes, Joe wrote a few letters on the front of it and propped it against the paddle on the dresser.

"W-what's going on?" Scott asked, as Joe turned back to face him.

"Seems a pity to waste all these, doesn't it?" Joe said, indicating one of the packets of envelopes.

Scott nodded, probably on automatic pilot. Joe would have bet anything he owned that Scott had no idea what he was talking about. It was just his newly found submissiveness answering for him. He'd have agreed with anything Joe said.

"You went first. Now it's my turn to invite you somewhere," Joe explained.

Scott's eyes went to the envelope and stayed there. "W-what d-does it say?"

Joe raised an eyebrow. "You'll just have to read it if you want to find out, won't you?"

Scott reached for the cuff that still trapped him on the bed.

"When I leave, you're free to take off that cuff, not before." Joe folded his arms across his chest and leaned back against the chest of drawers to wait and see what Scott would do.

Scott stilled. He was sitting near the top of the bed with his shoulder resting against the headboard and his legs folded beneath him. His softened shaft was completely exposed and still smeared with cum. He was bloody gorgeous and apparently not about to argue with Joe's commands.

Joe reluctantly looked down at his watch. He didn't have time to linger much longer. "I'm working the late shift at the club tonight."

Scott said nothing.

It was Saturday. Joe's boss would kill him if he was late on their busiest night of the week. Joe tried to convince himself that was important when it didn't feel even vaguely relevant.

There was no need for him to stay. The scene, such as it had been, was over. Joe knew all of that. Yet he still couldn't quite convince himself to head for the door.

Running a hand through his hair, Joe finally pushed himself away from the chest of drawers. "Here are the rules. If you want to play with me, you can only play with me. I don't share. Vanilla with other people is fine, but you don't get kinky with anyone else."

"Okay," Scott said, his voice barely more than

a whisper.

"I expect you to follow the orders I've left for you to the letter. If you're not where I told you to be, when I told you to be there, I'm going to assume that you've changed your mind about all of this. No second chances. If you want to walk away, now is the time to do it. But if you don't want to end this, then don't mess me about."

"I w-won't—"

Joe held up a hand and silenced him. "Do you understand the rules?"

"Yes."

Joe stepped forward until he stood directly in front of Scott with his legs pressed against the edge of the bed.

Scott followed his every move, tilting his head back to look up at him.

Sliding his fingers into Scott's hair, Joe made him tip his head back even further. No protest; no attempt to get out of the uncomfortable position. That deserved a reward.

Joe bent down and brought their lips together for the first time. Scott gasped as Joe pressed his tongue against Scott's lips, demanding access.

Scott didn't attempt to refuse him. He welcomed Joe into his mouth as if it never occurred to him to do anything else. Joe jerked Scott up onto his knees. A muffled yelp let him know that the cuff around Scott's wrist was dragging him back and stopping him short.

Not in the mood to make allowances, Joe didn't relent in the slightest. He kept Scott exactly where he wanted him while he thoroughly explored his mouth.

Scott was his, and the unexpected yet overwhelming need to mark his territory rolled through Joe's body like a seismic wave. Buildings toppled in his mind. Structures that had seen him through more casual relationships than he could count started to crumble.

Joe nipped at Scott's bottom lip, pulling a moan from him. Then Joe nipped at the same spot again, harder.

Breaking the kiss, Joe stepped back. Off balance and no longer able to support himself, Scott tumbled down onto the bed. His hair was disordered and his eyes glazed with submission.

Scott put one hand to his mouth. A drop of blood seeped from the spot where Joe had bitten him. Scott looked at his blood-smeared fingertips, then back to Joe. His eyes opened very wide with shock.

Joe took another step back. Partly because he was already cutting it fine if he had any intention of getting to work on time, but also because he wasn't actually sure what he'd end up doing to Scott if he stayed any longer. He'd never known a sub who made him want to own a person quite so thoroughly.

Turning toward the door, Joe only stopped to pick up his jacket and the remaining envelopes. He hurried out, slamming the door behind him. In the corridor outside Scott's bedroom, Joe paused, straining his hearing to pick up any sound of movement on the other side of the door.

Chains rattled, two light footsteps sounded on thin carpet, then paper tore.

Scott was opening his letter.

Joe took one step away from the door, then another. A smile twisted his lips as he turned and walked down the stairs, then out through the front door.

The first thing Scott had done once he had permission to free himself was open the letter. Joe's smile grew into a grin as he imagined Scott naked and sitting on the edge of his bed, reading his message.

As he reached his car, Joe glanced at his watch. Forget working out the travel time to the club. Calculating just how long it would be until he received Scott's answer to his invitation was much more fun.

* * * * *

Scott's hands shook so badly he had to rest Joe's letter on the bed to have any chance of reading it. Finally, the letters steadied themselves. Joe's scrawl was messy, but legible.

Arrive at the club at two am. Take the empty stool at the end of the bar.

No alcohol. No talking. No fidgeting. No underwear.

Expect to obey every order I give you. Disobedience will be punished.

Your safe word is still unicorn.

Scott took a deep breath. The lingering scent of sex filled his senses. Rolling onto his back, he stared up at the ceiling above his bed as if he had never seen it before.

He'd done it. Bloody hell, he really had. Joe was interested. Holding the paper above him, Scott read it again. Months of sitting in the corner of the club, watching Joe flirt with anything that moved, trying to build up the courage to speak to him and failing time and time again—it all seemed like a lifetime ago.

Scott rolled onto his stomach and inhaled deeply. The scent of Joe's arousal clung to his sheets. Closing his eyes, Scott relished Joe's lingering presence while he still had the chance.

He'd been granted exactly what he wanted. All he had to do now was hope like hell that he had the balls to follow through with it—to take the game out of his nice safe bedroom and into the wider world.

Shutting his eyes even more tightly, Scott pulled the blankets up over his head. Warmth and comfort surrounded him. It almost felt as good as it had when Joe had lain on top of him, pinning him to the mattress.

The letters on the front of the envelope rolled around and around inside his mind.

R.S.V.P.

Joe expected Scott to reply to the orders he'd left for him with complete obedience and Scott wasn't going to let him down.

Part Two: RSVP

There was no way anyone in the club could have guessed that Scott wasn't wearing underwear, but, as he tried to weave his way through the mass of gyrating bodies on the dance floor, he felt like there was a flashing red light floating above his head to signal that he'd left his boxers at home.

When yet another man tried to grab his arse, Scott started to wonder if that light also indicated that he'd be more than happy for every man in the club to cop a feel and check out his lack of underwear for themselves.

Scott pulled away as unfamiliar hands slid around his body and tried to draw him into the dance. He stumbled forward, deafened by the music blaring from the speakers. By the time Scott made it to the bar on the far side of the room, his head was spinning, and his heart was racing.

Gasping for breath, he pushed his hair back from his face. The moment he looked up, he saw Joe standing on the opposite side of the bar.

Joe looked Scott slowly up and down.

Forget underwear; Scott might as well have been stark bollock naked. Joe seemed to look straight through the black denim stretched over Scott's hard on, as if x-ray vision were par for the course in his own very special version of the world.

Scott's mouth went dry. His tongue stuck to the roof of his mouth. His palms turned slick with sweat. It was more luck than judgement that he didn't come in his jeans.

He screwed you just a couple of hours ago. He flogged you, screwed you and ordered you to turn up here minus your underwear.

Scott whimpered. Whatever stupid little part of his brain insisted on reminding him of those facts really wasn't helping him not to come before they even got started.

Without warning, a flailing elbow caught Scott painfully in the ribs. He looked over his shoulder, but the drunken dancer didn't seem to have noticed the collision. Scott rubbed absentmindedly at his side as he turned back to Joe.

Joe was frowning. Scott instantly wanted to apologise. He wasn't sure what he was sorry for, but the need to make Joe happy was damn near overwhelming.

Before Scott got a word out, Joe pointedly turned his attention toward an empty stool at the end of the bar. Every other seat was taken, but that one stood aloof from the crowd, with a reserved notice in the shape of a sharply pointed pyramid on top of it.

Take the empty stool at the end of the bar.

That was one of the orders Joe had put in his note. Scott hurried across, moved the reserved sign aside and clambered onto the high stool. He looked toward Joe, hoping for some hint of approval, but Joe was already serving someone a drink as if he'd completely forgotten about Scott.

Scott squirmed in his seat, and only partly because his arse was still a little sore from the combination of the leather flogger striking his skin, and Joe's cock sinking into him earlier that evening.

Never taking his eyes off Joe, Scott reached into the pocket of his coat and took out the note Joe had written for him. He glanced down at it. There was barely enough light to read by, but that was okay. Scott had already memorised every word.

Arrive at the club at two am. Take the empty stool at the end of the bar.

Okay, Scott had done that. He hadn't screwed up yet. The world was still spinning away on its axis. No need to panic.

No alcohol. No talking. No fidgeting. No underwear.

Scott shifted uneasily on the stool. All of those things could be mentally ticked off.

Expect to obey every order I give you. Disobedience will be punished.

"Stay there."

Scott jerked his head up. The lighting behind the bar did a great job of creating a brooding, sexy atmosphere, but it was bloody useless to actually see by. Their gazes locked. Joe's eyes were so dark, they looked completely black.

All too soon, Joe turned away. Scott was vaguely aware of another bartender calling out closing time and all the other customers being ushered toward the exits.

Your safe word is still unicorn.

Scott took a deep breath and slid the note back into his pocket. The important thing now was to not hyperventilate. Scott tugged at the neckline of his T-shirt.

No fidgeting.

Damn! He'd known that would be the hardest order to obey. Intertwining his fingers, Scott stared down at his knotted knuckles as the noise from the crowd faded away.

A door slammed, making Scott jump. His trainer slid off the foot rest attached to the legs of his stool. His hands skidded against the bar as he tried to brace himself against it, but somehow he kept his balance.

Closing his eyes, he cursed himself for a fool.

"You still want to lock up?"

Rather than peering over his shoulder to find out who had spoken, when Scott opened his eyes, he instinctively looked for Joe. He spotted him standing at the far end of the bar, mopping up spilt beer.

"Yeah, I'll be here a while yet."

Someone out of Scott's line of sight tossed a heavy set of keys to Joe.

Scott heard footsteps walking away, but the sound stopped registering with him when Joe turned toward him.

"Ever been behind a bar?"

No talking.

Scott remembered the command just in time. He shook his head.

"It's about time you corrected that, don't you think?"

It took far too long for Scott's brain to put the words together inside his head and work out what sort of order they represented.

"Get around here," Joe translated for him. "Now."

Scott looked both ways along the long length of dark wood, but he was damned if he could work out how the hell anyone was supposed to get from one side of it to the other. Joe offered no help or instruction. He just stood there with his arms folded across his chest. He'd given the order. He obviously expected it to be obeyed. How Scott managed to do that wasn't Joe's problem.

Messages fizzed through Scott's brain. Most of them came straight from his cock. Joe wanted him on the other side of the bar. Before he could think better of it, Scott had his palms pressed against the stained wood. Levering himself up, he clumsily swung his legs over the bar.

Dropping down onto the floor on the other side, Scott managed to steady himself without knocking over anything breakable through sheer luck. His body was still completely over-ruling his brain. His feet took him to stand directly in front of Joe before Scott even had a chance to consider his actions.

Joe didn't move a muscle. He merely stared down at Scott, somehow managing to seem a damn sight taller than the real difference in their heights implied he should be.

Scott blinked. As some small part of his brain came back on line, heat rushed to his cheeks. Dear God, he'd actually leapt over the bar in his rush to get screwed, hadn't he?

"I'm—"

Scott hadn't been sure what he was going to say, and he was never destined to find out what words he might have come up with. His back hit into the edge of the work surface behind the bar. Bottles rattled on the shelf behind him. An empty glass fell over and rolled along the countertop. All the air rushed out of Scott's lungs. But none of that was important, because Joe's lips were covering his, and Joe's hands were on his body.

Joe seemed to have far more hands than any one person should be able to lay claim to. He slid one hand into Scott's hair and gripped the strands tightly, holding Scott still so he could take complete possession of his mouth. But Joe's other hand somehow managed to be everywhere at the same time.

Joe slid his hand down Scott's back and tugged at his T-shirt, pulling the fabric up so he could caress the bare skin beneath. The next moment, Joe was working that same hand down the back of Scott's jeans, burrowing beneath the denim, obviously determined to see if the dress code had been obeyed.

Scott whimpered into the kiss. His limbs didn't seem to belong to him. While Joe was capable of doing all sorts of things that made Scott gasp and writhe against him, Scott could only fumble at Joe's body like a teenager who didn't even know where the best bits to grope were located.

Scott couldn't think, he couldn't breathe, but somehow, in his panic, he scraped up the coordination to push against Joe's shoulders with both hands.

Joe actually growled at him as he lifted his head and broke the kiss.

Scott stared up at him, wide-eyed in surprise.

"Do you remember what your safe word is?" Joe demanded,

Scott blinked. Moments passed. The world slowed down around them, allowing a few seconds to stretch out until they felt more like several consecutive life times. Finally, Scott managed to nod.

Joe's right hand now rested on Scott's neck, the thumb pressing up against his jaw, keeping his head tilted back. It didn't shift as Scott moved his head. It pushed unyieldingly against the sensitive skin on his throat.

"Do you want to say it?" Joe asked, his expression more serious than Scott could have ever believed possible.

Scott shook his head.

"Are you sure?"

Scott swallowed several times in quick succession. He nodded. "I'm so s-sorry, I'm j-j-just…"

No talking. Scott's words faded away to be replaced by mental curses.

"Go on, you're just…"

Scott glanced up again. Joe's voice had changed. It was softer now, more intimate. It invited both spoken words and something longer than a one-word answer.

"J-just n-nervous," Scott whispered. He closed his eyes, sure he sounded like an idiot, especially to someone like Joe—a man who probably did far more daring things several times a day.

Joe slid his hand slowly around Scott's neck and into the hair at his nape. Suddenly, Joe pulled him forward. Scott found himself pressed against Joe's body from shoulder to knee.

"There's no need to be nervous—"

"I k-know, I—"

"Hush." Joe's put his other hand on the small of Scott's back, keeping him where he was.

Speaking after that order had been issued,

gentle though it had been, was impossible.

"There's no need to be nervous," Joe repeated. "I've got everything under control."

Scott peered up at Joe. He was so confident about everything, so sure that everything would go according to his plans. So unlike Scott...

"Give me another ch-ch-chance?" Scott blurted out.

Joe's expression changed so quickly, it was as if someone had flipped a switch inside him. "You don't think I'm letting you go that easily, do you, darling?" Amusement danced on every word. He dipped his head to whisper into Scott's ear. "You offered yourself to me when you stepped in here tonight. You're mine and I intend to make good use of you. Nothing but your safe word will change that."

Scott was sure any sane man would find those words terrifying. Happily, he was even more sure that any sanity he'd possessed had packed its bags and flown away on an extended holiday the moment he'd set eyes on Joe.

There was no fear in Scott's world, only excitement. Adrenaline rushed through his veins so fast it was all he could do to stay upright enough to enjoy it.

Joe moved one hand to Scott's shoulder and pressed down.

Apparently, staying upright was no longer required.

Scott began to lower himself to his knees. His joints held strong until the last moment. An inch before he reached the floor, his control faltered. He landed heavily on the grubby floorboards. A jolt rushed through his body making the breath catch in his throat.

Scott's mouth dropped open.

Joe grinned and ran his thumb across Scott's bottom lip. Frozen in place, all Scott could do was stare up at Joe in awe.

"That's right," Joe said, sliding his thumb forward and pushing it between Scott's lips to casually penetrate his mouth.

Scott opened his mouth wider. In that moment, it felt right. It felt as if there was nothing he had to do but stay where he was, and do as Joe said, and absolutely everything in the whole damn world would be perfect.

* * * * *

"That's right," Joe repeated. He was barely aware of what he was saying; he doubted that it mattered what syllables fell from his lips anyway. Scott wasn't looking for complicated declarations and inspiring speeches. He just needed to hear the man in charge reassuring him that everything was fine. He needed the *tone* of Joe's voice.

At least, Joe guessed that was what Scott needed. Scott was so unlike the guys Joe normally played with, it was impossible to be certain.

Sounding certain however, that was a different matter. Joe smiled to himself—he was good at sounding certain. He slid his thumb further into Scott's mouth as he considered his options. Scott stared back at him, his eyes never leaving Joe's face.

Joe had no doubt that Scott was trying to work

out how to please him. The only difference between them was that Joe knew Scott would never guess that he was standing above him doing something similar.

It had been years since Joe had been willing to let another man see his emotions flash across his face that way. Almost as many years had passed since he'd had a sub that innocent.

No doubt any other sub who was as naive as Scott, would have had the sense to run for their life if Joe had approached them. But, Scott sucked gently around Joe's thumb as he met his gaze, and showed no inclination to rush off anywhere.

"I've been watching your mouth ever since we met," Joe told him.

A confused little sound vibrated against Joe's thumb, as if Scott had genuinely never noticed Joe staring at him like a ravenous wolf every time they were in the same room.

"Now, I'm going to do more than watch it."

Keeping his thumb in place, Joe slid a finger into Scott's mouth to join it. A wonderful combination of sensations surrounded the digits—wet heat, a soft nimble tongue, and just a touch of sharp teeth to make it interesting.

"I've wanted to have you on your knees back here for so long," Joe murmured, still letting his tone of voice do most of the talking for him. "Hell, I almost ordered you to get around here the first time I set eyes on you." He would have too, if it hadn't been so bloody obvious that Scott wasn't the type.

Joe's smile turned slightly lopsided. Apparently, God bless him, *Scott* hadn't realised he wasn't the type to do this...

Suddenly, Scott began to retreat. Joe's smile died. For a moment, he really thought Scott was trying to pull away. But no, Scott was just nodding his agreement. Relief rushed through Joe as he took his fingers out of Scott's mouth and moved his hand to the back of Scott's head.

Scott lifted a hand.

"Don't." Joe didn't know if Scott had intended to reach up for his fly or to wipe his own mouth. His order was the same either way.

Scott lowered his hand to his side. He closed his eyes for a moment. Then, very slowly, he opened his mouth in invitation.

Joe's cock throbbed with the desire to be lodged between Scott's lips. He quickly undid his zip. The silent offering was almost as erotic as the prospect of getting sucked off.

Scott obviously wasn't the kind of guy who invited relative strangers to cum in his mouth on a regular basis. Hell, Joe was willing to bet his own arse that he was the first man who had ever screwed Scott without being his boyfriend at the time.

Joe sighed his relief as he freed his cock from behind the tight confines of his jeans. Scott's mouth remained open. He was a quick learner; this time he didn't even blink at Joe's commando status.

Unable to resist testing him, Joe didn't rush to make use of Scott's mouth. He stroked his shaft, slow and easy, as if there were any chance he'd need something other than the sight of Scott on his knees to keep him hard.

Scott whimpered. He closed his mouth for just the briefest moment, moistened his lips with his tongue, and promptly resumed his offer.

"Good boy."

Joe took half a step forward. The tip of his erection brushed against Scott's open mouth.

Scott's frustrated moan sounded very loud in the deserted bar. His eyes fell closed, but his lips remained parted. Joe rocked his hips, pushing the head of his cock into Scott's mouth. Scott didn't move his jaw. He didn't close his mouth around Joe's cock. He merely remained perfectly still, waiting for permission, or for an order, or for whatever Joe was willing to offer him.

Joe tilted his shaft, pointing it down so he could rub the head against the soft, moist surface of Scott's tongue. A slow, controlled breath caressed his shaft. Scott blinked open his eyes and looked up at Joe, mutely pleading with him.

There were extra lights that Joe could switch on behind the bar, but the controls for them were all the way down the other end of the shelves. If Joe wanted to be able to see Scott clearly, he'd have to step away from him — he'd have to let his cock slip from between those full, pink lips.

Sod that. There would be other times, with better lighting, where he could stare at Scott to his heart's content. He wasn't stepping back for anything short of Scott's safe word.

Joe settled his hand on Scott's jaw and gently closed Scott's mouth around his shaft. A pleasure-filled groan vibrated around Joe's cock, coaxing pre-cum to leak onto Scott's tongue. Scott couldn't have sounded more pleased about the world if *he* was the one about to get the best blowjob of his life.

Joe tightened his grip on Scott's hair to hold him still, and pushed his hips forward, letting more of his erection into Scott's mouth. Scott made no complaint as Joe removed any free movement from within Scott's grasp.

It may only have been hours since Joe had come, but as he stood behind the bar with the sweetest little sub he'd ever set eyes on kneeling before him, it felt more like years.

Careful to keep his thrusts as controlled and shallow as he could, Joe made the most of whatever Scott's mouth could offer him. And Scott took it like a pro.

Joe frowned at the comparison. His concentration slipped. His hips took complete advantage of his brain's momentary distraction and lurched forward. Joe's cock slid deeper into Scott's mouth and nudged against the back of his throat.

Scott's eyebrows went up. His eyes opened very widely. At the same time, his hands came up and pushed against Joe's thighs. He jerked away, spluttering as he sat back on his ankles.

His panicked expression only lasted a moment before it was replaced by one of horror.

"Perfect," Joe murmured to himself. Not like a pro at all. He'd read Scott accurately from the start.

Scott looked up at him in confusion, and Joe realised he'd said the word out loud.

"Don't worry about it, darling," Joe ordered. "Give me a few months, and I'll have you trained to suck my cock exactly how I like it."

Scott nibbled at his bottom lip as he seemed to consider that plan from every angle. The sensitive

43

flesh was already flushed and swollen with an increased blood supply, it looked more suited to sucking cock than ever.

"Would you like that?" Joe prompted, idly stroking his shaft as he waited for Scott to compose himself.

Scott nodded. And, as if he hadn't already proved just how sweet and innocent he was, he blushed at the prospect. It wasn't easy to see his heightened colour in the dim lighting, but it was definitely worth the effort.

Joe chuckled as he slid his hand back into Scott's hair. He expected Scott to try to pull away, uncertain after his little mishap, but Scott opened his mouth as if nothing could come more naturally to him.

Bliss shot through Joe's body. No technically fantastic blow job could have compared to the rush Scott's instinctive submission gave him.

Scott's lips thinned into a pale pink line as he wrapped them around Joe's cock again. His cheeks hollowed out and he lowered his gaze to stare along Joe's shaft, as if eager to take in every detail so he could masturbate over it later. If he still had the right to jack off when Joe wasn't there to enjoy the show, of course. Whether or not Scott realised it, that right was no longer guaranteed.

As Joe held Scott's head still and moved his hips, Scott gradually seemed to gain the confidence to show him what techniques and tricks he had learnt before they met. He traced the vein on the underside of Joe's shaft and flicked the tip of his tongue against the head. He missed the sweet spot just beneath Joe's glans more often than he hit it, but Joe didn't care about that.

Scott was literally salivating with desire. His mouth grew wetter and slicker around Joe's cock by the moment; and every bit of pleasure offered to Joe's shaft raced around his body, setting off chain reactions that swept through his nerve endings.

"Yes, just like that," Joe murmured.

Scott's eyes dropped closed. He swallowed rapidly, working his mouth frantically around Joe's cock as if trying to milk his orgasm out of him.

Still keeping his thrusts as shallow as he could, Joe began to move more quickly. Scott knew he was close; as he opened his eyes and looked up at Joe, Joe saw the knowledge shining in his gaze.

One more thrust, and ecstasy rushed through Joe's veins. He came, spilling more of his cum across Scott's tongue each time he jerked his hips forwards.

Locking his knees when they threatened to give way, Joe tossed his head back and let out a triumphant yell. A pure, primal need to mark Scott as his own, and to warn all other men away from his territory, kept Joe pumping into Scott's mouth until he had nothing left to give.

Scott spluttered, but he didn't try to pull away. His hands came up to rest on Joe's thighs again, but Scott only tried to steady them both. There was no attempt to take control. The more feral side of Joe's dominance howled its approval.

Mine.

It was only breathlessness that kept the word inside Joe's head.

Finally, he managed to still his hips. Staring

down at Scott, he absorbed every detail of the beautiful picture presented.

As Joe took a step back and let his softening cock slip from Scott's mouth, he noticed that Scott hadn't been able to swallow quickly enough. Some of Joe's semen had escaped from between Scott's lips; his chin shone with moisture. A few drops of cum had landed on Scott's shirt too.

Scott was just as breathless as Joe. He swayed where he knelt, but he didn't try to get to his feet.

After a few seconds, Scott took his right hand off Joe's thigh, moving it toward his own lips.

"Put your hand back where it was."

Scott blinked in apparent confusion, but he also obeyed.

Joe's cock was still hanging out, but he lost all interest in tidying himself up. He swiped his thumb against Scott's chin and fed every scrap of cum that lingered there into Scott's mouth himself.

It took Scott a few moments to catch up with what Joe expected him to do; but once he was up to speed, he accepted each finger full of cum as if it was a delicious treat. When Scott had swallowed it all, Joe dropped his hand away from Scott's face.

Scott stared down at the grubby floor as if it was the most fascinating thing he'd ever seen. His hands remained obediently in position as the minutes passed by.

Gradually, their breathing evened out; Scott still didn't move. Joe was about to order Scott to his feet when Scott tentatively leaned forward and lapped very gently at the tip of Joe's cock.

He was licking him clean.

If Joe had been capable of coming again so soon, he would have.

Scott lifted one hand and tugged very lightly at Joe's jeans. Joe nodded his permission and Scott's movements became more confident. He gripped the pockets of Joe's jeans and pulled the denim down, until he'd completely exposed Joe's crotch.

Shuffling forward on his knees, Scott nuzzled the bared skin. Joe stroked his fingers through Scott's hair, keeping the floppy blond strands out of his way so he'd have a clear view of Scott's face as Scott tentatively began to lap at his balls.

Taking a step back, Joe leaned against the side of the bar and made himself comfortable. When Scott failed to keep pace with him without a blatant invitation, Joe beckoned him forward with a crook of one finger.

Scott hurriedly shuffled forward on his knees and immediately got back to work. He licked and mouthed Joe's balls with obvious enthusiasm, sucking them gently between his lips and placing delicate little kisses against the thickly furred skin.

Murmurs of pleasure filled the air as Scott settled in to worship Joe in the way only an instinctive submissive could. In that moment, Joe made a decision. Whether Scott knew it or not, he was destined to be on his knees in front of Joe on a regular basis.

* * * * *

Scott's jaw throbbed. The deep, burning ache on each side of his face demanded his attention more

47

loudly with every passing moment. He shifted his weight forward, trying to ease the stress on his knees, but somehow that only made the bare floor boards feel harder. Scott's cock ached. His balls were pulled up tight against his body, begging him to reach down and jerk off.

Scott's whole body seemed to be screaming at him, telling him what was wrong, but he couldn't bring himself to take any of those voices seriously. Nothing could be really wrong. Not when, for the first time in his life, it suddenly felt as if everything was right.

He tried to push any awareness of his insignificant little aches and pains out of his mind, but he couldn't stop himself whimpering as he tried to open his mouth wider and take Joe's cock back between his lips. For the first time since he dropped to his knees, it wasn't a sound filled with pleasure.

"That's enough for now." Joe pulled firmly at Scott's hair, tugging him away from his cock.

Scott shook his head, not caring if he yanked at Joe's grip on his hair. "N-no, I—"

"Do you remember your safe word?"

Scott blinked up at Joe. When he realised Joe was waiting for an answer, he nodded.

"Good, because just saying no to me won't get you anywhere."

Scott's cock jerked within the tight confines of his jeans. He still didn't understand why he loved the fact that Joe would ignore anything but his safe word, but he did. It called to something in the very bottom of his soul, something he was only just starting to investigate. It promised him that everything would be okay, because this was precisely the way things should be.

"I kn-know," Scott whispered.

"Good."

The lighting behind the bar cast deep shadows over Joe's face, highlighting his bone structure. His cheek bones appeared higher, his jaw stronger. He looked almost feline—not like a sweet little kitten with a pretty blue ribbon tied around its neck, but like the kind of big cat that stalked through the jungle and killed anything that didn't run away fast enough. He should have appeared terrifying, but Scott had never seen anything so beautiful in his life.

Without any warning, Joe caught hold of Scott's wrist and dragged him up onto his feet. He rubbed the pad of his thumb across Scott's lips. They were hyper-sensitive now, and Joe's firm touch sent pleasure bouncing through Scott's body like a pinball through an old fashioned gaming machine Lights flashed and bells rang inside him.

Scott moaned, desperate to let Joe know how much he loved him for granting him the pleasure of his touch. The sound morphed into something far more high-pitched when Joe placed his other hand on Scott's crotch.

Joe cupped Scott's fly in his palm, warming his cock and balls as he curled his fingers around his erection through the denim.

Scott's attempts to lift himself onto his toes only made Joe tighten his hold. His touch grew even rougher as he began to massage Scott through the fabric.

Scott grabbed Joe's shoulders, but only to

steady himself. As Joe's muscles flexed beneath his palms, Scott had no idea why anyone would ever want to push him away.

There was no gentleness in Joe's caress. His touch verged on painful, but somehow that only made more pleasure fly through Scott's veins.

Joe leaned forward and put his lips to Scott's ear. "If you've got any dates lined up, cross them off your calendar — even the vanilla ones."

He didn't stop rubbing Scott's cock for a second. It made it damn near impossible for Scott to think.

"W-what?" he mumbled.

"I don't want you to screw, or date, anyone else until I'm finished with you — not even for casual one-offs. No other guys. And no women either," he added. "If you swing both ways."

Scott desperately tried to keep back a pleasure-filled moan. As harsh as it was, Joe's touch was setting off rapid bursts of fireworks inside him — the kind that no gentle caress had ever put a match to. "Ok-k-kay," he managed to stutter out.

"Good boy."

A shiver ran down Scott's spine as those words hit the air. From anyone else, they might have seemed like little more than punctuation, just a response to getting their own way. From Joe, they sounded more like a promise that everything really would be okay — that Joe would make everything perfect for a man who proved capable of being a good boy for him.

"You're mine now, and no one else lays a hand on my sub without my permission," Joe went on.

The breath caught in Scott's throat. Every

picture he'd ever seen on the internet rushed to the front of his mind. Subs in bondage. Subs wearing collars bearing their owner's name. Subs walking at their master's heal on a thick leather lead. Belonging to Joe, being his...

Unable to speak, Scott simply nodded. Yes. Yes, to it all.

Joe pulled back, just far enough to look Scott in the eye. He smiled down at Scott not even trying to hide his triumphant expression.

He rubbed his hand against Scott's fly even more quickly. His fingers danced in a complicated routine that had obviously been choreographed by an actual sex-god. No mere mortal could have worked out how to force that much pleasure into a man's cock without even undoing his zip.

Scott's hips jerked forward. His vision blurred and, for the first time since he was a young teenager, Scott came all over the inside of his jeans

Ecstasy shot through him, tearing through his body, not caring what sort of damage it left in its wake. Any energy that Scott had left in him fled. He slumped forward, barely able to stay on his feet a second longer.

Bowing his head, he rested his temple on Joe's shoulder. Joe's hand was still on his crotch, still rubbing against him through the denim.

With his breaths coming in pants, Scott closed his eyes and watched the pretty patterns swirl behind his eyelids. As blissful as it was, he couldn't let himself indulge in his ecstasy for too long. He'd already come like a schoolboy; he'd be damned if he'd make the situation even more embarrassing by fainting like a schoolgirl too.

Joe didn't pull away from him or demand that Scott man-up and stand on his own two feet. He didn't stop stroking Scott's fly either. It was almost as if Joe hadn't noticed that he'd come. Or maybe as if he had noticed, but simply considered that fact irrelevant.

As they stood there together, it felt far more like Joe was touching him simply because that was what he wanted to do. He had the right, and he was exercising it because he could. Scott's orgasm might have been a vaguely interesting bi-product, but it hadn't been the aim.

It was the pleasure Joe got from playing with Scott's cock through his jeans that was the important thing, not the sheer ecstasy Scott had received in the process.

Scott bit down hard on his bottom lip. The bitter metallic flavour of blood filled his mouth, washing away the lingering taste of Joe's cum. That wasn't fair. Scott had wanted so much to make the sweet saltiness last, to preserve any evidence that this evening had really happened, and keep hold of it for the rest of his life.

"How's your back feeling?" Joe suddenly enquired.

Moving very slowly, very carefully, Scott lifted his head. "My b-back?" He blinked as he tried to make his mind work. Joe's hand had been on his cock, not his back. Scott was very sure of that. His shaft still throbbed with the aftershocks.

One brain cell finally bumped into another. Nerve endings whirled into action. Every inch of skin from the nape of his neck to the back of his ankles tingled.

Of course—the flogging! Scott shrugged his shoulders; his shirt rubbed against his sensitised skin. "It feels g-good."

Joe nodded, just once, as if that were nothing more or less than he'd expected. The universe was obviously operating in exactly the way Joe was used to. It was only Scott's world that had been turned upside down and shaken until every familiar landmark had dropped off it and scattered across the dusty floor around his feet.

"Th-th-thank you." Scott could barely make the words loud enough to be heard, but at the same time, they needed to be said.

Joe raised one dark eyebrow. His eyes danced with humour. "Are you thanking me for flogging you and screwing you? Or are you talking about me letting you suck my cock and allowing you to come?"

Scott stared up into Joe's eyes for a long time. All those things were liberties that Joe could easily have decided not to grant him. That fact had never been clearer. Whatever happened between them, it would only ever be because Joe allowed it. Scott's happiness was Joe's to permit or deny on a whim.

Scott's stomach turned over. Just because the idea was as hot as hell, that didn't stop it giving him a cold, foreboding feeling in the pit of his gut.

A sudden instinct for self-preservation made Scott try to take a step back, but he was pressed against the bar. He squirmed and shuffled his feet, but there was nowhere for him to go.

"I'm still waiting for an answer," Joe reminded

him.

What had he been thanking him for? The question whirled around and around in Scott's head.

"All of t-the a-above," he finally whispered. He'd never heard himself sound so uncertain.

A slow smile twisted Joe's lips, making him appear incredibly satisfied with himself. Relief bubbled up inside Scott. He hadn't said anything stupid. He'd been right to tell the truth.

"You have no idea how much of a natural sub you are, do you?"

Without a single word of warning, Joe stepped back.

The heat from Joe's body faded from Scott's skin. He frowned, wondering when he had lost the ability to warm himself from the inside; when his blood had begun to feel cold within his veins unless Joe was pressed against him. Suddenly, Scott felt dependent upon Joe for even that basic need.

Instincts screamed inside Scott, demanding that he step forward and close the gap between them, but his feet were rooted to the floor. "Can I h-help you c-clean up?" he blurted out.

"I think you've already done that," Joe said, as he tucked his freshly licked cock away.

In spite of everything they'd just done together, Scott felt heat rush to his cheeks at Joe's teasing. "No, I m-mean the club. I could help you—"

Joe cut him off with a shake of his head. "Not my job. My shift is over. I just have to lock up when we leave."

"Oh..." Scott shuffled his feet. His jeans were turning increasingly uncomfortable as his cum dried on the inside of his fly.

He glanced toward the door leading out of the club. He should leave. That was obvious. But whatever glue had been used to stick his feet to the floor was bloody stubborn stuff. All he could do was stand there like an idiot, staring down at his shoes.

Another pair of shoes appeared in his field of vision as black leather boots stepped between his trainers.

Scott jerked his head up.

Joe was right in front of him. "It's time to go."

Scott nodded, and then went right on staring at Joe, not moving an inch.

Joe placed his hands on Scott's shoulders and turned him around. A sharp tap on Scott's arse finally convinced him to move toward the gap in the bar that he hadn't been able to find before. It also sent a surprising wave of pleasure tingling through his body, and a whole host of possibilities racing through his mind.

With Joe right behind him, Scott reluctantly stepped out of the club and into the cool, early morning air. It had to be gone three a.m. and there was a decided chill to the air. No hint of dawn showed over the horizon yet. There wasn't a soul to be seen on the street.

Rubbing vaguely at his upper arms in an attempt to keep them warm, Scott lurked just outside the club as Joe locked up and pulled down the shutters.

Then, Scott had no excuses left.

Joe had said that he'd probably want to screw him again at some point, but Scott wasn't going to embarrass himself by asking when he could see Joe next. Dating and hooking up were different things. Hoping for the former rather than the latter would be silly.

Being Joe's back up option if no one better came along was fine with Scott. He took a step backward, away from Joe, then another, and another. Summoning up all his will power, he finally convinced himself to turn around and walk across the road to his beaten up old car.

"It's your turn."

Scott looked over his shoulder. "What?"

Joe reached into the pocket of the leather jacket he'd picked up on the way out of the club and took out a piece of paper.

Scott hurried back across the street and took what was now clearly an envelope from Joe.

"I don't understand," he admitted, staring down at the blank surface. The messy letters he'd hoped to see scrawled across the envelope were conspicuously absent.

"It's your turn," Joe repeated.

Scott continued to stare down at the envelope, still without the least clue what Joe was talking about.

"What do you want to invite me to do with you next time we meet up?" Joe prompted.

Scott opened his mouth. He closed it again, without saying a single word. There was going to be a definite, pre-arranged, next time. He was going to meet up with Joe, almost as if they had a date. They were going to do another scene and have sex. They were going to…

It didn't really matter what they did. Scott was

pretty sure he'd have a fantastic time if he was just allowed to sit and stare at Joe.

"Think about it." Joe flicked his finger against the envelope. "When you've made your decision, let me know. But remember what I said earlier—no one else lays a hand on you while I'm playing with you."

Scott silently watched Joe turn and walk away. Joe's long legs quickly ate up the pavement. Within seconds he'd turned the corner at the end of the street and disappeared from view.

Joe was playing with him. Scott couldn't help but picture a big cat toying with its prey, but the image didn't put him off at all. Neither did the fact that Joe hadn't said anything about both of them being obliged to remain faithful to the other.

Dropping his attention to the envelope in his hand, Scott made his way blindly back to his car. Unlocking it, he slid behind the steering wheel. Closing the car door, Scott took a deep breath and ran his free hand slowly down his face.

He needed a shower, several night's worth of sleep, a good meal, and at least a lifetime in which to process everything that had happened that night. But, in that particular moment, he realised that what he really needed, more than any of those other things, was a pen.

As he turned the key in the ignition, a smile crept on to Scott's lips. It was his turn, his chance to ask Joe for whatever he wanted...

Part Three: Written Request

Damn, but wasn't that a fantastic sight to come home to? A little of Joe's exhaustion faded away as he turned the corner at the end of the corridor leading to his flat. He smiled to himself as he paused to admire the view.

Scott was bent over right outside Joe's front door. His dark blue jeans were stretched taught over his buttocks. He was damn near begging someone to come up behind him and grind against his arse. As Joe watched, Scott straightened up. That was okay. Joe had already had plenty of time to etch the image indelibly into his brain—one more picture of Scott for him to treasure on those cold, boring nights when he had nothing but his own right hand to keep his cock warm and happy.

Scott took a step back from Joe's door before finally turning around. If he'd been a cat rather than a submissive, he'd have only had eight lives left to play with after spotting Joe. Scott's feet actually left the floor as he jerked with surprise.

"W-what are you...?" Scott began.

"What are you doing here?" Joe finished for him. "Isn't that my line?"

Scott blinked in confusion as Joe closed in on him.

"I'm the one who lives in this building, right?" Joe added.

"I...um..."

Joe studied Scott for a few seconds. He felt a

strange, protective desire to rescue Scott from his embarrassment, but he couldn't deny there was also pleasure to be had in watching him squirm.

Scott's cheeks became flushed. Ducking his head, he glanced up at Joe through his lashes. That was it.

Eventually, it became obvious to Joe that Scott had no intention of trying to speak up again. The rescuer in Joe finally won out. He extended a hand. Scott stared at it as if he'd never seen fingers or a palm before.

"You have an envelope for me," Joe hinted.

"I..." Scott looked over his shoulder.

Joe followed his gaze to the small gap beneath his front door. Stepping around Scott, Joe unlocked his flat and picked up the small white envelope laying just inside his hallway.

Scott shoved his hands deep into his pockets. If his jeans had been a little looser, he might have pushed them down to his knees in his rush to try to hide his nerves behind the denim. No such luck. Scott's trainers squeaked against the wooden floorboards as he shuffled his feet.

"That's enough," Joe said, as he turned back to him. "Stop fidgeting."

Scott froze.

Joe nodded his approval. Ripping open the envelope, he found a carefully folded piece of note paper.

If you don't mind, I'd really like to see you naked. Please.

Joe didn't chuckle. He didn't even allow himself to crack a smile. He ran his eyes over the neatly written words one more time. The 'please' was a nice touch. It was a very Scott-like touch.

"If you'd r-rather n-not—" Scott began.

"Be outside your house at ten o'clock tonight," Joe cut in. "And make sure you're wearing boots."

"B-boots? Um…okay?" Scott hazarded.

Joe put the envelope and the note in his jacket pocket, stepped into his flat, and closed the door behind him. A second later, he was peering through the peephole, checking on Scott's reaction.

Scott stared at Joe's front door for several long seconds. It was impossible to tell if he was shocked to get a third date that easily, or if he couldn't believe that he'd been abandoned on the doorstep rather than invited in.

As Joe watched, Scott pressed the heel of his palm against his crotch through his jeans. Whatever he was thinking, it had to be as hot as hell. Even with the distortion of the peephole, the line of Scott's erection was clearly visible through his trousers.

Nodding contentedly to himself at a job well done, Joe turned away from the door and wandered toward his bed. He set his alarm clock to make sure he woke up in time for their date and lay down, still wearing the same clothes he'd worn for a double shift in a sauna on the other side of town.

He was asleep almost before his head hit the pillow. In his dreams, there were no jeans blocking his view of Scott's arse.

* * * * *

Scott stared down at his sensible brown hiking boots. Rocking back on his heels, he pushed his hands deeper into his coat pockets in an effort not to fidget. It was almost ten o'clock. Joe might turn up any second. It wouldn't do for Joe's first impression of him that night to be a disobedient one.

Scott frowned as he resorted to wriggling his toes inside his boots. It didn't seem likely that Joe wanted them to go on a nice brisk walk in the middle of the night. Even if Joe was determined to keep all of his clothes on and never allow Scott to see a single bit of naked flesh, the idea of Joe and country rambles just didn't sit right inside Scott's head.

A low noise, somewhere between a purr and a roar, tugged at Scott's senses. He leaned forward, craning his neck to peek past the neighbour's overgrown hedge.

A motorbike rolled into view and pulled up at the kerb in front of Scott. Scott's mouth literally watered as he ran his eyes over each stunning inch of it. The machine was sex on two wheels — with an extra order of chrome and black paintwork thrown in for good measure; and Joe sat astride it like the king of the leather-clad world.

It had to be Joe, no one else would be able to look that hot — not even on a bike made out of pure sex appeal. Joe didn't bother to lift his visor, he just held another helmet out to Scott.

With his eyes still feasting on every perfect detail of both the man and the bike, Scott stepped forward and blindly took the helmet. Then, he just stood there and stared some more. It had never even occurred to him that Joe might pick him up on his bike rather than in his car.

He should have thought about it; he should have anticipated it. He should have jacked off thinking about it.

Joe impatiently revved the bike's engine. Scott snapped back into movement. He wouldn't put it past Joe to leave without him if he kept him waiting too long.

Scott fumbled with the helmet. Finally managing to get it on and secured, he scrambled onto the bike behind Joe. There was a little chrome hand hold behind the pillion seat. Gathering up all his courage, Scott ignored it in favour of wrapping his arms around Joe's body.

The bike was just like Joe—it lacked all middle gears. One moment they were idling at the kerb, the next, they were speeding headlong down the street. Suddenly, Scott wasn't just clutching around Joe for the chance to grope him. He clawed at Joe's leather jacket with his fingernails. The small part of his brain that wasn't praying they got to wherever they were going in one piece, hoped like hell that he didn't rip the leather in his panic.

Joe threw them along a tight, winding route, faster and faster. Pressed tightly against Joe's back, Scott had little choice but to lean into the corners with Joe—to follow Joe's lead, and hope like hell that was what a pillion passenger was supposed to do.

He closed his eyes and desperately tried to think of something other than how close the ground came to their knees every time they wavered from a perfectly straight line. Something like how bloody wonderful it felt to be pressed up against Joe that tightly.

The vibrations from the engine rolled up through Scott's body as he gradually managed to relax just a few of his muscles. His shaft throbbed inside his jeans. Every time either of them moved, Scott's cock rubbed against Joe's arse through their clothes, tempting him to imagine what it would be like if Joe ever allowed him to top.

Behind his helmet, Scott bit the inside of his cheek in an effort not to add his own groans of pleasure to the noise of the engine.

Finally, Joe brought the bike to a halt. The sudden silence made Scott's ears ring. The vibrations stopped, but Scott's body still trembled with the echoes of them. He was vaguely aware that time was passing, but he had no idea how long he sat there, clinging to Joe like a helmet-wearing limpet.

Joe shrugged his shoulders until Scott eventually managed to let go. Dismounting with practiced ease, Joe tugged off his helmet and turned to face Scott.

Scott didn't try to follow Joe's example and get off the bike. He wasn't sure his legs would support him. He reached for the strap on the helmet instead. His fingers wouldn't work. Panic at being stuck forever bubbled up inside Scott.

Joe stepped forward and unceremoniously pushed Scott's hands aside. He soon had the helmet off.

Shaking his head, Scott reached up and rubbed his hands through his hair. Joe looked tousled and gorgeous, but Scott suspected that he looked more like a bedraggled hedgehog in comparison.

"First time?" Joe asked.

Scott managed to nod.

"You did fine."

The praise was so unexpected, Scott could only blink at Joe in shock.

"Come on." Joe wrapped his arm around Scott's waist and half lifted and half dragged him off the bike.

Scrambling to raise his trailing leg over the saddle, Scott somehow managed to keep himself upright. For the first time, he looked around, trying to work out where they were. He didn't have much time to wonder, he was soon too busy hurrying to keep up with Joe's longer strides as he led the way into the low, shadowy building next to the car park.

Joe dropped some money on the counter just inside the entrance and took both of the keys the man working there offered to him.

Scott hesitated for a split second as he passed the counter, but Joe didn't order him to stop and get anything and Scott wasn't inclined to either take the initiative or to let Joe out of his sight.

He followed close on Joe's heels into some sort of locker room. He peered around the cramped space trying to work out what kind of place they were visiting. There were a few other guys in there, all of them in various stages of undress, just like in a gym changing room. But, somehow, he still got the distinct impression they weren't going to be doing any kind of conventional work out.

"Scott!"

He turned toward Joe just in time to catch one

of the keys when Joe tossed it to him. Scott peered down at the key as if he had no idea what to do with it, which wasn't actually too far from the truth. He looked up at Joe, tried to read his expression for some clue, and failed completely.

"Take your clothes off. Put them in your locker," Joe ordered.

"A-all of them?" Scott whispered, stepping closer, so they wouldn't be overheard.

"All of them," Joe confirmed.

Scott felt the blood drain from his face at the prospect.

"Except your boots of course," Joe added.

Scott's attention dropped to Joe's feet. He was wearing boots too—black military style ones. As discreetly as possible, Scott peeked at all the other guys' footwear.

Boots, boots and more boots.

As Scott watched, two men left the changing room, their bare cocks swinging freely with each step, their buttocks bright white compared to the tan covering the rest of their bodies. They'd kept their boots on.

"It's called a boots only night for a reason."

Scott nodded, as if that was the kind of event he attended every other week. It was several seconds before he actually processed the words. "Nobody wears *anything* but their boots?"

"That's right," Joe said, with a lopsided grin. "Not even me." As he spoke, he undid his jacket.

Scott half expected to discover that Joe wasn't wearing a stitch beneath his leather jacket, but he had a tight fitting black T-shirt on. Somehow, that fact didn't help Scott remember how to breathe as easily as it should have.

He was going to see Joe naked. Scott had asked for nudity, and he was going to get it. Admittedly, it had never occurred to Scott that he'd needed to specify that he would much prefer a private viewing, or to enquire if the price he'd have to pay for the pleasure would involve wandering around stark bollock naked in front of God knew how many equally naked men.

Scott slowly dragged his gaze up to Joe's face. Joe raised an eyebrow at him. Scott immediately scrambled to work out what he'd done to displease him.

His clothes. He was supposed to be taking them off. Scott fumbled with the zip on his coat. Undressing suddenly required an entire set of skills he didn't possess.

With most of his attention still fixed on Joe, Scott took his clothes off as if he were following an instruction manual translated from Chinese to English, by someone who didn't understand either language.

Joe hung his leather jacket in his locker. A second later, his T-shirt was gone. He had an intricate black tattoo on his right shoulder that Scott had never been lucky enough to see it up close before. Scott lost his grip on his own shirt buttons as he fought against the urge to reach out and touch Joe's ink without an invitation.

His need to run his hands over the complicated swirl of Celtic symbols was almost unbearable. So was the desire to lick it. Scott's mouth watered at the prospect. Hell, why stop with the tattoo. He'd love to lick every other bit of Joe too.

"Forgetting something?" Joe asked.

Scott blinked. Heat rushed to his cheeks as he went back to fumbling at his own clothes. Piece by piece, Scott put each garment in his locker. He didn't risk another glance at Joe until he'd removed everything and replaced his boots. He was completely naked from the ankles up — having his boots on only stressed that fact.

It was a locker room. There was nothing wrong with being naked in a locker room. Scott had been to gyms, if not regularly then, at least, on occasion. He'd got changed there the same as everyone else. He might not be entirely confident about his body, but he wasn't a prude. If he hadn't been sporting a very obvious erection, he might have been okay.

His fingers trembled as he turned the key in his locker. No one was going to swing a punch at him for getting turned on by all the naked men around him. There weren't going to be any homophobic straight men there. Everyone was gay or bi. There was nothing to be afraid of. None of those very logical thoughts actually helped Scott feel the least bit calmer.

When a hand brushed against the small of his back, Scott jumped forward and almost slammed himself face first into the row of lockers. He glanced over his shoulder. Joe was right there, and he didn't look the least bit happy.

Scott swallowed rapidly and tried to work out what was wrong. There were no clues in Joe's expression. His eyes revealed nothing. Scott wished like hell that he could believe his own poker face was just as effective.

* * * * *

Joe silently cursed himself as he stared down into a pair of big, blue, and very scared looking eyes. Scott really was a shy little thing. A man would have to be a complete bastard to drag him into a boots only night before they'd even spent a few hours naked and alone together.

Suddenly, Joe's amusing idea didn't seem so funny. It seemed less likely to nudge Scott out of his comfort zone and deeper into his submission, and far more likely to leave him scarred for life.

Joe lowered his gaze and saw that there was at least one part of Scott that appeared unaffected by his terror. Scott's cock was loving it. Talk about mixed signals.

"Do you want to leave?" Joe asked, cutting straight to the chase.

Scott's eyes opened very wide. "No!" He caught hold of Joe's bicep as if he thought Joe was the one who looked like he might run for the hills at any moment—as if he really thought he could stop Joe if that's what he decided to do.

"You look as if you're about to face a room full of serial killers," Joe pointed out.

A little bit of colour came back to Scott's face. Admittedly, it was an embarrassed blush rather than a healthy glow, but it was still better than the deathly pale version of Scott that had stared up at Joe just a few moments before.

"I just…" Scott took a deep breath and waved a hand toward his flourishing erection as if he thought it might have escaped Joe's notice. "I need a m-minute or two to get myself b-back under control," he whispered.

Joe looked from Scott's face to his hard cock and back again.

Was it really possible that Scott hadn't realised that everyone in the building was either going to be sporting wood or working on getting himself hard as soon as he could?

"No one's going to be insulted if you get turned on looking at them," Joe said.

Scott glanced up at him. "I guess I'm just n-not used to everyone else in the locker room being g-gay," he whispered.

"And you're not used to walking around naked and hard in front of strangers?" Joe suggested, with a smile. It was pretty much exactly what he expected.

Scott nodded. A lock of shiny blond hair fell forward into his eyes. He was so serious, so sweet, and since he seemed happy to stay in the pub it was impossible for Joe to resist upping the stakes.

"You don't need to worry," Joe whispered, dipping his head and bringing his lips to Scott's ear as if sharing a secret with him. "I never intended you to go out there *completely* naked."

Obvious relief rushed across Scott's face as Joe pulled back. A moment later, his expression morphed back into complete and utter shock.

"What the — ?"

Joe chuckled as he wrapped his fingers a little

more firmly around Scott's cock. "It's a cock ring," he said, as he fitted the flexible ring snugly in place at the base of Scott's shaft.

"I know w-what it is, I..." Scott's words trailed off as he met Joe's eyes. Of all the things he might have thought he'd be allowed to wear, a cock ring obviously hadn't made it onto his list.

"It looks good on you," Joe said, as he casually caressed Scott's hard shaft. Holding the length of Scott's erection steady, he checked the fit, making sure none of the short blond hairs at the base of Scott's cock were going to get caught.

Scott swallowed rapidly. For a moment, it looked as if he might protest, but he ultimately remained silent, accepting his "outfit" with true submissive grace.

Reluctantly releasing Scott's cock, Joe closed his own locker, took Scott's key from his unresisting hand, and tucked both keys into the side of his own boot. "Come on."

He was not going to jump Scott in the locker room, Joe reminded himself. Scott had wanted nudity and Joe was going to see to it that that was what Scott got. And he'd make sure Scott got it without being so stressed he gave himself a stroke.

Joe paused at the door leading out of the locker room and took hold of Scott's hand to reassure him there was no need to worry about anything. Then he led Scott purposefully into the bar area without giving him time to get more nervous.

There was an unoccupied table in the farthest corner of the room. Joe kept hold of Scott's hand and didn't release it until they'd reached the empty table.

Finally, freeing Scott's fingers, Joe sat down on the leather cushions that ran along the wall and settled his arm along the back of the seat.

A moment's hesitation, then Scott gingerly sat down next to him. Apparently, trapped between a desire to look around the room and a fear of being caught checking anyone out, he spent more time studying the table than anything else.

"You're allowed to look," Joe said. "That's the whole point."

Joe watched Scott's face as he took his advice and slowly ran his gaze over the room before turning back to Joe. His shoulders gradually relaxed. He unfurled his fists and settled his hands against the seat at his sides.

No matter which direction Scott looked, Joe never took his eyes off him. There wasn't going to be anything in the rest of the room that he hadn't seen a hundred times before. Scott was the first man who'd surprised him in a hell of a long time.

"You're n-not wearing…anything?" Scott observed when the silence seemed to get too much for him.

"No, I'm not," Joe agreed.

He'd have guessed that about two thirds of the guys there would be wearing a cock ring or butt plug. And even if they weren't, almost all of them would be either hardening, or at full mast by now. He didn't bother to look away from Scott to check out the other men's erections. They held no interest for him that night. Not even the sweetest arse could have made his attention stray from Scott's blushing face.

One thing was obvious. What he should have

given Scott to wear wasn't a cock ring, it was a collar. A strip of black leather would look damn good around his neck, marking him out as Joe's own personal property.

"Go up to the bar and fetch two glasses of Coke," Joe said, taking a fiver out of his sock and handing it to him.

"Coke?"

Joe nodded. "Coke."

Scott didn't say anything else. He stood up and made his way across the room. He might have been trying to hide his reluctance, but he failed spectacularly. Joe watched Scott walk up to the bar. His erection bounced slightly with each step. His buttocks clenched as his nerves increased with every foot he moved away from Joe's side. Any marks that the flogger had left on his skin last time they met up, had already faded away leaving a gorgeously-blank canvass.

With his attention never straying from Scott, Joe pulled one booted foot up to rest on the bench seat alongside him. Resting one elbow on his knee, he dropped his head back against the wall behind the cushioned seat.

A guy at the bar stepped up close to Scott. The place wasn't overly crowded. There was no need for any man to stand that near Scott. Joe tensed. He narrowed his gaze as he lifted his head away from the wall.

Words were exchanged. They spoke far too quietly for Joe to hear them, but whatever was said, it caused the man standing alongside Scott to look over his shoulder and toward their table.

Joe didn't move. He didn't even raise an eyebrow at the guy. But, he didn't rush to clear the frown from his forehead either.

All at once, there were several feet of empty space between Scott and the other guy.

Joe relaxed, once more satisfied with the state of the world. Within moments, Scott returned with their drinks. He paused when he saw Joe's foot on the seat, but chose to sit down on the edge of the cushion in front of Joe's boot, rather than move further down the bench and put any extra distance between them.

Scott kept his eyes firmly on the table as he set down their glasses and handed Joe the change.

"You're allowed to look at me, too," Joe pointed out. "That was what you wanted permission to do, wasn't it?"

Scott nibbled at his bottom lip. "Are you m-mad at me?"

Joe didn't think he was inclined to be easily taken aback, but he found himself blinking at Scott as if *he* were the naive little novice. "This isn't me mad," he finally said.

"Okay." That was it. Scott fell silent, once again completely fascinated by the table.

"If I was mad, I'd tell you straight out that I was pissed off. And I'd tell you exactly what you'd done that wound me up." Joe studied Scott's reaction very carefully.

Scott smiled slightly, as if being told that was something he needed to be grateful for. Then, he looked away, back to the oh-so-interesting table top.

Screw being patient—patience had never been Joe's strong point. Tucking a knuckle under Scott's chin, Joe made him face him properly. "I told you to ask for something. Why would I be mad at you for doing what you were told?"

Scott shrugged. He reached for his glass and took up a white knuckled grip around it. "Maybe you h-hoped I'd ask for s-s-something else?"

"I don't do mind games," Joe corrected. "If I think there's a chance you'll make a choice I don't like, I won't offer you the chance to make any decisions at all."

At least that coaxed a smile out of Scott. "I b-believe you."

"Good." Joe took a swig of his Coke and slouched a little more comfortably in his seat. His erection tilted back toward his stomach, a bead of pre-cum gathering on the tip. Joe ignored it. It was bloody hard to lose himself in the joy of being surrounded by naked, horny men when Scott stubbornly refused to act like the kind of sub he was so used to playing with.

Scott was an anomaly. He couldn't just be whipped, screwed and tossed aside; he had to be investigated. Joe mentally ran through everything he knew about Scott. Damn near nothing.

"What do you do when you're not writing letters inviting me to do kinky things with you?" Joe asked.

Scott looked up for a moment before quickly turning his attention back to his glass. Apparently, the dark bubbly liquid rivalled the sticky table top in terms of interest. "D-do?"

"Have you got a job?" Joe prompted.

Still looking ill at ease, Scott seemed to

consider the question very carefully. "Just a b-boring office j-job," he finally said. "I do the computer admin at a b-builder's merchants. Fill in the paperwork, make out the invoices, s-stuff like that. Why?"

Joe was pretty sure he could have told Scott that he intended to tie him up in the middle of the room, blindfold him, and whip every bit of skin off his back, and Scott would have been more at ease with it.

You're for sex, not for conversations.

It wasn't the first time Joe had sensed that thought in someone's head when he was playing with them. It was, however, the first time the idea pissed him off rather than suited him right down to his well-polished black boots. Joe tossed back another mouthful of Coke in an effort to wash away the bitterness on the back of his tongue.

"It doesn't pay g-g-great, but I p-p-pick up other work when I can," Scott went on. "Cut grass. W-walk dogs. D-deliver j-j-junk mail." His words were coming out faster now, and his stutter was getting more pronounced.

Joe took hold of Scott's wrist, the one attached to the hand holding his Coke, and guided it up toward his lips.

Words stopped. Scott drank steadily until Joe allowed him to lower his glass.

Relaxing back once more, Joe mentally corrected his impression of Scott's thoughts.

Sex makes me less nervous than talking to you.

It wasn't a thought he'd ever suspected any of his previous playmates of having, but it suited Scott far better than Joe's first reading of him. For some reason, the idea suited Joe, too.

"You know, answering my questions is no different to sucking my cock," he said, very casually.

Even though he'd already swallowed all the Coke he'd taken into his mouth, Scott managed to choke on it.

Joe casually rubbed Scott's back as Scott leaned over the table and spluttered.

His skin was warm and smooth. Joe's attention quickly wandered away from making sure Scott kept breathing, to enjoying the texture of Scott's flesh beneath his palm. Scott wasn't a muscle man, but Joe had played with guys with huge muscles before — they inevitably turned out to be less fun than Joe had expected them to be.

Scott glanced over his shoulder at him. Their eyes barely had a chance to meet before he dropped his gaze.

Joe's cock hardened a little more, showing off for Scott as Scott's eyes settled on his crotch. Joe could feel the bead of pre-cum forming on the tip of his cock growing fuller and heavier each time another erotic possibility nudged at his mind.

"Taste it," Joe ordered.

Scott glanced up at him. He blinked.

"Use your fingers, swipe up my cum, and taste it," Joe said again. He took another sip of his Coke.

Carefully setting his glass down, Scott turned toward Joe. A blush rushed to his cheeks as he tentatively ran a finger over the tip of Joe's erection.

Joe watched the digit disappear between Scott's lips. "If I order you to answer a question, that's no different," he explained. "An order is an order.

You obey me, and everything will be fine. Understand?"

Scott nodded.

"Good." Joe placed his glass on the table. "You said in your note that you wanted to see me naked."

Scott nodded.

"Is that all you want to do — to look at me?" Joe prompted.

Scott shook his head.

"What else?"

"Touch." The word was so softly spoken, even sitting as close together as they were, it was difficult for Joe to make it out.

Scott looked up. The desperation in his eyes was far louder than his whispered answer — it screamed both need and desire to Joe at the top of its voice.

"Go ahead."

Scott blinked.

Joe didn't say anything else. He just sat and waited to see what Scott would do with the permission he'd just granted him. With any other submissive, Joe probably wouldn't have bothered, but really, who could have realised that an unpredictable sub would be so hot?

Scott clenched and unclenched his fists several times before he finally reached out. His fingers came to rest on Joe's knee, where he'd bent his leg up to rest his boot on the bench.

Joe watched Scott as he ran his hand slowly up his thigh, brushing through the wiry dark hairs that decorated his skin. He tensed in expectation, but Scott didn't head straight for his cock. He moved his hand over Joe's abs instead. Palm flat against Joe's stomach, he spread his fingers as wide apart as he could, as if trying to touch as much of him as possible.

Joe's lips twitched into a smile as he saw Scott's self-consciousness fade. He was quickly losing himself in his explorations, and Joe wouldn't have had it any other way. Scott was beautiful when he wasn't aware he was being studied — perhaps not in an entirely classic way, but in a way that should have been guaranteed to appeal to any dom with a brain.

Joe made no attempt to control his body, or hide any of his reactions to Scott's touch, as the minutes ticked past. Scott's eyes shone with pleasure as he ran both his hands up to Joe's chest and slid his fingers into the thicker hair that grew in an inverted triangle there. Keeping his hands to himself for the moment, Joe contented himself with re-examining Scott's body with his eyes.

Scott's cock was thriving on the situation. He no longer needed the cock ring, and Joe no longer needed to worry that his nerves might make it impossible for Scott to remain hard in public; but it still looked very pretty on him.

Joe mentally replaced it with a chastity device. That would look even better on Scott. If it was locked and the key hung around Joe's neck, it would be perfect. Joe was aware that his smile had grown into a grin, but he didn't try to hide his pleasure at the idea.

Scott's hands strayed down Joe's body again. They skirted around Joe's cock to caress his thighs. Very slowly, Scott moved his hands closer together. With the fingertips of one hand he stroked around the base of Joe's cock, then up the shaft. At the same time, he slipped his other hand between Joe's thighs to cradle his densely furred balls.

His touch was gentle — too gentle. He'd have to be taught how to throw caution to the wind at some point. Joe added it as an extra item to his to-do list.

Scott seemed almost too embarrassed to linger over Joe's cock and balls for too long. Soon, he was working his way up Joe's body again. Eventually, his inspection reached Joe's shoulders, his fingers pressed harder there, exploring the layers of muscle more thoroughly, especially over his tattoo.

It was quite possible Scott had an undiagnosed massage fetish going on. Joe made another mental note about that. It could be a fun direction to take their explorations one night — but not tonight.

"Do you know why we're both drinking Coke?" Joe asked.

Scott shook his head.

"Because a man has no right to take control of anyone else unless he's in complete control of himself. I never drink if I'm planning to do a scene, if I expect someone to submit to me."

Scott couldn't have looked more stunned if Joe had announced an intention of taking him hot air ballooning.

Joe let his lips twist into a grin once more. "I'm going to screw you until you scream, Scott."

* * * * *

"Right now? Right h-here?" It was more luck than judgement which prevented Scott's voice from returning to soprano.

God help him, but if Joe wanted to bend him over the table and top him in front of all these naked strangers, Scott knew he wouldn't say no to him.

The idea of Joe and the word "no" existing in the same universe was insane.

Suddenly, Joe launched himself to his feet. Without a word, he grabbed Scott's wrist and headed for the door. Hurrying around the table, Scott stumbled behind Joe for several paces before he got his legs untangled and managed to catch up properly.

Joe wasn't the kind of guy who slowed down for anyone. The timely reminder of that made Scott's cock harder than ever. His shaft throbbed above the cock ring.

Scott was reasonably sure that, if he'd fallen over, Joe would simply have kept striding forward, dragging him along the bar room floor like a prehistoric warrior claiming his mate and rushing back to his cave to mark his new piece of property as his own.

It was pure luck that stopped Scott coming at the thought, untouched and without even his jeans to catch his cum this time.

He had no time to read the sign on a battered door before Joe pulled him through the doorway and slammed the door behind them. The door was barely closed before Scott found himself thrust roughly toward it.

Joe released Scott's wrist just in time to let Scott bring his hands forward and stop himself slamming head first into the peeling paint. Joe kicked the inside of each of Scott's boots, making him spread his legs like the suspect on an American cop show.

"Are we naked enough for you?" Joe asked, stepping forward so his body was pressed firmly against Scott's smaller frame. For the first time, skin met skin from shoulder to knee. Fireworks exploded through every inch of Scott that Joe rubbed against.

"So good..." Scott mumbled.

Joe made a satisfied noise in the back of his throat as he lined his body up against Scott's a little more perfectly. It sounded suspiciously like agreement and a declaration of ownership all rolled into one.

The hairs on Joe's chest rubbed against Scott's back as Joe rearranged his arms and legs so each limb found its mate. Joe's hands covered Scott's, pressing his palms more firmly against the door. His feet came to rest just inside Scott's boots, keeping him spread open and vulnerable. And, most importantly of all, Joe's cock rubbed against Scott's arse.

Scott moaned, pushing his backside out in blatant invitation. "Condom." That was important. Even if Joe was the hottest man on the planet, there was a little bit of Scott that still remembered that a condom was supposed to be considered important, although at that moment, he was damned if he could remember why.

"Why? Are you in a rush for something?" Joe whispered in his ear.

Scott frowned as he tried to make his mind work. It wasn't easy while Joe rubbed his cock along the cleft between Scott's arse cheeks, its strokes slicked by an increasing amount of Joe's pre-cum.

Joe moved his hands off Scott's, and ran his palms down Scott's arms. He reached around Scott and slid his hands across Scott's chest, only stopping once he found Scott's nipples. He caught the little peaks of nerve endings between his fingers.

"I'll remember everything that I need to do before I screw you. But it's still early. I have plenty of time to play with you first." As he spoke, he pulled Scott's nipples away from his chest, stretching the skin, sending wave after wave of unexpected sensations rolling through Scott's body.

As Joe scraped his thumbnails against Scott's nipples, they became more and more sensitive. They pebbled into tight little buds as Joe started to twist them. Scott whimpered, but he didn't try to pull away.

A quick caress was all any other man had ever offered Scott's chest—and that was all Scott had been interested in receiving. Now, he moaned, and helplessly arched his back, pressing his pecs against Joe's hands, looking for an even rougher touch, as Joe quickly convinced him to crave what he'd never even thought about before.

Pleasure rolled through Scott's body. He thrust his hips forward, desperate to feel something against his cock, but there was nothing for him to hump against.

"One day, I'm going to make you come just by playing with your nipples," Joe growled in Scott's ear.

Scott frowned, not sure that was physically possible.

"You will come from that," Joe informed him, without the slightest hint of doubt in his voice. "If I tell you to—you will."

Scott found himself nodding. Disobedience

obviously wasn't to be considered.

"I'm going to show you so many different ways I can make you come," Joe promised. He laughed then, a rough sound that had very little humour in it.

A shiver ran down Scott's spine. He wasn't at all sure he'd enjoy all of those ways—and even less sure that Joe would care if most of them came close to killing him from frustration before they finally brought him off.

Scott swallowed rapidly, still not really understanding why that knowledge appealed to him or what made him so desperate to submit to anything Joe wanted. He only knew that it rushed to his cock faster than anything any of the "nice guys" he'd tried to date had done for him.

Without any warning, Joe pulled away. Scott snatched his hands away from the door, turned, and reached out to stop him.

"Back as you were," Joe barked. "I didn't give you permission to move!"

Scott's body followed the order before his mind even caught up with the fact that one had been issued. He put himself back against the door, shuffling his feet apart without needing to be nudged into position again. A second's thought and he inched his boots even further away from each other, highlighting his invitation, even as his muscles protested at the extra stretch.

He heard something that sounded like paper tearing. The packaging from a condom? Scott didn't look over his shoulder to check if his guess was correct. Joe had said he'd remember, and he would.

Scott didn't need to worry about that any more. He didn't need to worry about anything...

As he stared at the woodwork, Scott felt someone take a tin opener to his skull. The moment the top of his head was removed, his brain floated away, no longer weighed down with his usual day to day worries. Scott didn't need thoughts now. Joe would take care of everything. Instincts and obedience were all that Scott required.

Joe's fingers were already slicked when he slid them between Scott's arse cheeks. Scott immediately rocked his hips, trying to push himself back onto Joe's fingers.

Joe slapped Scott's left buttock, hard. The sound echoed through the room. Scott gasped, relishing the unexpected flash of heat that radiated out from the smack, but the reminder still worked. He stilled his hips and gave over all control to Joe without needing to be told again.

A low, satisfied sound rumbled through Joe's chest in response. He finally stopped teasing, pushed his fingers forward, and penetrated Scott's arse — obedience well rewarded.

Helplessly moaning his pleasure, Scott gave everything he had to maintaining his position as Joe worked his fingers deeper inside him.

Joe didn't say anything when he took his fingers away. Every muscle in Scott's body tensed at the loss, but somehow, he managed to remain silent. His arms trembled. He dipped his head toward the door panels, but he didn't utter a single word of complaint.

A lifetime seemed to pass before Scott felt the

blunt pressure of Joe's cock against his well-prepared hole. Joe's shaft was slicked and latex-covered, but Scott was barely in any condition to notice such details. All he knew for sure was that it was Joe's cock and he wanted it buried inside him as far as was physically possible, then an extra inch deeper, just for luck.

For the first time in his life, it was the desire for a connection as much as for physical pleasure that drove Scott on. He didn't just need to come, he needed Joe inside him — needed Joe to take control of him and become part of him. Scott whimpered; unable to bring words to his lips, but equally unable to stay silent.

Scott closed his eyes. Leaning forward, he rested his temple against the door. Joe allowed that, but he grabbed Scott's hips with both hands and made sure Scott's arse remained exactly where he wanted it. He dug his fingers roughly into Scott's skin as he finally pushed forward, lodging his entire shaft inside Scott's body with one powerful motion.

Scott's whole body jerked. As much as he wanted Joe's cock, he wasn't entirely ready for the size of it. The breath rushed out of his lungs. His eyes tried to roll back in his head. Yet, somehow, he still found himself squirming within Joe's hold, desperate for more.

Joe made Scott remain still for what felt like forever, forcing him to take some time to relax and adjust. Years seemed to pass before Joe was finally willing to pull back and thrust hard into Scott again.

Scott clawed at the door's battered paintwork as Joe's movements became increasingly brutal and unyielding with every minute that passed. Scott could barely keep himself on his feet. If Joe's grip on him had been looser, Scott knew he'd have tumbled to the floor. But, while Joe's fingers dug into Scott's sides, collapsing simply wasn't an option.

There was no way for Scott to escape the rough pounding — or the ecstasy that raced through his body in response to it. It wasn't a comfortable way to be screwed, and it was nothing like being back on the creaking bed in his rented room. His knees trembled. Pleasure and something close to pain mingled inside him, making everything somehow better than pure bliss might have made it on its own.

Suddenly, Joe moved his right hand away from Scott's hip. He reached around Scott and grabbed Scott's cock.

Joe's grip was just a fraction too tight. He jacked Scott hard and relentless, not bothering to ask if that was the kind of caress Scott wanted, and maybe not even caring.

Scott thrashed helplessly between Joe and the door, unable to remain still, no matter how much he wanted to obey Joe's orders. He pushed himself back onto Joe's cock and forward into Joe's hand as if his life depended on it.

Trapped in the moment, Scott hurtled helplessly toward his orgasm. He bucked as his climax tore through him, his cum spilling into Joe's hand and onto the door panels in front him.

Just a moment later, Joe's rhythm escalated. He thrust his shaft deeper inside Scott, as he reached his own orgasm. The world came to a complete stop. Scott had no doubt that every man in the club froze, unable to do anything but wait out their bliss with them. There was no way that only two people could be aware of such a perfect moment existing in the world, there was no way it could ever have been kept a secret.

Scott didn't move. He couldn't move, not even when Joe ultimately pulled away. Scott wasn't sure if it was obedience, exhaustion, or simply an unwillingness to leave the ecstasy he'd found while leaning against that door.

He remained in position until Joe tugged at his shoulder and forced him to straighten up. Scott blinked down at the cum-stained door, his mind slow and hazy with afterglow. When Joe gave him no choice but to turn around, Scott looked at the room around them for the first time.

"Where a-a-are we?"

"Ladies' toilets."

Scott blinked.

Joe shrugged. "Not like anyone would be using them tonight." He sounded so confident, the fact they were standing in forbidden territory stopped feeling wrong to Scott. It couldn't be wrong — not when Joe chose it.

"I should p-probably, um..." Scott stepped clumsily around Joe, retrieved some paper towels from the dispenser on the wall and cleaned up his cum, only vaguely aware of Joe throwing away the used condom behind him.

Tasks completed, Scott glanced up at Joe, instinctively looking for an order. Joe said nothing, he merely slapped Scott's arse as he stepped past him, grabbed Scott's wrist and jerked open the door.

He led Scott out of the toilets, through the bar and into the locker room, apparently oblivious to the knowing looks every guy in the pub shot in their direction. Scott wished like hell he could have felt the same way. As it was, the only thing that kept Scott moving was Joe's grip on his wrist.

Joe seemed to make a point of giving Scott a few minutes to himself and allowing him to pull himself together while they each got dressed. Scott had never been more grateful for companionable silence in his life. He'd never enjoyed looking down at his own body while he got dressed and knowing that he'd soon be sporting a few bruises from a rough riding so much, either.

He didn't look up and meet Joe's eyes until they were both completely clothed.

Out of nowhere, Joe shook his head. His expression changed to one that appeared thoroughly disappointed in Scott. "You know, it's really not on for a man to have been out as long as you to have and to never have been to a boots only night."

Scott looked down. He'd obviously been crazy to think that he could keep the attention of a man like Joe for more than a couple of days. It was stupid to believe that, just because he'd thought their latest date put sliced bread in the shade, Joe would feel that way too.

Scott glanced up when he heard paper rustling, even though he knew it was hopeless to pray that it would be the sound of another condom being unwrapped.

All the air rushed out of his lungs when he spotted the envelope in Joe's hand.

Joe tapped the edge of the envelope against his chin, apparently deep in thought. "Yes, I think it's time someone started to introduce you to a whole new world, isn't it, Scott?"

Scott nodded enthusiastically, relief making his head spin and his lips curve up into a goofy grin. It didn't even occur to him to worry about what that might actually mean until after Joe had dropped him off outside his house with a final command that Scott leave the envelope sealed until the following morning.

There were only two words written on the outside of the envelope— Orders Enclosed.

Part Four: Orders Enclosed

Scott tapped the corner of the envelope against his car's steering wheel and stared vacantly through the windscreen. He didn't need to open the envelope and re-read the orders enclosed to be able to recall exactly what Joe had commanded him to do.

He had the whole damn thing memorised.

Drive to Carter's Rest.

He'd done that bit, no problem. The directions Scott had found on the internet had worked like a charm. He now sat outside a dingy-looking old pub on the edge of the city—which was apparently where Joe wanted him to be. Scott took a deep breath and let it out very slowly in an effort to calm his racing pulse.

Stay in your car until exactly 11pm.

Scott glanced at his watch for the third time in as many minutes and silently cursed himself. He shouldn't have left for their date so early. Excessive punctuality wasn't going to win him any prizes—it was just going to give him enough time to drive himself completely demented with nerves.

Running one hand down his face, Scott slumped back in his seat. At this rate, he'd be a wreck before he was even due to walk into place.

Letting out a sigh, he tilted his head back and stared at the underside of the car roof, as if the answer to every question in the universe might be written there—or at least a few pointers on how to please Joe. Forget all the bull about the key to perpetual serenity—the only thing Scott really wanted to know was how to keep Joe happy with him.

A neon light flickered on the wall in front of Scott, casting a strange intermittent glow over the car's interior.

Park in the first space to the right of the entrance.

He was exactly where Joe wanted him to be. Everything was fine. Scott rubbed his damp palms against his jeans.

He looked at his watch again. Then he looked at the clock on the dashboard to make sure his watch wasn't running fast.

11pm.

Gathering up whatever courage he could, Scott pulled himself out of his car. He peered into the shadows that extended for several yards on each side of the pub. There was still no sign of Joe's car, or his bike, anywhere in the car park.

Perhaps Joe had changed his mind about their date. Perhaps...

Scott shook his head. Orders were orders. They weren't to be questioned; they were to be followed.

He locked his car, sent up a quick prayer that it would still be there when he came out of the pub, and he turned toward the low, graffiti covered building. Pushing the door open, he stepped inside.

He'd thought the car park was gloomy, but as the pub door swung closed, a deeper kind of blackness closed in around him. A shiver ran down his spine.

It...well, it certainly wasn't anything like the sort of gay bars Scott had ventured into when he'd first come out. Clean lines and minimalist decor were conspicuously absent. No modern art hung on the walls, no fashionably dressed guys gathered in little groups, drinking cocktails and sneering at those not considered fashionable enough.

It wasn't like the club where he'd spent so many evenings staring at Joe either. There was no music; no dance floor filled with men grinding against each other in time to the beat.

Even somewhat obscured by the stale smoke that hung in the air, this looked more like the kind of place where Scott could imagine a serial killer picking up his victims.

Men dressed in grubby denim and well-worn leather stood along a dark, wooden bar that was scarred by what looked horrifyingly like knife marks.

Scott felt the men's eyes moving over him. Their gazes weren't so much like a physical caress, as like being grabbed by the throat and held helpless, his feet several inches off the floor as he was twisted around and inspected from every angle.

Scott took a step back. His shoulder hit the door. As quickly as he'd began to retreat, he stepped forward again, an unexpected wave of determination bubbling up inside him.

He had as much right to be there as anyone else. No, he had *even more* right, because he was there on Joe's orders.

Go through the door at the back of the main bar — between the jukebox and the door to the gents.

Head down, frantically trying to appear as inconspicuous as possible, Scott strode through the bar area as quickly as he could without breaking into a run. His jeans and shirt had felt like perfectly normal clothing a few minutes ago. Now, they marked him out as someone who didn't belong—as a potential victim.

Scott took a deep breath. His lungs filled with hot, smoky air. He almost choked on the stale stench of spilt alcohol.

Joe wouldn't send him somewhere that wasn't safe. Scott repeated that to himself several times, and hoped like hell his read on Joe was right.

Relief swept through Scott as he finally spotted the sign for the gents. A moment later, a broken jukebox came into view. Just as Joe had promised, another door stood between them.

Like a man who'd been wandering in the desert for several decades, Scott rushed toward the shimmering oasis. He half expected it to vanish like some imaginary palm tree, but the door handle was reassuringly solid. He pushed the door open and stepped into a smaller, even gloomier, room.

Cubicles lined one wall. It had obviously been the ladies room in some former incarnation of the pub—one where women had been more welcome. Scott shook his head, wondering if there was a special term for a gay man who had a fetish for ladies' bathrooms, and if Joe knew he had it.

Go into the second stall on the left.

Scott nudged the appropriate cubicle door open. Stepping inside, he automatically closed it and locked it behind him. A bare light bulb hung above his head, casting a ghostly yellow glow over the stains on the walls.

Barely a moment passed before Scott heard the door into the bathroom swing open, then click closed again. He held his breath, straining his hearing in the hope of identifying the man who'd just joined him.

Footsteps crossed the tiled floor. They sounded heavy, solid. Maybe the guy was wearing boots — maybe the kind of boots Joe liked to wear? The cubicle door to the left of Scott's stall squeaked. Two more footsteps echoed through the room. Another creak — whoever the guy was, he'd closed the door behind him.

Scott turned toward the rickety cubicle wall that now represented the only barrier between himself and the other man.

As if weighed down with concrete boots, his gaze descended as unstoppably as a mob informant until it reached the rough hole punched through the wall between the cubicles.

Scott's pulse raced faster and faster. He should have been horrified. He knew that deep down in a part of his brain that lay so close to instinct, Scott had never thought to question anything it had told him before.

His hand went to his fly and pressed against the dark blue denim. He hadn't been imagining it. He really was as hard as he'd ever been in his life. His grimy surroundings weren't putting him off. If anything, they were doing the exact opposite.

Scott stroked his shaft through the straining fabric. Adrenaline rushed through his veins, making him acutely aware of every part of his body, but his gaze never wavered from the glory hole.

He tried to take a deep breath, but there didn't seem to be enough oxygen. The man on the other side of the wall had stolen it all. Scott pressed the heel of his hand harder against his cock, massaging it firmly through the denim.

At this rate, it would be a toss-up if he'd came in his jeans or hyperventilated first.

The sound of a zip being drawn down filled the room. Scott looked away from the hole for a moment, quite prepared to believe his hand had unzipped his own jeans without giving his brain a chance to state an opinion on the matter.

No. He was still done up and neatly tucked away.

Scott looked back toward the cubicle wall just in time to see the tip of an erection appear through the glory hole. As he watched, several inches of shaft slid into view.

Kneel.

Suck.

The last two orders from Joe's note circled around and around in Scott's mind. Right on cue, Scott's mouth watered. He swallowed rapidly, trying to drag his brain back above his belt and failing. Curling his hand into a fist, Scott managed to move it away from his crotch.

Kneel.

Suck.

Joe's orders were very clear.

Even without his hand on his own cock, coaxing him to forget why he really shouldn't be thinking with his balls, Scott couldn't resist the urge to lower himself to his knees. Without any order leaving his own brain, Scott's body willingly followed the commands in the envelope and brought him eye level — mouth level, with the proffered cock.

He was where Joe wanted him to be, doing

exactly what Joe wanted him to do. That in itself was almost enough to make Scott whimper with pleasure. His skin prickled with the memory of Joe's touch from the last time they shared a moment in a deserted ladies' bathroom. Scott's nipples pebbled until just the friction of his shirt brushing against them was enough to make him shudder.

The light was too dim. His own shadow fell across the hole, making it even more difficult to make out the details of the offered erection.

It looked like Joe's cock—long, thick, uncut and flushed with arousal. Scott swallowed rapidly. It had to be Joe's—there couldn't be two cocks that gorgeous in the same city. And Joe wouldn't order him to go there and suck off a stranger...

Scott hesitated then.

Joe wouldn't do that. Would he?

Anxiety and adrenaline rushed through Scott's veins, mingling together so thoroughly it was impossible for him to know where one ended and the other began—where the part of him that wanted to be anywhere except kneeling in that cubicle blurred into that part of him that loved being there even more with every minute that passed.

It had to be Joe standing on the other side of the glory hole. Joe wouldn't want him blowing anyone else. Not when Joe had made it so clear that Scott wasn't allowed to have sex with anyone else and—

But maybe it didn't count as breaking the rules if Joe ordered him to go down on another man.

Scott's mind raced with so many different possibilities. They overlapped and interrupted each other inside his head, until they were nothing more than an unintelligible din.

Kneel.

Suck.

Those two words were the only ones that still came through clearly.

Scott gingerly adjusted his position on the dirty floor. There was nothing but stained tiles beneath his knees. His joints were already starting to protest their discomfort, but in some way that Scott still didn't understand, it felt like a good sort of pain—a kind that reminded him he was obeying Joe.

Scott swayed forward, instinctively moving closer to the cock protruding from the hole as he thought about Joe.

Kneel...

Scott leaned in further still and brushed his lips against the tip of the erection poking through the hole. The guy on the other side of the wall—Joe, it had to be Joe, didn't it?—pressed his cock more firmly against Scott's mouth.

After having to wait for so long for him to get started, Scott couldn't blame Joe—please, God, let it be Joe—for wanting more than a brief brush of skin against skin.

Scott pulled away, but only a fraction of an inch. He licked his lips, hesitating just one last time before he dipped his head and kissed the tip of the other man's cock properly.

The salty flavour of pre-cum quickly convinced Scott to open his mouth and wrap his lips around the head of the shaft. It tasted just like Joe had the last time Scott had gone down on him.

Murmuring his relief, Scott finally allowed himself to believe that there could be no doubt who was on the other side of the wall. He lapped at the tip of Joe's cock, relishing the taste of him.

Scott slid one hand between the wall and his face, and wrapped his fingers around Joe's shaft. His fingers brushed against a man's hand.

Before Scott could even try to peer through the hole and look for identifying features, the hand vanished. More of Joe's shaft slid through the hole as he altered his stance and allowed Scott the privilege of holding him steady without any assistance.

Gently drawing Joe's foreskin back, Scott ran his tongue over the sensitive glans it had covered, drawing a moan from Joe. The encouraging sound finally gave Scott the confidence to dip his head closer to the wall and take more of the shaft into his mouth.

Suck.

That order was so easy to obey now.

Instinct kicked in. Scott began to suckle enthusiastically around the thick shaft, glorying in the way Joe filled his senses. The taste of Joe, the scent of his pleasure; even if Scott couldn't look up and see Joe's face, his mind was full of him.

As Scott caressed the vein on the underside of Joe's cock with his tongue, it seemed to stiffen and swell even further within Scott's mouth.

Scott's mind spun. Dizziness threatened to overwhelm him. His vision blurred at the edges. Suddenly, Scott realised he'd been far too focused on sucking and hadn't been paying nearly enough attention to breathing. Desperate for air, he had to pull away. As Joe's cock slipped from between his lips, Scott sucked in deep pulls of air.

Silently cursing himself, he worked Joe's shaft with his hand, jacking him firmly, as he fought to catch his breath as quickly as possible. As soon as he could, Scott leaned forward and took the thick shaft back into his mouth. It felt so good inside him, so right and natural. It was where Joe's cock belonged, and it was so easy for Scott to believe that this was what his mouth had always been meant for; he just hadn't realised it until he found the right cock to fill it.

Scott slid his lips down Joe's erection until they kissed his hand, where his fingers were wrapped around the shaft. Moving his hand out of the way, Scott bowed his head even closer to the wall.

The girth of Joe's cock stretched Scott's lips. The head nudged the back of his throat. Scott moaned, pulled back until only the tip remained in his mouth, then slid back down again. He took as much as he could and thrived on every inch of it.

Carefully keeping his teeth covered, Scott bobbed his head more quickly, glorying in the increased friction against his lips. On the other side of the wall, Joe matched Scott's rhythm perfectly.

Scott looked up, eager to meet Joe's eyes. The only thing that stared back at him was graffiti praising another man's oral skills. Scott groaned his frustration around Joe's shaft.

A gasp from the other stall let him know that Joe really appreciated the vibrations. Bracing himself with his hands on the wall either side of the hole, Scott sucked harder around the length of Joe's erection, trying to draw another snippet of praise from him.

Joe's rhythm increased and Scott instinctively fell still so Joe could use his mouth in whatever way he pleased. That was the way it should be.

Even with the wall between them, Joe seemed to realise that Scott was trying to give up control to him. Dominant to the core, he didn't hesitate to take up the slack. A growl of approval echoed around the cubicles. Quickly establishing his rhythm, Joe thrust into Scott's mouth, deep and unrelenting.

In theory, at least, Scott knew he could pull away if he needed to. There was nothing stopping him — no hand on the back of his head, no bondage to prevent his escape. But he wouldn't, and even more than that, he knew he wouldn't need to. Even as Joe's thrusts sped up and grew more fierce, there was a sense of underlying control in his movements.

Joe knew exactly what he was doing. It stopped mattering what sort of pub they were in then. Scott had never felt safer, or more wanted.

His eyes dropped closed. His hands flattened out on the wall on either side of the hole. Scott whimpered his pleasure. He'd never been more turned on.

Scott tried to keep his mouth completely still, but it was impossible for him not to at least try to work his tongue against Joe's cock. Resisting the temptation to suckle around the head at every opportunity also proved to be far beyond Scott's capabilities.

Without any warning that Scott was aware of, Joe's rhythm disintegrated. He thrust into Scott's mouth several times, hard and fast, his movements jerky and lacking all his usual coordination. With a triumphant yell that everyone in the pub must have heard, Joe came in Scott's mouth.

Scott swallowed rapidly as semen spilled across his tongue. He was caught off guard, but he was still determined not to miss a drop. He scrabbled at the wall, pressing his face against the hole until Joe finally stilled.

Success rushed through Scott like a tidal wave. He'd made Joe come. Joe got off on what they were doing. As far as Scott was concerned, in that particular moment, he rocked!

In no rush to bring his moment of glory to an end, he remained where he was, letting Joe's shaft slowly soften in his mouth.

All too soon, Joe pulled away. Scott whimpered, but his wordless plea was ignored. Just a moment later, Scott heard Joe do up his fly. Even though he knew it was useless, Scott remained in position—his mouth open and offered up to the hole, his forehead resting on the wall just above it.

The door to the other cubicle squeaked. Footsteps echoed through the ladies' bathroom, getting quieter as they walked away. Scott heard the door leading back into the bar room swing open, then close again. Losing all interest in the hole now that Joe had left, Scott sat back on his heels.

Lifting one hand to his face, he traced his lips very gently with a fingertip. They were so swollen, so sensitive. Scott had no doubt they'd be reddened too. When he walked out of the ladies' room, everyone in the bar room would know what he had been doing in there.

Scott pressed his fingers more firmly against his sensitive lips, trying to hold back a sudden, light-headed, desire to giggle. He didn't take his hand away from his mouth until the urge had passed. Scott shook his head at himself. Everyone in the pub must have a bloody good idea of what guys went into the back room for. And he was pretty sure they'd guess that he was the kind of guy who much preferred to be on his knees.

Scott flicked out his tongue. The taste of Joe's cum still lingered on his lips. It sent another spark of pleasure rushing down his spine, straight to his cock.

He pressed the heel of his hand to his tenting fly once more.

Going to the pub on Joe's order, submitting to him, pleasing him — enjoying all of those things made perfect sense to Scott. Getting off on going down on his knees behind a glory hole when he had no guarantee that the man on the other side was Joe, was...

Scott frowned. Without fellatio to distract him, all his nerves came back. What had seemed certain while he had a cock in his mouth seemed tenuous now. The probability that he'd have to come to terms with having gone down on someone other than Joe doubled by the second.

Scott had no idea how long he knelt there before he finally dragged himself to his feet. Taking a deep breath, he pushed the stall door open and hoped like hell that he wouldn't meet anyone who was walking in while he was on his way out.

Luck was with him. Scott made it safely back into the bar room. Head down, he strode briskly toward the exit, praying that he wouldn't draw anyone's attention.

Pushing his hands deep into his jeans pockets, he tried to disguise his hard-on as best he could, but there was no way he could hide the stains on his knees. Scott heard someone say something about watching out for the quiet ones. A couple of guys laughed. Scott blushed and kept going.

His white-knuckled grip on his car keys tightened even further as he finally stepped out into the car park and pulled his hands out of his pockets.

He let out a sigh of relief when he saw that his car was still there. Hands shaking with an overload of adrenaline, Scott unlocked the car door and slid behind the wheel. It was only when he pulled the door closed that the full force of his evening's activities hit him like a punch to the gut. There was no way in hell it had been Joe on the other side of the glory hole.

* * * * *

Opening the passenger side door, Joe bent down and peered into Scott's car.

"What the—!" Scott cut himself off as he apparently realised who Joe was.

Joe grinned as he folded his tall frame into the small space, but his smile didn't last long. Whoever had sat in the passenger seat last had obviously been under three feet tall. After a couple of seconds groping around beneath his seat, Joe found the mechanism that allowed him to slide the seat back.

Finally able to breathe without his ribs hitting

into his knees, Joe turned in his seat and ran his eyes over Scott in a quick but thorough inspection. "You don't seem particularly happy to see me," he observed, keeping his tone casual and conversational.

Scott didn't say a word. He just stared at Joe as if he'd never set eyes on him before.

The flickering neon light lent a strange glow to Scott's face and made him appear even more freaked out by the world than he usually was. Joe was used to Scott finding it difficult to look him in the eye; he wasn't quite so accustomed to Scott staring at his crotch as if he thought Joe's cock might spontaneously jump out and do a little dance for him.

He reached out to put his hand on Scott's knee.

"I w-wouldn't if I w-were you."

Joe raised an eyebrow, and kept his hand hovering an inch above Scott's leg. "Feeling inclined to throw a punch, are you?"

Scott opened his eyes very wide as he shook his head. "Of c-c-course not!"

"Then what?" Joe asked.

Scott glanced down at his jeans. "The floor in there was r-really filthy. You don't want to p-put your hand on—"

Joe put his hand firmly on Scott's knee. Curling his fingers over the joint, Joe made sure his hand covered any bit of denim that might have come into direct contact with the floor. "I'll decide where I want to put my hands."

"I..." Scott blinked at Joe's hand, apparently more confused than ever.

"There's no fun in dirtying up a nice, clean-cut guy if you're going to be afraid to touch him afterwards, is there?"

Scott didn't laugh at Joe's teasing. He turned his attention from his knees back to Joe's crotch. He seemed fascinated by his fly. Joe glanced down. There was nothing special about his jeans. He couldn't even see the line of his cock through them that clearly, now that he was soft.

Joe lifted his attention to Scott's face. He'd planned to tease Scott about enjoying getting down and dirty in a rough pub, telling him he hadn't needed an order, just an excuse, but that plan obviously needed to change. "You took a while to get started in there," he offered, as an opening bid toward working out what the hell was going on.

The neon light outside was yellow. It made the blush that rushed to Scott's cheeks appear strangely orange. "I um…I w-was trying to work out if it w-was yours," he mumbled.

Joe's frown deepened. "What?"

Scott cleared his throat. "The lighting in there wasn't g-great. I…I was trying to work out if I'd be going down on you or—"

"Do you really think I'd have ordered you to go in there if there was *any* chance that someone else would be on the other side of the hole?" Joe demanded. He was aware that his grip on Scott's knee had tightened rapidly, but he couldn't seem to relax his fingers. The idea of Scott's mouth wrapping around anyone else's cock…

Scott shrugged. "Some guys g-get off on things like that, don't they?" he asked. "Sharing their…their…Sharing the m-men they're having s-s-sex with, with other men?"

"I don't," Joe bit out. Unable to shake the image from his imagination, he felt more anger flooding into him by the moment.

Scott hesitated several times, before he actually managed to speak. "It c-could have been a j-j-joke or something..." He shrugged again, the movement jerky and unsure of itself. Scott tried to straighten his leg, but Joe couldn't make himself let go of his knee.

"You've got a bloody strange sense of humour if you think that would have been funny..." Joe trailed off. His gaze narrowed. Scott wasn't that kind of guy. He wouldn't have thought that was in the least bit amusing. He wouldn't have played that kind of "joke" on anyone.

Forget anger, ice cold fury poured into Joe's veins. He tightened the hand that wasn't on Scott's knee into a fist. "Who?" he demanded.

Scott blinked, looking more innocent than ever — as if he really didn't have a clue what Joe was talking about.

"Who played that kind of sick joke on you?"

For several long seconds, Scott stared at him in silence, but Joe held his gaze, determined to get an answer.

Scott looked down, not at his knees or Joe's cock now, just down — like a man who had suddenly stopped believing he was worthy of looking another man in the eye.

Joe flexed his fingers, forcing them to relax out of a fist shape. Moving his hand to Scott's throat, he slid it up, until the edge of his index finger was right under his chin. Tilting Scott's head back, Joe made him look up.

"You've n-never been the guy on the outside l-looking in, have you?" Scott whispered.

Joe was used to seeing pain in a man's eyes when he was administering a harsh whipping — but it was always the good kind of pain. The man in pain was always a hard-core masochist. There was always pleasure in his eyes too.

The pure agony in Scott's gaze made Joe's heart race and his stomach clench. It would have been easy to look away, but Joe forced himself to keep Scott's gaze, no matter how uncomfortable the emotions that swirled around the car made him. "The outside?"

Scott's lips curved into a strange mockery of a smile. "You were the most p-popular boy in school, right? I'll bet both the boys and the girls were th-throwing themselves at you more quickly than you could w-work your way through them. And you s-sailed straight through your teens, looking all c-cool and gorgeous, didn't you?"

Joe didn't answer. He was still too busy trying to work out what the hell they were talking about.

"I... I was one of those kids who hit his g-growth spurt late. Add in skin you could play join the d-d-dots with, and me being scrawny as hell..." Scott's Adam's apple bobbed underneath Joe's palm as he swallowed several times in quick succession.

Joe stroked his thumb back and forth over Scott's jaw, as if he could actually make him feel better by doing that.

Scott gave a jerky shrug. "Kids can be cruel, but they've really got n-nothing on a certain kind of gay man. The guys I met just after I c-came out were all fashionable and gorgeous. They had m-muscles, and perfect skin, and expensive hair c-cuts. No w-wonder they thought I w-was an idiot."

Scott tried to laugh, as if there was anything funny about the way those guys had treated him. Scott failed, but Joe didn't even try to chuckle. His stomach twisted into a complicated knot as dozens of scenarios ran through his mind, each one worse than the last. He could easily imagine the kind of jokes some men would play on an easy target who was so desperate to please and be accepted. A bitter taste filled the back of his mouth. Fury bubbled in his veins. "I want their names."

If nothing else, the demand made Scott look Joe in the eye. Some of the pain in his expression gave way to confusion. "W-why?"

"So I can kill them."

Scott laughed. It was little more than a chuckle really, but it was genuine. The sound eased a little of Joe's anger, but he still wasn't sure he'd been joking. If any of the men who'd hurt Scott had been there, Joe would have happily throttled every one of the bastards, one after the other.

Joe's frown deepened. He never remembered being so desperate to hurt anyone who wasn't already an enthusiastic masochist. He'd never realised he could feel so protective of another man either. Suddenly, neither Scott's shyness nor his lack of confidence seemed so strange.

Joe forced the fingers on his right hand to uncurl. He even managed to turn his hold on Scott's throat into something that wasn't approaching a Vulcan death grip. "You still haven't answered my question," he said.

Scott shook his head. "It...it was y-years ago. I was still l-l-living at home. You d-don't know them."

That doesn't mean I can't track them down...

Joe cleared his throat. It was all he could do to keep those particular words back, instantly replacing them with more appropriate words was impossible. He sat in silence for a long time, replaying the scene in the back room of the pub over inside his head.

"It was me on the other side of the wall," he finally managed to say, determined that there would be no more misunderstandings on that point.

Scott glanced up at him through his lashes. "I'm g-glad," he whispered.

So was Joe. It was better than facing manslaughter charges against whoever had snuck into his place.

"I was watching you from the moment you stepped into the pub. I wouldn't have let anyone else get to the glory hole before me."

Scott silently nodded his understanding.

Joe took a deep breath, so far out of his comfort zone he had no idea how to get back into familiar territory. He had no map references for conversations this serious, no landmarks to guide him through deep, important discussions with a guy who'd just started submitting to him.

Joe glanced down at Scott's fly and the situation became far easier to handle. In spite of everything, Scott was still sporting a flourishing erection. He wasn't *that* traumatised by the glory hole.

A bright fluorescent sign flickered into life inside Joe's mind, completely overpowering the garish neon on the pub's wall. An erection was something Joe knew how to deal with. They were practically his speciality.

"Did you like it?" Joe asked.

"W-what?"

"The pub, the glory hole, did you like it?" Joe repeated.

Scott looked down.

Several heartbeats passed. Joe impatiently counted them out inside his head, but he didn't rush Scott along. He doubted Scott could have coped if he had.

Finally, Scott nodded. "I didn't th-think I would, but I...I really did." A blush crept back to his checks.

For damn near the first time since he'd entered the car, Joe felt no desire to frown. He smiled as he put his hand back on Scott's knee, then slid it a little further up his leg.

As easily as that, Scott appeared to lose the ability to breathe. He stared down at Joe's hand as if it was some sort of magical talisman that might do something startling and fantastical at any moment.

Joe leaned forward until his lips were within an inch of Scott's ear. "When you were in there, down on your knees behind a grubby glory hole, did you wonder what it would have felt like if I ordered you to stand there instead?"

It was Scott's turn to frown now. "S-s-stand?"

The way Scott's leg trembled under his hand, Joe wasn't sure if Scott would have been able to remain standing. The knowledge made Joe grin. "Yeah, stand," he said. "I could just as easily have ordered you to stand on one side, and knelt on the other side myself."

As Joe spoke, he undid Scott's fly.

It was impossible to tell if the mewing little whimper Scott let out was inspired by the way Joe's knuckles brushed against his cock, or by the pictures Joe was painting in his mind. Either scenario was fine with Joe.

Scott, once more, felt happy and safe. Anything that got them to that point was bloody fantastic as far as Joe was concerned.

"Didn't you know doms can go down on their subs?" Joe asked, all teasing surprise. "We can you know. I give *great* head."

Scott's head dropped back as Joe deftly freed his cock from behind the fabric and wrapped his fingers around it. After just a few strokes, he could tell Scott was already on edge.

"Push your seat back."

Scott blinked at Joe as if he were speaking a different language.

"It's a simple order, Scott. Just because I didn't write it down and stuff it in an envelope, that doesn't mean you can ignore it." Joe let just the tiniest note of dominance enter his voice. "Do as you're told. Push your seat back as far as it will go. Now."

* * * * *

Joe's words cut through every scrap of arousal and confusion clouding Scott's mind, and went straight to his nervous system. Messages rushed to his muscles; it was just a pity that none of them seemed to relate to co-ordination.

Scott scrambled at the plastic controls beneath his seat, damn near knocking himself out on the steering wheel in the process. It seemed to take a lifetime for him to find the leaver and free his seat. When his seat finally moved, it jerked so suddenly, Scott's head banged against the headrest.

That wasn't important though. Joe—Joe was what was important. Scott looked up and met Joe's eyes, desperate to see approval shining in them.

Joe smiled. Light-headed with relief, Scott offered him a goofy grin in return. The note of censorship he'd heard in Joe's voice seemed to be worlds away now, but Scott still needed to hear Joe to speak again, to check that Joe really had forgiven his mistake.

Scott held his breath, but Joe didn't say a single word.

Instead, Joe leaned forward. Dipping his head between the steering wheel and Scott's body, Joe wrapped his lips around the topmost section of Scott's cock.

The second that wet, silky heat surrounded the tip of his shaft, Scott's brain shut down. He was vaguely aware of someone letting out a strange noise somewhere between a yelp of surprise and a pleasure-filled scream, but he had no idea who it could have been.

Maybe someone in the pub had found the place even more shocking than he had? It was just about possible that there were guys out there who were even more inexperienced than him.

Scott lifted one hand, only to realise he didn't

know what to do with it. Putting it on the back of Joe's head was unthinkable. As much as he longed to wind his fingers through the glossy black strands of hair, he knew it wasn't his place to try to influence whatever Joe may or may not want to do. He couldn't risk doing anything that might cause Joe to stop.

Joe was a very good, and very honest man. That much was obvious. Scott was never going to have to wonder if Joe was lying to him ever again, because, stereotypes and conventions aside, Joe was a dom who could give better head than any submissive on the planet if he wanted to.

And, maybe because Scott had done something very good in a previous life, Joe wanted to. Scott closed his eyes and reverently thanked any previous incarnation of himself that might have been listening from an afterlife.

Joe didn't take a great deal of Scott's shaft into his mouth. He didn't have to. His lips and his tongue may only have worked on the top inch or so of Scott's erection, but they were inspired by genius.

Scott pressed his lips together, trying to keep his groans of ecstasy to a minimum. When he managed to drag his eyes open, he was blinded by neon light.

They were still parked right next to the entrance—clearly illuminated for anyone who happened to walk past his car.

All at once, Scott knew what he should do with his idle hand. He covered his mouth with his palm, pressing his head back against the headrest in an effort to muffle his moans and not draw any extra attention to the car.

It was impossible for him to see Joe's face or know if Joe gave a damn about being seen, but Scott had to guess he didn't care if every man in the pub came out to watch. Joe was all confidence. He wouldn't care what anyone thought. He didn't care about anything, except maybe, just maybe, the man he was with.

Scott couldn't see anything except the back of Joe's head. He couldn't hear anything over the pounding of his own heartbeat. All he could do was let his sense of touch fill in the gaps.

Joe's fingertips were even rougher than Scott remembered. He was aware of every callous, as Joe jacked the length of his shaft.

All of a sudden, Joe stilled his hand. He began to flex each finger in turn, starting with the little finger at the base of Scott's cock and working upward, as if he was literally going to milk the orgasm out of him.

The contrast between the coarseness of Joe's hand and the lush perfection of his lips and tongue sent wave after wave of pleasure rushing through Scott's body. His mouth opened behind his own hand and Scott sucked at the skin on his palm as he fought for air while still desperately trying to keep his makeshift gag in place.

Scott had never realised another man's mouth could be so silky and…

Scott frowned. No, not silky. Joe's lips weren't delicate—their touch wasn't insubstantial. They were stronger than that, and firmer, yet at the same time…

Leather!

Scott moaned his approval.

Yes, that's what they were like—like molten leather being poured over his cock. Hot and perfect and...

Scott barely had time to savour his success in solving the riddle before his brain dissolved. Like lava racing down a mountainside, the sensations Joe's mouth sent coursing through Scott's brain demolished everything in their path. No thoughts could survive that kind of onslaught.

As the thick layers of pleasure rapidly hardened into solid stone within his mind, Scott gasped. Joe dipped his head lower. The tip of Scott's cock rubbed against the back of Joe's throat. Pure ecstasy erupted through Scott's body.

Scott was powerless to stop himself thrusting up into Joe's mouth as he came, as helpless as any other man would be in the face of such a force of nature.

Scott managed to muffle most of his scream by biting down on the tender flesh between his thumb and index finger. All he was aware of then was the bliss cascading through his veins. Aeons passed by, mountain ranges rising from nothing before disappearing back into the sea as continents merged and broke apart again. Finally, Scott collapsed back in his seat, mentally and physically drained.

By the time Scott managed to open his eyes and peer at the real world around him, Joe was lounging comfortably in the passenger seat and studying Scott with rather obvious amusement.

Scott had no idea how long he'd sat there with his eyes closed, his cock hanging out and his hand still wedged between his own teeth. Blinking, trying to clear both his fuzzy vision and a mind still clouded by mental dust and ash, Scott sat up straighter in his seat.

He took his hand away from his mouth. For the first time, he realised just how hard he'd bitten down on it. There were clear teeth marks on both sides of his hand. Blood seeped from three points where he'd actually broken the skin.

Scott licked his lips as he registered the bitter metallic taste that lay heavily on his tongue, wiping away all the previous taste of Joe's cum.

Cum...

Scott turned his attention back to Joe.

Joe had gone down on him.

Joe had swallowed his cum.

Scott stared at Joe, completely unable to fit those facts in with any kind of recognisable reality.

Joe laughed, a rich, contagious sound, which made Scott smile. Even though he was aware that he was acting like an idiot, it still didn't feel as if Joe was laughing at him. He just sounded happy—as if Scott had made him happy.

As his laughter faded away, Joe took hold of Scott's wrist and pulled his hand forward so he could inspect it.

Scott immediately tried to snatch his hand back. "It's n-nothing."

Joe tightened his grip around Scott's wrist. "I'll be the one who decides that, not you."

He calmly tugged Scott's whole body closer as he turned his hand over to get a better look at the damage. Scott blushed, half at having made so much of a fool of himself and half because it really seemed like Joe cared that he might be hurt.

Joe turned on the car's interior light. Silently cursing, Scott fumbled to do up his fly with his free hand.

"Stop fidgeting."

Scott hesitated for a moment. It wasn't a tone of voice that invited disobedience. In an effort to compromise, he stilled, but left his hand resting over his softened cock.

Joe made no comment on that. All his attention remained on Scott's hand.

"You'll live," he eventually announced, releasing his wrist.

Scott hastily finished doing up his fly, but he had no idea what to say. The silence stretched out between them until Scott couldn't bear it a moment longer.

"Thank you."

Joe chuckled. "You're very welcome."

Scott shook his head. "N-not for the..." he waved a hand at his crotch. "I mean for...you said on our last d-date about showing me part of your w-world..."

Joe's smile seemed to turn a little gentler. "You're welcome for that, too. This was the first pub I went to after I came out — my first taste of what it was like to be gay."

Scott stared down at his hands, desperately trying to think of something to say in response.

"You know this means it's your turn next, right?" Joe asked, entirely out of the blue.

Scott glanced across the car at him. It took him a second to realise Joe was talking about the envelopes. "There's n-nothing about my life that you'd f-f-find interesting."

Joe shrugged, turning his attention to the wall of the pub. "Maybe you'd be surprised. You're nowhere near as boring as you seem to think you are."

Scott automatically studied Joe's profile, trying to work out if Joe was making a joke at his expense, and what the punchline might be, so he'd be ready to laugh along with it.

Joe frowned as he turned his head and met Scott's eyes. "I'm not laughing at you."

Scott looked down.

"Is that why you're interested in submission?" Joe asked, his tone becoming more serious by the moment. "Because you're so used to being bullied, you've decided that's the way you deserve to be treated?"

Scott opened his mouth, only to close it again without saying a word.

"Well?" Joe pushed.

"I just like doing what you s-s-say," Scott rushed out.

Joe's expression slowly eased. His smile came back. "Good, because I've got lots more orders to give you."

"I don't m-mind not having a turn," Scott offered, more than ready to give away any opportunity to screw up. "You could just—"

Joe cut him short with a shake of his head. Reaching into his back pocket, he took out a crumpled envelope. There was nothing written on it. It wasn't sealed. The piece of folded paper it came with was blank.

Scott took a deep breath, having no idea what he could possibly write on it that would please Joe.

"You don't need to fill it in now," Joe said. "Take a while to think about it. In the meantime, you can drop me off at my place on your way home."

Yes, driving. That would be a good idea. Scott frowned at the car's controls, wondering why they looked so different to normal. He reached out to the pedals. His legs were too short.

"You might want to pull your seat forward," Joe hinted. He didn't laugh, but Scott knew he was amused.

Strangely, it didn't feel like other men's laughter had in the past. Scott found himself genuinely smiling along with Joe.

Right then, inviting Joe to spend a little time in his part of the world didn't seem as scary as it had just a minute earlier. In a moment of uncharacteristic daring, Scott decided where he'd suggest Joe could meet him for their next date.

The moment Joe got out of the car, Scott wrote the invitation, before his courage could desert him.

Part Five: Cordially Invited

Joe stepped into the old fashioned elevator, turned to the highly embellished panel of controls and pressed the button for the third floor. The security guard on duty that night had let him in through the staff entrance at the back of the building, just as Scott had promised he would. Now, the guard was keeping a discreet eye on him from the middle of the department store's deserted foyer.

Their eyes met as the elevator doors began to slide together. The guard nodded politely to Joe and touched his uniform cap; but, just before the gap between the doors disappeared completely, Joe saw the guard's face split into a wide grin. Oh, yes. The last of Joe's doubts disappeared. The guy definitely knew that he and Scott were there to hook up.

Whistling tunelessly under his breath as the elderly elevator carried him slowly up to the third floor, Joe once again tried to guess what Scott had planned for them that night.

At 10 pm on Thursday, please go to Harrington's department store. There's a staff entrance at the back of the building and a security guard will be waiting there to let you in. Once inside please take the lift up to the third floor.

And that was it.

It wasn't really much to go on—just enough to have Joe spending damn near every minute of the three days since he'd received Scott's note, playing guessing games with himself.

A brass plaque listing the various departments

and which floor they were housed on hung on the elevator wall, but Joe made a point of not looking at it. Whatever surprise Scott was planning, Joe didn't feel inclined to spoil it at the last moment.

He smiled to himself. Apparently, being a nice guy and playing by the rules could actually be quite fun. Who could have known? And who could have guessed that screwing the same man over and over again could actually be so interesting?

Finally, a genteel ding indicated that the elevator had brought Joe to his destination. The doors slid open. Joe stepped out into what looked like some sort of kitchenware department. Raising one eye brow at the vanilla-looking fare on offer, Joe glanced around, trying to catch a glimpse of Scott between the displays of pots, pans, and useless gadgets.

Joe smiled when he eventually spotted him in the adjoining department. Scott was waiting for him within sight of the elevators, but his back was toward Joe. He couldn't have heard the elevator arrive, because he obviously had no idea he had company.

Joe took care to keep his footfalls as silent as possible as he approached. His attempts to remain undetected worked perfectly. Scott kept on staring out of a window overlooking the car park, oblivious to Joe's presence. Apparently, it had never occurred to him that Joe might park his bike in the alleyway on the other side of the building.

The thick carpeting helped to muffle Joe's footsteps as he crept closer still. He stopped a few yards away from Scott, unwilling to waste the opportunity of looking Scott over while he was unaware that he was being watched.

Scott's clothes were as conservative as ever — grey trousers, a pale blue polo shirt and sensible black shoes. Joe smiled as he ran his eyes down Scott's back and his gaze settled happily on his arse.

He wondered if anyone else knew how beautiful a body was hidden away behind that boring wardrobe? Or how kinky Scott could be, once he started obeying the orders of a dom who knew what he was doing?

No one knew. Or, to be more precise, no one else knew. Joe's smile widened into a grin. He was the only man who knew about that side of Scott's personality — and that suited Joe just fine. He slowly pulled his gaze up to Scott's face. Moving one step to his left, Joe was able to see more of his expression past the blond strands that fell into Scott's eyes.

Scott nibbled nervously at his bottom lip as he scanned the car park below the window. His lip thinned out — just like when he was going down on Joe's cock.

Joe rubbed his growing erection through his jeans. A moment passed. Scott freed his bottom lip from between his teeth. He hadn't bitten down that hard. There was no sign of blood. Scott took a deep breath and glanced at his watch.

"I'm right on time."

Scott spun around, his big blue eyes opening wide with surprise.

Every instinct Joe possessed demanded that he step forward and close the gap between them, that he grab hold of Scott and remind him exactly who he belonged to. It took every bit of self-control Joe could scrape together to remain where he was.

Scott had to be given time and space, Joe told himself, not for the first time. Scott was a novice sub. He had to have orders, but he also had to be permitted to be himself and not just become someone who did whatever his dom told him to do, regardless of his own wishes.

Joe folded his arms across his chest. He could do this. He could screw a novice sub without screwing him over.

"I d-didn't hear you come in," Scott said.

"I guessed that much."

Silence filled the room as Joe waited for Scott to tell him what was going to happen next, or to come closer, or to...well, to do pretty much anything, really.

Moments turned into minutes. They might as well have been playing musical statues. Scott evidently had no idea how to make the next move. As their eyes met, it was equally clear just how much panic was spiralling through his veins. Joe didn't need to press his fingertips against Scott's throat to know how fast his pulse was racing.

Joe did a quick but thorough inspection of Scott, looking for any clues that would help him take the scene forward in the direction Scott was hoping for. There was a logo on Scott's shirt. *Harrington's Department Store*. Next to it, was pinned a name tag. *Scott*.

They were playing dress up. Even if Scott's costume hadn't been bought from the back room of a sex shop, the fact Scott had taken such a leap of faith in his direction rushed straight to Joe's cock.

He cast a quick glance over the department they stood in, trying to guess how their surroundings fitted in with any kinks Scott might have.

Cushions, and curtains, and fabrics, oh my...

"I've known a few gay guys who *really* liked their interior decorating," Joe said. "But I'd never have pegged you as having a secret fetish for soft furnishings."

Scott blushed. He ducked his head, but he also smiled. Gradually, his shoulders relaxed into a more natural position. Joe could damn near see the tension pouring out of him.

"No cushion fetish?" he checked.

Scott shook his head. "I p-p-picked up some summer work here in my first year at university."

"Doing what?" Joe asked, leaning back against a stand full of throws and cushions as he pictured a version of Scott who was a few years younger and even less sure of himself than he was now.

"Mostly I just n-nodded, smiled, and pretended I was s-straight," Scott stuttered, with a chuckle.

Joe nodded his understanding, only just resisting the temptation to walk across the room and wrap his arms around Scott in a clumsy attempt to comfort him. It had never been more obvious just how different Scott was to Joe's usual hook ups, or how differently Joe felt about him, compared to his previous lovers.

Far more at home with offering kinkiness than comfort, Joe felt like he was stumbling forward in the dark with no way of knowing if he was about to step on a landmine. "How old were you when you came out?" he hazarded.

Scott tilted his head to one side, confusion

filled his eyes for a moment, before it quickly cleared. "No, I didn't m-mean... I came out before I went to uni. I just r-r-retreated into the closet for a while when I w-worked here..."

As he trailed off, Scott looked around them, at the big bolts of curtain fabric and shelves full of sample books. Joe was willing to bet Scott didn't really see any of it—not as it was now, at least.

Joe tensed. "Bigoted boss?" he asked, dragging Scott's attention back to him before Scott could mentally wander off into a past that Joe had no way of protecting him from.

Scott blinked, as if he had no idea what Joe was talking about. Then he shook his head. His embarrassed half-smile came back.

"If you're a straight m-man working in the textile department, people w-want you to fetch the heavier bolts of fabric or move b-boxes around in the store room. But, the moment you let on that you're gay in a p-place like this, everyone suddenly assumes you know what colours go with what, and what a t-t-triple-headed pinch is."

Joe relaxed back against the display stand and raised one eyebrow at Scott. "Okay—I'll bite. What is a triple-headed pinch?"

Scott shrugged. "I'm d-damned if I know," he admitted, pushing his hands into his pockets. "I was studying history, not f-f-fashion. It's probably something to do with curtains, but it always sounded a bit k-kinky to me."

"No, it can't be," Joe said, with complete confidence. "*You* might not know what it would mean if it was kinky, but *I* sure as hell would."

Scott met Joe's gaze properly for the first time that day, laughter shining brightly in his eyes.

Joe grinned back at him until Scott's expression gradually turned more serious.

Pushing his hands even deeper into his pockets, Scott shuffled his feet against the ugly brown carpet. "Whenever I wasn't w-working really hard at pretending to be straight," he said. "I'd creep over to one of the windows and look d-down into the car park."

"Oh, I see—this is all about a displaced car fetish," Joe said. He kept pace with Scott as Scott moved, seemingly without thinking about it, toward the window.

This time, Scott didn't chuckle in response to his teasing. Joe narrowed his eyes and studied Scott more closely.

"All the deliveries used to be m-made down there." Scott whispered the words very softly, as if the store's owner might race in and sack him for giving away company secrets unless he was careful.

Joe nodded, purposely keeping his own expression just as serious as Scott's. "So, what you're actually trying to tell me is that you stopped pretending to be straight every now and again, so you could ogle the pretty delivery men?"

Scott nodded. The blush tinting his cheeks deepened.

Joe stepped forward, glad he finally understood where this fantasy was heading. "Did you ever actually do anything with any of them?" he asked, pushing his jealousy aside as best he could.

Scott shook his head.

Joe moved closer still, possessiveness replacing any other emotion as he finally came within arm's reach of Scott. "But I'll bet you spent a lot of time thinking about it, didn't you?" He tried to lower his voice to match Scott's tone, but it didn't turn into a whisper — it became far more like a growl.

* * * * *

Scott looked over his shoulder. Joe was suddenly a hell of a lot closer than he'd expected him to be. No man should be able to move that silently in heavy boots.

Scott parted his lips to answer Joe, but his vocal cords seemed to have completely seized up. Or perhaps they were just suffering from an acute lack of blood flow. As soon as he'd set eyes on Joe, Scott's cock had become the only part of his body that his blood was interested in visiting.

All Scott could do was nod, and even that was a jerky little gesture. A string-less puppet could have probably done a better job pretending its brain was still above its waist.

Scott turned to face Joe properly, frantically trying to swallow his nerves and regain some control over himself. Joe took another step forward. Scott had to tilt his head back to look up at him.

Well aware that he was already several miles out of his depth, Scott took a blind step backwards, straight into the bin full of flowery cushions set to the left of the window.

He gasped and tried to turn around, but suddenly Joe was right in front of him. Scott no longer had enough room to turn around and check that the cushions weren't about to attack. Hell, he barely even had room to breathe.

Scott was trapped — helpless, hard, and happier than he had ever been in his life.

"What did you imagine?" Joe asked. He dipped his head as he spoke. The rough words sent a shiver down Scott's spine.

"I..." Scott licked his lips. A moment before Joe's arrival, the room had been a perfectly acceptable temperature. Now, it was more like a sauna. Scott tugged the neck of his polo shirt, wondering if Toby, the security guard, was buggering about with the heating.

Scott dropped his gaze, but that meant looking at the way Joe's body was pressed against him, at the way Joe had his hands on the storage bin's rim either side of him, keeping him exactly where Joe wanted.

Another shot of adrenaline rushed through Scott's veins. His heart pounded faster than ever.

Joe tucked a knuckle under Scott's chin, giving him no choice but to tilt back his head and lift his eyes.

"Did you imagine staying behind for a late delivery, Scott? Did you picture yourself waiting for one of those big, strong delivery men to turn up and catch you all on your own in the store?"

Scott blinked, and in that momentary darkness behind his lids, he saw it so clearly. Joe was wearing his usual jeans and t-shirt. It didn't take a huge leap of the imagination to put a clipboard with a delivery form in his hand. "I..."

Joe's lips twisted into a smile as he released

Scott's chin. He ran his hands down the outside of Scott's arms, until each hand encircled one of Scott's wrists.

Every inch of skin that Joe touched tingled. Scott had never thought of his arms as erogenous zones before, but now he knew he'd never think of them as anything else.

"What did you imagine your delivery guy doing to you?" Joe asked.

Scott took a deep breath, the scent of their combined arousal flooded his senses, making it even more impossible for him to think clearly.

"What shall I do with you, now that I've got you here, all on your own?" Joe rephrased.

That question was so much easier for Scott to answer. The appropriate response appeared inside his mind without him having to redirect a single drop of blood to his brain. "Anything you w-w-want," he whispered, still staring at the grip Joe had on his wrists.

It was one of those facts Scott didn't have to question. Tomorrow the sun would rise, gravity would still exist, and Joe should always do whatever he wanted with him.

"What do you think I would have wanted to do with you if I'd been the delivery man who found you here all alone?" Joe pushed, brushing his lips against Scott's ear as he spoke.

Another shudder ran down Scott's spine. His erection throbbed behind the thin uniform trousers that he'd dug out from the back of his wardrobe earlier that day.

The fabric was so restrictive, it was tempting to

believe his cock had grown a couple of inches over the last few years. Scott looked up at Joe. It was even easier to believe that nothing had ever succeeded in making him as hard as Joe could with just a few whispered words.

"I'm still waiting for an answer," Joe reminded him. He caught the lobe of Scott's ear between his teeth and nipped sharply at the delicate flesh.

Scott gasped, but he didn't try to pull away from the little spike of pain.

"I d-don't know," he blurted out.

Joe lifted his head and stared down at Scott, his disbelief obvious.

"I c-can't remember," Scott said, his voice now thin and raspy with pleasure. "I c-can't think when you're..."

Whether Joe believed him or not, he smiled at Scott's admission. He tightened his grip around Scott's wrists and pulled him away from the storage box.

Scott didn't hesitate to follow the unspoken order, once he actually recognised it as being an instruction to move. Within seconds, Joe had deftly pinned Scott's arms behind his back.

In one easy movement, he transferred both of Scott's wrists into the grip of one of his huge hands. Scott stared up at him, wondering if Joe really thought he could keep his wrists trapped against the small of his back with just one hand.

Joe's expression was completely serious but, no, Scott realised. Joe didn't think he was that weak. As Scott stared into Joe's eyes, he was sure that Joe knew that the physical hold he had on him was just a statement of where he wanted Scott to keep his hands.

It was the mental hold Joe had over Scott that actually made it impossible for him to move his arms. He would keep his hands behind his back until he was given permission to move them. That knowledge came from deep down, in a part of Scott's mind that he was still just beginning to explore, and there was no arguing with it.

Joe slid his free hand into Scott's hair. Wrapping his fingers around the disordered strands, he tilted Scott's head back and once more made Scott look him in the eye.

"Tell me what you remember," he ordered.

Scott frowned, trying to summon up details, but they were so hard to bring to mind. The past wasn't important. What he'd once dreamt of doing with other men was irrelevant. But, Joe's orders — they were vital. Scott concentrated harder.

"I r-remember thinking that whatever he did to me, it would h-hurt. But I...I remember being sure that I w-would like it — even though I knew I should hate it," Scott managed to whisper. "I...being treated like that, n-not having a choice...I like it..."

Scott's frown deepened, as he struggled to recall the specifics of a fantasy that had once filled his brain during every quiet moment for months on end. It was no use. Daydreams couldn't compete with Joe.

"If I'd come into this shop back then, everyone would have known that you were gay by the time I left," Joe suddenly informed him.

Scott nodded. It would have been obvious to everyone just by the way he stared at Joe. Joe wouldn't even have had to smile in his direction to out him.

"They'd have known you belonged to me, too," Joe went on. "That you're my submissive."

Scott stared up at Joe, loving those words. Whatever anyone else believed was irrelevant. Belonging to Joe, being his submissive, was everything he wanted from life. It was impossible for him to keep back a needy little whimper.

Joe tightened his grip around both Scott's wrists and Scott's hair in response. "They'd have all seen the way you submit to me, whether you wanted them to or not."

"Wh-what would you have done?" Scott whispered, as desperation kicked his vocal cords back into life.

"That would have depended on one very important fact," Joe said, his lips twisting into a humourless little smile.

"F-fact?" Scott echoed.

"Did you have my permission to come to work today or were you disobeying me?"

Scott swallowed. Unexpected guilt swarmed through his mind. Joe's voice had hardened again. Scott's stomach knotted. Every muscle in his body tensed. "I—"

"No," Joe cut in, drawing the word out, as if he was considering the matter very carefully. "You wouldn't disobey me like that, would you?"

Scott shook his head vehemently, not caring how hard he tugged at Joe's grip on his hair.

"No," Joe mused again, sliding his fingers down to rest, almost tenderly, on Scott's cheek.

At the same time, as if to balance out any hint of gentleness, Joe tightened his grip on Scott's wrists. There would be bruises there the next day. If Joe hadn't looked so serious, Scott would have grinned at being marked that way, at being allowed to wear Joe's marks beneath his skin for days to come. But Joe's usual smile was entirely absent.

"If I'd stumbled upon you in this store back then, it would have been the first time I set eyes on you." He seemed to be talking to himself.

Freed from any obligation to answer, Scott simply stared up at Joe, relishing their closeness.

"Do you remember the first time we met?" Joe suddenly demanded.

"I-in the fantasy?" Scott asked.

Joe's lips quirked into that lopsided smile; the one that always made Scott desperate to rise up onto his toes and kiss him.

"No, in the real world. Do you remember?" Joe asked again.

Scott nodded. Discomfort rushed through him. He twitched his hands behind his back. Joe immediately pressed his wrists more firmly against the back of his polo shirt — keeping them in place.

Scott remembered the first time he met Joe in perfect detail, but he knew he was the only one whose life changed that day. As easily as that, a more familiar reality returned to Scott's world. Without moving a muscle, he morphed back into the guy on the edge of the group who no one ever noticed, who —

"It was Valentine's Day last year," Joe said, slicing cleanly through every thought in Scott's head.

"You were the hottest sub there. I couldn't stop staring at you, wondering why the hell you were there on your own."

Scott blinked. He'd have been less shocked if Joe had announced he was an alien.

* * * * *

"You needn't look quite so convinced I'm a serial killer," Joe said, with a chuckle. He idly ran his thumb over Scott's cheek. Shocked was one hell of a good look on him. "What could be more natural than a dom noticing the stunning new sub who just walked in?"

"Are you s-sure you're talking about *me*?" Scott asked.

Joe used his grip on Scott's wrists to pull him closer so their bodies were pressed together from shoulder to knee. "Very sure." He was equally confident that Scott could feel his hard-on through their clothes.

"You really n-noticed *me*?" It was impossible to tell if Scott loved that possibility, or if he was too freaked out by it to feel anything at all.

"I really did," Joe said, managing to hold back another chuckle.

Scott closed his eyes, as if fighting for self-control.

If he was trying to resist the urge to hump Joe's leg, he lost that battle within seconds. His breaths turned ragged as he rubbed their bodies together.

A minute passed before, with a frustrated groan, Scott pried his eyes open and looked up at Joe.

It was obvious just how hard it was for him to make his brain work, but he stubbornly kept trying until he got some kind of thought process going. "You couldn't have k-known I'm a sub," Scott stuttered out. "You never saw me do anything the l-least bit kinky."

Of course he hadn't. Joe was certain there had never been anything kinky in Scott's life for anyone to see. That side of Scott belonged to him and no one else.

"I didn't need a demonstration," Joe said. "I still knew. The first time I saw you I wanted to pull down your jeans, turn you over my knee and spank you until you came in front of everyone in the club."

Scott whimpered.

It took all the self-control Joe had, to stop himself half-fulfilling that particular ambition right there, in the middle of the deserted department store. He cleared his throat. "If I'd walked into this shop a few years ago, I'd have known that you were a sub then, too."

"You w-would?"

"Yes," Joe left no room for doubt in his voice.

Scott glanced up at him and then quickly away, as if he wasn't sure where to look anymore.

"If we'd met then, it would have been back before I learned any patience." Joe dipped his head and nipped at Scott's ear again. "I wouldn't have waited for you to be ready to practice your letter writing skills," he whispered.

Scott arched his back, moulding his body against Joe's larger frame, pushing his erection against Joe leg. "What w-would you have done?" he murmured.

"Do you want me to tell you?"

Scott nodded.

Joe raised an eyebrow at him. "Really? Where's the fun in that?"

Scott instantly withdrew — if not physically, then mentally; as quick to lose confidence as ever.

"Wouldn't you prefer me to show you?" Joe asked.

He didn't give Scott another second in which to panic. He released Scott's hands, spun him around and pressed his erection against Scott's arse.

Scott tried to look over his shoulder, but Joe kept him exactly where he wanted him; holding Scott in place with his arms wrapped tightly around his body. Scott had no choice but to look straight ahead, at the shop where he had spent so much time fantasising about rough men not taking no for an answer.

"This would have been your first hint that anyone else was here — when you felt my body against yours," Joe told him. He thrust his erection against Scott's backside through their clothes. "And you'd have known exactly what I wanted from you, wouldn't you?"

Joe slid one hand down Scott's body and cupped his erection through his nice, sensible trousers. Scott wriggled helplessly as Joe massaged his shaft through the fabric. His movements only seemed to succeed in making him more frustrated.

"P-please?" Scott asked. He was so breathless, the word was barely audible.

Joe chuckled as he pressed a kiss to Scott's neck, letting Scott feel the vibrations from his amusement dance against his skin. "Do you really think I'd have let you have anything you wanted as easily as that? Perhaps it's a good thing you didn't know me back then."

"I'd have d-done anything you wanted," Scott promised.

"You're sure of that, are you?" Joe teased.

Scott nodded. "You'd have still b-been you." He sounded so bloody serious.

Joe might have just been talking dirty, taking dictation straight from his cock, but Scott was obviously speaking from the heart. Joe growled his approval, sharing a whole host of new vibrations with the same patch of Scott's skin.

It was a bloody good answer. It slipped straight past the part of Joe that was still trying to keep everything between them light and flirty; straight to the part of him that understood nothing but a feral need to possess Scott and own him completely.

Unzipping Scott's fly, Joe pushed his hands past the cheap fabric and guided Scott's erection through the openings of both his boxers and his trousers. Wrapping his hand around the shaft, Joe jacked Scott's cock, purposefully laying claim to each hard inch of his erection.

Scott froze; every muscle in his body tensed.

"I was a petulant little brat a few years ago," Joe whispered into Scott's ear as Scott began to tremble against him. "I'd have deserved to have been shot if I'd made a move on a sweet boy like you."

As suddenly as he'd frozen up, Scott thawed out. Without any warning, he twisted away from Joe,

137

trying to free himself and pull his cock away from Joe's hand at the same time.

"That's enough," Joe said, his words clipped and impatient.

Scott didn't seem to hear him. He continued to writhe against Joe, as if that would somehow help him prove he wasn't too sweet for a guy who'd been screwing most of the men on the local leather scene.

"You were a virgin," Joe snapped. He didn't bother to make it a question. He was already sure of the answer.

The calmly stated fact brought Scott back to him. He fell still, gasping for breath. A pretty red hue rushed to Scott's cheeks. If Joe had had any lingering doubts, that would have been all the confirmation he needed.

There was a very large part of him that wouldn't have minded being shot for having that particular pleasure. Joe tightened his grip around Scott's cock. "But you're mine now," he said.

The statement was three words longer than it would have been if he'd stumbled across Scott before he was old enough to really appreciate him.

Mine.

Scott nodded. "Y-yes," he whispered. "Yours."

Perfect.

Joe quickly scanned their surroundings. He silently cursed. Why the hell couldn't Scott have worked in the DIY section, surrounded by lengths of chain, and padlocks, and lots of other things that could easily be kinked up to fit his purposes?

The soft furnishings department offered him...

Joe squinted at the various racks and shelves

within sight. Ribbons? Lace? Joe was just about to give up and drag Scott off to a part of a store that sold more easily pervertable things, when he spotted some sort of red rope thing with a big tassel on the end.

"Put your hands behind your back." Keeping hold of Scott's cock, Joe led him across to the big countertop in the centre of the soft furnishings department by his erection.

"W-what are — ?"

"Hush." Joe snatched up one of the tasselled ropes on his way past.

As he reached the countertop, Joe realised two things. Firstly, it was too high for Scott to bend over it comfortably and keep his feet on the floor. Secondly, if Scott's feet were left to dangle helplessly a few inches off the floor, it would offer Scott's arse up at a lovely height for his own cock.

Joe grinned.

Snatching a cushion off a shelf to his left, Joe tossed it onto the edge of the countertop. He tugged both Scott's trousers and his boxers down until they bunched around his knees. Lifting Scott off his feet, Joe bent him neatly over his new makeshift bondage bench.

Stepping back, Joe considered the arrangement. Scott's chest lay against the countertop, his crotch was pressed into the cushion, his legs were hanging over the edge and, most importantly of all, his bare arse was offered up for Joe's personal pleasure.

A startled little yelp had been Scott's only contribution to proceedings. Even now, when Joe walked away, Scott remained speechless and kept his hands behind his back. Shock or submission — either way, it suited Joe.

On the other side of the counter, Joe discovered a row of hooks.

Moving aside a gigantic pair of shears which were far more intimidating than the equipment in most BDSM clubs, Joe secured one end of his newly acquired tassel to one of the big hooks.

"Perfect," he muttered to himself. Who needed a DIY section? Looking up, Joe met Scott's eyes. He had everything he needed right in front of him. "Give me your hands."

* * * * *

Scott slowly took his hands from behind his back and offered them to Joe across the highly polished countertop. He watched as Joe deftly secured them to a hook with a fancy curtain tie-back.

Scott frowned; he was reasonably sure the rope tassel wouldn't hold him in place if he made any sort of serious attempt to free himself. Suddenly, Joe's work on the knot pulled Scott's whole body an inch closer to the opposite side of the counter. Scott's bare cock rubbed against the cushion beneath him. Cool air caressed his arse. The tie-back became irrelevant. He could very happily spend the rest of his life in that exact spot without ever wanting to be free.

"Now I really can do whatever I want with you," Joe said. "Can't I?"

Scott nodded, still staring at his bound hands and wondering what else Joe might decide to tie him up with in the future. In that moment, Scott's world stopped being a place that contained innocent everyday things and, in a completely different mental category, kinky things that were designed to be used in erotic games.

The line in the sand disappeared — Joe's heavy boots stomped it out as he strode across it. A hundred kinky things followed in Joe's wake, spreading through Scott's world until there was nowhere he could hide from them.

Scott only managed to tear his gaze from the tie-back when Joe took a step back. That was wrong. Scott opened his mouth to protest, but no words came out. He might as well have been gagged.

Relief rushed through Scott, sweeping away his panic, as Joe failed to stride out of the room and leave him there, exposed and helpless. Instead, Joe walked around the counter and stood directly behind him, just an inch from his bare backside.

"Joe?" Scott finally managed to rasp out, as the silence stretched out.

Joe slid his fingertips down between Scott's cheeks to tease his hole.

Lightening sparked through Scott's body. His legs jerked. He kicked the side of the counter as he desperately tried to gain enough leverage to press his arse back against Joe's fingers.

It was no use. The side of the counter was just as smooth as its top. All Scott managed to do was rub his cock more firmly against the cushion and grind his crotch into the rough, tapestry surface.

Scott was stuck, unable to do anything other than accept whatever Joe chose to give him. He couldn't even spread his legs in invitation because his damn trousers were bunched up around his knees. He silently rattled through every curse he knew.

Joe hummed an unidentifiable little tune under his breath as he pushed the back of Scott's polo-shirt up, exposing another few inches of skin. A shiver danced along Scott's spine, more because of how vulnerable he felt than anything as irrelevant as temperature; and even more so because of how much that sense of vulnerability appealed to him.

"Joe?"

"Yeah?"

Scott peered awkwardly over his shoulder just in time to see Joe take a little tube of lube out of the back pocket of his jeans.

The next moment, Joe's hands left Scott's field of vision. Scott held his breath, mentally reciting every prayer he could remember. Someone was listening. All his desperate supplications were answered as Joe's fingers slid between his buttocks.

The lube was warm after being carried around in Joe's pocket. It was wonderfully slick as Joe circled Scott's hole with his fingertips, teasing him without trying to enter him.

Even while he knew it was impossible, Scott struggled to spread his legs. Moaning his frustration, he dropped his head toward the countertop as Joe slid his fingers inside him, very, *very* slowly. Scott only remembered how to breathe properly once those digits were buried so deeply inside him that he could feel Joe's knuckles pressing against the cleft between his arse cheeks.

Scott crammed as much air as possible into his lungs, not sure how long his ability to breathe without conscious effort would last this time. Joe crooked the digits and immediately found Scott's prostate.

Scott jerked, damn near putting his foot through the side of the counter as pleasure hit him hard and fast. Pain shot through his toes, but it couldn't compete with the pure bliss Joe pushed into him.

"If you stay still for me, I might give you permission to come."

Permission. Might. Those words registered in Scott's mind, even if nothing else did.

"W-what?"

"When you're at home playing with your cock all by yourself, you can come whenever you like — for now. But when we're together, you need permission."

"S-since when?" Scott blurted out.

"Since now. Since I decided it would be fun — for me, anyway."

Scott's brain was so full of pleasure he struggled to come up with an answer. Then he realised that he was wasting his time. It hadn't been a question. Joe wasn't asking him to agree to anything. Joe was telling him how things were going to be. The decision had been made. Joe thought it would be fun. Scott's opinion was irrelevant, and he now needed Joe's permission to come.

Under those circumstances, there was only one thing he could realistically say. "P-please?"

"Maybe," Joe said.

Maybe?

Scott whimpered, instinctively pulling at the tassel restraining his hands. The tie-back was far stronger than it looked. All Scott succeeded in doing was tightening the knot around his wrists.

He groaned as the rope chafed against his skin. There might as well have been another length of rope running beneath his torso to wrap around his shaft and ball sac because the sensation went straight to his cock.

Each tug against the tie-back seemed to pull Scott's balls up closer to his body, making him all the more frantic to come. The fact he needed Joe's permission before he could do that only increased his need. Scott clenched his teeth in a last ditch attempt to stop himself cursing Joe out loud.

"No."

Scott blinked open his eyes. He hadn't said anything out loud — he was sure of that. He had to have done something else that Joe disapproved of, but Scott had no idea what he could have done to make Joe so angry with him.

"Don't try to keep quiet," Joe ordered. "I've told you before, I want to hear you." He tilted his hand, rubbing the tips of his fingers more firmly against Scott's prostate.

Scott arched against the table top and let out a sound somewhere between a moan and a scream. He'd tentatively hoped that the noise might please Joe in some way, but it made Joe take his fingers away instead.

"N-no! Don't s-stop!" Scott pleaded, unable to form anything that resembled a complete sentence. "Please, I…"

Scott whimpered. Joe's fingers belonged inside him; he couldn't take them away. But Joe didn't take any notice of his protests.

Gathering up every scrap of energy he could find inside himself, Scott lifted his head and looked over his shoulder. One glance, and Scott knew he'd been wrong. Joe's fingers didn't belong inside him. They were designed for pushing Joe's clothing aside and for rolling a condom down his shaft. All at once, that was obvious.

Slicking the latex with extra lube, Joe positioned the tip of his cock against Scott's hole. He caught hold of Scott's hips and held him still, providing himself with a nice stationary target to thrust into.

Scott's trousers still kept his knees trapped together. His legs trembled as he strained against the fabric, but every bloody seam held true. All Scott could do was lie there and wait impatiently for Joe to thrust forward and bury himself inside his arse.

Scott couldn't stay silent any longer. Words began to tumble from his lips. He had no idea what he said. Begging, cursing, for all he knew he could have been speaking in tongues. But still, that first punishing thrust never came.

Joe leaned forward, pushing the tip of his cock against Scott's hole very gently, but even when his glans breached the tight ring of muscle, Joe didn't rush. He continued to slowly feed his shaft into Scott's body inch by wonderful inch. He stretched him and filled him so gradually that it seemed to Scott that Joe's cock was never ending. And each moment that passed only made Scott crave each little bit of Joe's cock even more desperately.

Scott bit down on his bottom lip before quickly

correcting himself and releasing the abused skin from between his teeth. He didn't have permission to keep his moans and groans to himself.

Oh, God — permission.

"P-please?" he gasped.

Joe stroked his hands up Scott's sides, from where they'd held his hips steady, to rest over his ribs on either side of his torso. Scott arched into Joe's palms. At the same time, he clenched around Joe's cock, relishing everywhere they touched.

Joe's hands were glorious; so was his crotch, pressed tightly against Scott's buttocks.

Time ticked by. The room was so quiet, Scott could hear the clock on the wall counting out the seconds. Eventually, Joe swayed back, gradually sliding out of Scott's hole. Scott held his breath. A lifetime passed before Joe finally ploughed back into him.

Again, then again. Joe finally began to move his hips a little faster on each stoke, until he was thrusting into Scott in earnest. He slid his hands back down and grabbed Scott's hips, holding him secure as he pounded into him.

The cushion beneath Scott's groin stopped his hip bones getting battered against the counter's edge, but the textured fabric rubbed against Scott's cock in time with each of Joe's thrusts. Scott felt his pre-cum soaking into the cushion cover, but he was as helpless to stop that as he was to control anything else.

Joe had stolen any power Scott might have once had. Like a masked thief creeping into an empty house in the dead of night, Joe took away both Scott's control and his desire for control.

Even Scott's ability to think seemed to have been scooped up and locked away in Joe's bag of stolen goods.

Scott whimpered in time with Joe's thrusts. He clenched and unclenched his fists, tugging against his bondage, not trying to get out of it but unable to remain entirely motionless.

Out of the blue, Joe took something from his hoard of stolen booty and tossed it back to Scott.

"Permission—" Thrust. "—Granted."

As he spoke, Joe tightened his grip. Digging his fingers into Scott's flesh, he forced Scott to tilt his hips and he thrust into Scott's arse harder than ever. The tiny alteration in the angle made all the difference.

Scott's whimpers morphed into a scream. If he'd been able to think clearly, he might have worried that Toby would start to take his job as a security guard seriously and rush up to the third floor, convinced that someone was being murdered.

As it was, Scott was unable to worry about anything. While Joe kept thrusting deep inside him and forcing more and more pleasure into his prostate, and while his cum was still spilling across the cushion beneath him, Scott was completely incapable of doing anything but descending through a spiral of orgasmic bliss.

As he clenched his internal muscles around Joe's cock, Scott felt Joe's rhythm falter. Joe came just a moment after Scott and he yelled out too—a harsh, triumphant sound that wrapped around Scott's bound body and gave him permission to sink even deeper into his pleasure.

Joe leant forward, resting his chest against

Scott's back. His weight pressed down on Scott, crushing him against the countertop.

With his forehead resting on the smooth, cream surface, Scott smiled to himself. He'd made Joe come. Forget everything else; right then, he was king of the world!

"Scott?"

Sleepy with satisfaction, Scott slowly blinked open his eyes. The room was just as it had been when he closed his eyes; it hadn't even changed that much from when he'd worked there.

This season's colours might vary a little from those that came before, but it was still the same place. Scott was the only thing that had changed.

Scott frowned slightly. Joe had said something to him, but he couldn't remember what. "P-pardon?"

"I said, do you have your wallet with you?" Joe repeated.

Scott tried to pull enough brain cells together to work out why that was important and failed. "Why?"

"We might need to buy the cushion you're lying on."

Brain activity once more failed to make itself known inside Scott's head.

"I doubt anyone else will want to buy it," Joe pointed out. "Since it's got your cum all over it and everything."

Everything finally clicked into place inside Scott's head. Heat rushed to his cheeks as Joe straightened up and pulled away from him.

Scott tried to follow Joe's lead. It was only when the rope pulled around his wrists that he remembered he was still bound.

Joe grinned as Scott looked over his shoulder and their eyes met.

"A-are you going to…?" Scott hinted, nodding toward the tie-back.

"I don't know," Joe said. "I like the way you look where you are. Maybe I'll leave you there."

Scott felt his blush deepen. Now that his brain was coming back on line, he looked over his shoulder and toward the elevator, convinced that someone might walk into the deserted building at any moment.

With his own fly already neatly fastened, Joe stroked his fingertips over Scott's exposed arse. "Really bloody stunning," he whispered, apparently to himself. He slid one finger between Scott's legs and stroked the back of his balls.

Scott helplessly arched his back as Joe teased the neatly trimmed hairs that covered his sac. It was impossible for him to get hard again so soon, but that didn't stop his brain sending signals to his cock and ordering it to try. Already uncomfortably sticky against the cushion, Scott's cock began to ache with increased blood flow too.

Finally, Joe seemed to get bored with that particular brand of teasing. He took his hand from between Scott legs and walked around the counter. He stopped directly in front of the hook he'd tied Scott's hands to, but he didn't rush to free him.

Joe took a piece of paper and an envelope out of the back pocket of his jeans. Leaning on the counter next to Scott's restrained wrists, he wrote out a note in seconds. He had it sealed in the envelope before Scott managed to decipher one upside down word of Joe's scrawl.

It was only then that Joe turned his attention to freeing Scott's hands. As he released each wrist, Joe checked that Scott's skin hadn't suffered too much. Scott automatically studied the same strip of skin. There wasn't a mark on him.

He was fine. The same couldn't be said for the tie-back.

"We'd best get this as another souvenir," Joe said, with an easy grin. "A man can never have too many..." His eyes narrowed as he studied it. His expression remained completely blank.

"Curtain tie-backs," Scott finished for him.

Joe nodded, apparently willing to take his word for it. He let go of Scott's wrists. "You're allowed to get up."

Joe made no effort to help Scott, he just leaned against the counter alongside him and watched as Scott wriggled his way off the countertop and squirmed back into his boxers. Scott's stomach and his cock were both tacky with the residue of his cum, but there was nowhere for him to clean up. All he could do was try to straighten out his trousers and shirt so they'd hide the worst of his embarrassment.

Scott picked up the cushion that had fallen to the floor when he'd levered himself off the counter. Joe had been right about them needing to buy it.

"Does the security guard know what we're doing up here?" Joe asked, as Scott dutifully left some money and a, not entirely accurate, explanatory note next to the till before sliding his purchases in to a carrier bag.

"He p-probably guessed," Scott said. "But he

won't tell anyone. I c-covered for him lots of times when I worked here."

"Are you going to blush when we walk past him on the way out?"

A touch of colour rose to Scott's cheeks just at the idea. "P-probably," he admitted.

Joe grinned as he pushed himself away from the counter and headed toward the elevator.

"But it was w-worth it," Scott blurted out.

Joe glanced over his shoulder. "What?"

"It was worth a b-bit of embarrassment," Scott repeated.

Joe smiled and held out an arm toward Scott. "Come on."

Scott stepped forward.

Joe slid his arm around his waist and pulled him close as they walked toward the lifts. "You can hide your face in my shoulder if you get too embarrassed," he offered.

As they rode down in the elevator, Scott felt an envelope being pushed into the back pocket of his trousers. Smiling to himself, he leaned into Joe's side a little more confidently. To hell with a bit of embarrassment, the knowledge they'd be going on another date was worth it— it was worth damn near anything!

Part Six: For His Eyes Only

Scott stood on the pavement outside a very fashionable hair-dressers — the kind that charged more for a quick trim than he made in a month. He'd read the note Joe had slipped into his pocket at the end of their last date a dozen times. He'd been sure he'd known the address where he was supposed to meet Joe off by heart, but apparently not. And, of course, sod's law, he'd already sent his taxi away.

Frowning at the darkness behind the shop window, glad it was closed so that he didn't have an audience to his stupidity, Scott dug into his coat pocket and pulled out the latest envelope from Joe. Hopefully, the right address was close by, so he'd be able to run there and not be late. Carefully extracting the note, Scott re-read the address. He looked at the number on the building, and then at the street sign on the corner. Everything seemed to match.

The sudden roar of a motorbike turning into the street made Scott smile. Even if the hair-dressers didn't look like Joe's type of place, that definitely sounded like Joe's kind of ride.

The physical memory of the vibrations that had danced through his body when he'd been permitted to ride pillion behind Joe, rushed straight to Scott's cock. He immediately began to harden. Scott couldn't bring himself to be surprised. Everything about Joe had the same effect on him. The guy was super-strength, leather-clad Viagra.

A hulking mass of silvered chrome and shining

black metal rolled to a stop alongside Scott.

Hastily pushing the note into his pocket, Scott did his best to force his features into something resembling a sensible smile, rather than an idiotic grin. He had as much control over his face as he had over his cock.

Joe pulled his helmet off and shoved his hand through his hair, shaking out the dark strands. "Turn around."

Scott obediently turned through three-hundred-and-sixty degrees. He did his best to remain calm, but his mind was racing like a stallion being whipped by the most sadistic of jockeys.

Joe hadn't mentioned anything about needing to dress up for their date. Maybe if he —

"No," Joe corrected, patiently. "Turn to face the shop window, then stop."

"Oh, s-sorry," Scott mumbled, dutifully turning his back on Joe.

"Do you remember what your safe word is?"

Scott swallowed several times in quick succession. In his reflection on the dark window pane, he saw his Adam's apple bob. "I r-remember," he whispered.

"Good. Stay where you are. You don't have permission to move."

Scott refocused and watched Joe put his crash helmet in the case on the back of his bike and take something out of one of the panniers.

Being able to see what Joe was doing helped calm Scott's nerves a little, but he knew he hadn't been given permission to make use of Joe's reflection that way. As adrenaline rushed into his blood stream,

Scott dropped his gaze.

It was so easy to feel as if he was a naughty boy who'd been sent to stand in the corner until it was time for his spanking. Scott only just managed to bite back a whimper at the possibility of being turned over Joe's knee. The idea of Joe's hand falling against his bare arse again and again... Scott closed his eyes.

A fantasy version of his first ever spanking appeared in his mind. Joe would be dressed, of course. He hardly ever seemed to take off any clothing unless it was absolutely necessary or specifically asked for. Scott could almost feel his own naked erection rubbing against the rough denim that covered Joe's legs as each smack made him rock against Joe's thighs.

Sudden pressure against his eye lids jerked Scott out of his day dream. He tried to open his eyes, but something was covering them. He lifted a hand to his face. His fingers brushed against a cool, smooth surface when he tried to touch his eyes.

Picking at the edges of it, Scott desperately tried to tug it off his eyes, but he couldn't get a grip on it. All he succeeding in doing was scratching his forehead. Whatever covered Scott's eyes wrapped itself all the way around his head. He felt it move against his hair as it completely encircled his scalp.

Scott wanted to cry out, but he couldn't make his vocal cords work—not even when the thing pulled him backward, stealing all his balance from him.

"You're only going to hurt yourself if you keep struggling."

Scott froze. "J-j-joe?"

"Who else would it be?"

Scott relaxed, cursing himself for a fool. He'd have rolled his eyes at himself, if he'd been able to open them.

Fingers moved against the back of Scott's head, the thing over his eyes cinched tighter. Joe was doing up some sort of fastening.

Suddenly, Scott felt Joe's hands move to his shoulders. They spun him around, almost sending him crashing to the ground.

Unable to rely on visual cues, Scott swayed and groped for any solid point of reference. His hands landed on Joe's forearms. Scott clenched the sleeves of Joe's jacket, relishing the increasingly familiar feel of leather, as well as the strength and solidity Joe represented.

"I'm still waiting for an answer," Joe said.

Scott frowned behind his...his blindfold, he supposed. "An a-answer to what?"

"Who else would be blindfolding you?"

Scott chuckled. It took him a moment to realise that the icy atmosphere had nothing to do with the chilly breeze. Joe was seriously asking him who else he'd been playing with.

"N-no one," Scott said. "It wouldn't have been anyone else—it c-couldn't be." Scott listened very carefully as he struggled to gauge Joe's reaction. A car engine purred as it no doubt drove down one of the side streets nearby. A dog barked in the distance. Joe said nothing.

The only way Scott could be sure that Joe was still there, was by the warmth from Joe's hands seeping through his coat and into his shoulders. Scott tightened his grip on Joe's jacket, sure Joe wouldn't leave without that, even if he couldn't have been blamed for walking away from such a clueless idiot.

"No one else," Scott whispered. "I w-wouldn't do that." He wasn't even sure who he was trying to convince now, himself or Joe. The idea of him screwing around behind Joe's back was insane. But, the probability that Joe still had a string of other lovers on the side was —

"Come on." Joe turned Scott around again and pushed him forward. "Small step up."

Scott edged cautiously forward. His toe tapped against a step. Joe reached past his shoulder and Scott heard a key turn in a lock, followed by the light, pleasant sound of a shop bell tinkling above his head. They were going into the hair-dressers?

Lifting his hands, Scott held them out in front of himself, blindly feeling for obstacles in his way. He searched his memory, trying to remember what he'd seen of the layout inside the shop when he'd peered through the window. Damn! He hadn't actually looked through the window for more than a second.

Joe's grip on Scott's shoulders tightened. "I won't walk you into anything by accident."

His tone of voice was off. It sounded more like, when he did walk Scott into something, it would be on purpose. Scott still dropped his hands to his sides, instinctively needing to hand over control to Joe, even if he knew it would get him hurt.

"That's better," Joe murmured.

The pleasure his words sent racing through Scott was worth any number of stubbed toes or bruised limbs. Scott's cock strained against the inside of his trousers. Joe could walk him into whatever he liked.

They seemed to make their way further back than the shop could possibly run, passing through a series of doors along the way. If there were any obstacles, Joe guided Scott around them rather than into them. The only bruises on him when they reached their destination were the very faint marks that still lingered on Scott's hips from when Joe had held him still to be screwed, three days ago, in the department store.

Finally, Joe stopped, bringing Scott to a jerky halt.

Scott's hearing told him nothing about the kind of room they were in now. "J-Joe?" he asked.

"Yes?" Joe's hands left Scott's shoulders.

Scott turned, following the sound of Joe's footsteps as they walked away from him. "Am I allowed to ask w-where we are?"

"You can ask."

Scott opened his mouth to do just that.

"But you won't get an answer."

Scott brought his lips back together.

"Take off your clothes," Joe ordered. "All of them. Leave the blindfold on."

Scott fiddled with one of the buttons on his coat. "Is a-anyone else here?"

"Why? Would you disobey me if we had an audience?" Joe countered.

Twisting the same button around and around until it was a wonder the thread held, Scott thought about that very carefully. "No, I'd s-still obey you," he admitted.

"Good. But tonight is for my eyes only," Joe said, from a few feet away. "I'm the only one who'll see what happens in this room. That's why you're blindfolded. Not even you get to share the view tonight."

Scott tilted his head back as he sensed Joe come closer, until he stood right in front of him. The blindfold was effective. Not a single ray of light made it past the padded leather. There was no way Scott could actually look up into Joe's eyes.

Without any warning, something brushed against Scott's lips. He opened his mouth and let out a shocked gasp. Joe's tongue brushed against Scott's bottom lip as he traced the line of Scott's teeth with its tip.

Finally, Scott's brain caught up with events. He reached out. Finding Joe's shoulders, Scott clung to him like a drowning man grasping a life raft in a storm.

Scott had already learned that kisses from Joe were rare. They had to be savoured. Temporary blindness was no excuse for screwing that up.

Tentative, not wanting to do anything that Joe might take offense at, Scott lapped gently at the tip of Joe's tongue as it slid further into his mouth. Joe moved one of his hands to the back of Scott's head and wound his fingers into those strands of hair that weren't trapped by the blindfold. He forced Scott to tilt back his head even further, then kept him trapped at that angle.

Joe deepened the kiss and took complete possession of Scott's mouth as if it was the easiest thing in the world. More than happy to follow Joe's lead, Scott let it happen.

Without his sight, his other senses seemed determined to work overtime. Arching his back, Scott pressed his body against Joe's. Even the sensation of his own clothes rubbing against his skin had him shivering with need until, as suddenly as Joe had begun the kiss, he ended it.

Joe took a step back, breaking all contact between them. Scott stretched his arms out, but Joe was no longer within his reach.

"Unless you intend to use your safe word in the next three seconds, I suggest you start stripping, because, if I have to remove your clothes for you, there's no guarantee they'll be in any fit state for you to put back on when you leave."

It wasn't fair—Joe sounded so bloody calm, and Scott could barely remember how to do anything other than pray for another kiss. Eventually, Joe's warning sank in.

Scott shrugged off his coat, but once he had it in his hand, he had no idea what to do with it, had no way to know if there was anywhere suitable for him to put it.

"I'll take it." The coat slipped from Scott's grasp as Joe claimed it.

Scott reached for his shirt buttons. They were smaller and more fiddly to undo. Without his sight, Scott was clumsier than ever.

Joe made no comment when Scott eventually handed the shirt over.

Crouching down, Scott removed his shoes and socks. His trousers and boxers were next. Once they were removed, Scott stood completely naked. He assumed he was doing that directly in front of Joe, but he really didn't know. Not being able to see made Scott acutely aware of how vulnerable he was. His hands formed into nervous fists at his sides.

"Joe?"

"I'm not going anywhere," Joe promised.

Scott took a step to his left, shuffling his bare feet on the cold tile floor as he desperately tried to find a posture that might make him look like less of an idiot while he stood around, naked and hard, waiting for another order.

Folding his arms across his chest would look defensive. Trying to cover his cock would be pointless. Pockets, Scott realised — that was what he needed, pockets he could push his hands into and —

"Come here."

Scott turned his head toward the sound of Joe's voice. Hesitant, waving his arms about in front of him and feeling along the floor with his toes, Scott made his way toward where he hoped Joe stood.

His fingers brushed against something. It felt a bit like leather, maybe like some sort of leather cushion?

"Sit down," Joe ordered.

Joe was doing something as he spoke. Metal rattled against metal, but Scott couldn't work out what made those sounds as he turned and perched nervously on the edge of the seat, waiting for another order — preferably one that involved taking off the damn blindfold.

"Sit back properly," Joe corrected. "There's a back support. Lean against it"

Scott wriggled further onto the seat, trying not

to think about his hard-on bobbing in front of him every time he moved. He reached behind him, trying to find the back of the chair. It seemed to slope away from him at a really strange angle. Frowning behind the blindfold, Scott leaned back well over forty-five degrees, until he finally lay against it.

Whatever the chair was upholstered with was cold against his skin, but it quickly warmed up. That was good...

Scott took a deep breath and tried to remain calm, but he was incapable of slowing his racing pulse. Far too much adrenaline raced through him as he waited for Joe to really get their date started — possibly by telling him why he'd brought him there of all places.

Another metallic rattle. This time it came from somewhere just above Scott's head. He tilted back his head, automatically trying to see what it was.

Scott jumped when Joe wrapped his hand around his wrist, but it wasn't until Joe guided his hand toward something above his head and fastened some sort of restraint around his wrist that every muscle in his body tensed.

* * * * *

When Scott tried to pull his hand away, Joe automatically tightened his grip on the cuff he'd placed around Scott's wrist. It wasn't difficult to keep Scott's hand where he wanted it. Joe waited a moment, to see if Scott wanted to speak up and yell his safe word at the top of his lungs. But Joe's initial instinct seemed to have been right. Scott's reaction was borne of surprise rather than any real objection to being tied up.

Fastening the first cuff to the metal rail at the top of the bench, Joe repeated the process with Scott's other hand. Just as Joe suspected, Scott made no attempt to pull away this time. He accepted the bondage with apparent pleasure. His erection remained firm, pointing straight up toward the ceiling of the salon's back room.

Joe smiled, his own cock growing harder at the sight of Scott's natural submission. Making his way around the bench, Joe took hold of one of Scott's ankles. Momentary tension filled Scott's leg, before he relaxed and gave Joe his silent consent to bind his ankles as well.

Instead of reaching for another cuff, Joe lifted Scott's leg and placed it neatly in one of the stirrups attached to the salon's waxing bench. Scott's blindfold shifted slightly as he frowned. Joe stared down at him, wondering if Scott had guessed what he intended to do with him yet.

"Joe?"

Nope. Joe's smile morphed into a grin. Scott obviously didn't have a clue.

"Yes, Scott?" Joe asked, his tone as innocent as he could make it. Lifting Scott's other leg, he placed it in the stirrup on the other side of the bench, before stepping back to admire the picture he'd created.

Naked and helpless, Scott had never looked more gorgeous. Joe moved closer and stood between Scott's spread legs. He ran his fingers through the fine blond hairs that covered Scott's balls and the area around his cock. Before long, Scott was going to look even better.

"W-what are you...?" Scott began. "I m-mean...?" He cleared his throat, apparently unable to find a whole sentence that fitted the situation.

Joe didn't rush to help him out. Stroking his fingers through the strands of hair above Scott's cock, he followed the light blond trail all the way up to his navel, then back down to the root of his erection.

"What are you g-going to do to me?" Scott finally blurted out. He didn't sound scared as such — more like nervous and fascinated in equal measure.

"I'm going to get rid of all this," Joe said, tugging lightly at a few of the strands. "Shave you nice and clean for me."

Joe studied all that was visible of Scott's face, but it was impossible to read his expression accurately past the blindfold. He half expected a loud "no", quickly followed by Scott's safe word, but it didn't come.

A few more seconds of silence passed.

"Any comment?" Joe prompted.

Scott's chest rose and fell as he took a deep breath. He shook his head.

Joe's eyes narrowed as he waited for the gesture to become a lie when Scott finally got around to voicing his objections. But no, Joe's lips quirked into a smile as his frown eased. That really was it. Scott was his to do with as he pleased.

Joe dropped his gaze to Scott's cock. Trailing his knuckles along the underside of Scott's shaft, he watched the way Scott's stomach muscles tensed and relaxed, making his cock twitch, almost as if it were doing a little dance for Joe.

Now completely focused on the scene before him, Joe trailed his fingers over the light blond curls on Scott's balls one last time. With his other hand, he reached for the electric trimmers he'd placed on the metal tray next to the waxing bench.

Scott flinched as the clippers whirred noisily into motion. He pulled at the cuffs and lifted his arse off the edge of the bench as he kicked out against the stirrups. The sturdy piece of furniture didn't even sway.

Joe caught hold of Scott's cock and forced the rigid shaft to point down toward the stool he sat on, giving no weight to any consideration other than what would make his task easier to complete.

Scott gasped.

"Uncomfortable?" Joe prompted, glancing up.

"A-a little," Scott admitted. "But…but I don't m-mind."

"Good boy." Joe scooted forward to sit on the very edge of his stool and placed the shaver on the edge of Scott's pubic hairline. As he brought it forward, pale blond hairs fell away.

Scott whimpered and pressed his head back against the waxing bench. Joe flicked his gaze between Scott's face and his crotch as he swept another strip of hair away.

Pausing, Joe ran his fingers over the tiny spikes of hair the clippers had left in its wake and brushed away all the loose strands. Scott lifted his hips off the bench and pushed his crotch up, as eager for his touch as ever.

Pre-cum leaked onto Joe's hand as Scott's shaft slid against his other palm.

Joe nodded his approval as he worked the clippers over the rest of the hairs around the base of Scott's cock, taking each strand down to just a few millimetres in length.

Scott let out a breath of relief when Joe finally allowed Scott's cock to rise back into its naturally erect position. A murmur of pleasure followed as Joe traced his fingers over Scott's partially-shaved skin.

"Speak up," Joe ordered. "Tell me what you're thinking."

Scott parted his lips and flicked his tongue out to moisten them. "I…"

Joe rubbed his thumb over the almost-bare skin again.

"H-hot. Your hand feels hotter without any h-hair there," Scott offered.

"Go on," Joe said.

"But I…I can't picture it, the hair n-not being there anymore."

"Good." Joe picked up the clippers again, switched them on and carefully began to work them over Scott's balls. More blond strands tumbled toward the floor as he worked.

"G-good?" Scott whispered, as if speaking at full volume might distract Joe into cutting off far more than hair. However, his voice was also rough with desire. Any fear he felt wasn't turning him off at all.

"I told you tonight would be for my eyes only, didn't I?" Joe reminded him. "I'm going to be the only one who knows how you'll look without a single strand of hair hiding any of this skin from me." He had to alter his position on the therapist's stool to give his own cock more room in his jeans as he spoke.

Scott's Adam's apple bobbed.

"Maybe I won't let you see yourself at all," Joe mused, doing his best not to let on just how fast that prospect made his heart race. "I'll order you to keep your cock covered as much as you can, and to close your eyes whenever you take a shower. I'll blindfold you whenever we have sex. You'll never see your balls again. Would you like that?"

Scott shook his head.

"Good." Joe chuckled. "That would be half the fun." He carefully stretched the skin covering Scott's balls as he continued his task.

Scott remained very still, and Joe was sure that was only partly because sharp blades were whirling against his testicles. Scott really didn't get it.

"Dominants aren't always nice guys," Joe pointed out. "They don't always like giving their subs orders that they'll enjoy following. Knowing that a man is doing something against his own inclination because he wants to obey you more than he wants his own way, it's..." Joe paused and took the clippers away from Scott's skin as he tried to find the right words. "For a dom, it's the mental equivalent of an expert blow-job."

Smiling to himself, Joe returned most of his attention to his self-appointed task; but he couldn't quite stop part of his mind going off on its own tangent. For the first time, he found himself wondering what the sub might get out of that particular scenario.

"Some subs like getting those kinds of orders, too," he finally decided. "I'm damned if I know

166

why — but some guys really get off on obeying commands they don't actually like following."

* * * * *

Because knowing I've pleased you feels better than any orgasm ever could.

Scott's chest shook as he took a deep breath. He managed to keep the words back, but he couldn't deny that they were true. If it was a choice between knowing what he looked like shaved or knowing that he was pleasing Joe — that he was pleasing his dom — by remaining ignorant, there really was no competition.

A shiver ran down Scott's spine. He desperately tried to stop it in its tracks, sure that any false move would have him singing soprano for life, but he was as powerless to stop it as he was to disobey Joe.

The sound of the clippers finally disappeared from Scott's darkened world. Joe ran his fingers over Scott's balls. It was obvious that his touch was entirely practical. Joe was just assessing his work with the shaver; he wasn't even trying to pretend otherwise. There was nothing of a lover's caress in his actions. But that didn't change the way the heat from Joe's palm soaked into Scott's balls when he cupped them in his hand, or the way bliss radiated through Scott's body with each movement of Joe's fingers.

Scott moaned as he closed his eyes very tightly. Part of him still remembered being a school boy and being so proud that the blond curls around his cock proved that he was finally becoming a man rather than a boy. Another part of Scott's mind was far more interested in being the kind of man who was capable of keeping Joe in his life for as long as possible. His cock really just wanted to come and —

"What the — ?" Scott jerked forward as far as his restraints would allow. He tried to look down to see what the hell Joe was doing to him now, but all he saw was the black interior of the leather blindfold.

"It's just shaving cream," Joe said, his voice tinged with amusement. "Can't have you walking around with stubble all over your balls, can we?"

Scott automatically shook his head, but he wasn't at all sure he wanted the last traces of hair removed from his skin. He frowned behind his blindfold, but he didn't go so far as to actually say anything to stop Joe. The cream felt warm and slick, just like lube, as Joe spread it down between his arse cheeks. Scott couldn't help but squirm.

"It's in your best interests to remain very still from now on," Joe informed him. He seemed to have finished applying the cream.

Scott's mind instantly conjured up an image of a huge knife, a cross between an old straight edge razor and a machete. He swallowed rapidly. Every muscle in his body tensed.

Joe placed his fingers on Scott's stomach, just alongside the edge of the cream, and stretched his skin taught. Scott helplessly pictured the blade descending toward his cock.

As a high pitched whimper escaped from the back of Scott's throat, he gritted his teeth, and concentrated on remaining completely motionless. He barely felt the razor scrape across his skin. All he was really aware of was the cream being swiped away in sections.

His hair was going with it. Scott knew that, but he still couldn't picture it. Even his imagination seemed to be obeying Joe's orders. For Joe's eyes only. This night belonged to Joe. For tonight at least, *Scott* belonged to Joe. He was Joe's sub; Joe was his dom.

A droplet of pre-cum dripped onto Scott's stomach as Joe bent his erection to one side to access another patch of soon to be hairless skin. Scott was so desperate to come that his balls felt ready to explode as Joe worked on them, but Joe didn't seem to be in any sort of rush. No hairdresser at the salon could have been more determined to do a perfect job.

Something that Scott guessed had to be the razor, clicked against something else metallic. Suddenly, both of Joe's hands were on Scott's body. Every one of Joe's fingers trailed over Scott's crotch at the same time. All at once, Scott realised that there was absolutely nothing, not even the shortest stubble, between him and Joe's touch.

A shiver ran down Scott's spine. Instead of feeling colder though, Scott felt the heat build up just beneath his skin. Joe moved his fingers over Scott's crotch again, smoothing something into his skin.

Some kind of after-shave lotion, Scott guessed. It seemed to seep into his skin as Joe worked; within seconds, the heat from his cock was speeding through his muscles, making him tremble within his restraints.

"Does that feel good?" Joe asked.

Scott nodded.

Joe stroked his fingers down the cleft between Scott's arse cheeks. Scott would never have believed that removing the few fine hairs that had been there at the start of the day could have made so much difference to how sensitive his skin was.

"You look good," Joe said. "Really good..."

Scott felt a new wave of heat rush through him — this time to the cheeks on his face. He blushed. There was nothing that wasn't worth it, if it meant hearing that sort of approval in Joe's voice.

Out of nowhere, a cool rush of air brushed across Scott's cock. Scott frowned. It took his arousal-addled mind far longer than it should have to realise that Joe was blowing against his bare skin.

As he groaned, Scott pictured Joe's head bent over his cock and balls with his lips pursed. Every sensation was suddenly highlighted one hundred fold.

"Speak up," Joe ordered. His breath caressed Scott's cock as he spoke.

"Why the hell didn't I d-d-do this years ago?" Scott blurted out.

* * * * *

"*You* haven't done anything," Joe corrected. "*I* did this."

Scott thrust his hips forward, bucking off the bench in his enthusiasm, but Joe was pretty sure that Scott was still entirely oblivious to the way he was thrashing around. Joe ran his eyes over Scott's body once more, taking in every taut line of muscle.

With his hands clenched into tight fists above his cuffs and his chest rapidly rising and falling in time with his ragged breaths, Scott was stunning.

170

And his newly shaved skin was amazingly tactile; Joe couldn't stop stroking his fingers over it. It was his new addiction, and he fully intended to indulge it whenever possible.

Dipping his head, Joe blew against Scott's balls again. Scott whimpered, making Joe grin. He dipped his head a little further and ran the tip of his tongue over the smooth skin just to the right of Scott's cock.

"Oh, G-G-God..."

Turning his head, Joe let the almost-two-o'clock-in-the-morning shadow on his jawline brush against Scott's groin.

Scott didn't even seem capable of asking for heavenly intervention this time. The sound that left his throat didn't contain anything recognisable as a syllable.

Joe stood up. The legs of his stool scraped across the floor.

"Where are you g-going?" Scott demanded, trying to sit upright, only to slump back when his cuffs stopped him short.

"Wherever I want to," Joe said.

It was an automatic reply — little more than punctuation designed to reinforce Scott's lack of control, and the fact that Scott didn't need to try to control anything at all when they were together. But it was in that particular moment that Joe realised that, for the first time he could remember, he had absolutely no interest in walking away from someone — and not just because he was painfully hard and determined to come.

Being with Scott, controlling Scott, claiming ownership over Scott — it all felt so right.

Joe's hand went to his fly; his body more than happy to take over while his brain was occupied with complications his cock didn't give a damn about.

Scott lifted his head again. He turned his blindfolded eyes toward Joe's crotch as if he thought the leather might disappear if he stared hard enough. Joe shook his head. That wasn't going to happen, not while Joe was the only one who had a say in the matter.

Joe pushed his jeans down his thighs. Ignoring his hard-on for now, he ran his fingers through the thick dark thatch of curls above his cock. He looked back and forth between Scott's shaved skin and his own pubic hair, glorying in the differences between them and, even more than that, relishing the fact that he was the one who had created those differences.

As glorious as the contrast was, it wasn't long before Joe had to move his hand to his cock. He stroked himself a couple of times before stepping forward and letting his thighs come to rest on the edge of the waxing bench.

Releasing his cock, Joe leaned forward and grasped the metal bar that Scott's cuffs were attached to. Scott frowned again, as if he once more found it impossible to work out what was going on.

Joe leaned a little further. His cock brushed against Scott's newly shaved skin. They both gasped at the same time.

Joe stared down at Scott's blindfolded face as he rolled his hips, rubbing their cocks together, letting his balls brush against Scott's shaved sac—hair moving against bare skin, a dominant moving against a submissive.

Dipping his head, Joe brushed his cheek against Scott's, just below the line of the blindfold. Scott had obviously shaved his face before their date; Joe had made a conscious decision not to.

The contrasts between them extended far beyond their balls.

Scott whimpered. He turned his head. Their lips met. Joe instantly took control of the kiss. There was no dramatic physical difference between their mouths. Nothing there marked either of them out as seeking a different role. It was all about action now, and Joe thrust his tongue into Scott's mouth, demanding that Scott follow his lead.

Scott parted his lips in welcome, lapping at Joe's tongue, sucking on the tip as it slid in to and out of his mouth.

Joe's grip on the bar behind the waxing bench turned white-knuckled. His movements sped up. Pre-cum slicked their movements as Scott squirmed beneath Joe's thrusts.

Joe nipped at Scott's bottom lip, ordering Scott to calm down. When Scott gave a shocked little gasp and froze in position, Joe forced himself to fall motionless too. He stared down at Scott for several long seconds before beginning to move again. This time, he made a point of emphasising the control he had over *both* their bodies.

He slid his hands along the bar until they rested over the chains attached to Scott's cuffs. Joe's hold on the metal links effectively shortened the chain and took away a little more of Scott's freedom.

Dipping his head, Joe put his lips to Scott's ear. "You have permission to come, make the most of it because you never know how long it will be before I give you another chance."

Scott groaned with frustration and need. It was music to Joe's ears.

Joe made his thrusts slow and deliberate as he looked down between their bodies to watch their cocks slide against each other. The contrast was glorious. Glancing up at their hands sent an extra wave of pleasure rushing through Joe's veins; Scott's wrists in cuffs were dazzling too.

Scott tossed his head back. His occasional moans and whimpers became a steady stream. Within what felt like moments, they grew into a raging torrent. Scott thrust his hips up off the table in jerky little movements that were obviously beyond his control.

Without any warning, Joe was caught up in the same river of ecstasy Scott seemed to have been swept away by.

It was no pretty little brook that people picnicked alongside. White water rapids surrounded Joe and tossed him against the rocks. His hearing cut out, overpowered by the roar of an upcoming waterfall. Joe's eyes dropped closed.

Scott cried out as he tumbled over the falls. The sound seemed to come from a very long way away. Joe grabbed hold of Scott's wrists, determined not to lose him in the deep, swirling pool at the base of the drop.

Joe's own yell was drowned out by the pounding in his ears as he came, thrusting violently against Scott's crotch as they both spilled their loads between them.

As he finally stopped, gasping for breath and still barely able to get his head above the surface of the water, Joe slumped forward, letting his full weight come to rest against Scott.

* * * * *

Scott tried to breathe. It wasn't easy, but very little of that was down to the pressure of Joe's body-weight on his chest. Scott wasn't sure it was physically possible to drown in pleasure, but the bliss that had swirled through him had taken his breath away and made his head spin, just as if he were deep underwater.

They were pressed together so tightly, Scott could feel every beat of Joe's heart. He could almost swear their pulses had fallen into sync as they remained there recovering together. Even if he'd been free to sit up, Scott wouldn't have had the desire to move—especially when he was exactly where he knew he belonged.

Turning his head slightly, Scott brushed his cheek against Joe's hair. It was the only kind of caress at his disposal. In his mind's eye he could easily picture the thick black hairs that covered Joe's head. They decorated most of his body too, far more sparsely in some areas than others, but still…

Scott took a deep breath. The only place where his own, far fairer, body hair had been really thick and noticeable was around his cock and balls, and now…

Joe made a pleased sound in the back of his throat as he straightened up. An unpleasant chill ran

175

through Scott as cooler air replaced the heat from Joe's body, but Scott knew better than to ask to be allowed up straight away.

He'd be freed as and when Joe wanted to release him—not before. And that was fine with Scott. Leaning back against the bench, trying not to wonder how insane he had to look—bald, spread-eagled, and cum-stained—Scott took a deep breath and let it out very slowly.

He listened for the sounds of Joe straightening up his clothing. Instead, he felt Joe's hand came to rest on his stomach.

Scott lifted his head. "J-Joe?"

"Yeah?"

What are you doing? But by the time Scott had the words lined up in his head, there was no reason for him to ask. He'd already realised what Joe was doing. He was rubbing both loads of their cum into Scott's skin.

Slowly, carefully, as if determined not to miss a single smudge of semen, Joe massaged it all in. Across Scott's stomach, and down over his cock and balls, it seemed to Scott as if Joe gave his complete attention to applying a nice even coating all across his body, ensuring it would soak in perfectly.

A whimper escaped from the back of Scott's throat. He'd never really thought of cum as something a man might use to mark his territory, but he had no doubt that was what Joe was doing.

The scent of their combined pleasure hung in the air all around them, and Scott knew it would cling to his skin until he took his next shower. Any man who got too close to him in the meantime would be bound to smell the scent of sex and satisfaction all over him; and then the guy would know that Scott had already been claimed by a man who knew how to make him cum like never before. He'd know Scott had no need of another lover.

Eventually, Joe seemed to be done. Scott sensed him step back. Then came the familiar rustle of clothes that Scott had been waiting for. Scott had no idea how long he was left in his bondage before it finally pleased Joe to free him. In truth, he was lost in far too much of a post-orgasm daze to really care.

Even when Joe guided his legs off whatever they'd been trapped by, Scott was content to let Joe move his limbs in whatever way he chose. Joe soon freed Scott's arms too. Scott sat up and reached for the blindfold, his movements stiff after his arms had been held in the same position for so long.

"No. Get dressed first." Joe pushed Scott's clothes into his hands.

"But…?"

Joe laughed. "Did you really think I was joking about not letting you see yourself tonight?"

Scott looked down, as if it were possible for him to see the clothes in his arms.

"Get dressed," Joe ordered again.

Scott clumsily began to obey.

"Tonight or f-f-forever?" he stuttered out, when he was half dressed.

Apparently those few words were enough to make sense, because Joe didn't ask for an explanation.

"As hot as it would be not to let you see your cock forever, it wouldn't be practical," Joe said. "Not when I expect you to keep yourself shaved for me from now on. You can look first thing tomorrow morning."

Scott nodded his understanding. It didn't occur to him that he either could or should object. Anyway, he had a far more immediate concern and it made him wince as he tucked his cock away. "You do this on purpose, d-don't you?" he asked, before he could stop himself.

"Do what?" The reply came from where Scott guessed the room's door to be. He could easily picture Joe leaning casually against the door frame as he enjoyed watching him struggle.

"You always make me try to get hard again s-straight after I come," Scott mumbled. "Hurts l-l-like hell."

Joe laughed again, a rich cheerful sound that hinted that Joe might have enjoyed their time together that evening just as much as Scott had.

Scott found himself smiling too as he pulled his coat back on. He turned his blindfolded face toward Joe's laugh, but he wasn't sure Joe would actually tell him if he'd put anything on upside down or inside out. He had a feeling that was the kind of thing Joe would let him learn the hard way.

"You forgot one thing," Joe suddenly said.

For reasons his conscious mind wasn't even aware of, Scott held out his hand, palm up, in expectation.

"You're pretty damn sure of yourself, aren't you?" Joe asked.

Scott's pulse rate doubled. The only reason he kept his hand out, was because horror had frozen him in position.

"Good," Joe said. "About time you realised any man who likes leather would have to be a fool to walk away from a sub as good as you are." He put what could only be an envelope in Scott's hand.

Scott felt his jaw drop. Being able to frame a response was out of the question.

A touch against the back of his head and sudden white light filled Scott's world. He closed his hand tightly around the envelope Joe had given him, determined not to drop it as he lifted both his hands to shield his eyes.

His vision slowly came back to him. Scott couldn't bring himself to look around the room to see if any of his guesses about his surroundings had been correct. He blinked up at Joe, keeping all his attention on him. "Hi," he whispered.

Joe's amused little smile morphed into a full blown grin. "Hi, yourself. Come on." He took Scott's hand and led him out of the back room. He was still holding Scott's hand when they stepped out of the shop.

"Where's your car?"

"It k-kind of died. I got a t-t-taxi here, but it's not that far, I can w-w-walk back and —"

"I'll give you a ride home."

It was a statement, not a question. There was no need for Scott to answer. Any protest he made wouldn't be taken as a polite attempt not to make his friend go out of his way. It would be read as disobedience to his dom, and that was out of the question.

Scott was soon settled behind Joe on his bike. His lips were still tingling from Joe's last kiss. He was tempted to write a note there and then, requesting that Joe would kiss him goodnight when they reached his doorstep, but no.

By the time they were halfway back to his place, Scott was determined to ask for something that would last for far longer than even the best kiss in the world — to ask that Joe mark him more thoroughly than ever before, and in a way that wouldn't wash off the moment Scott stepped into the shower.

Part Seven: Yours Sincerely

"Did you think I might want to spank you *im*properly?"

Scott looked up from the glass of Coke he'd been staring into for the last fifteen minutes, while he patiently waited for Joe to finish his late shift at the club.

The words in the note he'd handed over at the start of their date played through Scott's mind as he met Joe's eyes across the bar top.

I'd like you to spank me properly, please.

Joe raised an eyebrow; he obviously wanted an answer now, and not whenever the hell Scott felt like giving one.

Playing for an extra few seconds to pull his thoughts together, Scott took a hasty sip of his drink and cleared his throat. "I just m-meant that you wouldn't have to hold b-back on my account." He peered down into his drink as he turned his glass around and around on the bar. "I know you've been d-doing this for years and I'm just getting s-s-started, but you don't have to m-make allowances for me." He risked a glance up.

Joe had his arms folded and was resting them on the bar directly opposite Scott. His expression didn't change as their eyes met.

Someone working further down the bar called time. Everyone began to make their way toward the door, except Scott—he remained on his stool. Even if he hadn't been sure that was what Joe expected him to do, looking away from Joe was unthinkable.

The room fell silent around them. Scott's heart beat faster and faster. Finally, Joe's lips quirked into a smile and the world kicked back in motion. Joe walked a little way down the bar. Scott glanced into every shadowy corner of the room, checking no one else was around. He took a deep breath. They were the only ones there.

If this was going to happen, it was going to happen now. Scott wiped his hands on his jeans as his palms turned slick with sweat. The skin across his buttocks tingled, and Joe hadn't even looked at his arse, let alone struck it.

Adrenaline rushed through Scott's veins, and his throat went dry. He was going to be spanked by Joe. He grinned at that knowledge, unsure how he'd managed to get so lucky.

Incapable of sitting still for another moment, Scott clambered down from his high barstool. His trainers squeaked against the floorboards. Joe looked up from whatever he'd been doing on the other side of the bar.

Scott froze. "Sh-should I...?" He waved a hand toward the empty room.

"Should you what?"

Scott fiddled with the end of his belt as he tried to think of a sensible way to finish the sentence. Should he set up whatever Joe needed in order to spank him? Should he bare his backside in readiness?

"Your arse will get hellish cold on the ride home if you drop your jeans now," Joe warned, when

Scott failed to utter a single word.

"H-home?" Scott repeated blankly.

"What?" Joe asked, turning to face Scott properly. "Did you think I was going to spank you here? And then what, send you off home before you could even sit comfortably behind the wheel of your car?"

"Um...Yes?" Scott said. "Or in a t-taxi anyway — turns out my car's a write off and..."

His words died as Joe shook his head in apparent disbelief.

"Well, like you said. I know what I'm doing. You don't." Joe pushed himself away from the shelf behind the bar. "You're coming home with me tonight."

Joe stepped out from behind the bar, picked up his jacket and headed for the door. Scott hurried after him. He only just reached the front door in time to slip out before Joe pulled the shutters down and ended up locking him inside.

Joe tutted. "Keep up, Scottie."

Scottie? Folding his arms across his chest, Scott just stood there, feeling very much like a spare part while Joe locked up the club.

Joe never hesitated. His movements were strong and confident. It didn't matter that he wasn't doing anything kinky at that particular moment; Scott was still enthralled by every movement of Joe's body.

Scott was so busy admiring the view, he was caught completely off guard by a set of keys suddenly being thrown in his direction. He missed the catch and had to pick them up off the pavement.

"In the panniers on my bike, there's a spare

helmet, some gloves, and a jacket; put them on."

Scott obeyed; it didn't occur to him to do anything else. Obedience was what his dates with Joe were all about. Every command made Scott's cock harder.

All things considered, Scott was quite proud of how steady his hands were as he undid the lock, took out the garments, and re-locked the panniers.

Shutters were still rattling down behind Scott as he pulled the helmet on and clawed at the chin strap, determined he wouldn't make a fool of himself by fumbling about with the damn thing in front of Joe again. Scott let out a relieved breath as he realised he'd completed that part of his assignment before Joe joined him alongside the bike.

The helmet muffled the sounds of the outside world and made them hard to distinguish, but Scott didn't worry about that as he pulled on the gloves. The leather was thick. They limited his sense of touch just as thoroughly as the helmet reduced his hearing.

Scott wasn't sure if it was the muffled sound of footsteps that alerted him to Joe's approach, or if it was some sort of sixth sense, but he turned just in time to see Joe step up alongside him. In the comparative privacy of the helmet, Scott was free to grin like an idiot.

Joe pulled on his jacket. Quick to follow his lead, Scott reached for the one he'd placed over the bike's saddle. The bulk of the helmet made it difficult for him to look down to see what he was doing as he tried to zip up the jacket. The gloves were too big for him and made it feel like he was working through a dozen layers of thick cotton wool.

The visor blurred his vision, mostly because there was a smudge of something on the bit just in front of his right eye, but he was still able to recognise Joe's bare hand as it calmly brushed his gloved fingers aside.

Joe had been sensible enough not to put his gloves on until he'd done up all the fiddly little buckles and clasps on his own jacket. Scott could only stare down, feeling helpless and childlike as Joe finished dressing him.

"All done," Joe announced. He left Scott standing idly next to the bike as he threw one leg over the saddle and settled himself comfortably astride it. He slid his helmet on as easily as if it had been moulded specifically for his head. Finally, Joe nodded to Scott to get on behind him.

Scott already knew how amazing it felt when he was allowed to wrap himself around Joe for a ride. He didn't need a second invitation. He slid his arms around Joe's waist and took as firm a grip on him as the oversized gloves would allow as Joe started the bike and pulled away from the kerb.

Joe rode fast, still unwilling to make any sort of allowance for Scott's lack of experience. Scott chuckled within the privacy of his helmet, lightheaded with a sudden rush of endorphins.

God, he'd been an idiot when he wrote that last note. He'd been stupid to think Joe might go easy on him during the spanking just because he was a novice submissive. Joe never did anything by halves.

It was always all or nothing with Joe, and Scott wanted it all.

As they turned a hair-pin corner, Scott clung

even more tightly to Joe. Eyes closed, he made no attempt to track their progress across the city. It was only when Joe killed the engine that Scott realised they'd reached their destination.

Stumbling off the bike on shaky knees, Scott did whatever Joe nudged him to do. Helmet and jacket off, he soon found himself following Joe into the block of flats. Then, before he knew it, Scott was standing just inside Joe's front door, looking around as if he'd never visited anyone's place before.

Clearing his throat, Scott squared his shoulders and did his best to make himself look like less of a nervous idiot than he actually was. Perhaps it would have been worth the effort if Joe had bothered to look in his direction.

"The living room's through there." With his back still toward Scott, Joe waved a hand to an unassuming door halfway down a short hallway.

Scott cautiously made his way toward it while Joe took off his coat. The hall was bland, white, and empty apart from a row of hooks that held nothing but leather garments. There was no other hint of Joe's personality. It gave Scott no idea what to expect as he peeked into Joe's living room for the first time.

When he finally found the light switch, a bare bulb flickered to life from a central ceiling rose and illuminated...well, not a lot. Scott walked into the centre of the empty room.

"I come home to sleep or screw, not to play interior decorator. Although I do have a cum-stained cushion around here somewhere, and a tie-back."

Scott glanced over his shoulder. Joe stood in the living room doorway, leaning against the plain wooden frame. Turning back to face the blank space, Scott ran his eyes over the stripped floorboards. Two tall windows occupied the furthest wall; there weren't any curtains. Scott paced across to the right-hand window, his footsteps echoing loudly around his featureless surroundings.

The view outside was as drab as the interior. The brick wall of the adjacent block of flats didn't even have any graffiti on it. No one could see in, but it was impossible not to feel very exposed. Scott stepped away from the window, instinctively crossing his arms in front of him.

"I want you naked by the time I get back."

Joe was gone before Scott had turned around.

Scott glanced nervously at the uncovered window, but he was already reaching for the edge of his T-shirt. Joe wanted him naked. If some Spiderman impersonator climbed up the opposite building and peeked through the window, they'd just have to deal with the sight of a grown man getting his bare arse spanked.

Scott could hear Joe moving around somewhere else in the flat. Not sure how long he had before Joe would be back, Scott scrambled out of his clothes and tossed them all toward one corner of the room. It wasn't until he was down to nothing but his watch that he paused and took a deep breath.

A moment's thought and he removed his watch, too. Naked meant naked. Orders weren't meant to be messed with. Scott pushed his hands through his hair. He was officially as ready for this as he'd ever be. A sudden click made him spin around, his hard-on pointing straight out in front of him.

187

Joe stepped calmly away from the now closed living room door. Walking into the middle of the room, he placed a battered kitchen chair beneath the room's central bulb. He was completely naked.

Scott couldn't have been more shocked if Joe had walked into the room wearing a fancy dress costume. He hadn't specifically requested nudity in his letter, and he hadn't expected to get any. The unanticipated treat scattered his thoughts.

Scott couldn't help but run his eyes slowly over Joe's body and take in every gorgeous detail. As he studied the inverted triangle of dark hair on Joe's chest, and traced his way down toward Joe's pubes, Scott stroked the freshly shaved and hairless skin alongside his own cock.

He hadn't thought about body hair for years before he met Joe. Now that he was over the initial shock of Joe choosing to get naked, he found it impossible to convince himself to think about anything else.

* * * * *

For a second, Joe thought that Scott was taking a truly unacceptable level of initiative by daring to play with his cock when they were together without asking for his permission. But, when he focused in a little more closely and realised what Scott was actually doing, Joe smiled. "How does it feel?"

Scott blinked. He stopped staring at Joe's body like a hungry hyena, looked up, and met his gaze. "F-feel?"

"Being shaved," Joe specified, sitting down on

the kitchen chair and casually extending his legs out in front of him. His cock was already hard. Joe gave it a few strokes, mostly to remind Scott that *he* didn't need anyone's permission to do that.

"It's… okay," Scott said, dropping his hand to his side.

Joe leaned back in the chair and folded his arms across his chest. "You want to try being a bit more vague?"

"It…I don't know. Everything just f-feels so much m-more sensitive," Scott said, very softly. Whether he was aware of it or not, Scott's hand crept back to his crotch as he spoke. He ran his knuckles over his shaved skin.

"Does it get you hard?"

Scott nodded. "All the time." He shook his head. "Even when I'm at w-work."

Joe's smile grew wider as he imagined Scott going through his day completely unable to control his cock. "Good. I want you hard and ready for me all the time."

Scott nodded, apparently entirely on automatic pilot.

Joe was pretty sure Scott had no idea what he was actually agreeing to anymore, he just knew that he wanted his dom to be pleased with him—that he wanted to submit to Joe's will more than he wanted to get his own way. Joe straightened up in his chair. "Come here."

Scott walked toward him, his bare feet making no sound on the floorboards. He stopped directly in front of Joe, halting just short of making physical contact with him.

Joe placed his hands on either side of Scott's body and pulled him an inch or two closer, until Scott was standing neatly between Joe's own comfortably splayed legs.

Running his hands down Scott's sides and over his buttocks, Joe relished the strength tangible in the muscles hidden away beneath Scott's surprisingly soft skin.

His fingers reached the backs of Scott's legs. "Tell me why you want to be spanked," he ordered, as he massaged the flesh he was about to punish.

"What?"

Joe moved his hands back up and settled them on Scott's arse to contentedly cup the firm, round globes. "Tell me why you asked me to spank you," he repeated.

Scott peered down at Joe as if he was speaking a different language.

Slipping his hands further around Scott's body, Joe dipped his fingers down the cleft between Scott's buttocks and ran a fingertip over the sensitive strip of skin right above Scott's hole.

Scott had shaved himself there too. Joe ran his eyes over Scott's crotch. There wasn't even a hint of stubble anywhere. Such a good boy...

"Have you done something you think you need to be punished for?" Joe looked up, and their eyes met.

Scott blinked first. He looked down, but the gesture wasn't accompanied by any sort of attempt to speak.

"It's a simple question," Joe pushed. "All it requires is an honest answer."

Scott politely covered his mouth as he cleared his throat. "I d-don't think I've done anything wrong."

"You don't *think* you've done anything wrong?" Leaning back in his seat, Joe broke all contact between them, re-folded his arms, and raised an eyebrow. "You don't know?"

Scott shuffled his feet. His erection swayed in front of Joe's face.

"Have you come without permission when we're together?" Joe asked.

Scott shook his head.

"Have you done anything with another guy?" The very thought of it made Joe tense, but he managed to keep his voice level.

Another shake of the head.

Joe relaxed. "Have you committed murder, treason, anything like that?"

Scott smiled slightly. "No, n-nothing like that."

"So..." Joe prompted.

Scott glanced away for a moment. When he met Joe's eyes again, it was obvious how much effort it required. "N-no," he said, his voice softer than ever. "I haven't d-done anything I think I need to be p-punished for."

Joe nodded his approval. It might have been like getting blood out of a stone, but the satisfaction he received from hearing Scott say those words was worth it. "So why a spanking?" he asked.

Scott shrugged. His arms hung idly at his sides as if he wasn't sure what to do with them; or perhaps as if he felt the need to receive an order before he was *allowed* to do anything with them. As Joe watched,

Scott twitched his fingers and formed a half-fist several times in quick succession.

"Because it's something you think I want?" Joe suggested.

All that question did was convince Scott to meet Joe's gaze for another few seconds. No words left Scott's mouth; he just managed to look more nervous than ever.

"I do want to spank you," Joe added, just in case Scott harboured any doubts about that. "You have a fantastic arse. I've imagined you turned over my knee since the first day I met you. I've jacked off to the idea of it dozens of times. Hell, if you hadn't done such a good impression of a man who didn't know he was a sub, this would have happened months ago."

Scott's Adam's apple bobbed. He still didn't speak.

"And you *are* a sub," Joe went on. His grip on his opposite biceps tightened. His forearms pressed against his chest, threatening to squeeze the air out of his lungs as he forced himself not to reach for Scott just yet. "You're submissive enough that I know that you'd volunteer to do something you think you'd hate, just because you thought it would please me."

Scott's fingers curled into a full-fist at his side. His knuckles turned white. Every muscle in his body seemed to tense before Joe's eyes, but Scott's erection didn't falter. "I w-want this," he whispered.

They couldn't have been any closer unless Scott was sitting on Joe's lap, but the words were still on the edge of Joe's hearing. "What do you want?" he pushed.

"I want you to s-spank me."

Joe didn't move.

Scott cleared his throat; then tried again, louder. "I w-want you to spank me." He paused for a moment. "Please."

Joe couldn't stop his lips twitching, but he managed to stop himself laughing out loud. So bloody polite... "You think you'll like it?" he asked.

"Yes."

"Because you liked it when I used the flogger on you the first time we did a scene together?"

Scott nodded. A bead of pre-cum formed on the tip of his cock. Joe had stayed still for long enough, and Scott had earned his touch with his honesty. Joe swiped up the droplet and offered it to Scott's lips on his fingertip.

Very slowly, Scott opened his mouth and accepted the treat.

Joe took his finger away once it had been licked clean. "Good boy." He leaned back in his chair. "But this won't be anything like what I did with the flogger."

Scott shuffled his feet, once more making his cock do a little dance for Joe's amusement, but he remained silent.

Sod it. There was only so much talking, so much one-way conversation, a man could be expected to live through. "Turn yourself over my knees."

Scott took a step back and stared down at Joe's lap, as if he needed to literally look at the task from a new angle before he could work out how to follow the command.

Joe brought his legs together and guided Scott

around to stand at his side. Scott's attempt to bend over Joe's lap may have been intended to be cautious and graceful, but in reality it was as clumsy as hell. Scott's cock poked into Joe's thigh as Scott landed heavily across his legs.

Joe's cock rubbed very pleasantly against the underside of Scott's torso as Joe tugged him into a more appropriate position — one which allowed Scott to reach forward and steady himself with his hands on the floor in front of him.

A few moments went by while Joe nudged Scott into the exact pose he wanted him to assume, and made sure Scott's erection wouldn't get trapped too painfully beneath him while he was being spanked. Finally satisfied with their arrangements, Joe settled his right hand gently on Scott's arse.

Scott jerked forward as if Joe had struck him with all of his might. Joe made no comment. Instead, he stroked Scott's arse and legs, gentling him down, encouraging him to relax.

When he spoke, Joe made a point of keeping his voice level and matter of fact. "That first flogging I gave you was very gentle for good reasons. I didn't know how much you'd done or what you were really into, but I doubted you had much experience. I wasn't going to risk scaring you off, or take the chance of freaking you out just before my shift started."

Scott squirmed, as if he believed there was some way in hell he was actually going to find an entirely comfortable position when he was head down and arse up over Joe's lap.

"The flogger didn't hurt at all, did it?" Joe asked.

Scott shook his head.

Joe ran his hand all the way down Scott's leg, from thigh to ankle, then back up. "It just felt good, right? Hot and tingly. All it did was make you want more."

Scott gasped when Joe slid his fingers between his arse cheeks to circle his hole. "Yeah," he moaned. "R-r-right." He rocked his hips, pushing his cock against Joe's leg.

"This spanking won't be like that," Joe said. "This will hurt."

Scott froze mid-thrust.

"If you turn out to be a masochist, you'll really like that," Joe went on in that same purposefully conversational tone of voice. "But if it turns out that you're not into pain, then you won't like it." He paused for a moment, considering the possibilities. "That's not a deal breaker, it's just something that is what it is."

"I c-can—" Scott began.

"Hush."

"B-but—" Scott tried again.

"I knew a man a few years ago who didn't like pain for its own sake, but he loved being spanked because he knew how much his master enjoyed spanking him. Another guy I played with a while back really got off on having marks on his body, even if he didn't enjoy actually getting them."

Scott lay very still over Joe's lap, apparently thinking about everything he said very carefully. "That was okay w-with you?" he finally asked.

"If I wanted someone who always matched my kinks perfectly and was always completely predictable, I wouldn't bother screwing anyone. I'd just close my eyes and make up some cute little fantasy to jack off to." Joe stroked his hand over Scott's arse again, relishing the way Scott's muscles clenched and flexed beneath his palm. "It's the reality of owning another man that makes dominating him hot—not the fantasy."

Scott pushed his shaft against Joe's leg again.

"So I expect you to be honest about how much this hurts and how much you either love or hate it. Understand?" Joe said, letting his tone of voice turn deadly serious for a few seconds.

"Yeah, I—"

Scott broke off abruptly when Joe brought his hand down on his arse for the first time.

* * * * *

Scott jerked forward. His fingers slipped against the floorboards. The noise of the smack echoed off the bare walls, making it sound far harsher than it had actually felt. Warmth spread through Scott's right buttock, but very little pain followed in its wake.

He twisted his neck, trying to peer over his shoulder and see if there was any kind of mark left on his skin. It was silly to get his hopes up so soon, but the urge to check was impossible to resist.

"Oh no you don't." Joe ruffled Scott's hair as he pushed his head back down. "This is about how you feel, not about how you look. Vanity can come later—if you're good."

Scott gazed down at the floorboards between

his hands. There was a dark, twisted knot right in the centre of one of the boards. He let his eyes rest upon it while he made a concerted effort to redirect his thoughts toward the mild stinging sensation in his right buttock and push everything else out of his mind.

Joe caressed the skin he'd just struck. It was the most tender touch Scott ever remembered receiving. He frowned at the realisation. Tonight wasn't supposed to be about gentleness.

"I—"

Scott cut off as Joe brought his hand down on his left buttock. He was just a little more ready for it that time. His first impressions had been correct. No pain, just heat.

The sound raced through the air, then warmth washed over his skin. Just a moment after that, something else radiated out from the point of contact. It spread slowly through Scott's body until it reached the tip of every finger and toe, and filled him to the brim with its presence.

It wasn't pain. It wasn't heat. Maybe it was something like a combination of both — with a heaped spoonful of perfection added in too.

Scott closed his eyes, struggling to concentrate on what was going on inside his body while most of his brain wanted nothing more than to slip into neutral and just coast along for the ride of its life.

It wasn't long before Joe brought his cupped hand down again. Scott gasped as Joe struck the exact same point that he'd spanked before. The heat was more intense this time. It coiled and snaked through Scott's muscles, causing them to tense and relax outside of his control.

Joe didn't wait around now. He struck Scott's left buttock.

Scott squirmed, trying to move himself into a more comfortable position over Joe's lap, as another wave of endorphins flew through his veins.

All the blood was rushing to his head. His toes cramped as he tried to maintain his awkward position. Both things diverted his attention from the way Joe's hand was warming his arse, and Scott couldn't accept anything distracting him. He needed to be able to focus—not just because Joe told him to, but because every cell in his body demanded it.

Something within Scott screamed that this was important. It wasn't so much that a particular part of him *liked* the way the spanking felt. Every bit of him was completely fascinated by it—that was closer to the mark.

Until that point, Joe's left forearm had rested lightly over the small of Scott's back. Now, Joe tightened his grip on him; holding him down and leaving him no choice but to accept the position he was in.

Without uttering a word, Joe still managed to make himself heard loud and clear. There was no point in Scott fidgeting—he wasn't going anywhere.

Freed from any temptation to try to rearrange himself, Scott fell still. Either his ears honed in more effectively once he stopped wriggling, or the spanks grew harder and louder. The sound filled Scott's head. Like the beat of a lover's heart or the regular rhythm of a war drum, it called to him and sent adrenaline pounding through his veins in perfect time with his spanking.

More and more heat built up in the skin as Joe struck his buttocks. No single blow was hard, but as Joe layered the spanks, one over another, they morphed into something different to anything Scott had ever known.

He whimpered as scorching flames seeped deeper into the thick layers of muscle. Somehow, they wove their way through his body until they reached his cock.

His shaft was so hard it throbbed in time with each beat of Scott's heart. Trapped beneath him, Scott's erection rubbed alongside Joe's thigh each time Scott swayed from the force of a spank, but that bit of friction offered no hope of anything other than increased frustration.

There was no chance of relief unless Joe decided to grant it—even if Scott was dizzy with pleasure, he still knew that.

Scott gasped as Joe brought his hand down upon the sensitive flesh where the top of his thigh met his buttock. Scott's fingers slid away from him as his toes lost their tenuous purchase on the wooden floor. All of Scott's weight came to rest on Joe's lap. The air rushed out of Scott's lungs, but Joe didn't even lose his rhythm.

Joe kept on going as if he hadn't even noticed a change. It was easy for Scott to believe that nothing would stop Joe now. Empires could rise and fall. The earth could spin out of orbit and spiral in toward the sun and certain destruction. But Joe would still be there, holding Scott firmly in place so he could keep spanking his bare arse without pause.

Scott whimpered at the idea. As soon as the sound left his mouth, he was powerless to stop other pleasure-filled noises following it. His moans and grunts of bliss filled the silence between the sounds of Joe's cupped palm connecting heavily with his arse.

The chair legs creaked as they slid several inches across the bare floorboards. It didn't occur to Scott to try to stop himself toppling off Joe's lap. It didn't seem possible that he could fall—that Joe wasn't in complete control of that as well as everything else in the world.

Scott's mind was blank. Unable to think about anything that had happened in the past, or anything that might happen in the future, he was trapped in the moment.

Joe was the only man Scott could think about. In his own mind, even Scott himself ceased to matter. Joe was the centre of the universe, everything else was just dust in his orbit.

Nerve endings that had barely whispered through the first twenty-plus years of Scott's life sung out as if they'd been secretly training for the stage. Sweat broke out across his skin, and still Joe kept bringing his hand down on Scott's arse.

Pleasure and pain. Pain and pleasure. Scott no longer knew the difference—he wasn't even sure there was a difference.

Then, there was nothing.

For a moment, Scott thought he might have passed out. Panic rushed through him at the possibility that the spanking might be continuing uninterrupted, but his conscious mind simply wasn't there to enjoy it anymore.

Scott managed to open his eyes. The floorboards were blurry, but they were undeniably there. His eyes were working, and so was every other part of him.

He hadn't stopped processing the spanking. The spanking had stopped.

No! That was even worse. It couldn't be allowed to happen.

For the first time since Joe had tightened his hold on him, Scott began to struggle. He must have done something appalling to make Joe stop. That was the only explanation.

Scott had to get up. He had to be able to face Joe so he could work out how to fix everything. It was Scott's only hope of keeping his sanity.

Joe pressed down even more firmly against the small of his back, refusing to give him permission to rise.

Scott shook his head. Scrabbling at the floor with his fingertips, he kicked out against thin air, desperate for some sort of leverage. The chair legs scraped against the floor again.

"Enough!"

The word kicked down the door and forced its way into Scott's senses. It grabbed that part of him that so desperately needed to please Joe and shook it by the shoulders. Scott froze. He gasped for breath, still draped face down over Joe's lap.

"I'm going to help you stand up," Joe said. "But you're not going to make any movements I don't tell you to make. Understand?"

Scott nodded. The room moved around Scott as Joe guided him onto his feet. The room was blurry.

Scott's knees trembled as he risked a glance at Joe's face.

For some reason, Joe was blurry too.

There was no smudged helmet-visor to blame this time. Scott lifted a hand to his eyes, wondering if being upside down had somehow distorted his sight.

His knuckles came away from his eyes wet. He was crying.

Joe stood up. Before Scott even had a chance to swipe at his face and wipe away any evidence of such mortifying silliness, Joe wrapped his arms around him. Scott parted his lips to apologise, but a surprised yelp replaced any words he might have hoped to utter when he found himself tossed unceremoniously over Joe's shoulder.

The back of Scott's thighs burned as Joe gripped the recently abused skin. Each bit of flesh sent frantic signals racing through Scott's body. Endorphins and adrenaline sprinted through his veins.

His heart raced, his head spun — and Scott was reasonably sure that was only partly due to the fact he was once more upside down.

Walls rushed past Scott on either side. Trying to both wipe his eyes and cling to Joe for grim death, Scott didn't gain any sort of impression of the space they moved through.

As suddenly as he'd picked Scott up, Joe dropped him.

Scott's arms flailed. He tried to cling to empty air. "What the — ?"

He bounced as he landed on a firm mattress. It might as well have been a bed of nails against Scott's flaming arse. Instinct kicked in. He swiftly rolled onto his stomach.

Wiping his eyes once more, Scott cleared his vision well enough to take in his surroundings. Bed. Wardrobe. Lots of complicated looking leather bondage gear. He was in Joe's bedroom. And suddenly it was obvious why Joe couldn't afford a sofa for his living room. Every penny Joe made obviously went straight into his toy collection.

Scott gawped, slack-jawed, at the three rows of black leather toys hanging on the wall alongside Joe's bed.

"I didn't bring you in here to admire the scenery." Joe nudged impatiently at Scott's hip. "Move over."

Obediently wriggling toward the other side of the bed, Scott turned his attention to the one thing a sub might reasonably find even more fascinating than a room full of leather — a naked dom. A naked Joe.

* * * * *

Joe picked up a pillow and tossed it against the headboard. Leaning against it, he stretched his legs out toward the foot of the bed, but he didn't turn his attention toward Scott straight away. He made a point of giving Scott a few moments to catch his breath while he made himself comfortable.

Even when he finally turned toward Scott, Joe didn't pressure him to meet his gaze. For several minutes, Joe was happy to admire the fine blush that he'd spread across Scott's arse. A spanking looked good on him. If Scott's flourishing hard-on had been anything to go by, the spanking had felt good while it was being administered too.

Finally, Joe judged the moment right. He caught Scott's eye.

Scott quickly dropped his gaze. There were still tears clinging to his lashes.

Joe beckoned Scott toward his side of the super-sized bed. "Come here."

Scott crawled across to him.

Joe brushed his thumb across Scott's cheek, wiping away some of the lingering moisture.

Scott immediately tried to pull away. "I'm n-not crying."

"Yes, you are."

"No, I'm n-not. I—"

"It's nothing to be embarrassed about," Joe cut in.

But Scott wasn't listening. He shook his head. "No, I'm not. It d-d-didn't even hurt that much!"

Joe folded his arms across his chest. He'd already discovered that Scott was one of those men whose brain connected directly to his lips when he was flying high on endorphins. He was pretty sure that Scott had no idea what he'd blurted out while being spanked. Nothing had been too personal or too embarrassing for Scott to share with his lover then. And now, Joe was perfectly willing to wait out another round of babbling if that's what he needed to do.

As Scott kept talking, Joe tuned out his lies and watched his lips instead.

He had a beautiful mouth, and it wasn't fair to expect Scott to control it right then. There was no control in Scott now, and no desire to control anyone either. Soon, he'd learn to hand command of himself over to Joe and everything would change, but, for now, Joe simply watched Scott take his first shaky steps into his submission, and smiled.

Gradually, Scott came to a stuttering stop. He stared at a centre point on Joe's chest as if the little patch of skin over his sternum might have all the answers to his questions.

Joe kept his breaths slow and even, just in case Scott was paying attention to that. "The word you're looking for is intense," Joe said, as the silence stretched out. "It felt intense."

Scott glanced up at him.

Joe wiped the last of the tears from beneath Scott's eyes. "There's nothing wrong with that. I'd be more worried if you hadn't shown any reaction. And I know that these are very different than the kind of tears someone cries when they're upset."

Scott's Adam's apple bobbed as he swallowed rapidly. "Th-thank you…"

Joe pushed his hands through Scott's hair. Tugging him up the bed, Joe brought their mouths together.

Scott gasped into the kiss, apparently more than a little shocked by it. Joe buried his hands deeper in Scott's hair, holding him still until he was sure that Scott would keep his head in place of his own volition.

Soon, Scott was lost in the kiss. Joe slid his hands down Scott's body and settled them on Scott's freshly reddened arse.

The moan Scott let out went straight to Joe's

cock; so did the way Scott bucked his hips. Joe pulled Scott down more firmly against his body. Scott pushed his arse back into Joe's hands, then thrust forward, rubbing their cocks together. "Please," Scott whimpered into the kiss.

"Tell me what you want."

Scott groaned. He dug his fingers into Joe's shoulders as he seemed to scramble for the right words. Finally, he pulled away from the kiss—just an inch. "Screw me. P-please, screw me." He spoke loudly and clearly, there was no need for Joe to make him repeat the request.

In one movement, Joe rolled them both over. Pushing Scott onto his back, he pinned him down against the bed. Scott jerked as his arse hit the bed sheet. It was as if the soft cotton had completed an electrical circuit that had lain dormant inside Scott's body for years. He tensed with pleasure, until his whole body became as stiff as his cock.

Joe caught hold of Scott's ankles. Pushing his knees back toward his shoulders, Joe lifted Scott's sore arse off the bed. Scott looked up at him, his eyes open very wide with shock. It was a moment before he seemed to catch up with events. Grabbing hold of his knees, Scott took over holding his legs back.

That left Joe's hands free. He grabbed a condom and a tube of lube from the shelf beneath the mirror hanging on the wall above his bed. Quickly sheathing his cock in latex, he slicked the entire length of his erection with a generous coating of lube. Smearing more lube onto his fingers, he quickly worked two digits deep inside Scott, moving as fast as he thought Scott could handle.

The second that Scott had relaxed enough to take him, Joe moved Scott's ankles up onto his shoulders. Leaning forward, Joe settled his hands on either side of Scott's body and lined his shaft up with Scott's waiting arse. Their eyes met as Joe's cock kissed Scott's hole for the first time that night.

Scott stared up at him, unblinking. His breaths were already ragged. Everything in Scott's expression begged Joe to hurry up, but Scott didn't speak. There were no demands, no orders. As desperate as Scott obviously was, he still seemed to submit to Joe's decisions as if it was his first and only nature to do so.

Scott gasped as Joe yielded to his silent pleas and finally gave them both exactly what they wanted. Scott's eyes fell closed as Joe pushed forward, sheathing himself to the hilt and bringing his hips to rest against Scott's upturned and reddened arse.

Scott seemed to forget how to breathe then. His lips parted, but no sound escaped. Ecstasy transformed Scott's face into something more beautiful than Joe had ever seen. Joe growled his triumph as he swayed back and thrust deep into Scott again.

There was little Scott could do to compliment Joe's movements. All he could do was lie there and accept it. That suited Joe perfectly. He'd given Scott pain and been completely in control of every second of it. Now, he needed to be the one who controlled the pleasure Scott received.

Joe stared down, watching bliss and emotions rush across Scott's face like a whole team of sprinters racing for the finish line.

Scott was his — and he hadn't been the only one

who'd found the spanking intense. With Scott pinned beneath him and almost folded in half by their position, Joe's need to come was only equalled by a sudden need to protect what was his—and Scott was definitely his.

Joe scrambled for control as he pushed deep inside Scott again. Scott's arse seemed to be hotter and tighter than ever. From the first thrust, Joe had been on edge, desperate to spill his cum deep inside Scott's body.

Scott squirmed as he seemed to fight to hold back. But it wasn't until he looked up at Joe, with mute pleading in his eyes, that Joe was willing to believe that Scott was just as frantic to come as he was.

"Come," Joe ordered.

Scott, natural submissive that he was, obeyed him without question. On the very next thrust, Scott came. His cum spurted between them, landing in long creamy ropes across both of their chests, and smearing against their skin, as Joe kept going through Scott's orgasm.

Joe didn't try to hold back a second longer than that. He came. Fireworks whizzed through his veins and exploded behind his eyes. Pretty coloured Catherine wheels, and even more beautiful firecrackers filled with ecstasy, took over his world.

As suddenly as it had begun, the fireworks display ended. All of Joe's strength drained away. Somehow, he managed to stop himself collapsing on top of Scott, but only just. He used his last scraps of energy to roll over onto his back, dragging Scott with him so he could keep his cock buried in his arse a little while longer.

Time passed. They gradually caught their breath, and Joe carefully parted their bodies, but he stopped Scott short when he would have moved away.

Scott made no protest against the decision. He didn't need any extra encouragement to rest against Joe's chest.

Sliding his hands down Scott's back, Joe rested his hands on Scott's arse, just as he had when they first lay in the bed together.

Pressing his head back into his pillow in a lethargic effort to get a better view, Joe studied Scott's face. His eyes were closed; he looked impossibly angelic for a man who had just been screwed to within an inch of his life.

"Thank you," Scott murmured. He sounded as if he was already more than half-asleep. He snuggled into Joe's body as he spoke, seemingly desperate for contact and reassurance after his first taste of pain.

Joe shook his head, wondering how the hell Scott had thought they could have done this scene in the club and gone their separate ways the moment they'd zipped up.

As if reading Joe's mind, Scott began to lift his head. "Shall I—?"

"Sleep," Joe ordered.

Scott let out a soft little sigh as he settled comfortably against Joe's chest again. Joe stroked his fingers gently down his back. He'd never seen Scott so at peace before, and Joe had never been so desperate to hold a man—to hold *onto* a man—in his life. Looking up at the ceiling, he ran the evening's events over in his mind.

There were so many things he wanted to do with Scott, it was almost impossible to decide what he wanted to invite him to do next. It was no use looking to Scott for hints of what he'd prefer. Scott wasn't the kind of man who would ever find it easy to make his desires known to a dom.

Luckily, it wasn't difficult for Joe to guess what kind of thing Scott would love—even if he was equally sure it was something Scott would always be way too embarrassed to mention.

Joe glanced down at Scott once more. If Scott had chosen to be spanked specifically because he thought it would please him, then it only seemed right that Joe should choose something that Scott would enjoy—even if it was something close to his personal idea of torture.

Joe nodded to himself as he made his decision. If there was one thing he was more certain of by the day, it was that Scott was the kind of sub it would be worth spending a night in purgatory for.

Part Eight: Be There

7 P.M. The corner of Churchill Street and Victoria Avenue.

Be There. (Wear a tie.)

In Scott's opinion, the last note he'd received from Joe contained three things that he needed to panic about.

Firstly, there was the time of day. Dates with Joe almost always started late at night. Standing on a street corner and waiting for Joe while it was still daylight simply wasn't natural. Robbed of the shadows he'd become used to over the last few weeks, Scott felt exposed and vulnerable in an entirely new way.

He stared down at his shoes for a few moments. When he looked up, he was immediately confronted by the second reason why hyperventilating seemed like a perfectly reasonable reaction — the location.

A street lined with expensive bars and restaurants, and situated in the most fashionable part of the city, wasn't Scott's natural habitat. Hell, a polar bear in the Sahara would have had more chance of blending in.

Every expensively dressed person who walked past him seemed to instinctively realise that he didn't belong there; none of them bothered to hide their disapproval when they stared down their noses at him.

Scott took a deep breath. This wasn't Joe's usual part of the city either. Joe belonged in a world full of noisy bar rooms, and leather, and clubs where men did kinky, painful, glorious things to each other.

Tucking two fingers into his shirt collar, Scott tugged at the restrictive fabric. He felt like a schoolboy who'd been forced into his Sunday best to visit his posh relatives; which brought him very neatly to the third problem inherent in Joe's commands.

Wear a tie.

That was the full extent of the command. Joe hadn't actually given him permission to wear any other garments. Scott swallowed, his Adam's apple fighting its way past his shirt collar with great difficulty. He had a nagging suspicion that Joe always intended his orders to be followed precisely.

Scott looked down at his neatly pressed black suit and his well-polished black shoes—neither of which had seen the light of day since his grandfather's funeral. If Joe turned up and told him he had to strip off everything but his tie—right there in the middle of a nice polite street, surrounded by couples out on nice polite dates then...

Then Scott had the horrible feeling that he'd do it. He'd probably get slapped by a passer-by, then arrested for indecent exposure. But, God help him, if Joe issued the order, Scott knew he'd do it, and—

"I should have guessed that you'd be here ridiculously early."

Scott spun around. Joe stood less than a foot away from him. Scott took a clumsy step back. Joe looked...not like Joe at all.

212

"You're n-not wearing any leather," Scott blurted out, as his shock got the better of him.

He pulled his gaze up to Joe's face just in time to see his lips twist into a smile. Closing his eyes, Scott mentally cursed himself. "I'm s-sorry, I…"

Scott opened his eyes very wide as Joe put his hand over Scott's mouth and silenced him.

Technically, there was nothing stopping Scott stepping back and regaining the ability to say whatever the hell he wanted. But technicalities didn't mean a damn thing when Joe was around. Scott's feet remained rooted to the same spot of pavement.

He stared up at Joe. Even if he hadn't been gently gagged by Joe's palm, he wouldn't have been able to think of anything to say. All he could do was stare.

Joe had shaved. His usual whatever-o'clock shadow was gone. Scott's hand itched with his desire to stroke his fingertips down Joe's cheek, just for the novelty of it. He'd never known any part of Joe to be entirely hairless.

Heat rushed to Scott's face as he thought about just how smooth Joe had ordered him to keep certain parts of his own body. His cock immediately tried to rise. His shaved balls became more sensitive than ever, and he whimpered behind Joe's hand.

Joe's smile widened, as if he could read Scott's mind, and he loved making him squirm.

Scott glanced to his right, then his left. They were still on a public street. No one was staring at them, but that had to be more by luck than by judgement. He turned his attention back toward Joe.

Joe didn't seem the least unnerved by the

possibility of the whole world seeing them getting kinky. A shiver ran down Scott's spine and immediately spread over every inch of skin on his buttocks.

Joe looked as if he wouldn't hesitate to turn Scott over his lap and spank him where they stood. Scott's knees trembled at the prospect, but he couldn't deny that it also made his cock harder than ever.

Joe took his hand away from Scott's mouth, but only so he could rub his thumb over the heated skin along Scott's cheek bone.

"I like making you blush."

Of course, that only made Scott's face get hotter than ever.

"I...you said I should w-wear a tie," Scott blurted out.

"And you're a very good boy for doing as you're told." Joe calmly straightened the knot in his tie.

Scott stared at Joe's neck. He'd have put money on Joe not even owning a tie, let alone an entire suit, but this evening Joe could easily have passed for an up-market business man. There was no hint of the bartender about him except, maybe, in his eyes. Scott risked a glance up.

Yes, Joe's eyes still promised that he wasn't someone who'd back down from anything or anyone — that he was the kind of guy who didn't merely screw someone, but who took possession of the people he had sex with, body and soul.

Scott shifted his weight from one foot to the other. Even if there was nothing kinky about a man straightening his date's tie, it was still an intimate thing to be seen doing on the street.

"Are you out to everyone in your life?" Joe suddenly enquired.

Scott frowned, wondering if he had missed an entire segment of the conversation. "Yes."

"Good, so you can stop looking like you're ashamed to be seen with me."

Scott opened his mouth. No words happened. He closed his mouth, then tried again. "I'm n-not ashamed of you! I j-j-just..."

Joe raised an eyebrow. He obviously expected Scott to finish the sentence, so it was a pity that Scott had no idea how to do that. Scott looked down for a moment. When he lifted his gaze, he squared his shoulders. "J-just nothing," he finished. "I'm not ashamed of you and I n-never could be. There's nothing else to s-s-say."

Joe nodded. Approval shone in his eyes. "That's better." He tucked a knuckle under Scott's chin and held him still as he dipped his head and brought their lips together. The kiss was brief and sweet. Only the way that Joe nipped at Scott's bottom lip reminded him that, suit or no suit, Joe was still all dom.

When he pulled back, Joe took Scott's hand in a firm grip and led him across the street toward an expensive looking restaurant.

Scott was more than willing to follow Joe wherever he wanted to go, but he couldn't help but let out a mental sigh as he took in a few more details of their destination.

It was one of those places where he couldn't afford anything on the menu, and while his credit card could probably help him disguise that fact, it wouldn't be any help in finding something that looked both recognisable and edible. It was going to be all frogs' legs and fish spawn. His stomach turned over at the thought

Forcing a smile onto his lips, determined to keep it there no matter what, Scott stepped into the restaurant at Joe's side.

"We have a reservation for two under the name Joseph Stuart," Joe said briskly.

A snooty looking maître d' ran a manicured fingertip down a list of bookings propped up on a small podium just inside the entrance. "Yes, indeed. Mr. Stuart." He made a quick notation on the list. "If you'll follow me."

He hurried them toward a small table tucked away in the furthest corner of the restaurant, as if he wanted to make sure as few people as possible noticed the presence of two working class gay guys in his establishment.

Joe pulled Scott's chair out before Scott had a chance to do it himself. He knew he should protest at being treated like a girl, but he couldn't seem to bring the words to his lips—being fussed over by Joe felt too good. Even as he blushed, Scott felt his smile become more genuine.

Joe didn't speak as he took the seat opposite Scott. Menus handed over, the maître d' strode away. Scott had hoped that the friendly, if rather sexually charged, atmosphere that had extended over their previous dates would return now that they were alone, but it didn't.

Joe looked just as tense as Scott felt. His

shoulder muscles were all bunched up beneath his jacket. Scott cleared his throat and he tore his gaze away from Joe's body before he made himself even more flustered. He opened the menu and peered at the starters on the first page.

"Do you see anything you like?" Joe asked after a few moments.

Scott took a deep breath. He didn't see a damn thing that he'd willingly pick for himself. When inspiration struck, it was manna from heaven. Joe liked making his decisions for him, didn't he?

"M-maybe you should o-order for both of us?"

Their gazes met across the table.

Joe's eyes narrowed. "I'm going to ask you a question. Don't think about the answer, just tell me the first thing that comes into your head."

Scott nodded his willingness to obey that order.

"What's your all-time favourite meal?"

Scott couldn't help but follow Joe's command. He didn't think before his lips started moving. "Hamburger meal from McDonalds." He cursed himself the moment the words hit the air. "But I l-like this kind of food too," he rushed to add.

Joe stared straight into Scott's eyes for several seconds. Then he nodded, just once, as if making a decision. Standing up, Joe held out his hand to Scott.

Pure instinct made Scott place his hand in Joe's palm. Joe pulled him unceremoniously to his feet. Scott had little choice but to try to keep up with Joe as Joe strode across the restaurant, still holding onto Scott's hand.

Heads turned to watch them go. Scott was sure

he would have blushed bright red, if it weren't for the fact he'd felt every drop of blood drain from his face when he realised just how badly he must have offended Joe.

"Sorry, mate," Joe said, as he brushed past the maître d' without even slowing down. "Change of plans."

It was all Scott could do to stay on his feet as Joe strode on, his long legs eating up the ground at an astonishing pace. When they reached the pavement outside the restaurant, Scott knew he had to do something. He dug his feet in as best he could, and tugged hard against Joe's grip on his hand.

His elbow and wrist protested, but Scott held his ground until Joe looked over his shoulder and came to a stop. Joe's expression was a mixture of surprise and confusion; as if it had never occurred to him that Scott would try to bring them to a halt without his permission.

"I'm s-so sorry," Scott blurted out. "I really d-didn't mean to blurt out something s-so stupid. I m-mean, you went to all this t-t-trouble and — "

"Do shut up. There's a good boy," Joe said.

Scott shut up, took a deep breath, and braced himself for the worst.

Releasing Scott's hand, Joe undid his own tie and the top button of his shirt. He let out a sigh of relief. "Damn, but I'm glad that's over." Joe pushed his hand through his hair and the thick black strands immediately resumed their usual disordered style. He rolled his shoulders, as if working out a week's worth of tension from the muscles.

Scott blinked. Suddenly, he was face to face

with the Joe he had come to know and… Scott's mind rebelled at that point, refusing to even consider what word might best finish that particular sentence.

But that didn't change the fact that the man who stood before Scott now looked a lot more like Scott's familiar version of Joe—and a dozen times hotter than the imposter that had tried to take his place.

First things first. "You're n-not pissed off with me?" Scott checked.

* * * * *

Joe rolled up his tie and pushed it into his pocket. Taking his uncomfortable suit trousers off in the middle of the street probably wasn't a good idea, but it was tempting. He'd have given damn near anything for a well-worn pair of jeans or leathers.

He glanced at Scott as he turned his attention back to the conversation. "Why would I be pissed off with you?"

"Because you set up a b-big fancy date and I r-r-ruined it?" Scott suggested.

Joe chuckled as he shrugged his suit jacket off and slipped his finger through the loop inside the neck so he could toss it over his shoulder. "That just proves you've got good taste. Bloody awful place, wasn't it?"

Scott said nothing.

Joe stopped wishing that he'd thought ahead and brought a change of clothes along with him. He studied Scott more carefully. "I thought that kind of place would be right up your street." He rubbed his jawline as he frowned, mildly annoyed with himself, but not altogether disappointed he'd read Scott wrongly in this instance. "I still have a bit of work to do on understanding the whole vanilla romance thing, don't I?"

Scott blinked, as if he really hadn't had a clue why Joe had booked a table there until that moment. "You don't n-need to—"

"To do whatever the hell I want?" Joe finished for him. "Pity, because I fully intend to. Do you know this part of town?"

Scott shook his head.

Joe looked down each of the cross roads. There wasn't a McDonalds in sight— another reason to hate the posher part of the city. "Got your car with you?"

Scott seemed to have reverted to his completely mute mode. He shook his head again.

"Good, because we're taking mine." Joe strode off toward the side street he'd parked on. It took him a few seconds to realise that he could only hear one set of footsteps. Turning around, he clicked his fingers to get Scott's attention.

Scott came obediently to his side. Joe looped his arm casually around Scott's shoulders. "We're going to have to work on your ability to walk at heel." When Scott seemed about to speak, Joe kept going without giving him the chance. "Here's the deal. Unless I tell you to stay, I expect you to keep up with me. Imagine you're a puppy. If I walk away, you follow me. Understand?"

"Yes, sir."

Scott came to a complete stop the moment the honorific hit the air.

Joe chuckled, tightened his hold around Scott's shoulders and nudged him into resuming their progress toward his car. "I'm not going to complain if that's what you want to call me, Scottie," he whispered in his ear. Hell, if it was pet commands that brought out Scott's subbiest side, Joe had no problem with that.

Scott blushed, but that was probably less at being treated like a pet and more from blurting out the honorific for the first time. He didn't utter a single word during the drive across town, to the last McDonalds Joe could remember passing. He didn't speak when Joe stopped his car, in the nearest on-street parking space to the McDonalds either.

Joe turned in his seat. If it hadn't been for the fact Scott's hard-on was tenting his trousers, Joe might have thought he was having a full blown panic attack.

"They had a really strict dress code in that restaurant," Joe said, conversationally.

Scott glanced in his direction.

"No tie, no table."

Scott swallowed, but he still didn't speak.

"Of course, that wasn't the only reason I told you to wear a tie."

"I'm n-not sure what you mean," Scott finally whispered.

Joe reached out and tugged Scott's tie, tightening the knot. "It's not leather cuffs, but it will look just as good tied around your wrists as it does around your neck."

Scott peered down at the pale blue fabric as if he had never seen it before. "I prefer you when you're l-like this." His expression changed, making it obvious that he'd had no intention of saying that out loud.

"Like this?" Joe raised an eyebrow.

"Kinky s-suits you."

Joe chuckled. Leaning forward, he brushed their lips together. "Submissiveness suits you," he said, against Scott's mouth.

Scott looked down, resting his forehead against Joe's temple.

"So does confidence," Joe murmured as he trailed kisses back toward Scott's ear. "They're not mutually exclusive, you know?"

Scott took a deep breath and closed his eyes.

Joe gave him a minute before he spoke up again. "Now, go and fetch some food for us, okay?"

Scott nodded. Taking his wallet out of his back pocket, Joe tossed it to Scott. One glance at Joe's expression and Scott seemed to realise that who would pay wasn't up for debate. He didn't bother to argue, he merely listened to Joe's menu order and nodded again before leaving the car.

Joe watched in the rear view mirror as Scott disappeared into the building. Just as he'd suspected, Scott's jacket was long enough to hide his embarrassment. No one was going to spot Scott's hard-on unless Scott wanted them to.

A few minutes later, Joe saw Scott step back onto the pavement; two brown paper bags and Joe's wallet in one hand, and a cardboard tray containing two drinks balanced precariously in the other.

For some reason, Scott seemed to think that there was a curse attached to the wallet. The moment he was back in the car, Scott set the bags of food on his lap and pushed the wallet into Joe's hands as if he couldn't wait to get rid of it. "The bill c-came to—"

"I don't ask men to trust me to tie them up, or spank them, unless I'm willing to put my trust in them in return," Joe cut in. He slid the wallet back into his pocket without checking its contents.

Scott glanced up at Joe through his lashes as he offered him one of the bags of food.

"No. You hang on to it for now. I know the perfect spot for us." Joe pulled away from the kerb. The park he had in mind was close to the edge of town. Their luck was in. There wasn't a single car parked by the lake when they arrived. Joe pulled into the furthest parking spot from the path. Perfect...

The sound of rustling paper filled the car as they both opened their bags. While Scott kept his eyes firmly on his meal, Joe barely even noticed what he was eating. His attention was all on Scott. But, no matter how hard Joe stared at Scott, it was impossible for him to tell what was going on in Scott's mind. He didn't seem to be on the verge of a panic attack at that very moment—but that never seemed to last long with Scott.

Eventually, Scott glanced across the car at him. Joe made a point of catching his eye, more for the joy of making him blush than anything else.

"If anyone s-sees the windows all steamed up, they're g-g-going to think we're screwing each other in here," Scott offered.

"Give me a minute to finish this burger, and they'll be right."

Joe reached out and rubbed Scott's back as

Scott choked on a fry.

"I..." Scott shook his head, apparently giving up on the idea of talking altogether. He dropped his head back against the headrest as he caught his breath. By the time he turned toward Joe again, he seemed to have composed himself slightly.

"Joe?"

"Yeah?"

"The th-thing outside the restaurant, when you s-s-straightened my tie," Scott said.

Joe frowned as he scrolled back in his memory. "What about it?"

"I expected you to b-be ashamed to be seen with me, n-not the other way around."

"Then you're an idiot."

Scott smiled as if he thought that was some sort of endearment.

Joe rolled up all their empty wrappers. One sort of hunger had been dealt with. He was more than ready to move on to another. Getting out of the car, he tossed the wrappers in a rubbish bin attached to the fence around the car park. His car looked sexy, but it was damn near impossible for two reasonably tall men to actually do anything kinky in there. Rather than get back in the car, Joe ducked his head and peered in at Scott.

Scott kept staring straight at the misted up windshield until he seemed unable to remain still under Joe's gaze. He turned and met Joe's eyes through the open driver's side door.

"Get out and come around here."

Scott obediently exited the car and joined Joe. Joe locked it and turned to Scott. Neither of them had kept their jackets on while they ate and they were now both in their shirt sleeves. Joe quickly undid Scott's tie and took it from around his neck.

Scott smiled and let out a quiet little sigh. Apparently, he felt a lot better about the world now that he knew he was about to be tied up and that he would have no control over whatever happened next.

Joe grinned. He'd known there was something he loved about Scott.

* * * * *

"Are you ready to play?"

Scott nodded so quickly he almost gave himself whiplash in his enthusiasm. "Yes." He paused for a second, gathering his courage. "S-sir."

The honorific felt good on Scott's lips, but the way Joe smiled when he heard him say it was nothing short of amazing. Scott grinned, not caring how goofy his expression might be.

"Come on." Joe caught hold of Scott's wrist and led him into a wooded area to the left of the car park. Within moments, they'd both clambered over the fence—Joe with easy grace and Scott with, if not elegance, then at least with real determination to follow Joe.

Soon, they were completely surrounded by trees. It was hard to believe that they weren't in the middle of nowhere, out of sight and sound of all civilisation.

Twigs snapped beneath their feet as Joe led Scott deeper into the woods. Finally, Joe stopped. There was just enough moonlight for Scott to see the way Joe's eyes glistened with desire.

Joe had brought Scott's tie with him. It only took him moments to have one end of it wrapped securely around Scott's right wrist. Scott watched with a detached kind of interest, happy to hold his hand still while Joe worked; but not the least interested in learning how to tie complicated knots himself.

Joe slid a finger between Scott's skin and the fabric, apparently checking the fit. Then, he seemed to lose all interest in both Scott and his tie. He turned away. Joe had almost revolved a full three hundred and sixty degrees when he set off toward a large tree growing a few metres further into the forest. Most of the trees had plants and bushes clustered around their bases, but the trunk of the one that had caught Joe's attention stood straight and proud, isolated from all the other greenery.

Using Scott's tie like the kind of lead another sort of man might attach to a dog's collar, Joe led Scott to the chosen tree and positioned him facing the trunk. "Stay."

Another canine command, but at least Joe didn't suggest Scott cock his leg against the trunk.

Joe walked around the tree, taking his end of Scott's tie with him. It wasn't possible for Scott to stay *exactly* where Joe had left him. He had to step closer to the tree trunk — it was that or detach his arm from his shoulder.

"Give me your free hand."

Scott reached around the tree toward Joe's voice.

Joe started to knot the other end of Scott's tie

around the skin just below Scott's watch. The tie was only just long enough. Even when Scott pressed his torso hard against the rough bark in an effort to make it easier for Joe to restrain him, it seemed like the tie was barely able to bridge the gap between his wrists.

Scott's pulse raced as Joe finished restraining his wrists. Each time he took a breath, his ribs pushed against the tree's trunk. He barely had room to get air into his lungs. He tried to turn his head, but that was impossible too. The only bit of the forest he could see was that segment directly in front of him.

A rustle of leaves from somewhere behind him made Scott tense.

"Sweetheart, if anyone else is out here at this time of night, it's because they're looking for a quiet little spot to do exactly the same thing," Joe whispered into Scott's ear, as he stepped behind him. "There's no reason to be afraid—well, not of anyone but me, anyway."

Scott gasped as Joe pressed up against his back. Scott had heard of people hugging trees, but he was sure they weren't supposed to have erections that threatened to drill a hole in the trunk while they did it.

He squirmed, frantically trying to push himself back against Joe's body, but it felt like he had even less freedom than he'd had on any of his other dates with Joe.

The fact that there was so much open space around them only made the bondage feel tighter and more restrictive. It made Scott's cock harder too. He whimpered against the tree. Everything in the forest was free—every bird, every bug, everything—except

him.

Scott tensed as he felt Joe worming his hand in between his crotch and the tree. Scott pushed his arse out, instinctively trying to create enough space for Joe to do whatever he wanted to him.

"Good boy," Joe whispered. He cupped Scott's cock and balls through his trousers as he spoke, massaging his aching hard-on, and making him moan.

A moment later, all the sounds of the woodland were drowned out by a zip being tugged down. Everything that lived among the trees seemed to hold its breath to listen. Moments passed, and all the small furry animals gradually resumed the day to day business of their lives. Only Scott remained trapped in place, helpless to do anything as his trousers and boxers were tugged down until they bunched up around his ankles.

"J-Joe?" Scott managed to stutter out.

"Yeah?" Joe ran his hand over Scott's exposed arse and massaged his buttocks. "You wanted to ask me something?"

Scott nodded as best he could in his current position.

"Ask then," Joe ordered. He settled both of his hands on Scott's buttocks and slid his thumbs down the cleft between Scott's cheeks, pulling them apart.

"C-can't remember," Scott mumbled.

"Well, you just let me know if you do remember, okay?" Joe said. He spoke very kindly, but his voice sounded like it had come from far lower than it should have.

Joe palmed Scott's buttocks again, making him

arch his back and push his arse out in invitation. Joe pulled Scott's checks apart, completely exposing his hole.

The only warning Scott received was a breath of air brushing against his arse. It wasn't enough of a warning. Scott let out a startled yelp as Joe circled his hole with his tongue.

Scott jerked away in surprise, then swayed back. His body seemed unable to decide if it wanted to be shocked or merely completely thrilled at receiving such an unexpected treat from his lover.

"Do you like that, Scottie?"

Scott nodded rapidly, not caring how the bark scratched his face. He stopped giving a damn about anything when Joe brought his mouth back to his arse.

He ran his tongue around Scott's hole again and again, sending tidal waves of pleasure rushing through his body. Scott's knees trembled, but there was no way he could fall while he was tied around the tree – he was as safe as he was helpless.

Scott tried to move his feet further apart to give Joe more room to work, but his bunched up trousers made that impossible. Scott gasped as another upsurge of bliss rushed through his body. Even though he knew Joe's views on him trying to keep himself silent during sex, Scott be bit down on his bottom lip, closed his eyes very tightly and desperately tried to keep his moans and whimpers to a minimum. Suddenly, both Joe's hands and his lips disappeared from Scott's world.

Scott blinked open his eyes. He peered over his shoulder as best he could, but there was no need to struggle to turn around. Joe stepped into his field of vision and held up something just in front of Scott's face. It was impossible to tell what it was in the gloom.

"Open your mouth."

Scott obeyed.

Fabric brushed against his lips. "Now, stop worrying about being heard," Joe ordered. "I don't want to have to remind you about trying to keep yourself silent again."

Scott cautiously investigated the make-shift gag with the tip of his tongue. It didn't take him too long to work out that it was Joe's tie. Scott closed his eyes again. He was almost willing to swear that he could taste Joe's own unique flavour on the fabric. Joe filled all of his senses, overpowering the rest of Scott's world, as Joe dropped back down to his knees behind him.

Joe set to work on Scott's arse again. Scott lost his grip on reality as Joe pressed his tongue flat against his hole, bringing a million different nerve endings to life.

All the pleasure rushing through Scott's body made him feel like he was floating in the air above them; held aloft by wings of ecstasy, and staring down at the scene playing out below him.

Scott knew that Joe's hands were more tanned than his own arse. It was so easy for him to picture the long, slim digits, holding his buttocks apart, and to imagine Joe dipping his head so his tongue could drive Scott to the edge of madness and beyond.

Scott squirmed, pushing his crotch painfully against the rough tree trunk. Joe didn't seem to care about that. He didn't even seem to notice Scott's desperate wriggling.

Joe stopped when, and only when, he wanted to stop. Scott had as little choice over when the rimming ended as he had about when it had begun.

Joe's fingers pushed against his hole, slicked only with Joe's saliva. With no artificial lube to ease its way, Joe's touch was rough, and even more perfect because of that. Scott pushed back eagerly against the digits, begging into his gag as he writhed against the tree trunk.

"Careful, sweetheart. There are some places even a masochist doesn't want to get splinters."

Scott heard Joe's amusement as Joe whispered the words against his ear. Neither Joe's laughter, nor his advice, could convince Scott to fall still. His cock rubbed against the tree with every movement. The bark was far too rough to feel good against his shaft, but any kind of friction was better than nothing.

A zip being drawn down, a condom wrapper being torn open—Scott heard it all, but his senses were fuzzy, and the sounds seemed to come from miles away. It was only when Joe lined up behind him, and Scott felt the heat from Joe's body against his back, that he was able to believe that Joe was really there.

Scott bit down on Joe's tie, anxious to keep his screams of frustrated need to himself. Joe's hands came to rest on Scott's hips and took up a tight grip on him.

Scott stilled. There was no time for wriggling now. Anything that slowed down the speed at which Joe had his cock lodged deep within Scott's arse was unthinkable.

* * * * *

Joe leaned forward and pressed the tip of his cock more firmly against Scott's hole. A thin smear of pre-applied lube coated the condom and glistened under the thin streaks of moonlight that passed between the tree branches overhead.

His tie wasn't completely silencing Scott. Just as Joe had hoped, he could still hear every whimper. The need in the muffled sounds rushed straight to Joe's cock. Rocking his hips, he teased the tight ring of muscle around Scott's hole.

One heartbeat. Two.

Joe thrust forward. Scott's body welcomed him, and Joe slid in, all the way to the base of his cock.

Joe tossed back his head and stared up at the leafy canopy as white hot bliss raced through his body. Scott twisted within his bondage, trying to push back against him. He clenched and unclenched his hole around Joe's cock.

Scott's garbled moans and pleas filled the air, but Joe was in no mood to rush. He remained completely motionless, relishing both the tight channel of flesh around his shaft and his complete control over the situation. He didn't move a single muscle until he was good and ready. Even then, he refused to be hurried.

Pulling leisurely out of Scott's body, Joe stared down between them and watched his cock emerge. He thrust back into Scott just as slowly, drawing out

232

both their pleasure.

His trousers slid down as he moved, exposing his bare arse to anyone who was wandering around the forest at that time of night. Cool air brushed against Joe's skin, but it was no match for the inferno burning inside him.

Pulling a deep breath into his lungs, Joe filled his senses with the scent of their mingled desire. When he dipped his head, his lips brushed against the side of Scott's neck and he kissed the skin just below his ear.

Scott whimpered.

Another slow, deep thrust, and Joe ran his tongue over Scott's neck. He felt Scott shudder in response and thrust forward again. At the same moment, Joe bit down on the sensitive patch of skin he'd stumbled upon.

A high pitched whine made it past the makeshift gag. Joe grinned as he sucked rhythmically against Scott's neck in time with his thrusts, ensuring that a vivid mark would appear there, clearly marking out Scott as his property.

A love bite wasn't ideal, but it would do until a proper collar could be arranged. Joe's thrusts sped up as both his mind and his body dragged him closer to his orgasm.

Scott was his. Joe knew without any shadow of a doubt that he owned Scott in every way that mattered. He could do whatever he wanted with Scott. He was responsible for him. That knowledge felt just as good as Scott's tight arse wrapped around Joe's cock.

Even Joe wasn't sure which it was that finally

pushed him over the edge and sent his climax racing through him—his body or his brain, but it was all the same in the end.

As he thrust frantically into Scott, helpless to hold back a moment longer, the tiny bit of Joe's mind that was still capable of rational thought realised that he wasn't the only one who deserved their climax.

"Come."

Scott must have been holding on to his self-control by the skin of his teeth. His hole clamped down around Joe's shaft as he pulled desperately at his restraints; his whole body jerking with the force of his orgasm.

Wave after wave of adrenaline and endorphins flooded Joe's world as he came just a moment later. It carried him along on a sea of pure pleasure until the tide receded just as quickly as it had attacked the shore.

Joe slumped forward, pressing Scott against the tree. Half their clothes were still in place, stopping their bodies from properly resting against each other's skin, but Joe didn't have the energy to fix that.

It took all that Joe had in him to gasp for breath. He was acutely aware of each breath Scott took too—and if Scott tried to pull oxygen into his system any quicker, he was going to hyperventilate.

Something unexpected brushed against Joe's forearm. He opened his eyes just in time to see his tie drop onto the leaf strewn ground. Now free of the gag, Scott murmured his complete satisfaction.

Joe smiled at Scott's profile. Scott's eyes were open, but he didn't seem to be able to focus on anything. He was just staring off into the night;

content and apparently more than a little sleepy now that he was sated.

Joe gave himself another minute to enjoy the warm cocoon of Scott's arse wrapped around his softening shaft before he finally convinced himself to pull away and separate their bodies. As he tidied himself up, Joe ran his eyes over Scott's moonlit form.

His arse was beautifully displayed. The evidence of his first spanking had faded away. His skin was gorgeous; pale and unblemished, it just begged to be marked.

Stepping closer, Joe brought his hand down hard on Scott's right buttock, spreading his fingers so each digit would leave its own mark.

Scott yelped. His brow creased into a frown as he tried to peer over his shoulder. Their eyes met and Scott's frown melted away. He smiled slightly. If he hadn't been bound so tightly to the tree, Joe had no doubt Scott would have tried to duck his head in that shy little way he had, once he knew he hadn't been struck as punishment.

Joe grinned as he walked around the tree and began to undo the fabric from Scott's wrists. By the time Joe returned to Scott's side of the tree, his hand print was blossoming very nicely on Scott's arse. It was almost criminal to let Scott hide it away, but Joe forced himself not to protest as Scott clumsily pulled his trousers up.

Neither of their ties looked salvageable. Joe pushed them into his pocket anyway; strangely loath to toss them aside the way he would have if he'd carried out the scene with any other man.

"Come on."

Scott obediently began to stride forward.

Catching hold of his shoulders, Joe turned Scott around and pointed him toward the car park before he ended up getting himself completely lost in the woods.

"Oh, um. Yeah, th-thanks..." Scott cleared his throat and fell silent.

Back at the car, they slouched down in their seats; Joe once more behind the wheel, and both of them apparently satisfied to sit in silence and simply exist for a little while.

With his head resting back against his seat's neck support, Joe slowly turned his face to his left so he could admire Scott's profile again. There didn't seem to be any scratches where Scott's cheek had been pressed against the tree bark, but that didn't mean his cock wouldn't have to be checked for splinters at some point. A very detailed and thorough inspection was obviously called for.

A shrill ringing sound cut through the air. Scott closed his eyes very tight.

"I'm guessing that's your phone," Joe said.

Scott nodded, without opening his eyes.

"Good, because otherwise there's something else in your trousers making a really strange noise."

"I'm s-so sor —"

Joe reached out and put his hand over Scott's mouth to stop him short. "There's a difference between a spanking given for pleasure and one that's a punishment. Next time you apologise to me without a damn good reason, you're going to get the latter, and it won't be nearly as much fun as your last spanking was." He took his hand away. "Answer your phone."

Pulling a small handset out of his pocket, Scott pressed the screen and held it to his ear.

He closed his eyes and pushed his free hand through his hair. Finally, the person on the other end of the phone seemed to stop speaking for long enough for Scott to respond. "Hi, M-mum."

Joe leaned his elbow on the car window and grinned as he watched Scott's cheeks grow hotter and hotter.

A few more stuttered answers and Scott quickly ended the call with a promise to call back the following day. "Next time, I'll r-r-remember to switch it off before we m-meet up."

"Was that what you promised your mum you'd do too?"

Scott shook his head. After a few seconds he seemed to realise that Joe wanted a damn sight more than a yes or no answer.

"To try t-t-to relax m-m-more."

Joe tried to work that out and failed.

"I only s-stutter when I'm n-n-nervous."

Joe raised an eyebrow. Apparently, he made Scott hellish nervous every time he stepped into the same room as him, because he couldn't ever remember Scott getting a whole sentence out without a stutter.

Joe filed that fact away to think about later. Part of his mind was already on other things — things it should have dealt with a long time before. "What's your number?"

Scott blinked as if Joe had just suggested something unexpectedly rude.

Joe owned Scott. He was very certain of that. He might not be as attached to his phone as most guys he knew, but not having the mobile number of a man he owned was wrong on so many levels he couldn't even begin to count them.

Joe frowned as he realised how much of an idiot he was for not having demanded the number before. Hell, he should have had it from him that first night he'd visited him in his room.

Pulling out his own phone, Joe added the number Scott gave him to his address book and quickly texted Scott his number in return.

"If you ever need help, that's the first number you ring."

Scott gave him a strange look, but Joe merely held his gaze until Scott gave up and nodded his understanding.

"Remember what I said about punishment spankings?" Joe asked.

Scott didn't hesitate to nod that time. "Yes, I r-remember."

"Good, because there are some things that aren't negotiable. Not calling that number when you need help is one way to be sure you won't sit comfortably for a week."

Scott looked down at his phone for a second before pushing it back into his pocket. When Joe did the same, a piece of folded paper rustled beneath the fabric.

Of course—the envelope. Joe pulled it out of his pocket.

Scott's attention instantly focused in on it. That was good. It made Joe feel a little less stupid for not wanting to allow Scott out of his sight until he knew exactly when he would see him again.

"Do you already know what you want to ask me for?" Joe said.

Scott nodded without looking away from the envelope. "Yes."

"Good. I want you to write it down and give the envelope straight back to me."

After a little bit of scrabbling around in the glove box, Scott unearthed a pen. Joe kept his gaze averted until Scott had sealed the envelope and was ready to hand it back over to him.

"I'll give you a choice," Joe offered, to his own surprise as much as Scott's. "Do you want me to open it now, or shall I wait until after I've dropped you off?"

Scott took a deep breath. "I'd p-p-prefer you to wait, if you d-d-don't mind."

At least he didn't apologise for having a preference—Joe was willing to call that progress of a sort.

"I'll text you if there's anything I need you to know before our next date," Joe said.

Scott nodded. Joe smiled as he pushed the envelope back into his pocket. Now, there was only one thing left that he had to do that night, and it was a job he'd been looking forward to ever since they got back to the car.

"Undo your fly."

Scott blinked at him.

Joe smiled as he switched on the car's interior light. "Time to check your cock for splinters."

Part Nine: By Hand

Show me what you really like, please.

As invitations went, Joe had to admit that Scott's latest one was open to a great deal of interpretation. But Joe was hardly going to complain about that. When a sub was that vague about his preferences, it obviously fell to the dom to take up the slack, and Joe was more than happy to oblige.

As he put the finishing touches to his preparations, Joe whistled tunelessly under his breath, very happy with the world and his place in it. Taking a few paces back, he ran a critical eye over his bedroom. Yes, it was all exactly as he wanted it. He was just about to glance at his watch when a knock sounded on his front door.

Joe smiled; punctuality was such a nice trait in a sub. He made his way to the front door, neither rushing nor making a point of keeping Scott waiting. There was no room for games like that in his plans for the evening.

He didn't bother looking through the peephole before he opened the door.

Scott smiled as their eyes met, but his expression quickly changed as he took in Joe's outfit of choice. Apparently, he'd never seen a man open his front door stark bollock naked and very ready to screw.

Scott's lips formed a perfect O. He moved his attention all the way down to Joe's feet before bringing it slowly back up his body. When Joe felt Scott had been given enough time to gawp, he stepped back and welcomed him into the flat.

It would have been wrong to say that Scott pulled himself together at that point. Joe wasn't sure he'd ever seen Scott actually achieve "together" in all the time they'd spent with each other. But Scott stepped inside the flat and followed Joe to his bedroom without hyperventilating, and Joe was very willing to consider that close enough.

"That's n-new, isn't it?" Scott indicated the huge flat screen TV set up on a low cabinet opposite the foot of Joe's bed.

"It's new to my place. I borrowed it from a friend," Joe replied, casually moving to stand alongside the bed.

"Oh…" Scott's brow furrowed in confusion.

"You asked me to show you exactly what I like," Joe reminded him.

Scott nodded. A second later, everything seemed to click together inside his head. "Of course. Porn!"

Columbus couldn't have sounded more thrilled with his discovery when he stumbled upon America.

"Yeah," Joe agreed. "Porn." He even managed to keep a straight face as he said it.

Scott headed toward the DVDs stacked up next to the screen.

"Aren't you forgetting something?" Joe asked.

Scott stopped and looked over his shoulder.

"I'm naked. You're not," Joe hinted.

"Oh, I'm s-sorry." Scott hurriedly grabbed the

hem of his T-shirt and pulled it over his head.

Apparently, in some ways, Joe already had Scott better trained than he'd realised. Scott stripped himself down to his bare skin without any hint of shyness or hesitation; he was already getting hard, but he made no attempt to hide his cock.

All thought of DVDs forgotten now, Scott simply stood with his hands at his sides and waited for another order. Such a good sub.

Joe sat on the bed and settled himself comfortably against the pillows he'd propped up against the headboard in preparation for their scene. "Come here."

Scott climbed onto the bed and crawled across the expanse of dark blue sheets until he knelt next to Joe. He licked his lips in apparent anticipation, obviously expecting Joe to give him permission to go down on him.

Catching hold of Scott's wrist, Joe deftly re-arranged him so they sat side by side with both of them leaning back against the headboard and their legs stretched out toward the TV.

Joe picked up the DVD remote from his bedside table and pressed play. A hard cock appeared on the TV, almost completely filling the screen. There was a man's hand wrapped around the shaft, pumping it in strong determined movements. A groan of pleasure filled the air as the TV speakers kicked into action.

A spurt of pre-cum left the tip of the actor's cock. He caught it in his palm and used it to slick his touch. He gasped, obviously already close to coming.

Joe turned to Scott; he was staring at the

screen, wide-eyed and completely mesmerised. If Scott had seen gay porn before, he was a bloody good actor. His impression of a man who hadn't so much as caught a glimpse of anything rated above PG was Oscar-worthy.

Reaching across the thin strip of blanket between them, Joe wrapped his fingers around Scott's cock. Scott jerked as if receiving an electric shock. Forget static, this seemed more like the voltage that inspired little yellow signs showing men and lightning bolts.

Scott glanced toward Joe and then back to the screen, apparently unable to cope with both at the same time.

Joe watched Scott's reaction with great interest. He also made a point of keeping his hand in place while he waited out Scott's momentary panic. There would be no backing off today. He wouldn't take it easy on Scott just because he was so obviously innocent. Today, Scott's only outs were his safe word or a full blown panic attack.

With plate tectonic haste, Scott relaxed enough to be able to lean back against the pillows rather than sit ram-rod stiff, ready to leap out of the bed at the next sudden movement.

Scott looked rapidly from Joe's face to the screen and back, occasionally dropping his gaze to look at the way Joe's hand encircled his shaft. A minute passed and a fourth point appeared on Scott's itinerary — Joe's cock. By the time another sixty seconds had slipped away, Scott had stopped looking at anything but Joe's erection.

It was difficult to be sure if he was fascinated

by Joe's hard-on, or if he was scared that it might attack him if provoked. Joe's lips twisted into a half-smile. Scott was safe for now. Joe had a few other things planned first. Attacking wouldn't come until later.

Joe caught hold of Scott's wrist. Allowing no time for first, let alone second, thoughts on Scott's part, Joe closed Scott's fist around his erection.

It was a nice arrangement; each of them had a cock to stroke, each had the pleasure of another man's hand around his shaft. And they both still had a wonderful view of the screen.

"*No.*"

Scott gasped in obvious dismay. His eyes were filled with horror as he turned to Joe. An apology was no doubt already rushing toward his lips.

With a nod toward the screen, Joe reminded Scott that theirs wasn't the only scene going on in the room. The word hadn't been directed toward Scott.

Scott turned his attention to the TV once more.

Whatever doubts Joe might have harboured in the past, they all vanished in that instant. No one was that good an actor; Scott really hadn't seen proper leather porn before.

His expression didn't grow in the least bit less shocked as the camera gradually zoomed out to show that the man who was jacking himself off was trapped by several thick leather straps that completely encircled his body.

The guy's only free limb was the one he was using to play with his cock. The heavy restraints were fastened by huge padlocks that kept the rest of him bound to a wooden post in the middle of a squalid room. Paint and plaster flaked off the wall in the background. The floor was nothing but rough concrete. But Joe doubted that Scott was in any condition to take in the interior decor.

Scott's attention was all on the dom standing next to the bound porn star. Joe studied Scott's gaze a little more closely. His hand tightened around Scott's cock, purposefully pulling Scott's mind back to him.

Swallowing rapidly, Scott turned toward Joe, but he didn't focus on him the way he had upon the actor on the screen. Joe tensed at the realisation. He only grew less impressed when it took Scott several seconds to lift his gaze high enough to look him in the eye. But then their eyes met, and everything became clear.

Submission.

That was the only thing visible in Scott's expression. Oh, there were probably bits and pieces of other things in there. Shock and shyness were never far away where Scott was concerned. Lust tended to make itself known quite often too. But it was submission that owned Scott right then.

He hadn't looked at the guy on the screen like that. Curiously, yes. Warily, quite possibly. Maybe even with a kind of fascination. But he hadn't looked at the actor with any inclination to submit to him.

Joe nodded once in approval and looked back to the TV. Scott followed his lead.

"You don't come until I give permission," the porn dom announced.

Joe began to move his hand over Scott's cock in slow, easy strokes. With his eyes still fixed on the screen, Scott automatically began to raise and lower his hand in echo of Joe's actions, jacking Joe's cock at the exact same speed.

It was almost sweet, just how fascinated Scott seemed to be with the film.

"Keep that hand moving!" the porn dom demanded.

The poor sod tied to the post whimpered as he obeyed.

The two competing orders, to prevent himself coming while constantly pushing himself closer to the edge, must have put him in a special sort of hell. The fact that his only bit of freedom existed especially so he could torment himself probably messed with his mind just as thoroughly as his hand messed with his body.

But really, Joe could only guess why the sub was playing the game. For a moment, he looked away from porn sub and turned his attention to the porn dom. He knew what a dom would be thinking in that scenario. He would be glorying in being in such complete control of another man, in being able to do whatever the hell he wanted with another guy.

And, if they weren't just strangers the director had thrown into a scene, but a real dom and his sub, as the website Joe had downloaded it from had claimed, that wouldn't be all the porn dom felt. Playing with someone he knew would feel very different. Joe was only just starting to realise how true that was.

Joe turned his attention back to Scott, and paused the action on the film with his free hand.

* * * * *

"That's w-what you like?" Scott asked, as the image on the screen flickered and stilled. He tried like hell not to sound breathless and already desperate to come, but knew he failed spectacularly.

Joe might have halted the action on the screen, but Joe's hand was still wrapped around Scott's cock, and it was moving just as unstoppably as the screen sub's had.

Scott gathered his wits as best he could and cleared his throat in the hope of sounding calm when he spoke again. "You'd like us to d-d-do that?"

"I like control," Joe corrected. "I like being in control of you."

Scott risked a glance at Joe, but it was impossible to stare at him as if he were no different than some random actor. Scott had to drop his gaze almost the moment that their eyes met, but even that fraction of a second was enough. The strength of emotion in Joe's eyes was unmistakable.

"And you l-l-like deciding when guys g-get to come," Scott added with complete certainty.

"That too," Joe confirmed.

Scott bit back a needy little sound. He already wanted to come more than he'd ever thought possible before meeting Joe. He looked down at his cock and the way Joe's hand encircled it.

Control. Being under another man's control. That was what made watching porn feel so different now compared to in the past. It was what made the images on the screen stop being fantasies and become possibilities.

Scott took a deep breath. "Okay."

"Okay?" Joe didn't need a bright light to shine in anyone's eyes. He had an amazing way of growling questions that made them sound like an interrogation even while they were sitting companionably next to each other.

"I p-promise I won't c-come without p-permission," Scott whispered. "Even when you're n-n-not there."

"Good."

And that was it. Joe casually accepted control of a huge part of Scott's life as if it was nothing more than his right to receive it.

Scott glanced down at his cock. He might have needed Joe's permission to come during a scene for quite a long time, but that wasn't the same as needing it all the time.

Joe's hand was still moving over Scott's shaft in slow, persistent strokes. It was only then that Scott realised he was moving his own hand and caressing Joe at exactly the same speed.

"I like knowing that you'll do whatever I say." Joe seemed about to add something else, but appeared to decide against it at the last moment.

Unwilling to risk overstepping unspoken boundaries and asking questions Joe might prefer he didn't voice, Scott remained silent and let the moment slip away.

The TV went momentarily blank. Another picture appeared. With the remote on the other side of Joe's body, it wasn't easy for Scott to see when Joe reached for it or pressed a button.

Scott had no warning before he found himself staring at a man being whipped.

It wasn't as sterile as any of the images of punishments that Scott had found on the internet. There was no air brushing here, and no pretending. There was no turning the camera away at the last moment so it was impossible for the audience to tell if it was all sound effects and trickery. No imagination was required here. The dom was holding a real whip, and he wasn't afraid to bring it down hard and unrelenting upon a sub.

The crack of thin leather against unprotected skin filled the air. Vivid red lines appeared on the submissive's back. Pain flashed across his features.

It hurt him. There was no escaping that fact. This was nothing like the spanking Joe had given him. That had been all pleasure, this was...

Scott took a deep breath. "You l-l-like hurting people." The words came out strangely lacking in any kind of emotion.

"Yes." Joe said, without any hint of apology. It was several moments before he spoke again. "But only guys who like being hurt."

Scott turned toward him.

Joe's lips quirked into a strange mockery of a smile. "Some guys might like to hurt a man who hates it, and if that man freely agrees to take it, that's fine with me. But I've never seen the point in whipping a guy who isn't an enthusiastic masochist."

Joe suddenly released Scott's cock. Before Scott had a chance to promise he'd learn how to take any degree of pain that Joe wanted to inflict upon him, and to beg Joe not to give up on him just yet, Joe had already transferred his grip to Scott's wrist.

Lightheaded with relief, Scott was more than

happy to let Joe rearrange them on the bed. Before he knew what was happening, he found himself sitting between Joe's spread legs and leaning back against Joe's larger body.

"Look again," Joe ordered, dipping his head to whisper the words in Scott's ear like a secret that was vital to national security. "This time, don't just stare at the bits that demand your attention. Look at all of it."

Scott did as he was told. He'd already seen the marks appearing across the sub's back. He didn't need to see that again. He looked elsewhere.

The sub could easily have escaped the pain if he'd wanted to. As Scott concentrated on the details rather than the fireworks exploding on the actor's back, he realised that was actually the biggest difference between this man and the first one he'd watched.

There was no bondage this time, nothing was holding the guy in place. Nothing, perhaps, except his desire to remain within range of his dom's whip. And…yes, now that Scott looked properly, he could see it. There wasn't just pain in the sub's expression. There was pleasure there too. Maybe it wasn't the same kind of pleasure that Joe's spanking had made dance within Scott's veins, but it was clear that the sub on the screen didn't just *like* what the dom was doing to him, he loved it.

Scott took a deep breath. His back rubbed against Joe's chest. The dark, wiry hairs there bristled against him. Further down, he could feel Joe's erection pressing against the small of his back and smearing pre-cum onto his skin.

"He l-likes it," Scott whispered.

"Yes, he does." Joe's voice was filled with approval of that fact.

Scott slowly took in other details—ones which he was less certain about the implications of. The sub on the screen was built like a brick out-house, all muscle and tattoos. And it wasn't just the man's crotch that was shaved. There wasn't a single hair on the actor's head.

Scott lifted a hand to push it through his own hair as new uncertainty swirled inside him. Joe caught hold of his wrist and stopped him before he accidentally blocked Joe's view of the screen. A second later, he released Scott's other wrist and resumed masturbating him.

"I'm n-n-not like the g-g-guy on the screen," Scott said, unable to avoid the obvious a second longer.

"No, you're not."

Scott swallowed. It wasn't even as if the guy could be considered some sort of "after" picture—the image of a man Scott might become over time. A razor might give him the same haircut, but no amount of physical training could make him that man. He'd never have that guy's build; come to that, the man's attitude was just as far out of Scott's reach.

The man might have been a masochist, he might even have been a submissive, but there was nothing shy or uncertain about him. He looked like he could hold his own in any situation. He was the kind of guy who swaggered when he strode into a room and—

"If I wanted to screw him, or his double, that's what I'd be doing. There are hundreds of men out there who look like him, and who act like him. Been there, done that."

Joe's grip tightened around both Scott's wrist and his cock.

Scott's fingers curled into fists in response but there was no way he could reach for Joe's cock. In their new positions, there was no way he could touch anything. He couldn't even grip the blankets without reaching over Joe's thighs and making it obvious that he was already scrabbling for control.

"You d-don't want that, w-want him?" Scott said, as calmly and conversationally as possible.

"No. I don't screw second bests." The frustration in Joe's voice was clear, possibly because he didn't seem to be making any attempt to hide it. "And I sure as hell don't come back for more from someone unless he's something pretty bloody special!"

Scott leaned to one side and looked over his shoulder at Joe. "So I should j-just shut up and enjoy the sh-sh-show without freaking out, r-right?"

"Smart boy," Joe said, with one of his strange half-smiles.

He released Scott's wrist and pressed another button on his remote. Apparently, he'd programmed everything very carefully, long before Scott had arrived on his doorstep. The next scene sprung into existence without either of them having to sit through boring titles or adverts for other releases.

Scott was almost ready for it this time. He did his best to remain composed and take in the most pertinent details without letting another rush of anxiety get the better of him.

One dom, one sub. That was good. Joe still hadn't announced any desire to bring anyone else into a scene with them. Scott happily ticked that off his list of things to hyperventilate over.

The sub was on his knees, staring up at his dom with a look of pure devotion in his eyes. If he hadn't known better, Scott might have thought the sub was looking up at some sort of religious artefact rather than another mere mortal. But, as he stared in the other sub's eyes, Scott realised just how much better he knew.

That's how I look at you.

Scott kept the words back, but it was a near run thing. There was no denying the truth. Scott knew, deep down, that that was the way he looked at Joe. The knowledge made his heart race so fast it was almost impossible to believe his rib cage would remain intact.

The dom on the receiving end of all that adoration stepped forward and fed his cock into his sub's eager mouth. Whimpering his pleasure around the thick length, the sub took it as if he'd never even heard of a gag reflex.

A blowjob; that was what Joe was showing him!

Scott had never been more relieved to realise anything in his life. Forget adoration and silly sub-ish ideas. Joe was a practical guy who enjoyed straightforward things. He was showing him a film about blowjobs.

Scott immediately tried to turn around. Joe apparently wasn't in favour of the idea. He held Scott in place. For once, Scott battled against whatever it was inside him that continually screamed out its need to obey and fall in with Joe's plans.

He tugged at Joe's grip on him, as if there was nothing that had passed between them that could make anyone think that one of them had more right to call the shots than the other.

"Do you want to say your safe word?" Joe asked.

Scott shook his head. "No! I w-w-want to suck your cock."

That announcement seemed to make Joe pause for thought. Scott hesitated, then stilled to wait for Joe's verdict.

"If you want to move from where I put you, you should tell me that. If I approve of your reason, I'll give you permission."

The words rushed toward Scott's lips before he had a chance to edit them for suitability, sense, or to see if they contained anything he actually wanted to say. "Please may I t-turn around so I can s-s-suck your cock, sir?"

Silence met his request.

Scott twisted around as best he could and peered over his shoulder. It looked as if Joe was fighting back the urge to laugh.

The fact he wasn't mad at Scott was obviously a good thing, but still...
Scott frowned both his confusion and his disapproval. "I w-w-wasn't joking."

* * * * *

Joe gave up trying to hold back his grin. "I

know, pet. It wouldn't be half so funny if you hadn't been so serious."

Scott's frown deepened. Apparently, he was completely unaware of the inherent humour in a man asking for permission to go down on him, as if the man receiving a blowjob deserved his gratitude for putting up with his strange and perverted inclination to give head.

Joe released Scott's wrists in favour of moving his hands to either side of Scott's face and holding him still to be kissed. Making no allowances for Scott's tendency to need a few minutes to catch up, Joe kissed Scott the way he loved to kiss him—like he was laying ownership over a sub he had no intention of giving up at the end of the scene.

Scott moaned against Joe's lips but he'd barely even pulled himself together enough to bring his tongue out to play before Joe pulled away. Scott was still frowning, but now it seemed to be all about disappointment at his pleasure being cut short.

As Joe watched, Scott ran his tongue over his bottom lip, trying to find some lingering trace of the kiss to savour.

"Permission granted."

Scott blinked. "Permission to come?" He sounded so hopeful.

"No, permission to move so you can suck me off."

"Oh!" Without any sign of disappointment, Scott shuffled around and knelt between Joe's spread legs.

Joe shook his head. That wouldn't do at all. Mentally calculating angles and viewpoints, Joe rearranged them so he lay across the bed with Scott once more kneeling between his legs. Leaning back on his elbows, Joe nodded his satisfaction. Yes. This would work perfectly.

Scott accepted their wriggling around without comment. As Joe stared down his body at Scott, it was easy to believe that it didn't even occur to him to ask why they needed to position themselves that way.

It was Joe's decision, and apparently, that automatically made it good enough for Scott.

With a glance up, to check that he had permission to begin his much longed for fellatio, Scott dipped his head and took the tip of Joe's cock into his mouth. He'd come a long way since his cautious attempt to please Joe behind the bar.

Now, Scott worked with all the confidence of a submissive who knew exactly what his dom liked and was certain of his ability to give him that.

Joe pressed a button on the remote. Right on cue, another of the snippets he'd harvested from various DVDs and pay-per-view websites snapped into life.

Scott glanced to his left. If he had ever wondered about their positions, he probably assumed that Joe had just wanted them both to be able to see the screen. If he only knew...

Joe didn't need to glance at the scene on the TV screen. He remembered it clearly. It featured two guys in a club, completely surrounded by other men. More importantly, it showed two men who only had eyes for each other. The noise and commotion around them didn't make any difference to either guy, neither did the fact they were being filmed. Their scene was their own. No one else mattered.

Scott paused for a moment. His lips remained around Joe's shaft and his tongue pressed firmly against the tip of his cock, but all his attention was on the screen.

Joe let Scott look his fill. It was impossible for anyone to see those actors and not realise they were together in real life. Anyone who was the least bit kinky had to see just how much the sub loved being owned by his long-term master and how proud and delighted the dom was with his boy.

Scott seemed quite fascinated. Several seconds passed before he apparently remembered that he was supposed to be giving some of his attention to something else. A blush rushed to his cheeks as he quickly dipped his head and took as much of Joe's erection into his mouth as he could.

A full minute of exquisite pleasure surrounded Joe's cock before Scott peeked up at him through his lashes. His eyes silently begged forgiveness for his lapse in concentration.

Joe smiled and pushed his hand through Scott's hair in a gentle caress, letting Scott see how pleased he was with him.

If he'd been able to find a suitable clip of a guy blushing for the strangest of reasons, he'd have had to have added it to his list of turn-ons. It was a crying shame that so few porn stars had retained the ability to blush the way Scott did.

Joe ran his fingers over Scott's cheek, feeling the heat there and, at the same time, feeling the way his skin hollowed out as Scott sucked and created a glorious little vacuum around his cock. Put together, the effects sent a bolt of pleasure shooting through Joe's body. Innocence and eroticism bounced off each other, making each just a little more fantastic.

Scott seemed completely unaware of how stunning he looked; how perfect a demonstration of submission he was giving. He glanced toward the screen now and again, but kept most of his attention on the wonderful blowjob he was providing. Just like the sub in the film, it seemed impossible for him to care about anyone else for very long.

Focusing on his dominant—on his master—came to Scott as naturally as his desire to breathe. Joe slid his hand through Scott's hair again, making no attempt to control Scott's movements, only to praise each and every one of them.

Scott dipped his head again and again, taking a little more of Joe's shaft each time. The minutes passed by and Scott only seemed to become more enthusiastic. But Joe noticed the moment Scott's intent changed. Hell, Joe had even made a point of setting aside a part of his mind to watch out for it, while the rest of him laid back and enjoyed it all.

Apparently, Scott had decided that it was time to stop messing around and give everything he had to trying to make Joe come as soon as humanly possible.

Tightening his grip on Scott's hair, Joe guided his mouth away from his cock. Scott looked up at him reproachfully, but he seemed to be waiting for more information before he went so far as to actually complain.

Maintaining his grip on Scott's hair, Joe tugged him up until their mouths met. Rolling Scott over onto his back, and pinning him down beneath his larger frame, was the work of a single second.

Scott gasped into the kiss, so sweet and so confused. But, even if his mind lagged behind, his body was obviously completely up to speed. He squirmed beneath Joe in a determined effort to spread his legs for him.

That invitation couldn't be refused. Grabbing lube off the bedside table, Joe slicked his fingers and found Scott's hole. Scott relaxed beautifully for him, eagerly accepting an increasing number of digits inside him until he was ready to feel something more than mere fingers thrusting deep into his arse.

Their wriggling had turned them around on the bed. They now lay diagonally across the wide mattress. Scott's arse was toward the TV. Neither of them were the least bit interested in what might have been playing on the screen.

Joe grabbed a condom and rolled it down his shaft. Slicking it with extra lube, he pulled Scott around and arranged him on his hands and knees across the centre of the bed.

Scott followed Joe's every nudge and hint as if they were all orders yelled at the top of a sergeant major's lungs. There was no need to tie him up to make a point. Scott's submission already went deeper than any set of cuffs could reach. Invisible ties already bound him to Joe, demanding that he submit to his every whim.

Joe's cock ached at the thought. He settled his hands on Scott's hips and quickly brought their bodies together. He thrust his cock into Scott's arse, all the way to the hilt, in one smooth motion.

Scott jerked. His hole clenched and unclenched

around Joe's erection as his body fought to adjust to his girth.

Scott whimpered. His arms were shaking and, while Joe held still inside him, Scott carefully lowered the front of his body down so he could support himself on his forearms. He dropped his head toward the mattress until first his forehead, then his cheek rested against the bed sheet.

"Turn your head the other way."

Scott obediently turned his face toward the screen. His eyes remained closed. There was no chance of him being able to see what was playing, but Joe didn't issue any further orders.

As soon as he sensed Scott could take it and enjoy it, Joe thrust into him again. Scott murmured. The sound was all pleasure, and every noise that followed proclaimed Scott's love of being screwed hard and fast. He pushed back into every thrust, his hole clenching tightly around Joe's cock.

"Scott."

A vague noise was Scott's only response.

"Scott!" Joe demanded.

Scott slowly opened his eyes. "Y-yes, sir?"

"Don't come."

Scott closed his eyes again.

Joe gritted his teeth as he fought for control of his own body. "Scott?"

"I-I understand," Scott said.

"Good."

Joe swayed back and thrust into Scott once more, not even trying to make it easier for Scott to ride out the pounding he was taking. It was Scott's job not to come. It was not Joe's job to make it easy for

him.

He pushed into Scott's arse again and again, enjoying every wave of adrenaline and endorphins that flooded into his veins. Finally, he could let go and allow himself to simply glory in the joys to be found deep inside Scott's body.

No thoughts; no higher brain function at all. Nothing was allowed into Joe's world to cloud his ecstasy. He was all pure animal pleasure now. Joe tightened his hold on Scott. Thrusting harder and faster than ever, he shouted his triumph up to the ceiling as he came.

Wave after wave of deep, dark, satisfaction rolled over him until they completely enveloped him. There was nothing warm or cosy about it. It robbed the air from the room. And for every bit of pleasure it gave, it quickly presented its bill.

Joe collapsed forward as all the energy that had buzzed through his veins deserted him. He gave little thought to how comfortable Scott might find being pinned beneath him. Every time Scott took a breath, Joe felt it. He sensed every beat of Scott's heart.

Scott was fine and, just as importantly, Scott was his. Joe smiled against Scott's shoulder before slowly lifting his head and taking some of his weight onto his elbows. Scott didn't rush to follow his lead right then. He kept his cheek pressed firmly against the blanket.

"Are you going to move?" Joe asked.

"Might c-c-come if I do." The response was mumbled, as if Scott was afraid that even moving his lips might trigger his orgasm.

Chuckling, Joe took matters into his own

hands. The moment their bodies were separated and the condom had been disposed of, Joe rolled Scott onto his back.

Scott gasped. His hips bucked. His cock thrust up into the empty air. But he didn't actually come. Very slowly, Scott opened his eyes and peered up at Joe. His need was obvious. His expression was filled with a silent plea to be allowed his own release.

"When I give permission," Joe reminded him. "Not before." As he spoke, he reached out and ran one fingertip up the line of Scott's cock.

* * * * *

"Ready for round two?" Joe asked, barely a moment later.

"R-r-round two?" Scott asked, unable to tear his eyes away from Joe's finger as Joe ran the tip of it up and down his erection.

Suddenly, Joe moved his hand away from Scott's aching shaft. He took hold of Scott's wrist, and tugged until Scott sat up on the bed.

As Joe once more re-arranged them, Scott nibbled on his bottom lip, unsure how to ask if there had been something wrong with round one; if there was something that had stopped Joe enjoying it properly, or something about it that had left him unsatisfied.

He also wanted to know if he'd be allowed to come during round two. Did it make him a bad submissive to want to ask that?

Scott cleared his throat, not one hundred percent sure which question was going to leave his lips. "J-Joe?"

Joe shook his head. "Unless you want to say your safe word, we'll talk afterwards, not now."

Scott pushed his hand through his hair and tried to force his brain into some sort of clear thought process, but there was no point trying to formulate a carefully worded question now. There was no way he was going to push the issue and risk displeasing Joe further.

Scott's need to come faded. His erection softened as Joe's obvious lack of satisfaction during round one sent a shiver of panic down his spine.

Before Scott knew it, they were once again leaning against pillows propped up against the headboard. Joe picked up the remote.

Scott turned all his attention toward the screen. His desire to learn more about what Joe really liked was now a harsh, desperate need. He could feel Joe slipping further away from him by the moment. He had to work out how he'd screwed up, how he could do better in round two.

The screen lit up more slowly this time. It showed...Joe's empty bedroom? Toys hung on the wall; the bed was directly opposite the camera and it was unmistakably Joe's bedroom. There were no people visible.

Lines appeared across the picture as Joe fast forwarded.

He was going to show Scott what he'd enjoyed doing with his past lovers. Scott had no doubts about it. Joe was going to show him a recording of himself screwing another man; or maybe dozens of other men, one after another. And he was going to point out all the ways they were better lovers than Scott, and all the things they did more effectively than him.

Panic scattered Scott's thoughts. He couldn't do this. He couldn't sit there and let it happen. But he was helpless. He remained frozen in place, unable to object as a naked image of Joe blurred onto the screen. Joe stopped fast forwarding just in time for them to see another man step into view.

Scott's lips started moving without permission from his brain. "That's m-m-me!"

"You asked me to show you what I like," Joe said, perfectly calmly. "It's about time you faced the fact that you're one of the things I like."

The image on the screen began to remove his clothes. Scott's eyes opened very wide.

"Maybe from this angle, you'll be able to see how hot you are," Joe continued.

Scott shook his head.

No.

He didn't want to play this game anymore. He turned away from the screen. After seeing all those porn stars putting on expert displays, he knew how pathetic his own attempts to please Joe would look. Maybe Joe didn't realise that yet, but he would soon enough and…

No.

Scott scrambled away from Joe and toward the edge of the bed nearest the door.

"I'm not going to force you to stay and watch it," Joe said, his feelings on that fact impossible to guess. "But I'm not going to switch it off just because you leave."

Scott paused, sitting on the edge of the

mattress with his feet already on the floor alongside it. Leaving Joe before he was ordered to felt wrong in every cell of his being, but the tiny bit of his mind that was still interested in sanity and self-preservation screamed that he'd be a fool to stay. He could—

"I love it when you do that."

"W-What?" Scott couldn't help but glance at the screen. Joe had paused the image. It showed Scott standing at the bottom of the bed completely naked, his head tilted back so he could look up at Joe.

"That moment," Joe said, his tone relaxed and almost conversational. "You're always a sub, and, even when you're not submitting to someone, I'm sure you're the kind of guy who'll fall in with someone else's plans whenever you can. But that moment when you look up at me at the start of a scene and you hand over control to me; the moment when you start to relax and all need for responsibility seems to leave you. It's beautiful."

Scott peered at the screen. All he saw was a pale, skinny guy standing around like an idiot and staring at the most stunning man the world had ever seen. Scott frowned as he risked a glance at Joe, sure there had to be a punch-line coming.

"I don't joke about things like this. You made a request. You asked me to show you what I like. I'm honouring that request." Scott had never heard Joe sound so serious.

"I'm s-s-sorry," he whispered.

Joe said nothing. He simply sat there, one leg bent up so he could rest his forearm on his raised knee.

Gathering up as much courage as he could,

Scott waved a hand toward where he'd been sitting next to Joe just a few minutes before. "May I?"

Joe gave one nod to indicate his willingness to accept him back. As Scott shuffled closer, Joe even raised his arm, inviting him to curl into his side and rest his head on his shoulder.

The moment Scott stilled, the image began to roll forward. There was no sound, but it was easy for Scott to fill in the words from memory.

"I like giving hand jobs," Joe said as the images on the screen began to jack each other off. "Don't get me wrong. I love screwing and sucking too. But it's a control thing; literally holding you in the palm of my hand is a huge power trip."

Scott nodded, as if he understood, but he didn't. It was impossible for him to comprehend how anyone could look at the two men on the screen and not realise that Joe was completely out of his league, that he was—

Joe tapped Scott firmly on the thigh with the remote control. "Pay attention. No daydreaming. And no doubting what I say is true."

"S-sorry."

"Don't apologise. Just do as you're told."

Scott glanced up—at the real Joe rather than the one on the screen. Joe was smiling. He actually seemed to really be enjoying watching them together. Scott dropped his gaze. Yep, Joe was definitely enjoying the sight. They'd barely caught their breath since round one, and Joe's cock was already hardening.

Scott's shaft had softened in his panic when he'd doubted Joe's satisfaction with round one. His concerns might not have evaporated, but curling up against Joe's naked body had already made sure his erection was once more oblivious to any mental hysterics.

Joe seemed to notice that Scott's cock was hard again. Glancing away from the screen for a moment, he wrapped his hand around Scott's shaft, just as he had the last time they watched the screen.

Scott gasped. Joe had only moved his hand around Scott's shaft a few times before Scott was right on the edge of coming.

"You have the most amazing mouth," Joe informed him.

He must have fast forwarded when Scott was too busy trying not to come to have noticed what Joe's other hand was up to. On the screen, Scott was going down on Joe with obvious enthusiasm. He remembered the sensation of Joe filling his mouth so perfectly. The taste of Joe's pre-cum flooded his senses. Joe's hand never stilled on his cock.

The combination was like an exquisite form of torture. Scott needed to come so badly that Joe's touch offered more pain than pleasure, but he couldn't bring himself to try to pull away or reject anything that Joe was willing to offer him.

Joe had seen all the men who'd filled the screen just a few minutes ago. He'd had the chance to compare Scott to all those guys, and somehow he still wanted Scott in his bed.

And alongside that, even though his shaft ached more with each moment that passed, Scott was starting to realise that there was something in him that actually seemed to like, no, that seemed to *love,* being balanced on the very edge, afraid of falling, yet at the same time almost equally terrified of *not* falling.

Like a tightrope walker who's suddenly realised that there are guys underneath him who are rolling up his safety net and walking away with it, Scott knew falling was out of the question. But, having looked across and realised that someone had magicked away the platforms at either end of his rope, he also knew that trying to keep his balance forever would just be more painful in the long run.

"Come."

Scott fell. Joe's order slid beneath him, catching him before he could hit the sand in the circus' centre ring. But, rather than set him down gently, the order scooped him up and whisked him higher, way above the big top and any mere illusion or tricks that had been performed there.

Scott flew on wings of adrenaline, caught up on air currents of endorphins. And he had permission to fly. Maybe even better than that, he had permission to believe he was worth the effort of flight.

He reached a peak of perfection set high up in the sky before he felt himself floating gently back down to earth. He had no idea how much time had passed; only that he was now in Joe's bed, in Joe's arms, and there was nowhere else he wanted to be.

The room was silent. Their dates so far had included so little time merely laying together and luxuriating in each other's presence. Scott kept his eyes closed, just in case opening them might inspire Joe to pull away. Scott didn't move; he barely even dared to take a deep breath.

A chuckle from Joe almost made Scott falter in

his resolve and open his eyes, but he held firm and kept himself in darkness.

"I know you're back with me," Joe said. "But don't worry, pet. I'm not going to make you move just because you've let on that you're conscious."

* * * * *

Joe tightened his hold around Scott's shoulders, feeling more protective of him with every minute he spent in his presence.

Scott blinked and opened his eyes, but he didn't try to lift his head from Joe's shoulder or meet his gaze. Not sure what to say, Joe took the easy way out and started up the recording again. It was impossible to think that anything could make it easy for Scott to watch the film, but now that he was full of afterglow, he seemed to find it a little more manageable.

Scott curled into Joe's side, ignoring the cum drying on his stomach, and made no protest as the film played on.

"You're gorgeous when you submit to me," Joe said. "Don't get me wrong, you're hot all the time, but when you submit, that's when you come into your own."

And it was at those times that Joe felt his need to protect, as well as dominate, Scott come to the fore and refuse to be denied. It was at those times he knew that he was going to find it impossible to ever walk away from Scott.

Scott was his. That meant Scott's problems were his problems. If he ever wanted Scott to be a content and confident collared sub in the future, Joe would have to fix those problems. He'd have to do whatever it took.

No excuses. No pulling back. No taking the easy road and thinking that sex could take the place of big, serious, real world issues. He couldn't just leave Scott floundering while he enjoyed having his own way all the time.

Dominance didn't just mean being allowed to be bossy. It also meant taking serious issues seriously, and making sure that the orders he gave were the right orders for everyone involved.

Joe glanced at the envelope on his bedside table. He hadn't written the note to go inside it yet, but he knew then what he needed to invite Scott to do. It wasn't his idea of fun, but it was very much what a good dom would do.

Scott deserved a good dom.

Part Ten: Plain Brown Wrapper

South Street Sauna. 11 PM Friday. Go straight to reception – the guy behind the desk will take care of you.

"Take care of you" meant that the guy behind the desk would tell him where Joe was. Scott reminded himself of that several times as he walked down South Street.

He'd seen saunas that specialised in catering to gay and bi men before, from the outside at least, so he knew what to expect. It would be discreetly tucked into a basement property. Very few signs, and none making it clear that it catered to men who had no interest in the possible health benefits of a sauna.

It would be the kind of place that men ducked into while hoping that no one spotted them. Forget relaxed, gay friendly spaces—most of the men in a sauna wouldn't even be out.

Scott was almost at the end of the directions Joe had texted him when he finally dragged his eyes up from the pavement to get a good look at his destination.

Forget everything he'd predicted. The sign above the door was huge and featured several very attractive men wearing very small towels. Forget cramped basement properties—this sauna occupied the entire building.

Scott shuffled his feet on the pavement outside for several minutes, trying to re-jig his expectations. Whatever Joe had planned for him tonight, it wasn't going to be like their visit to the glory hole in that rough pub. Joe wasn't trying to show him the seedier, rougher side of gay sex tonight.

No longer needing to be concerned that he might be stabbed or mugged, Scott now worried that he might be expected to purchase a membership that cost more than his annual salary.

"First time?"

Scott jumped.

There was a guy behind him. He was older than Scott, perhaps in his mid-forties, and wearing a business suit.

Scott blinked at him.

The man laughed, but not in a particularly unkind way. "Yes, definitely a first timer."

Scott felt the blush rush to his cheeks. The man opened the door and held it for him. "After you."

Scott hesitated for a second before rushing forward. He was halfway through stuttering out his thanks when he spotted the reception desk. His pulse doubled.

The man he'd met outside put his hand on the small of Scott's back. Scott jumped forward liked a scalded cat. The man chuckled again, but Scott had very little attention to spare for him.

His focus was all on the man standing behind the reception desk. Joe. The world was instantly a more manageable place. The guy behind the desk really would take care of him.

Joe raised an eyebrow. That was all he needed to do to make Scott jerk into action.

Go straight to reception.

Standing around just inside the door wasn't

part of Scott's orders. He hurried up to the reception desk.

"My young friend here is a first timer," the man from outside said as he stepped up alongside Scott.

Scott opened and closed his mouth, but he had no idea how to explain that he really wasn't friends with the man, especially when the guy was standing right there.

Joe didn't even blink. "You must be Mr. Evans." He glanced at the computer as if checking something. "You booked an introductory visit with an eye to taking out an annual membership. Right?"

Scott nodded on the familiar principle that Joe was always right about everything.

"No problem. I'll just sign in the gentleman behind you, then I'll be right with you."

Scott nodded again; and when Joe glanced at a patch of floor just to Scott's left, Scott moved to stand there.

Joe took a card off the guy who was obviously a regular visitor to the sauna, swiped it through a machine attached to the computer, pressed a few buttons on the keyboard and handed the guy a key. "Enjoy your visit, Mr. Leonard."

Mr. Leonard looked Scott pointedly up and down. "I'm sure I will." He winked at Scott before heading through the door to the left of reception leaving Joe and Scott alone.

"I m-m-met him just outside. I—"

"Scott," Joe cut in.

Scott fell silent.

"I'm not an idiot. The man didn't even know

your name. And even if he did, I'm hardly going to think you came here to play with *him*, am I?"

Scott took a deep breath and nodded to himself. Everything was fine, well mostly. "I haven't come since last time we m-m-met up." As soon as the words tumbled from his lips, Scott regretted them. He put his hand over his mouth, but Joe just chuckled as if he saw nothing wrong with him making that sort of declaration in a public place.

"Good boy."

Scott relaxed enough to smile when Joe said that. They really were wonderful words.

A door opened behind Joe and a red-headed man about the same age as them stepped through.

Joe turned to him. "Perfect timing, Ben. You can hold down the fort while I take Mr. Evans on a tour of the facilities."

Scott was vaguely aware of Joe typing something into the computer, but he couldn't think of anything useful to contribute. He remained still and silent until Joe stepped away from the desk and ordered him through the same door Mr. Leonard had used.

It might have sounded like a polite, business-like invitation, but Scott still knew it was an order. He followed it immediately, but any hopes he had of speaking to Joe in private died as Joe led him into a locker room where several men were already getting changed.

Joe opened a locker. "If you'd like to leave your clothes here, Mr. Evans." He took a towel out of a locker and put it on the bench next to Scott.

Scott glanced around. Other men were also

getting undressed. He'd survived the boots only night, he could survive this too. He started to undo his shirt, only to stall when he saw that Joe was also getting undressed.

Joe opened a locker a few down from Scott and put his T-shirt in it. He took out a towel and placed it on the bench next to Scott's.

Scott watched the way Joe's muscles moved on his back when he bent down to take off his trainers.

His desire to worship Joe's bare skin hadn't decreased since the boots only night. Scott's legs trembled, begging him to drop to his knees and rub his face against Joe's skin, but he managed to resist.

Joe straightened up and undid his fly. Scott watched as Joe undid each button. Joe wasn't wearing underwear, of course; Scott wasn't actually sure Joe owned any.

Joe's pubic hair was revealed, quickly followed by his cock. Saliva flooded Scott's mouth. He tried to keep back a needy little whimper and failed. It had been less than a week since he sucked Joe's cock, but it felt like years.

Joe didn't try to hide his cock, or to show it off either. He moved around completely naturally; placing his clothes in his locker, then taking a few things out of the small space before closing and locking it.

Scott loved every inch of Joe's body, but his attention kept reverting to Joe's cock. No longer entirely soft, his glans was just starting to peek past the end of his foreskin. Scott licked his lips.

"Less staring, more obeying."

Scott snapped his attention up to Joe's face at

whiplash speed.

Joe smiled, but it was nothing like the polite expression that had graced his features in the reception area. His lips twisted up at the same angle as before, but his eyes looked feral. It wasn't a friendly expression, and it went straight to Scott's cock.

Scott swallowed rapidly, feeling very much like a rabbit trapped in a set of extra bright headlights.

"Now."

Scott finally regained power over his limbs. He scrambled out of his shirt and shoved it haphazardly into the locker. He tossed his trainers and socks in on top of his shirt, not thinking clearly enough to care how crumpled he'd look when he left the sauna.

Obeying Joe's orders was all that mattered. Jeans off and crammed into the locker, Scott only had his boxer shorts left.

He reached for the towel that he'd seen Joe place on the bench behind him earlier, but it was gone. He turned to Joe.

"The regular members have green towels," Joe said, conversationally. "Blue is for members of staff. Red is for guests." He indicated the two towels he'd picked up and draped casually over one knee.

Neither towel did anything to hide his cock, which was now flushed with arousal and rising away from his crotch.

Scott managed to nod his understanding of the colour code without looking away from Joe's cock. He waited patiently, happy to enjoy the view until Joe wanted to pass him the red towel.

Several minutes passed. Neither of them moved. Finally, Scott looked up. Joe raised an eyebrow.

"M-m-may I have my towel, p-p-please?" Scott asked.

"You're not undressed yet."

Scott shifted his weight from one foot to the other and tried to find the right words to explain to Joe that he wanted to wrap the towel around his waist and struggle out of the boxers underneath it; the same way he had changed into swimming trunks at the beach when he was little. No words left his lips. For once, that had nothing to do with his stutter.

He obviously didn't have Joe's permission to hide his crotch while exchanging the boxers for the towel.

"Problem?" Joe asked.

Yes, there was, and Scott was well aware that Joe already knew what it was. Scott hadn't stepped foot in a changing room since Joe ordered him to keep his pubic area shaved. He had no interest in displaying his hairlessness to strangers.

"Did you forget to shave?" Joe asked.

Scott frowned, wondering why Joe would think that. He shook his head.

"So you're not trying to hide your disobedience, then?"

"N-n-no!"

Joe smiled, just a little less evilly than before. "How many men are in the changing room at the moment?"

Scott tore his gaze away from Joe and looked around. The other guys had all left.

"I'm the only one who'll get a good look at you — unless you keep stalling until other guys turn up, of course."

Scott hurriedly shoved his boxers down and kicked them off. He tossed them in the locker and tried to take the towel.

Joe pulled it out of his reach. Seconds stretched out and felt like hours as Joe kept him standing there, completely exposed to anyone who might walk into the room, while he ran his eyes slowly over Scott's body.

Scott felt the heat rush to his cheeks. Soon, they were going to match the colour of the guest towel.

"J-Joe?" Scott finally stuttered out.

"There are flip flops in the locker. Put them on."

Scott looked at each door leading into the locker room, but it was no good worrying about who might come in. The only way he was going to get his towel was to obey Joe's orders. His pulse raced, but he couldn't deny that Joe's minor demonstration of the control he had over him made his cock rise.

He dug beneath his clothes until he found the flip flops. He dropped them on the floor and clumsily pushed his feet into them.

"Good boy."

Scott looked hopefully at his towel.

"There's a wrist wallet in there. You'll need that as well." He lifted his hand and showed Scott a small black pouch he'd secured around his wrist.

Scott whimpered at the delay, but dutifully fumbled through the locker until he found it. He couldn't fasten it around his wrist. His hands were shaking—although he wasn't sure that was from an overload of nervousness or arousal.

Joe stood up.

"I'm s—" Joe put his hand over Scott's mouth.

"I warned you that I'll spank you next time you offer me an unnecessary apology. I have no problem turning you over my knee right here." He took his hand away.

Scott kept his mouth shut, sure Joe wasn't bluffing.

Joe smiled and fastened the thing around Scott's wrist. "Perfect." He dipped his head and brushed his lips against Scott's mouth.

Scott ached to lean into the kiss, but he remembered how business-like Joe had acted when there were other people around and he held back. "I d-d-don't w-want..." he managed to stutter out.

Joe lifted his head. "Nothing will happen that you really don't want," he promised. "You still remember your safe word, right?"

Scott shook his head and grabbed Joe's hand to stop him pulling away.

"I d-don't want to g-g-get you in t-trouble," Scott managed to finish.

For once it was Joe who looked shocked.

"You're at w-w-work," Scott reminded him, carefully.

Joe laughed. "If I was willing to screw five guys a night in the middle of the busiest room in the building, my boss wouldn't fire me, he'd give me a raise."

Scott blinked at him. Heat rushed to his cheeks. Even if he'd always known that Joe wasn't bound by the same rules as him, Scott had let himself pretend that Joe wasn't screwing anyone else. Gradually, part of what Joe had said nudged its way to the front of Scott's mind.

"You're not w-w-willing to?"

"I never have taken well to other people telling me who to screw, or when, or where."

Scott stared at the centre of Joe's chest, caught between hoping that Joe would announce that he hadn't screwed anyone else since they'd met; and hoping that Joe wouldn't say anything at all, because the truth was probably far from monogamy. For better or worse, Joe remained silent on the subject.

Someone had to say something to break the hush. "You could s-s-screw me wherever you w-w-wanted. If you th-think that would h-help," Scott offered.

* * * * *

Joe stared down at Scott. Fair play, Scott was obviously doing his damnedest not to look too horrified at the prospect of a public performance. However, he was a bloody awful actor. Hard core exhibitionism wasn't his thing. Joe was sure it never would be. The offer was a desperate attempt to please, nothing more.

"One day, I might take you up on that." Joe let himself imagine it for a few seconds. He couldn't deny the exhibitionist in him would thrive on it. But no. That wasn't something for them. Scott would probably always want a solid barrier between them and any audience, and Joe wasn't going to push him on that score.

Scott made no comment. He just stared up at Joe, waiting for an order.

Happily, Joe had plenty to give him.

"I'm going to show you around. You're going to pretend that we've just met. As far as anyone will know, we're strangers. Understand?"

Scott frowned slightly, but he didn't question the commands.

"If anyone asks, you and I just met," Joe repeated.

Scott nodded, although he didn't look entirely happy. Joe wasn't about to change his plans just because Scott had no idea why he wanted them to play the part of strangers, but he couldn't leave Scott looking so dejected either.

This time, he didn't just brush their lips together. He caught hold of Scott and pulled him forward so their naked bodies were pressed tightly together.

It was less a kiss and more a statement of ownership. Once he caught up with events, Scott was more than happy to give, but Joe still didn't ask; he took.

Scott leaned up into the kiss and moulded himself against Joe's body. Joe had never known Scott to launch himself into a kiss with such energy. A less confident dom might have been intimidated, thinking that Scott was trying to take control, but Joe loved it. If he had thought it was a display of confidence rather than a plea for reassurance, it would have been perfect.

When Joe pulled back, they were both

breathless. No one had joined them in the locker room, but Joe knew a herd of marauding elephants could have trampled through and he wouldn't have noticed. It was more luck than judgement that no one knew they were together. He'd have to be more careful.

Hiding their relationship as they walked through the sauna wasn't going to be easy; but it was going to be worth it, Joe reminded himself. Still, Scott was a man who dealt much better with statements of fact than he did with hints and nudges. It never hurt to make the facts clear to him.

"Just because no one else is allowed to know you belong to me, that doesn't mean you're allowed to forget that I'm your master."

Master.

Scott mouthed the word rather than attempted to say it out loud. It seemed more because he was in awe, than because he was trying to avoid stuttering.

"Didn't you know that I'm you master?" Joe teased. "That you're my sub?" Joe didn't push him to offer a verbal answer. He stepped back, tossed Scott's towel to him and smacked him once, very firmly, on the bare arse as he stepped past him and picked up his own towel.

Scott let out a high, startled noise and leapt forward when the smack connected.

Joe grinned as he wrapped his towel around his waist. Both of them were tenting the fabric in front of them as he led Scott out of the locker room and into the main part of the sauna, but that wasn't a problem. There wasn't a single patron who wouldn't see a noticeable erection as a very positive thing.

With his towel wrapped casually around his waist, Joe was content to allow the end he'd tucked in, to keep it in place. As Scott stepped forward, Joe noticed that he was the only one who felt that relaxed. Scott's grip on his towel was white-knuckled.

"Everything's fine," Joe reminded him, in a hushed tone. "Just because we're playing a different game, that doesn't mean you'll be out of my sight for a second."

Scott smiled up at him. He seemed reassured. That was something Joe was still getting used to. No other man had ever raised such a protective urge in him. He'd never spent so much time and energy making sure another man was as confident and as happy as he could possibly be. Who would have thought it could feel so good?

Warmth enveloped them as they stepped through another doorway. It wasn't a sauna room, but there weren't many areas of the building that weren't kept at a high temperature.

The business owners weren't idiots. They knew men weren't going to walk around damn near naked in frigid temperatures. Everything was bigger at higher temperatures; including the company profits.

Joe led the way down a corridor. About a third of the way along it, one wall turned transparent.

"It's a one-way mirror," Joe said, bringing them to a stop and turning to look through the glass at the men showering behind it. Six men were under the spray. "They have no idea that we are here," Joe said. "Of course, they'd probably only enjoy themselves more if they knew."

Three of the men weren't even pretending that

their groping had anything to do with massaging shower gel into each other's bodies. The man getting most of the attention was older than the others and even though it was impossible to hear what he was saying from outside in the corridor, it was clear that he was in charge and he could have any of the other occupants of the shower on their knees or grabbing their ankles with a word.

Unable to feign interest in the live porn about to take place in front of him, Joe turned to Scott, eager to see his reaction. His blush was beautiful and, just as Joe had expected, a wall between him and the show made him far more relaxed.

Joe smiled. As sweet as it was to watch Scott's embarrassment climb, it wasn't actually the aim tonight. He lowered his voice to a whisper. "Come on, Scottie. Lots more to see."

He led Scott into the sauna's bar room. It was designed to look like a normal coffee shop at first glance. It was only on closer inspection that it became clear that the low sofas were sized large enough to comfortably hold a three-way, and that the huge TV screens hanging high on the walls played gay porn rather than the more PG-rated team sports often displayed in other pubs and bars.

There were more guys in here, and no wall between Scott and those men. Joe sensed Scott move to stand nearer to his side. As much as he loved the way Scott looked to him for protection, that wasn't going to help his plan.

"I need to speak to one of my colleagues for a few moments, Mr. Evans. Perhaps you'd like to get a drink from the bar. Everything served here is complimentary and included as part of the standard membership fee."

Joe would have bet his job that the only reason Scott didn't object was because he heard the order concealed beneath the business-like invitation. Joe walked across to the man working behind a counter on the other side of the room and took up a position where Scott would be within his line of sight.

While Thomas—the sauna's resident gossip extraordinaire—babbled away, Joe watched Scott approach the bar.

Freddie, the man working behind the bar that night, had been married and monogamous ever since it was legal; but he wasn't shy about letting a cute guy know it was only his wedding ring stopping him from making a play for him.

Joe smiled to himself. If seeing himself submitting on a wide screen TV hadn't convinced Scott that he was stunning in all the ways that count, then seeing the number of guys in the sauna who would make it clear they desperately wanted to screw him the moment they set eyes on him was bound to do it.

There wasn't a man alive who wouldn't get a confidence boost from that, was there? Joe nodded vaguely to whatever Thomas was telling him. Tonight was going to lay to rest all of the demons Scott had acquired when he'd first come out of the closet. Joe was determined about that.

Scott politely took a bottle of Coke from Freddie. He turned. His blush was brighter than ever. He looked toward Joe, but Joe told him with a tiny shake of his head that he wasn't allowed to approach yet.

Scott looked around the room and, still maintaining a death grip on his towel, headed straight to the quietest area. He perched on the edge of the low slung sofa and clumsily took the top off his drink. He tipped his head back and poured a good amount of Coke down his throat, as if he was trying to drown his nerves with the sugary soft drink.

Joe bit back a chuckle as a guy approached Scott's sofa, and Scott promptly choked on his Coke. The guy sat down next to Scott and rubbed his back.

Joe's inclination to laugh died. He'd planned on a lot of flirting on the part of other men, and a lot of blushing and polite no thank yous on Scott's part. Touching had not been part of the deal. Any man but him touching Scott was not part of any plan.

Scott scooted away, moving down the sofa to put some space between himself and the guy hitting on him. Joe felt slightly better about the world when he saw Scott's reaction, but when the guy moved closer again and stroked his fingers over the hand with which Scott maintained a death grip on his towel, Joe knew that the tour of this particular room had gone on quite long enough.

He arrived beside the sofa just in time to hear Scott stutter out a reply to whatever it was the guy had asked him. It was difficult to guess what the question had been because Scott's answer was garbled by nerves, but Scott was making it clear that his answer was no. That was all that really mattered.

"Are you ready to resume your tour, Mr. Evans?" Joe asked, with false cheerfulness.

Scott jumped like a puppy caught rooting

through the rubbish bin. "Y-Y-Yes!"

The guy on the sofa laughed. Damn it, that was just as unacceptable as the touching. Joe might find Scott's nerves and blushing amusing, but that didn't mean other men could take liberties like laughing at him.

He turned away before he forgot what he was supposed to be focused on that day in favour of making it clear that Scott was his by smacking some sense into the other guy. Joe headed for the door on the opposite side of the bar room to where they'd entered, and Scott hurried along in his wake.

"I w-wasn't encouraging h-him. I'd never b-break your rules about th-th-that."

Joe paused a few steps into the corridor and turned to face Scott. Scott appeared even more worried than usual.

"I haven't accused you of anything," Joe pointed out, gently.

Scott looked sceptical.

Joe walked back to him. "It's never even occurred to me that you want anyone else," he said, honestly.

Words only did so much to reassure. They were alone in the corridor and he knew one thing that always helped Scott feel better about the world. He kissed him.

He could damn near feel the fear and nervousness draining out of Scott's body. It was probably in sync with the way the blood drained away from his head and rushed to his cock. Joe smiled to himself as he stepped back. "But you're not going to distract me from this tour, no matter how hard you try."

Scott parted his lips and was obviously about to protest until he saw Joe's teasing expression.

"Come on, Scottie."

He opened a door and stepped back to allow Scott in first.

"The swimming pool is one of the most popular areas in the complex," Joe said in his best attempt at a detached professional voice. He ran a quick eye over the men enjoying the area.

Two guys were making out in one of the Jacuzzis. A three-way was taking place in the shallow end of the pool. As Joe ran an assessing eye over the situation, another man swam over and joined them. The guy getting screwed was now completely surrounded and obviously enjoying all of the attention. There wasn't room for him to drown. No one would have to play lifeguard.

Joe turned his attention back to Scott. He found himself already the focus of Scott's gaze. It was impossible to tell if he'd even glanced at the guys in the water.

"Can you swim?" Joe asked.

Scott nodded.

"Ever been screwed in the deep end?" he asked, more quietly.

Scott shook his head.

"Something for the bucket list," Joe said.

Scott didn't have a chance to answer before a whistle cut through the air.

"Hey, new boy."

Joe looked over his shoulder and traced the call back to one of the men in the Jacuzzi.

"Want to find out what men really come here for?" The guy offered.

Joe met his gaze.

"If you ever decide to screw where you work, you know you've got a standing invitation too, Joe! The more the merrier—especially when they've got a cock like yours!"

The moment the man turned his attention toward him rather than Scott, Joe was happy to consider him harmless.

"Maybe next time," Joe said—just like he always did.

"You said that last time," the other man in the Jacuzzi protested.

"Yeah, but one day, I'll mean it and it will definitely be worth the wait." It was easy talking to someone like that. Joe could do that on auto-pilot. It wasn't like speaking to Scott, where each word was important and Joe had to weigh each syllable.

Leading Scott away from the guys in the Jacuzzi and out into another corridor, Joe didn't give them time to hit on Scott again.

Glory holes lined one wall of the passageway. Many were surrounded by one-way mirrors—some of them allowed a man to see who would be sucking him, while the others allowed the man getting the blowjob to be seen without knowing who was on the other side.

Joe caught Scott's eye. "In most areas, this sauna can compete with any place in the city; but there are one or two activities where we lose hands down to other venues."

Scott was obviously reliving the same memory

that filled Joe's mind. It would be a different experience for Scott to play with a glory hole in a sparkling, modern building.

Joe was tempted to order Scott to wait there while he hurried around to the other side of the wall and got behind one of the glory holes that would allow him to see Scott when he went down on him. No. Tonight wasn't about showing Scott how much *he* wanted him. Being wanted by one man would never get his confidence up high enough.

Joe opened another door and once more stepped back to let Scott go first. "Just follow the corridor. You can't get lost. Keep going. I'll be right behind you. You won't lose me."

The moment Joe stepped into the part of the sauna affectionately nicknamed the labyrinth and closed the door in their wake, almost all the light disappeared from the world. Heat replaced it. It reminded him of some of the stricter religions' idea of hell.

Hot, dark, full of steam and, just like those same religions promised, it felt like it was home to every gay man who had ever lived. There was no way Scott could walk through there and leave without knowing just how wrong the first gay men he'd met had been when they told him that no one would ever be interested in screwing him.

Muscular, naked shapes moved around them as they took a few steps forward. Scott came to a complete halt.

Joe stepped up behind Scott. He put one hand on Scott's shoulder, and the other on his waist. "Do you remember your orders?"

* * * * *

Orders. Yes. Scott had orders to follow. Even if Joe was playing the part of tour guide, every word that left Joe's lips still represented a command. All Scott had to do was obey. He just had to follow the corridors and trust that Joe would be right behind him.

It wouldn't be the first time that he'd had to trust that Joe was there and watching over him, even when he couldn't see Joe for himself.

Scott thought back to the rough, glory hole pub once more. Even naked and horny, the men here weren't anywhere near as scary as the denim and leather clad guys in that pub had been.

It soon became apparent, however, that the men in the sauna were far more touchy-feely.

Hands slid over Scott's body. They weren't threatening. They weren't hurting him. There wasn't even the sense that they wanted to do anything that he wasn't willing to allow. But, they weren't Joe's hands.

In the dim lighting and steam, all Scott could see were vague shapes and glimpses of naked skin, slick and shining in the heat. The caresses felt more like invitations than demands, but that didn't help. Scott knew Joe's touch, and he knew these caresses belonged to strangers.

Scott kept walking down the corridor, but far from leaving the people who were interested in him behind, he only found more of them. Far from telling him to get the hell out of there or laughing at him for thinking he could ever be hot enough to be wanted in a place like this, they called to him with whispers and caresses. They invited him into their games — and into their mouths and arses.

If they'd known he was with Joe, perhaps it would have made sense. Then it would have been obvious they were only making a move on him because they knew Joe would be part of the deal. As things stood, their actions remained entirely inexplicable.

But, one thing was obvious. If that number of guys were willing to make do with him, Joe had to be getting mobbed by a whole legion.

Unease made Scott shiver despite the heat. Joe had said he would be right behind him, and Joe kept his word. Joe wouldn't let anyone else stop him. Even if he was tempted by a better offer and intended to go off and play with someone else, Joe would tell him first — and he'd even do it kindly.

Scott tightened his grip on his towel and kept pushing forward, speeding up his search for the exit with each minute that passed.

The corridor got narrower. The only way to keep going was to rub up against the men he needed to squirm past. Hard, strong bodies, and even harder cocks seemed to surround Scott completely. Mumbling excuse mes and apologies as he went, Scott kept wriggling forward.

A few guys tugged playfully at his towel, but Scott kept a death grip on it and refused to stop or even slow down.

A door. Thank God!

Scott pushed it open and stumbled out into the

light. Cold air hit every part of his body at once, shocking him into coming to a sudden halt in the middle of a wider, more brightly lit, corridor.

He put out an arm and steadied himself against a blindingly well-lit white wall. Every inch of him was damp with a combination of steam and sweat. His hand slid against the paintwork. The door clicked closed behind him. Scott took a deep breath but he couldn't bring himself to turn around and stare at the door while he counted the seconds until Joe followed him out of the sauna-come-maze.

Hands landed on Scott's shoulders.

Joe.

As addled and out of his depth as Scott felt, he still had no doubt who grabbed him. He knew Joe's touch. Relief ran through him as he realised Joe must have left the sauna at the same time as he had. Joe really had been right behind him.

Joe spun him around. The next thing Scott knew, his back was against the cold wall and Joe's steam-hot body was pressed against him, pinning him in place. Scott moaned against Joe's lips as Joe plundered his mouth in a kiss that seemed to be fuelled less by desire than anger.

Joe caught hold of Scott's chin and forced him to tip his head back before Scott had a chance to do it of his own free will. His fingers bit into the skin on Scott's jaw just as Joe nipped at the tip of Scott's tongue.

Scott scrambled to keep up. It was a familiar feeling. He was used to Joe's kisses taking him by surprise, but he had no idea what he'd done to make Joe so angry.

Determined to do anything and everything possible to make Joe pleased with him again, Scott frantically tried to root out any hints that could tell him what Joe would most like him to do. He leaned into the kiss, but that just made Joe make an angry sound in the back of his throat, almost like a growl.

He tried to kiss Joe back and reach out to pull him closer—making it clear that Joe could do whatever he wanted with him, but that just made Joe pull away entirely.

Scott looked up at him, far too panicked to say anything for several seconds.

It hadn't been his overactive imagination making him think that Joe was angry. As he met Joe's eyes, it was obvious that Joe really was furious.

"Come on." Joe grabbed Scott's wrist and headed off down the corridor. They passed several doors and several areas where walls had been replaced by mirrors or panes of glass.

Inside the rooms, men were having sex. Some of them were having sex in complicated numbers that involved far more limbs and penises than Scott would ever be able to cope with.

Was that why Joe was mad? Had he expected Scott to get involved with some of the guys in the sauna maze? Was he disappointed in him? Had he hoped they'd exit the other end of the maze with one or more extra guys in tow?

Suddenly, Joe jerked Scott through an open door and slammed it shut behind them.

There wasn't anyone in the room. They were alone. That was good.

Another glance around the room informed him

that part of one wall was mirrored. Scott had no idea if that also meant guys outside could see in, but he had more important worries than exhibitionism anyway.

"I'm s—"

Joe roughly covered Scott's mouth with his hand. "What did I tell you about apologising for no reason?" he demanded.

Scott's heart raced so fast he thought he might have a heart attack at any moment, but he still waited until Joe took his hand away before answering. "You s-s-said you'd spank m-me."

"I meant it." Joe caught Scott's gaze and held it.

"If it w-would m-m-make you feel better, you can," Scott offered.

For several seconds, Joe continued to glare at him, looking pissed off and gorgeous in equal measure. Then he broke into a grin and gorgeousness won out completely.

Scott smiled back, thrilled that he'd somehow stumbled upon a good suggestion. He glanced around the room again. There wasn't a kitchen chair, like the one Joe had sat on last time he'd spanked him, but there was a bed.

Scott pointed to it. "W-w-would there be ok-k-kay?"

"Will I only be marking my territory just to make myself feel better, or do you like the idea too?" Joe whispered in his ear as he stepped up behind him. His erection rubbed against Scott through their towels.

Scott wasn't sure what the right answer was. Joe taking hold of both their towels and tossing them away didn't help him come up with any ideas.

"W-w-whichever you prefer?" he hazarded.

Joe made Scott turn to face him.

He studied Scott through narrowed eyes. "You have no idea why I just jumped you, do you?"

"I know you're a-a-angry with m-m-me," Scott ventured.

"You haven't done anything wrong. I've got no reason to be angry with you."

Scott nibbled on his bottom lip. Joe sounded really serious about that. The grin was gone.

"You did as you were told, didn't you?"

Scott nodded.

"So, I've no reason to be angry with you. And even if I was angry, I've no right to take it out on you, do I?"

Joe still sounded serious, but ran his hands over Scott's body as he spoke; and that made it so damn difficult for Scott to think clearly.

"Possessive," Joe whispered in his ear.

Scott took a deep breath and tried to make sense of the word.

"You know they all wanted you, don't you?"

Scott looked down at Joe's wandering hands. His touch felt so different than all the other men who'd tried to cop a feel in the labyrinth.

"Y-yes, but I didn't w-w-want them," Scott whispered.

Joe spun him around so they once more stood face to face.

It had obviously been the right thing to say. Scott saw the success in Joe's eyes; felt it in the raw, sexual energy pouring off Joe.

"I w-want you," Scott blurted out.

"Be careful what you wish for, pet."

Scott frowned.

Joe caught hold of Scott's shoulders and twirled him around again. Before Scott had time to catch his balance, Joe had one of his wrists twisted up behind his back.

"Are you sure you wouldn't prefer one of those nice, polite businessmen from the labyrinth, someone who'd be all gentle and considerate with you?"

Scott knew that teasing tone of voice. Joe already knew the answer. The question was just part of the game; a hoop Joe wanted him to jump through for his pleasure.

Scott shook his head. "I w-want you."

Joe reached around Scott's body with his free hand and pinched his right nipple.

"Maybe one of them would let you have everything just as you want. A nice, vanilla guy who'd let you have all the freedom in the world."

Scott shook his head even more vehemently. He tested Joe's grip on him as fear of suddenly being freed from Joe's tight grasp shot through him.

Joe kept Scott in place, easily twisting his arm even further up behind his back. His arm wasn't meant to achieve that position painlessly. Scott knew his shoulder would be sore in the morning, but all he felt right then was relief at being held; at being wanted by the one person he desperately wanted to want him.

To hell with guys who'd told him he wasn't good enough in the past. The offers he'd fended off in the dark heat of the labyrinth were irrelevant. Joe wanted him.

"I don't want to play nice tonight," Joe whispered in Scott's ear. His tone made the words a clear warning.

Scott swallowed rapidly. He'd been out of his depth ever since he'd first offered himself to Joe, but suddenly, he was well aware that he might never have actually ventured out of the shallow end.

Even after all this time, Joe was still babying him, taking it easy on him.

Need peaked inside Scott. The need to please Joe. The need to have Joe throw everything he had at him. Need. So much need.

"Good!" Scott got the word out without a single stutter. He tested Joe's hold on him again, with far more determination this time.

"You want it rough?" Joe asked. He laughed, and for once it sounded like he thought that the joke might be entirely on Scott, but Scott didn't care; he nodded rapidly.

"Yes!"

Joe pushed him forward. The front of Scott's legs hit the edge of the bed, but Joe didn't seem to care. He kept pushing until Scott managed to get his knees onto the edge of the mattress. Joe's grip on his wrist twisted Scott's shoulder, making him arch and bow his spine as he was unceremoniously put head down, arse up.

"Lube," Joe demanded.

Scott's heart rate doubled. Lube! Why hadn't it occurred to him to bring lube?

He tried to stutter out an apology and an

explanation at the same time, but quickly gave up, knowing that everything he'd said had been unintelligible.

"D-d-don't need it," Scott promised. Even as he said it, he knew he was an idiot. Joe was hung like the devil. This was bound to hurt, but Scott carried on anyway. "S-s-spit is f-fine. I can—"

"On your free wrist," Joe cut in, but he didn't ease his hold on Scott's other wrist so he could reach for the complimentary wallet that had been in the locker—the one that Joe had ordered him to wear.

Scott awkwardly scrabbled at the Velcro that fastened the thing in place with his teeth, and then at the zip holding it closed.

Years seemed to pass, but he eventually managed to tip the contents onto the bed. Several sachets of lube and condoms blurred as he tried to make out the writing from the corner of his eye. There were all sorts of sizes, colours, flavours, and God only knew what else. Some of the sachets were decorated with flames, fireworks, and weird symbols he didn't understand. There was no time for deep, complicated thoughts. He grabbed one packet of lube and a condom at random and clumsily handed them to Joe.

Joe didn't say a word.

Scott took a deep breath and tried to relax as he waited for Joe's fingers to push into him, slick and demanding.

He heard Joe tear open two packets— presumably the lube and a condom—but he didn't feel Joe's fingers against him. A few seconds passed, then the round, blunt tip of Joe's cock pushed against his hole.

Joe had obviously chosen to only lube up his cock, and leave Scott's hole to take care of itself. And this time he hadn't rimmed Scott to help him relax, the way he had when they'd ventured into the woods. Scott's breath caught in his throat as Joe pushed the head of his cock inside his arse.

Scott hadn't remembered how to breathe before Joe thrust forward, lodging another two inches of his shaft inside Scott's arse and pushing against his prostate. Scott's mind spun. Pleasure pounded through him. There was pain too, but against all his expectations, it wasn't enough to override the bliss of having any part of Joe inside his body.

Scott bucked, trying to push back against Joe's pelvis, but Joe wouldn't allow it. He held Scott motionless on the edge of the bed, his fingertips biting into Scott's wrist and shoulder.

Scott had no idea how long Joe made him remain still. He only knew that he hadn't remained silent for more than a moment. His whimpers filled the air over and over again, until, without warning, Joe released his grip on Scott's wrist, dragged Scott upright, and pulled him back to lean against his chest.

Scott let out a triumphant yell as Joe finally gave him what he wanted and lodged his cock in him to the hilt. Their bodies joined firmly together, Joe turned them and took a few steps forward. With both his hands free, Scott was able to brace himself against the wall alongside the door. It was the mirrored wall.

Scott stared at himself, wide-eyed and trembling with the effort of remaining on his feet while his body was still trying to adapt to the deep penetration.

"Rough enough for you, Scottie."

Scott nodded.

"Words!"

In between panting for breath, Scott managed to stutter out; "Y-yes, sir."

Joe met his eyes over his shoulder in his reflection. Triumph burned brightly in his gaze. But whatever he felt about the honorific, it wasn't enough to distract him from what he was doing.

He didn't stand around waiting for Scott to relax around his shaft or for him to get comfortable in the new position. He started a series of deep, powerful, thrusts that threatened to have Scott tumbling to the floor at any moment — although Scott had no idea if it would be lack of balance that took him down to the floor or going literally weak at the knees with pleasure.

There was no way in hell he could take a hand off the mirrored wall to jack himself off. But, he'd come from nothing more than the ecstasy of having Joe's cock in his arse before. He really hoped he could do the same again, because he needed to come so badly.

"Remember that I own your cock," Joe growled in his ear. "Come without permission and I'll have you locked in a chastity cage for the rest of your life."

Scott tried to speak, but he only managed to utter mangled syllables. Forget stuttering, any kind of speech was beyond him now.

Joe reached around Scott's body.

Scott thought he was going to reach for his cock; but at the last moment, he grabbed Scott's balls.

The grip he took on Scott's nuts was just as

fierce as the one he'd had on his wrist earlier. Joe twisted his hold.

Scott's whole body jerked.

He tossed back his head and screamed — not in pleasure at his orgasm flooding through him, but in despair at having it snatched away at the last moment.

As he felt Joe thrust harder and faster than ever, Scott looked down at his own cock. He was completely soft now. His shaft didn't even twitch as he felt Joe come deep inside him.

Joe bucked his hips and tossed his head back, but he didn't completely release his grip on Scott's balls until he finally fell still. Scott stared down at his cock as he fought to catch his breath.

"Head up," Joe suddenly ordered. "Don't you want the guys in the corridor to be able to see your face?"

Scott obediently looked up. He watched as his reflection blushed. "They c-can see us…s-sir?"

Joe's reflection grinned. He looked content and sleepy after his orgasm, and more than a little smug too.

"I th-thought…" Scott reconsidered whether he wanted to finish that sentence, but when he saw Joe raise an eyebrow at him, he knew that he wasn't going to be able to get away with doing whatever the hell he wanted. He cleared his throat. "You s-said that no one was s-supposed to know we're t-together, sir."

"Yeah, well, they wouldn't have hit on you if they knew you were mine, would they? And you wouldn't have seen how hot they all were for you and realised that I'm telling the truth when I say how lucky I am to have you for a sub, would they?"

He separated their bodies and turned Scott around.

Leaning back against the wall, Scott stared up at him. Joe looked very serious. Scott swallowed several times in quick succession.

"But that was then," Joe said. "This is now. It's important that they know you're not actually on the market. And even more important that you know I have no problem with anyone seeing me with you."

Scott stared up at him, relishing his words.

"I have no problem with anyone seeing me with my sub," Joe said, in a softer tone of voice. "And you are my sub, aren't you, Scottie?"

Scott nodded rapidly. "Yes, s-sir."

"Good boy." Joe brushed their lips together. It was a gentle touch, but after the earlier, rougher, kisses, it was still enough to send shivers down Scott's spine.

"Now, aren't you going to thank me?" Joe asked.

Scott blinked at him. A moment later, he felt a new blush rush to his cheeks. "Th-thank you for h-helping me b-build my confidence, sir."

Joe smiled, but he shook his head. "I will see that you lose all this self-doubt rubbish, but that's not something I expect you to be grateful for."

Scott felt his blush deepen. "Thank you f-for wh-what we j-just did." He shook his head. "Sex," he blurted out, knowing he was an idiot for still finding it hard to say out loud when they weren't actually screwing.

Joe chuckled and shook his head again.

Scott hesitated.

"Aren't you glad I made sure that you don't have to spend the rest of your life in a chastity cage?" Joe whispered in his ear.

"Yes!" It felt surreal to be thanking someone for grabbing him by the balls that way, but who was Scott kidding? Joe had had him by the balls since the first time Scott set eyes on him. "You m-made sure I d-didn't screw up," Scott said, realising how true that was as he said it. Joe had made sure that he didn't let him down. "I am g-g-grateful for that, sir."

"Good boy." Joe gave him another brief kiss as a reward. Reaching into the wallet he wore on his own wrist, he made it clear why he'd needed the lube and condom from Scott's wallet earlier.

Almost all the space in Joe's wrist wallet was taken up by a blank envelope and piece of paper.

Joe handed it over. "You are going to have permission to come the next time we meet up, so you don't need to waste your turn just asking me for an orgasm."

Scott nodded his understanding.

When Joe stepped back, Scott straightened up and moved away from the wall. It was only when he turned around that he remembered that it was a one-way mirror that he'd been resting his arse against.

He looked at the envelope. Maybe he should ask that their next date take place somewhere where there weren't any see-through walls?

He glanced at Joe—he was resting on the bed now, looking as relaxed and as carefree as it was possible for a man to be.

But he did care. Joe cared enough to try to get

him over his stupid self-consciousness and show him that he was good enough to be of interest to other men. Joe cared enough to go easy on him and play nicely, even though he was used to guys who knew what they were doing and had to be bored to tears by babying him for so long.

When Joe beckoned him closer, Scott lay down next to him and rested his head on his shoulder. As Joe dozed and Scott's cock hardened in response to their closeness, Scott turned his attention back to the envelope.

Joe didn't need to be so careful and patient with him. Scott wasn't an idiot. He'd never let himself believe that he'd be able to keep Joe interested in him forever. This was lust, not love, for either of them.

However, there was nothing Scott would refuse to do if it kept Joe interested in him for just a little longer. It was time Scott made that one hundred percent clear.

Part Eleven: Fragile – Handle with Care

Please show me what you would be doing with me if you thought I could handle anything and everything you are into, sir.

Scott had been aware that his latest request could lead damn near anywhere; but, while he was on the back of Joe's bike and had his arms wrapped tightly around Joe's waist, the destination didn't seem important.

Being pressed up against Joe's back, the vibrations of the bike, the smell of leather, and even the sound of the hulking great engine, all went straight to Scott's cock. But, even more than that, they went to the part of Scott's mind that was labelled Joe in big shiny chrome letters.

Joe.

Scott smiled wryly in the privacy of his helmet. He didn't smoke. He drank very little. He'd never taken a drug stronger than aspirin. Yet somehow he'd still managed to fall down a rabbit hole and become an addict. He might have more survival instinct than to fall in love with Joe, but he was definitely addicted to Joe; and he trembled like a junkie who'd gone too long without a fix.

In real-world time, it hadn't been long since he visited the sauna. The bruise around his wrist had only just faded away. But, in the timescale of addiction, it had still been far too long.

Scott tightened his grip around Joe. He had no idea how far they'd ridden. He'd had his eyes closed most of the time, simply clinging to Joe's back and enjoying being so close to him. By the time Joe brought the bike to a halt and killed the engine, they could have been anywhere.

Scott opened his eyes. If anything, the world got darker. They were in an alleyway. There were no street lights. The moon was out, but it only provided enough light to see the larger obstacles.

Joe got off the bike and moved confidently around as if one of his many superpowers was better night vision than a predatory big cat. Scott moved more like a new born herbivore who had yet to work out how to operate his knees, or realise that big cats were dangerous.

The second time Scott cursed himself and whatever the hell he'd just tripped over, he sensed Joe turn his attention toward him. Unnecessary apologies were wrong. Scott got that. Unfortunately, he still didn't have a clue how to work out which times counted as necessary.

He was still trying to work it out when Joe slid his arms around his waist. Scott tilted his head back, more than happy to be kissed anywhere, anytime, but Joe bent down, put his shoulder to Scott's crotch, and tossed Scott unceremoniously over his shoulder.

Scott screamed. He wished there was a more dignified word for it, but was well aware that the sound he'd let out was very definitely a scream. And to think that he'd thought it would be embarrassing if he'd tripped over...

Being upside down didn't make it any easier for Scott to get his bearings. He was aware of Joe walking a little way down the alley, then opening a door and carrying him inside a building.

Joe set Scott back on his feet. A second later, blinding white light filled the world. Scott covered his eyes. Several seconds passed before he managed to adjust his vision and blink at his surroundings.

"Well?" Joe prompted.

Scott turned to him. Joe was leaning against the wall just inside the door with his lips twisted into a smirk.

"I..." Scott cleared his throat. He looked around again. He'd never realised that so many types of bondage furniture existed. "I g-g-guess we don't need to w-worry anyone phoned the p-p-police when they heard me s-s-scream. P-people who live around here, m-must be used to it."

Joe laughed, light and carefree. "Good boy. Good answer. Now, strip."

Scott was so tempted to look around and check that they were the only ones there, but he managed not to. It wasn't as if he'd ever seriously objected to Joe telling him to get naked in front of strangers anyway.

He took off his clothes with as much coordination as he could pull together while Joe was just standing there, fully dressed, watching him. The look in Joe's eyes didn't help Scott redirect any blood from his erection toward his brain.

"Give me your clothes."

Completely nude now, Scott handed all his

clothes to Joe.

"Stay there."

Without another word, Joe disappeared through a door to their left. Scott no longer had anything to distract him from the equipment visible from his position just inside the door.

He could recognise some of it from the internet. Others were familiar from films set in the medieval period. Stocks. Pillories. Racks. A human-shaped cage hung from the ceiling. Scott frowned, sure he'd heard what one was called in an old movie, but unable to recall the term.

Because that was the real problem — not that he was faced with a dozen different set-ups that were all a million miles out of his comfort zone; but that he lacked a complete vocabulary of historical torture devices.

"See anything you like?"

Scott spun around to face Joe.

Joe looked him up and down, his gaze finally settling on Scott's erection. "I'll take that to mean you don't find anything so scary it isn't still hot."

Scott blushed. If he hadn't felt the heat in his cheeks, he would have known from the way Joe's smile gentled.

"It's a pity, really," Joe said, his expression becoming rueful.

"P-p-pity?" Scott asked. He considered their location and added; "s-sir?"

"The first thing you'd have already tried out by now, if you were more experienced when we first met, is a cage."

Scott looked over his shoulder at the cage

hanging from the ceiling.

"Think smaller," Joe ordered.

Scott turned back to face Joe, still completely confused. Holding out his hand, Joe showed him a much smaller cage. It was made from shiny silver metal. The bars were curved and shaped like a flaccid cock.

Scott stared at it, somewhere between horror and fascination.

"If you found the idea less erotic, this bit wouldn't be necessary."

Before Scott could ask what that meant, Joe took his other hand from behind his back and put a bag of crushed ice directly on Scott's crotch.

Pain shot through Scott. His erection died. His entire package tried to retreat inside his body. But, it still never occurred to Scott to step back and try to escape whatever sensations Joe was willing to offer him.

"Good boy."

Scott gasped in relief as Joe finally took the ice bag away.

Suddenly, Joe dropped to his knees in front of Scott.

Still not entirely up to date on current events, Scott's cock instantly tried to rise to an occasion that might include a blowjob, but the ice had done its job well. Joe had no problem tugging his balls through a small metal ring, or fitting the metal cage over his soft shaft.

Scott whimpered as Joe slid a lock into place and clicked it shut.

Joe sat back on his heels.

"It's good that you've remembered to keep yourself shaved. It hurts like hell if a pube gets caught in the cage—or so I've been told." Their gaze met. Even with Joe on his knees before him, Scott had never been more aware that Joe was the kind of man who took control of other guys' cocks, and not someone who would ever end up in a chastity cage himself.

Joe straightened up. "How does it feel?"

"Ok-k-kay."

Joe raised an eyebrow.

"A b-bit heavy, but ok-kay, s-sir."

Joe stood up. "It will make sure you get through the tour without coming without permission. Its main purpose is to help you obey that order."

Scott nodded.

"Its other purpose is to look as hot as hell."

Scott took a deep breath and let it out very slowly.

"When the tour is over, I'll take it off and let you come."

"Y-yes, sir."

"If you're very good, I might not lock it back on you before I take you home tonight."

Scott met Joe's eyes. It was impossible to tell if he was teasing, or if he really was considering making him stay in chastity until their next date. Against all logic, the idea made Scott's cock try to get hard inside the cage.

"Come on." Joe held out his hand to Scott.

Taking his hand, Scott walked forward at Joe's side. Each step reminded him of the cage around his cock. Each movement seemed to tug gently at the top of his shaft and, as the effect of the ice faded away, his cock responded by swelling and starting to harden.

"What do you think?" Joe asked, as he brought them to a stop next to a spanking bench padded in deep red leather.

"I l-loved it w-when you spanked me before, s-sir," Scott offered.

"Yes, but that was with my bare hand. Now, it's time to try something new. Pick a number between one and ten."

An order was an order, even if it didn't make much sense. "F-five?" Scott hazarded, at random.

Joe pointed to the wall alongside the bench. There was a cabinet there with lots of differently shaped and sized doors — each one numbered. "Go and see what you've picked."

Scott cautiously approached the cabinets. The doors weren't in number order. It took him a few moments to find number five. The door was tall and narrow. Scott opened it and took out a crop. The tip was cut into the shape of a butterfly, which seemed like a very un-Joe-like thing.

"Not a bad choice," Joe said.

It felt odd in Scott's hands, as if a deep instinctive part of him knew that he wasn't someone who should be wielding it. It belonged in the hands of a dom. Scott quickly carried the crop across to Joe, but hesitated a step away from him.

It seemed wrong to just hand the thing over as if it was no more interesting than a sandwich. Scott knelt down, resting the crop on both of his palms, and offered it to Joe, in rough imitation of pictures he'd seen on the internet.

"Good boy." Joe reached past the crop and stroked Scott's cheek. He brushed his thumb against Scott's lips before casually penetrating his mouth with it. "So good." He picked up the crop with his free hand, but didn't rush to take his thumb out of Scott's mouth.

Scott's shaft strained against the bars of his cage. His mouth watered in the hope that Joe would offer him his cock to suck on next, but Joe helped him up off his knees instead.

"Sh-should I?" Scott pointed to the spanking bench.

"No, we're not stopping here. If I get you on a spanking bench now, we'll never finish the tour." Rather than offer Scott his hand again, he tapped Scott on the arse, quite firmly, with the crop.

Scott lurched forward, more in surprise than pain, making Joe laugh. Scott smiled back at him. The crop had looked both odd and intimidating when it was in the cupboard. It had looked unwieldy while Scott held it. But, it looked very different in Joe's hand. Once Joe was in control of it, it became something that looked natural and comfortable. Scott was sure it would provide far more pleasure than pain.

For better or worse, Scott couldn't say the same for some of the equipment they walked past. Bloody hell, most of it would have been rejected by the Inquisition as too extreme.

"Try it out for size."

Scott turned around very slow, his mind racing with guesses as to what Joe was pointing out behind him.

A cage.

Scott stared down at it for several seconds. It looked like a mini version of the kind of cages used by old fashioned circuses, except it was way too small for a lion — maybe more the size for a largish dog — or a man on his hands and knees.

A shiver of anticipation ran up Scott's spine, mixed with relief at Joe having picked something that Scott was reasonably sure he could cope with.

Scott lowered himself to his knees and set his hands on the floor in front of him. The cock cage pulled in a slightly different direction now. It took him a few seconds of shuffling awkwardly on his knees before he could pick up the pace and crawl past Joe toward the cage door.

Joe helpfully opened it for him.

"In you go." He gave Scott a couple of taps with the crop to encourage him forward. The impact still wasn't enough to hurt, just enough to sting pleasantly, and to make Scott wonder what it would feel like when Joe finally decided he was willing to use it in earnest.

The cage door clanged when Joe closed it. Something that small should never have been able to make that much noise. Scott squirmed, attempting poses that would challenge most yoga instructors, in his desperation to face the door — to face Joe.

"I've seen a lot of guys locked in this cage over the years," Joe said, crouching down so they were closer to eye level with each other.

"You c-come here a lot, s-sir?"

"I've worked here off and on for a few years."

"Is there anywhere in the c-city to d-d-do with

sex that you haven't w-w-worked?" Scott blurted out.

Joe laughed. "Well, there's one lesbian pub on the outskirts of the city which, for some reason, has never offered me a job. Apart from that, not really. The phrase sex sells exists for a reason. Places like this pay well. Even in a recession, people still want to get laid, and they want to get whipped. Some even want to be put in cages."

Scott tried to sit back on his heels and straighten up, but there wasn't enough head height. He had to keep his hands on the floor in front of him and his body bent forward.

"What usually h-h-happens to guys when they're in the c-c-cage?" Scott asked carefully.

"Depends what they're into?"

"You," Scott replied.

"I'm your fetish?" Joe asked, with obvious amusement.

But Scott wasn't joking. He nodded, perfectly seriously.

"Some guys blow whoever sticks their cock through the bars of the cage. Others get teased." Joe seemed to think for a while. "If I put you in there, it would be so you could feel safe while you had a rest between rounds. I'd pull up a chair and rest my feet on top of the cage — have a chat to some old friends while you have a nap — or at least get your breath back — you'd probably be too frustrated to actually sleep."

Long before Joe had finished the first sentence, Scott's cock was straining against his cage. The image expanded to fill his whole mind.

"Then, when I thought you'd rested for long

enough, I'd release you." Joe picked up something from a container alongside the cage. "But, if the club was actually open, I wouldn't be letting you wander around on your own. I'd want to keep you close at heel, wouldn't I, Scottie?"

He reached through the bars of the cage and slipped a chain link collar around Scott's neck. "Of course, this is just a practical bit of bondage, it isn't a *real* collar. A real collar would have a tag on it saying Property of Joe, and it wouldn't ever leave your neck."

Property of Joe.

It was all Scott could do to hold back a whimper. He had no idea how a man went about earning a "real" collar, or a tag like that, but gaining one shot to the top of his list of Joe flavoured fantasies.

While Scott was lost in his thoughts, Joe retrieved another item from alongside the cage. A black leather lead. He clipped it onto Scott's collar. Another practical bit of bondage.

When Joe opened the door, Scott crawled out of the cage. He automatically started to stand up, but stopped short, not sure if that was something he had to have permission to do now. He looked at the lead, then up at Joe, who raised an eyebrow at him in silent query.

"D-do I s-stand up, s-sir? Or do you w-want me to stay l-like this?"

"If it was full here, you wouldn't be allowed to move around on your hands and knees — I've seen far too many crawling subs get stepped on in crowds, but, since we're the only ones here..." He smiled.

Scott nodded. Putting his hands on the floor in front of him, he crawled forward a few feet before looking up at his surroundings.

A whimper rose up inside him. If the equipment in the club had looked intimidating when Scott was standing upright, from his new point of view, it was terrifying.

* * * * *

Joe stared down at Scott's back. If his new posture made it more difficult for Joe to see Scott's cock or his face, then at least it gave him a fantastic view of Scott's arse. Joe slowed down to let Scott move a little way ahead of him, so he could properly admire how his buttocks clenched and released as he shuffled forward.

Scott, however, ignored all the slack on his lead and kept close to Joe's side. If Joe had been interested in Scott's ability to play the part of a good puppy rather than the joy of being able to perv on Scott's arse, it would have been perfect.

He gave Scott a gentle tap with the crop to encourage him on ahead. Scott shot forward as if there'd been a hot ember on the crop tip.

He looked over his shoulder, obviously startled, but as soon as their eyes met, Scott smiled and ducked his head; a blush tinted his cheeks.

And Scott being slightly ahead of him provided a bonus completely separate from the view. Unable to follow Joe's lead, Scott had to pick which piece of equipment to head towards next. Joe strolled along behind him, fascinated to see where Scott might crawl and what that might tell him about any kinks that lay undiscovered within him.

Water sports.

Scott headed straight for that part of the club as if there was a lighthouse, a homing beacon, and a SatNav all guiding his way.

Scott stopped at the archway that separated the wet rooms from the drier parts of the club. A two-foot wide metal grate extended from one side of the arch to the other. It probably wasn't a comfortable thing to crawl across, but Joe had seen plenty of guys do it without coming to any harm. If Scott was as into water sports as his internal GPS implied, the grating wouldn't stop him.

Joe stepped forward and leaned against the arch so he could study Scott's profile more easily. He'd expected fascination, or perhaps uncertainty, because he didn't know if Joe would share that particular kink.

Scott just looked bemused.

As Joe watched, Scott's attention moved from the grating to the various parts of the tiled wet room. Pure confusion. He had no idea what he was looking at. Joe grinned.

As if sensing his amusement, Scott looked up at him.

"Want to guess what guys do in there?" Joe asked, confident that playing in there wouldn't be high on Scott's list of kinks if he didn't even recognise the possibilities in the set-ups.

"W-w-water torture?"

"Close," Joe said with a chuckle. "Water sports."

He waited a few moments to see if Scott would recognise the term. He saw the moment when the penny dropped. "You m-mean when guys p-p-pee on each other?"

"That's the basic idea."

"You…" Scott trailed off.

"It's not my thing, but there aren't that many things I haven't tried at one time or another."

Scott glanced through the archway again. He still didn't look enthusiastic.

Joe laughed. "Come on. I'm sure there are some other parts of the club that will fit your kinks better."

Rather than let Scott pick the direction again, Joe resumed control. He led Scott, who still hadn't complained about crawling at his feet, toward a high-backed metal bondage chair on the western edge of the club. There were trays of equipment on each side of the chair, and a frame that could hinge down over someone as they sat in the chair. Scott was too low down to see most of the things on the trays.

"Guess what it's set up for," Joe ordered.

"I th-th-think I'm too focused on the w-w-word torture. I c-can't think of anything else," Scott admitted.

"Well, I'd call it nipple play, but some people do call it nipple torture—depends what sort of games you like to play, I suppose."

Scott pulled back. From observing just that one reaction, it would have been easy to think that Scott hated the idea. But as Joe kept watching him, Scott shifted his weight and swayed toward the bondage chair.

Joe smiled to himself. He'd seen the way Scott had reacted to having his nipples toyed with on their previous dates and his instincts hadn't been wrong. Scott wasn't so much retreating from the bondage chair as he was squirming at the possibilities it held.

"Before you started writing your letters to me, you'd never even thought about nipple play, had you?"

Scott shook his head.

"Have you thought about it since?" Joe prompted.

"I've thought about w-when you..."

It sounded like he'd enjoyed the memories they'd made together, but hadn't gone so far as to work on any new fantasies. "We can improve a hell of a lot on what I've done with you in the past," Joe said. "Hop up."

Scott must have worked out what Joe was going to order him to do, because he didn't hesitate to get up into the chair. He even managed to keep his body language quite calm. It was only when their eyes met that his need for continued reassurance became clear.

"I always knew you'd look amazing in this sort of set-up." Joe moved behind the chair as he spoke and lowered the frame down so it blocked Scott's easiest escape route.

"If I intended to keep you in this chair all night—which I definitely will next time I put you in it—I'd put all the restraints in place." He placed his hands on Scott's shoulders.

Scott tilted his head back to try to look at his face.

"You won't be able to do that next time," Joe warned. He showed Scott the restraint attached to the headrest. "This would keep the back of your head pinned in place."

Scott straightened his head and pressed it against the headrest.

"That's right," Joe said. "Just like that. I'd trap your arms against the armrests, too. Elbows, wrists, shoulders—all secured in place." As Joe walked around the chair, Scott arranged himself neatly. His desire to be bound was obvious, but Joe didn't indulge him this time.

"Your legs would be trapped too."

Scott dutifully positioned his legs against the bondage. Obviously well into the right mind set, he didn't move his head to look down.

He was perfect. Cock caged, neck collared, but without anything binding him to the chair apart from his own will, he'd never looked better. The expression in his eyes, that steel strong determination to please his dom, along with that slight uncertainty that he'd prove capable of doing that, was the most glorious finishing touch.

"Perfect."

Joe stepped closer and pulled a stool forward so he could sit comfortably at the right height to play.

Reaching past the frame, Joe rested his elbows against the solid steelwork and took each of Scott's nipples between his thumbs and forefingers.

Locking his eyes with Scott's, Joe began slowly. Being willing to show Scott a little of what he would do with him in the future wasn't the same as being stupid enough to throw him into the deep end. No real pain for now; nothing to scare Scott away before he really got started. Joe just toyed with him, gradually increasing his sensitivity as he held his gaze.

"People are wrong to think that it's only women who have sensitive nipples. Guys are just as capable of getting off on this kind of play."

Scott's expression faltered. He frowned slightly, but rather than nod the way Joe expected, Scott whispered, "Y-yes."

A shot of pleasure raced down Joe's spine as he realised that the bondage Scott was pretending passed across his forehead had stopped him communicating with one of his favourite gestures. Joe tightened his grip, pinching Scott's nipples more firmly as he rolled them between his fingers. He gave Scott a few moments to get used to that before he altered his grip and let his thumb nails join in on the fun.

Scott's breath caught in his throat. He swallowed rapidly. Joe felt each movement of Scott's chest as Scott breathed deeply and tried to wrap his mind around the sensations racing through his body.

Scott closed his eyes and bit down on his bottom lip.

"I came here this afternoon and set everything up. I brought every toy I could possibly need with me. Blindfolds, hoods, every type of gag you can think of," Joe said, casually. "I wouldn't even need to dip into the toys the club owns."

Scott blinked at him. Realisation dawned in his eyes. "If you w-w-want me blind or silent, you'll d-d-do it yourself."

It was almost a direct quote. Joe nodded his approval. "Until then, assume that I want to be able to look into your eyes and hear you whimper for me."

As if unable to hold back for another second, Scott whimpered. The sound seemed to be dragged from every cell in his body.

"Good boy. Let me hear how frustrated you are."

The shock in Scott's expression made Joe chuckle. "Yes, I know. Playing with you and making you desperate to get off while keeping you caged is evil. But sometimes I like being evil."

That, combined with a sharp pinch to each nipple, earned Joe a higher pitched whimper.

"I told you I didn't put you in the cage *just* because it would help you not to come until you have permission, didn't I?"

Scott groaned. It was as close to a verbal answer as Joe suspected he was capable of right then. He didn't press him for actual words.

Joe released Scott's nipples. They were already flushed and slightly swollen. Joe took two small silver clamps from his pocket.

Gripping Scott's right nipple and pulling it away from his body, Joe put the rubber tips against his already sensitised flesh and slid the adjustment ring up to tighten it in place. Scott moaned. His eyes rolled. Joe gently tugged at the clamp, then tightened it a little more before repeating the process on the other side of Scott's chest.

Joe hadn't expected Scott to be able to resist looking down to watch what he was doing but, God bless him, he didn't move his scalp away from the headrest for a second.

His breathing was more rapid now, a little faster than was ideal. Joe wanted him on edge and loving it, but hyperventilating wasn't part of the plan. He ran his knuckles up and down the centre line of Scott's chest. "Good boy. That's right. Take a minute and slow it all down now."

There were small weights attached to the clamps; they moved with each breath Scott took.

When Joe sensed Scott was mentally ready, he indicated the frame in front of him and continued his tour of that particular piece of kit. "This is to let someone put tension on the clamps." He pulled one weight away from Scott's body and stretched Scott's nipple out toward the frame. "There are so many games we could play in this chair."

"Yes, s-sir."

"But there are some things we can't do in it."

Scott met his gaze, obviously hoping for some clue as to what Joe wanted to do to him next. As careful and gentle as Joe was being, he could see how far out of his comfort zone Scott was. There were so many things someone could do to him in that club, and so many things that he obviously knew he didn't have a clue about.

But at the same time, Joe had no doubt that Scott was hoping for information so that he could prepare himself and make sure he didn't disappoint Joe by doing anything wrong. His desire for information had nothing to do with any inclination towards self-preservation. He was more under Joe's control than any man had ever been, more dependent upon him, more willing to do whatever he wanted.

He was more of everything that Joe had always wanted in a sub, and more of the things he hadn't realised he wanted until he met Scott, too.

Joe lifted up the frame.

Scott tensed up, but he still didn't move out of his psychological bondage.

"Perfect."

* * * * *

Scott nibbled at his bottom lip. Obviously perfect was a good thing — it might not be an accurate thing for Joe to call him, but it certainly wasn't an insult. Scott took a deep breath and let it out slowly. The clamps Joe had put on his nipples tweaked different nerve endings in response. Scott closed his eyes for a moment, but quickly opened them.

Joe had told him to keep his eyes open, and Scott couldn't fail him now. He swallowed as the pressure to remain what Joe seemed willing to consider perfect weighed down against him.

Joe reached out and ran a fingertip across Scott's forehead. "Pretend this bit of bondage is unfastened now."

Freedom was a dangerous thing. It was far easier to do nothing imperfectly when he couldn't move any part of his body. Scott would have much preferred to stay frozen in place, but he knew Joe giving him permission to move was tantamount to an order to alter his position.

Scott cautiously tipped his head forward and looked down at his own body.

Joe picked up one of the clamps, holding it

away from Scott's body so he could study it more easily. The movement twisted his nerve endings again. The sensation went straight to his cock. Tearing his gaze away from the clamp and the small silver weight attached to it, Scott looked to the cage around his shaft.

He was leaking pre-cum through the tip of the cage. His stunted erection was pressed against the metalwork so firmly that his flesh seemed to bulge against the gaps between the bars.

Scott swallowed and looked back up at Joe.

"It's hard to work out which bit of jewellery looks better on you," Joe said.

Scott licked his lips. They were dry with either nerves or desire, but he didn't actually manage to comment.

Joe released his hold on the nipple clamp and stood up. The weight swung down and bounced against Scott's chest. Ignoring that as best he could, Scott tilted his head back to look at Joe, but he couldn't hold his gaze for more than a second.

"Imagine all your bondage has been released. You're free to move however you want."

Scott suspected that Joe meant he was allowed to stretch out any muscles which were threatening to cramp up. But he couldn't help himself taking complete advantage of the permission. He slid out of his chair and landed at Joe's feet.

His knees hit the ground hard, jolting his body and making the weights attached to his nipple clamps bounce and tug at invisible lines connected straight to every pleasure centre on his body. He ignored all that, leaned forward and rubbed his face against Joe's fly.

Joe didn't yell or order him away. That was all the encouragement Scott needed. He pressed open-mouthed kisses against the front of Joe's jeans. His own cock was still trapped in the cage and unable to harden, but Joe didn't have the same problem. His erection flourished, just a thin layer of denim stopping it rising proudly away from his body and standing to complete attention.

Scott tried to move his hand up to undo Joe's fly, but Joe slid his hand into Scott's hair and pulled his face back into his crotch.

Scott whimpered and licked the denim, willing to make the most of what he was offered; but it wasn't enough. He needed Joe's cock inside him. Joe had done as he had asked; he'd shown Scott how he'd have treated him if he had more experience. Now, Scott desperately needed Joe to show him that he still wanted to screw him even though he was as clueless as hell.

"P-please," Scott mumbled in Joe's lap. "P-please, Joe. Please, S-sir."

Joe let him whisper and beg for a few minutes as he worshiped his cock through the fabric, but all too soon, he crouched down in front of Scott, rendering his crotch completely inaccessible.

"I haven't finished showing you what I'd have done with a more experienced man."

Scott hesitated, but only for a moment. Despite his desire to howl his frustration like a wild wolf caught in a trap, Scott knew that Joe's preferences would always be more important than his own. "W-w-whatever you w-want," he gasped out.

"Good boy." Joe kissed him — hard, fast, but all

too brief. Before Scott knew what was happening, Joe was already straightening up.

Scott sat back on his heels and stared up at him. His lips were sensitive after spending so long working against denim. The kiss had left him raw and desperate, but Joe picked up the handle of Scott's lead and gently tugged him forward.

"Come on, Scottie."

As soon as he leaned forward, Scott gasped. The new angle completely changed the way the nipple clamps pulled at him. The silver weights were teardrop-shaped and swung back and forth beneath his body every time he moved a limb. If he managed to go any distance without either moaning out loud or coming despite the cage, Scott knew it would be a miracle.

Dividing his time between looking up at Joe to try to read every hint of expression that passed across his face, and glancing in front of him to make sure he didn't make a fool of himself by shuffling head-first into a piece of bondage furniture, Scott crawled at Joe's heel toward the other side of the club.

Joe brought them to a stop in front of a length of wood. One-half of it was attached to the ground by huge metal bolts, the other half was hinged up. There were four semi-circular grooves cut out of each section.

"S-s-stocks," Scott blurted out. He'd seen them in old Robin Hood movies. He knew what they were. He was sure he would be out of his depth again soon, but for a few seconds, he felt like a man who knew the answer to a question.

"Got it in one," Joe said, ruffling Scott's hair in

praise. He nudged Scott forward. "Go ahead and try them out."

Scott obeyed. Shuffling around to sit on the ground on the other side of the stocks, he placed his ankles in the centre two cut-outs and tried to line his wrists up with the two outside ones. He had to arch over in a really weird position, and even then his wrists didn't line up as they should.

Sitting up, Scott pushed a hand through his hair. It wasn't easy to think clearly when his entire nervous system screamed out in a complicated mixture of need, desire, and frustration.

It was several minutes before he managed to work out why the position didn't feel quite right. He quickly rearranged himself, putting his ankles in the outside slots and his wrists in the inside ones. Everything lined up a bit better, but he still didn't seem to be in a very useful position.

He frowned at the stocks. His heart raced faster and faster as he tried to work out what he was doing wrong. He was letting Joe down with his stupidity, and —

"T-two!" he blurted out as he realised what he was doing wrong. He looked up at Joe. "The stocks are for two m-men, aren't they, s-sir?" He peered into Joe's eyes, begging Joe to tell him that he'd guessed right, even if the idea that Joe might intend to bring another guy into the game scared the hell out of him.

"It could be used for two guys. I've seen them used that way. Or, there are a few different ways it can be used on one guy."

Scott looked at the four cut-outs again, willing his brain to come up with the right solution.

Joe crouched down next to him.

Scott parted his lips, but Joe cut him off with a shake of the head. "Before you say anything, have I ever given you a row for not knowing how to do something?" Joe asked.

Scott took the question as rhetorical, until Joe remained silent for so long it became obvious that he wanted an answer.

Scott shook his head.

"So you have no reason to apologise. I'm far too turned on to want to give you a punishment spanking before I screw you, so no apologising for anything. I have no problem ordering you how to do things exactly the way I want you to do them."

"P-please?" Scott whispered, looking up at him, more than ready to beg if an apology wasn't acceptable.

"Of course," Joe said, easily.

The moment the orders started flowing, Scott's pulse steadied. Nothing could go wrong now. Everything would be fine. With the world broken down into command-size bites, Scott had nothing to fear.

Move onto your hands and knees. Put your ankles in the outside dips. That's right. Now, lean forward. Put your cheek on the floor. Reach back between your legs and find the dips where your wrists fit in.

It all became so obvious when Joe took control. Head down, arse up. It not only made far more sense than any of the positions Scott had attempted, it also hinted that Joe might finally be finished with the tour and Scott might finally get Joe's cock inside him.

Mouth or arse, Scott was flexible on the details.

He just needed Joe's cock; needed to feel Joe finding his pleasure inside his body.

In position, Scott waited expectantly, but for what felt like hours, nothing happened.

Scott tried to lift his head and catch a glimpse of Joe.

"I'm still here, just admiring the view," Joe said. A second later, a hinge squeaked and Scott sensed the stocks come together over his wrist and ankle joints, trapping him in place.

Scott tensed. He was trapped — far more so than when he'd been in the bondage chair. The stocks weren't a figment of his imagination. They weren't going to disappear the moment he stopped pretending they were there.

He was trapped until Joe chose to release him. It scared him almost as much as it excited him.

"Such a pretty pose," Joe said, running his hand down Scott's back. He was obviously sitting directly behind Scott now. He slid one hand over each of Scott's thighs.

Scott tried to relax, but it was as if every muscle Joe touched had a mind of its own — or, perhaps, as if his body was more interested in obeying Joe's touch rather than Scott's own brain.

He wasn't in control of anything anymore. He closed his eyes and relished the knowledge.

"Tell me what you want."

"Your cock in m-my arse." Scott was so desperate for it; he wasn't even embarrassed to blurt it out. "P-please, J-Joe. P-please." Begging, pleading, anything which convinced Joe to screw him was worth it.

"You sure?" Joe asked, rubbing his hands over Scott's backside. "There's nothing else you want me to do first?"

"No, nothing else." Scott let out a high-pitched whimper and shook his head, pushing his face into the floor. "P-please, let me have your cock!"

Joe chuckled, but he didn't say no, and that was the only thing that mattered to Scott right then. Joe pressed two lubed fingers against Scott's hole and started to prepare him. Scott guessed that was what Joe had been hinting at when he talked about doing something else first, but he was giving him his prep whether he'd remembered or not.

At least Joe wasn't going teasingly slow. His movements were quick and deft, and Scott loved him for it even if they made his cock ache more than ever within its cage. He moaned as he tried to compliment Joe's movements and make his enthusiasm clear.

Maybe that made a difference, maybe it didn't. It was impossible to tell if Joe would have done anything faster or slower without his efforts. All that really mattered was that Scott soon felt the blunt tip of Joe's cock pressing against his slicked hole.

One movement. Harsh and fast, Joe buried his cock in Scott all the way to the base.

Scott yelled out as Joe's cock stretched his hole wide open and Joe's hips collided with his upturned buttocks. Like a lightning bolt shooting straight into his body, pleasure and pain sparked and scorched through him, burning up everything in its path until it hit his prostate and earthed itself in his cock. His cock jerked inside the cage. If he'd thought that he'd been frustrated by the chastity device while wandering around the club, he quickly learned that he hadn't even known what frustration was until he'd been screwed while caged.

But the cage also did its job. It was the only thing that stopped him coming from just that first thrust.

Instinct made Scott try to buck and struggle as if he could somehow get the chastity device off, but the stocks made any kind of real movement impossible. All he really did was moan and repeatedly clench his hole around Joe's erection.

It was only when Scott managed to halt his attempts at frustrated wriggling that Joe began to move. His thrusts were slow, but by no means lazy. He pulled out until only the tip of his cock remained inside Scott's body, then rammed back in to the hilt. Each time, his hips connected hard with Scott's buttocks and made him jerk against the stocks.

Joe's aim was spot-on. Every thrust connected hard against Scott's prostate. He felt pre-cum spurt from the tip of his cock in response. The angle at which he was bound meant it landed on his forearms. It did nothing to make him less frantic to come.

Time seemed to stretch out so each of Joe's thrusts lasted hours, and Scott felt each millimetre of Joe's cock spread him wide open. By the time Joe's rhythm finally faltered and Scott sensed Joe's orgasm overtake him, Scott was whimpering in time with Joe's thrusts.

Scott gasped for breath as Joe finally stilled. Joe let out a groan full of satisfaction, but didn't rush to pull his cock out of Scott's arse, he just leaned forward and rested his hips against Scott's buttocks.

"Are you ready to hear what I was going to offer to do before I screwed you, or are you still too impatient to let me have my say?" Joe asked when he'd caught his breath.

Eyes closed and face pressed against the rubber matting, Scott frowned. "Sir?"

"I thought you might have liked it if I'd taken the cage off," Joe said, conversationally, as he separated their bodies.

Scott heard clothing rustle as Joe tidied himself up, but he couldn't move a muscle — not to speak, not even to open his eyes, until he sensed Joe moving around. By the time Scott opened his eyes, Joe was sitting, neatly dressed, on the floor within his line of sight.

"I m-m-missed my chance," Scott realised. His breath caught in his chest. His torso ached as if his heart was actually breaking.

Joe grinned. "You missed your first chance."

Scott peered awkwardly up at him from his bound position. He was desperate to ask, but unwilling to risk interrupting. From now on he was simply going to listen to Joe and take every opportunity to hear any offers of any sort of chances.

"You lost the chance to come when I screwed you, but that's never been the only thing I've wanted to do to your arse," Joe said. He picked up the crop. "You remember your safe word?"

Scott nodded.

"If you say it, you'll still be allowed to come, but if I think you didn't say it when you needed to, I promise you you'll spend so much time in chastity you won't even be able to remember what an orgasm feels like by the time I unlock you again."

And with that, Joe removed the cage.

Scott couldn't see his cock, but he felt his erection spring free and straighten to point up toward his chest.

He gasped his relief. Even the bliss of being free enough to harden made his mind spin.

He heard Joe move again, but when he opened his eyes, the only part of Joe within his field of vision was one black boot. A tap against his upturned arse told him that Joe had picked up the crop again.

At any other time, Scott was sure he would have been as nervous as hell, but there wasn't room for nerves inside his head. His entire being was too full of need and desperation.

Joe brought the crop down against Scott's right buttock, slightly more firmly than he had before. It still wasn't painful, more a tease than anything else. Scott helplessly moaned his frustration. If Joe expected him to come from nothing more than the crop's kiss, he'd need Joe to offer him a far more intense sensation.

"P-please?" Scott blurted out. "Joe, s-sir, m-m-master? Please!"

Joe didn't reply, but he brought the crop down just a fraction harder. Begging worked! Scott was more than happy to beg if it got him more of whatever Joe was willing to offer him.

Words fell from his lips in a steady stream. He had no idea what most of them were. He didn't care. As long as Joe kept bringing the crop down slightly harder each time, it was worth saying anything.

The leather slapped against his skin again and

again. Scott moaned and whimpered in between his pleas, desperately trying to rock his hips and find something to hump against.

There was nothing within his reach. He was more helpless than he had ever felt in his life. The skin across his buttocks burned, but it was nothing compared to the ache in his balls. The need to come overwhelmed everything else in the world.

He had no idea how much his sanity had come to depend on the repetitive sharp slaps against his buttocks until they suddenly stopped.

Scott's pleas stuck in his throat. Silence fell over the world.

Suddenly, another sensation came to Scott's rescue. Nothing touched his cock, but he felt Joe's fingers enter his hole. Scott held his breath until the air rushed out of his lungs when the crop suddenly came down on his right buttock again.

Scott jerked and tensed all his muscles, including the ones wrapped around Joe's fingers.

Another slap on the other buttock; Scott clenched around Joe's fingers again. The tip of one rubbed against Scott's prostate.

His orgasm raced through him. His cock jerked. His cum exploded from the tip of his cock. It felt like part of his soul went with it. Some of his semen landed on the floor beneath him, but his position meant most seemed to hit his arms and chest.

If he hadn't already been as flat on the floor as his bondage allowed, his orgasm would have felled him. Scott smiled against the rubber flooring under his cheek. His arse, his cock, his bound limbs, his whole body in fact, ached and throbbed. And all was right with the world.

"I can put you in the same position using a spreader bar and a set of cuffs at home," Joe said as he ran his hand down Scott's spine.

Scott murmured a response, glorying in the gentle, reassuring touch.

"Would you like that, being trapped head down and arse up whenever I wanted, for as long as I wanted? Would you like turning up at my place never knowing if this is where you'd end up?"

Scott nodded as well as his position allowed. He could see it all so clearly in his mind. He knew he'd love it just as much as he loved everything Joe did to him.

If it involved Joe, Scott would love it. If it included an orgasm as well, nothing could compare to it.

"Don't move until I tell you to," Joe said.

Scott sensed Joe lifting up the top part of the stocks, but obediently remained in position. He wasn't actually sure if he could move on his own; every limb and joint had seized up.

The order to move never actually arrived — not as a verbal command anyway. Joe simply caught hold of Scott's shoulders and levered him up.

Scott gasped at the sudden movement. His head spun. Pain spiked through his body as muscles that had been contorted into a strange position were jerked out of it without warning.

"The pain will pass. Just breathe through it." Joe moved around in front of him and guided Scott to lean forward and rest against his body.

A few minutes passed. Joe took off the nipple

clamps without a warning. It was like being struck by lightning. Scott couldn't keep back a yell. His body took over and tried to curl him into a tiny ball, but Joe wouldn't allow it. He pulled Scott around and made him sit up.

Licking his thumb, Joe gently caressed Scott's right nipple before blowing on it. Even the air brushing against it made Scott tremble. He looked up at Joe — he was smiling.

"You still haven't answered my questions," Joe reminded him.

Scott trawled through his memories. Most of them were fuzzy. It wasn't easy to remember words when both his nipples were on fire. "Yes, s-sir."

* * * * *

Joe chuckled. "Do you even remember what I asked?"

Scott frowned.

Joe gave in to the temptation to circle one of Scott's nipples with a fingertip while he waited for an answer. Even that gentle touch sent a shudder running through him.

"Your p-place. Spreader b-bar."

"Good boy, that's right." Joe moved his attention to the other nipple.

"Answer is still the s-same. Yes, s-sir." He looked up and met Joe's eyes; such pure peace and acceptance in his expression.

The breath caught in Joe's throat. God, but Scott was perfect.

"And clamps," Joe pointed out. "I have lots of

them at home."

"Yes, sir. Any t-time you want."

Joe pulled Scott up for a kiss. Part of him wanted to make it sweet and reassuring, but he couldn't help but take possession of Scott's mouth — to take the control Scott offered him so instinctively, so completely.

"Good boy," he whispered against his lips, before he went back for that slightly sweeter kiss.

Finally, he made himself stand up and help Scott to his feet.

"We're leaving, s-sir?" Scott asked, tentatively.

"Not immediately. We have some cleaning up to do first."

Scott glanced at the play station with the stocks and the cum stains on the mat he'd been bound on. "Yes, s-sir."

"And you should probably dress before we go," Joe said. "As much as I'd love for you to ride home behind me nude, it's too cold today."

"Yes, s-sir."

Joe grinned. If he'd ordered him to leave nude, he was sure Scott would actually do it. His submission was that deep. No survival instincts now; not even any nerves, just complete trust.

"Anyway, I'm looking forward to seeing you squirm when you feel your clothes against your skin." He palmed Scott's buttocks with one hand, pulling him close so Scott's nipples rubbed against his chest.

Scott whimpered, but the only words that left his lips were another, "Yes, sir."

So perfect, Joe thought to himself. And that gave him so many options. The possibilities were endless with Scott. As they made their way around, cleaning up the stations they used, Joe couldn't help but realise that Scott's depth of submission meant he might be able to enjoy doing things with him that rarely appealed to him with less spectacular submissives.

Joe's cock hardened behind his fly. Yes, Scott was one of those guys he really did want in that very particular way. He had their next date planned already.

Part Twelve: First Class

My place. Friday. Midnight. Expect to stay the night.

Scott would have felt better if there had been a little bit more information contained in Joe's note. Or, maybe not. Scott was reasonably sure he was never going to be able to turn up for a date with Joe without feeling his stomach tying itself into knots.

It was equally impossible to believe that he'd arrive at Joe's without his cock being so hard it was testing the strength of the stitching around his fly, but he was quite happy to keep popping wood every time he visited Joe. It was a far more pleasant sensation than nervousness, and he didn't want to stop finding Joe as hot as hell.

Scott smiled at the idea that Joe could ever be anything other than hellishly erotic. Just at that moment, the door swung open.

"That's a nice surprise," Joe said.

Scott blinked. "Surprise?" He peered down at his wrist-watch. "I th-thought—"

"I meant the smile," Joe cut in. "It's good to see you looking more relaxed, more confident."

"Oh..." Scott dutifully tried to ignore the fact that he was now as tense as any man could be.

Joe chuckled and shook his head in mock exasperation, as he stepped back and let Scott in.

Scott shuffled his feet against the hall carpet, unable to think of anything to say that didn't revolve around the fact that Joe had decided to wear clothes when he answered his door tonight. It would have been rude to complain that Joe's foray into nudity had been so brief—like Scott thought he could make demands and state expectations.

Obviously, Joe had the right to wear whatever he wanted. He wasn't the one who was frequently ordered to—

"Strip."

Joe couldn't have timed it better if he'd been able to read Scott's thoughts straight out of his head. In the middle of setting down his overnight bag, Scott hesitated. The possibility of Joe being privy to all the crazy babbling that bounced around inside his mind was almost enough to make him want to turn tail and run.

"Any time you're ready," Joe prompted.

That was all he needed to say to pull Scott back into the moment. He pushed aside his irrational panic regarding sudden psychic abilities and focused on the far more sensible brand of panic that came from having kept Joe waiting.

At least that was something he could fix.

Placing each item of his clothing neatly on top of his bag in turn, Scott revealed his body with something closer to composure than he'd ever thought possible. He'd done it so often now, it almost felt natural.

After all this time, Joe was unlikely to realise that he was way out of Scott's league and that he didn't want to have sex with him after all.

Completely naked, Scott turned to look at Joe along the stark white hallway.

Against all logic, Scott couldn't help but think that Joe looked nervous tonight too.

No. Not nervous. That didn't make any sense. Joe wasn't an anxious sort of guy. But, stressed-out, maybe?

"Have you had a b-bad d-day?" Scott blurted out.

Joe's eyes narrowed. "Why would you think that?"

Scott shrugged. "You just seem d-different tonight."

It was obviously the wrong thing to say. Joe's shoulders noticeably bunched up beneath his T-shirt as he tensed.

"But no less h-hot," Scott rushed out, eager to add anything that might erase Joe's displeasure with him.

"Oh?"

Scott studied the floor between them. Unfortunately, there was nothing interesting there for him to stare at. His gaze soon migrated toward Joe's boots. "You know d-damn well that you're the hottest g-guy around." Hell, even Joe's footwear was making Scott desperate to come.

He saw Joe's boots moving closer, but he couldn't bring himself to look up.

"Have you been taking some sort of survey on the subject?" Joe asked.

Scott swallowed. As Joe stepped forward again, Scott dragged his gaze up to Joe's well-worn jeans. There were a couple of rips on the legs, but the material around the fly seemed to have been put to even more use than the rest. It was faded and thinning, and Scott itched to reach out and run his fingers over it.

His courage failed him; his arms remained at his sides. Still unsure if Joe was pleased with him or not, he couldn't work out what the hell felt so different about tonight.

"Well?" Joe asked.

A trawl through his short-term memory brought up Joe's last question. "Guys who s-stand on the edge of the crowd and watch everything from the s-side-lines see things that men in the m-m-middle of all the action can miss," he said, quietly.

"Such as?"

Joe moved even closer, but Scott kept his gaze at fly height. Joe was just as hard as Scott was; knowing that always made Scott feel a bit better about the world.

Scott cleared his throat. "Every man who w-w-walks into a club where you're tending b-bar can't take his eyes off you. You're the first m-man they look at, the first one they ch-check out. After that, they m-measure everyone else against the standard you s-s-set." Scott took a deep breath and pushed on. "They might leave with another g-guy, but I'll bet you're the one most of them are th-thinking about when they c-c-come."

So what the hell are you doing with me?

The thought seeped into Scott's mind unbidden, sliding along the all too familiar channels in his thought processes; the ones that were years old and would probably never disappear completely.

Scott shook his head, struggling to turn those thoughts around and force them to retreat. Joe wanted him. He'd made that clear in every possible way. Joe wouldn't be with him unless he wanted him. He didn't screw men he didn't want. And he wanted Scott to believe that.

"I think you're projecting, Scottie."

Scott lifted his gaze slightly and frowned at the T-shirt material covering Joe's abs. "W-What?"

A hand appeared at the edge of Scott's vision. Before he could react, Joe's fingers were already on his throat. His knuckles pressed against the underside of Scott's chin, demanding that he tilt his head back and look Joe in the eye.

"Projecting," Joe repeated.

Scott stared into Joe's eyes, completely incapable of looking away without permission, or of making his brain work.

"You only think that because that's what you did. Because you focused on me, you assume everyone else must have done the same," Joe said. "I'll bet just as many guys were checking you out."

Scott tried to shake his head, but Joe caught hold of his chin, making that impossible.

"I'm right." When Joe sounded that confident, it was hard to argue, but Scott fought against every instinct and made the effort.

"Maybe I'm not the only one who's projecting?"

Joe grinned. That had to mean he wasn't mad at Scott for disagreeing with him, didn't it? Scott smiled his relief back at Joe.

Without any warning, Joe dipped his head and brought their lips together. Scott's smile disappeared as the kiss instantly took complete control of his world. Without any hesitation, he tipped back his head, parted his lips, and gave himself over to Joe in every way he knew how.

Every one of his senses came alive. Gripping Joe's biceps through his T-shirt sleeves, Scott let his thoughts slip away; the better to focus upon what he felt. There was no need for him to think about anything, no need for him to worry about anything.

He was under Joe's control now. Worrying was Joe's responsibility. There was only one thing Scott needed to do, and that was please Joe.

Arching his back, Scott pressed his body against Joe's more muscular frame. He felt Joe's erection through his jeans as he thrust against him. As wonderful as Joe's clothes felt as they rubbed against his bare skin, rough and gorgeous and so very Joe, Scott couldn't help but wish he was thrusting against bare skin instead.

Scott whimpered, a low needy sound that came from the very depth of his soul.

Joe slid his arms around Scott and held him even tighter. His hands were strong and confident against Scott's back. When they grabbed hold of Scott's arse, they were even better.

Scott imagined that Joe's hands would leave beautiful red marks in their wake, just like the crop had the previous week. Until he'd been spanked — first by Joe's bare hand, and then with the crop — Scott hadn't realised how wonderful wearing a lover's marks under his skin could be. Now, he longed for it to happen again and again.

As the seconds ticked by, Scott became vaguely aware that he was being led somewhere, but that wasn't important enough to make him take any of his attention away from the kiss. They weren't in a club where anything went. Joe probably wasn't walking him out of his flat and into a public part of the building.

He was most likely taking him into his bedroom. Considering that was the only furnished room in the flat, Scott had to consider that a good thing.

And Scott's guess was right. By the time Joe lifted his head and ended the kiss, they were standing in his bedroom. Scott looked from the rows of toys on the walls to the big double bed. The flat screen TV was gone.

Scott tried to focus on the remaining contents of the room. Nothing else had appeared to take the screen's place, but the kit on the wall had to represent more than enough entertainment to last a lifetime.

Crops. Whips. Paddles.

Gags. Cuffs. Hoods.

Scott had no idea if Joe had anything particular in mind for them that evening, but he had complete faith in Joe being able to make it one of the most erotic nights of his life. He glanced up at Joe through his lashes.

For once, Joe didn't rush to announce his plans. His expression remained unreadable. He didn't say anything; he just stared down at Scott in return.

If Joe was looking for some particular bit of information to be offered up to him, Scott had no idea what it could be. Joe not instantly stepping up to the plate to take charge felt odd.

As one silent minute slipped into another, it

seemed more and more like Joe was waiting for him to do or say something.

Scott took a deep breath. He had to at least try to give Joe something. Everything Joe had said about him being more confident and more certain his submission would be well received came back to the front of his mind.

"So," Scott said, in as close to a flirtatious tone as he had ever managed in his life. "Are you g-going to screw me now?"

"No." There was nothing flirtatious in Joe's tone. He was all seriousness.

For several seconds, Scott was sure he had tripped over some unspoken rule that meant submissives weren't supposed to ask questions like that.

Maybe it had sounded like he was demanding sex from Joe? Or perhaps it had seemed like he thought that he was the one who should decide what happened between them, and when? Scott's heart raced faster and faster. Maybe—?

The thought died unfinished as Joe finally spoke up. "Tonight, Scottie, you're the one who's going to screw me."

* * * * *

"I don't want to be a dom!"

Joe had mentally prepared himself to deal with a few different reactions, but that was one he'd completely failed to anticipate. All the stress that had been building in him through the day dissolved.

Laughter bubbled up inside Joe, more from a

348

combination of relief and the realisation that he'd been an idiot to imagine Scott would react in any other way, than from amusement, but it still felt wonderful to let it out.

Scott's look of horror faded. A small, self-mocking smile appeared in its place. He joined in with Joe's laughter. "You r-really had me g-g-going there! For a s-second I actually thought you were s-serious."

"I was. I still am."

Joe's laughter trailed off into a chuckle before drawing to a perfectly natural conclusion. Scott's laughter cut out as if something had pressed a mute button.

It was several seconds before Scott found the remote and was able to break the silence. "P-pardon?"

"I was serious," Joe repeated. "And I still am — perfectly serious." He stepped forward.

Scott already stood close to the bedroom wall. One step back and he was pressed firmly against the paintwork.

Joe placed his hands on the wall either side of Scott's shoulders. Dipping his head, he brought his lips to Scott's ear.

"You are going to screw me, sweetheart. But don't, for a single moment, think that means you'll be the one giving the orders."

"I...um..." Scott swayed toward Joe and his naked skin rubbed temptingly against Joe's clothes.

Scott's nerves only made Joe more confident that he had made the right decision. As Joe pulled back far enough to study Scott's expression, Scott took a deep breath and tried to calm himself a little.

349

Now that he was trapped safely against the wall, he seemed to find that a far more manageable task.

A minute passed. Scott's attention seemed to focus in on Joe's lips, but Joe couldn't tell if that was because Scott found it so hard to believe what he had just said and was waiting for more words that would explain everything, or because he wanted another kiss. Joe gave him neither.

Another minute of silence.

"Yes, s-sir." For Scott, the words were spoken with surprising tranquillity. That in itself raised a red flag in the most protective part of Joe's mind.

Joe stepped back from Scott and folded his arms across his chest to make sure he didn't reach out to Scott before he should. It would be far too easy to lose focus and make the wrong decision if his senses were alive with the sensation of Scott's skin beneath his hands.

Joe even made himself keep his gaze up on Scott's face, away from all that wonderful naked skin. "Are you just saying that because you think it's what a sub should always say to a dom?"

"More because it always f-feels like the right thing to say to y-you," Scott whispered.

It would have been hard for him to have picked a statement more likely to head straight to Joe's cock, but Joe steeled his resolve and forced at least a little of his blood to aim for his brain rather than his shaft.

"Before tonight, have you ever thought about screwing me?" he asked.

Scott shifted his weight nervously onto the balls of his feet and back. The movement made Joe look momentarily down, and Scott's erection bob temptingly.

"It's not a trick question," Joe promised, dragging his gaze back up to Scott's eyes.

Scott gave a jerky nod. "Yes, I've th-th-thought about it."

Something inside Joe relaxed. He wasn't pushing Scott into doing something he didn't want to do after all. Scott wanted to screw him, and Joe had never imagined he could be so thoroughly overjoyed by finding out a guy wanted to top him.

It wasn't that he'd been worried about making a fool of himself when he announced his plans for the night, of course he hadn't. He wasn't the type. Joe had always done whatever the hell he wanted without worrying about what anyone thought and...and he really wasn't fooling himself with that line of bull anymore.

Things were different with Scott; and whatever way Joe tried to twist the facts, it was bloody fantastic to know that the limb he'd crawled out on wasn't going to be cut off when he least expected it.

Joe allowed himself a small smile. "I've thought about it too." He finally let himself move, but rather than close the gap between himself and Scott, he strode across to his wall of toys. "And I promise you, there wasn't a single scenario that passed through my mind that featured *me* as a sub."

Scott licked his lips. He was still nervous, but now, unless Joe was very much mistaken, that was all due to anticipation. Scott's only concern now revolved around finding out which toy Joe intended to introduce him to.

Joe ran his palm over a paddle. His fingers flirted with a whip. Scott would love them—their session with the crop had left Joe more convinced of that than ever. But, when he finally took an implement down from its hook, it wasn't anything that might fall against Scott's skin and redden his arse.

Scott let out a soft little moan of pleasure as he saw the handcuffs Joe had selected. The moment Joe stepped toward him, he held out his wrists to be cuffed.

"No."

Scott's gaze jerked from the restraints up to Joe's eyes.

"Behind you."

The words had barely had time to leave Joe's lips before Scott turned around and put his hands behind him, offering his wrists close together at the small of his back.

The cuffs weren't the kind sold in the high street sex shops. There was no furry padding around them, no safety release function. When the metal curled around Scott's wrists, it sounded serious. That only seemed fitting to Joe, since he'd never been so serious about a guy. Scott, however, damn near jumped out of his skin.

It only took Joe a moment to have Scott's other hand restrained.

Scott squirmed, instinctively testing his bonds, even though they both knew he'd never actually want to escape them.

"They're not supposed to be comfortable," Joe told him, stepping closer and trapping Scott's hands between their bodies. This time, when he put his lips to Scott's ear, he nipped sharply at the lobe. "They're supposed to remind you who's in charge." As if there could ever be any doubt...

"Y-you are," Scott confirmed, leaning back against Joe without any apparent care for the comfort of his own wrists.

"Smart boy," Joe said. He stepped back. It was only the fact that Joe reached out and caught hold of his arms that kept Scott on his feet once his support was taken away.

"I'm sorr—"

Scott's words cut out with a shocked little gasp when Joe released Scott's left arm and brought his hand down sharply on Scott's naked backside.

"What did I tell you about unnecessary apologies?" Joe asked.

Scott looked over his shoulder and met Joe's gaze. "I..." he frowned. "I'll k-keep working on it?" he hazarded.

"Good idea." Joe grinned as he released his hold on Scott and moved away.

Now very ready to play, Joe pulled his T-shirt over his head and tossed it aside. Stripped to the waist, he sat on the end of his bed to undo his boots.

Scott stood and watched. There wasn't much else he could do while his hands were cuffed behind his back. Joe tugged one boot off and set it aside.

There were certain things that were difficult to ignore, no matter how determined a man was to forget about them, or how engrossed he was with his lover. The way the plug that Joe had lodged in his arse shifted around when he sat down was one of his top ten in that category. The way it moved when he leaned forward and untied his laces was right up there, too.

Boots and socks off, Joe stood up and undid his fly.

The messages his prostate sent shooting through his body were an unfamiliar distraction. That was his only excuse for not realising that Scott had moved until Scott was already down on his knees, positioned directly in front of him with his mouth open.

Joe's jeans were still around his hips, his cock barely exposed, but he abandoned all thought of undressing further. Priorities were priorities. He nodded his permission.

Scott shuffled forward. The first kiss he placed upon the tip of Joe's cock was very gentle, almost chaste, but any idea of anyone ever being pure or innocent died the moment Scott wrapped his lips around the shaft.

Internal muscles that weren't entirely under Joe's conscious control tensed. The plug pressed ever more firmly against Joe's prostate.

Scott sucked around Joe's cock as he dipped his head forward; his tongue did fantastic things against every inch of flesh that slid past his lips.

Joe put one hand on Scott's shoulder, although he wasn't sure which of them he thought needed steadying. His other hand went to Scott's hair. Sliding his fingers through the thick blond strands, Joe took up a tight grip on them. He made no attempt to influence anything Scott did, but as Scott tipped back his head and peeked up at him through his lashes, they both knew that Joe could assume control at any time, and that Scott would obey his every whim.

Scott dropped his gaze. He moaned as he dipped his head again before slowly pulling back. His lips thinned into little more than a pale pink line as he sent wave after wave of pleasure crashing through Joe. Each rolling wall of white water battered at his defences, tempting him to make everything very simple and just come in Scott's mouth.

Sirens blared through Joe's mind, warning him that he had to run for higher ground if he didn't want to be swept away by the tide. Joe ignored all that and stayed right where he was. Scott was going to get the time he needed in order to find his proper headspace and reassure himself that everything was still the same between them as it had always been. Every other consideration was secondary.

Joe would never deny that he thoroughly enjoyed every sensation that Scott offered him. But, the moment he sensed Scott was ready for other things, Joe tugged on Scott's hair, pulled Scott's mouth away from his cock, and dragged him up onto his feet.

One kiss was all Joe allowed by way of transition from one part of the night into another; and he barely gave Scott time to gasp against his mouth before he took another treat from his lips.

Scott made a soft, disappointed, sound in the back of his throat, but he voiced no actual complaint.

Joe quickly kicked off his jeans. He was building up momentum now. He didn't hesitate before he snatched up the supplies on his bed-side cabinet. Tearing open a condom wrapper, he deftly sheathed Scott's cock with the thin latex.

Their eyes met as he looked up from his task.

With his hair mussed, his eyes slightly unfocused by pleasure, and his cock ready to go, Scott looked as gorgeous as ever, but as wary as ever too.

"You've topped before?" Joe asked.

Scott nodded.

"Topped a dom before?" he specified.

Scott swallowed rapidly and shook his head.

"I know what I'm doing," Joe promised.

Scott relaxed, but only a fraction. His shoulders remained tense. Behind his back, Joe was sure Scott's hands were clenched into nervous fists. "You've d-done this before, sir?"

The sir was a nice touch, Joe thought. Being asked to top had only made Scott more determined to remind the world that he was a sub through and through; as if who topped could really make any difference to any of that.

Joe smiled down at Scott. Yep, in so many ways, Scott was still as innocent as hell.

* * * * *

"I've occasionally had a sub top me in the past," Joe said, but his tone made it sound like he was thinking far more than the words relayed.

Scott studied his expression very carefully. Joe smiled far more often now than he had when Scott had only known him from the clubs, but he still didn't let his emotions show easily. A man had to seek out little hints if he wanted to know how Joe might feel about the world around him, but Scott was tentatively beginning to consider himself a master of that art.

Joe's lips twitched. His eyes sparkled a little more brightly than usual. For some reason, he seemed to find Scott's question amusing.

"It's not something I want all the time," Joe went on. "But being topped now and again can be fun. Even for a dom."

"I d-didn't mean any off—"

A shake of Joe's head cut Scott short. "None taken." He wrapped his fingers around Scott's cock.

That settled the matter. An offended man would never want to stroke so much pleasure into a guy's erection. Scott moaned. Unable to fight against a rush of pure instinct, he pushed his shaft more firmly into Joe's fist.

As suddenly as Joe's hand had arrived in Scott's world, it vanished. Scott hadn't realised he'd closed his eyes until he found himself opening them again. He blinked at Joe, then looked down and saw the lube covering the condom.

There never had been a hand job on offer.

Scott took a deep breath and let it out very slowly. No, there was no hand job; Joe was offering him his arse instead.

Scott hadn't lied when he said he'd fantasised about topping Joe, but the idea had been so insubstantial in his mind, a pure fantasy. He'd wondered about it the same way he daydreamed about what it felt like to fly or be able to breathe underwater. He'd never actually considered that Joe would allow anyone, let alone permit *him* to—

Every thought vanished from within Scott's head as he watched Joe calmly reach behind himself and withdraw a large butt plug from within his hole. It was impossible to tell how long he'd been wearing it, but it had obviously been there since before Scott arrived at his apartment.

It had been there while they kissed, and while he sucked on Joe's cock. The whole time they'd been standing there, Joe's arse had been filled by the shiny black plastic and —

"Get on the bed."

Subjected to far too many surprise attacks, Scott's mind simply gave up. His body took over complete control. That was a good thing.

It was far easier to let his brain concentrate on simply filing everything away in his memory, so that he'd be able to look back upon it all later, assess everything, and work out whatever the hell it all meant, when he was alone.

For now, bodily obedience was all he needed. Clumsy with his hands still tied behind his back, Scott scrambled onto the bed.

The mattress dipped as Joe joined him. Scott remained kneeling in the centre of the bed, waiting for another command.

Joe moved with complete confidence. Scott couldn't help but admire that, as well as the large amount of naked skin Joe was favouring him with that night, of course. Each of Joe's muscles was beautifully defined — especially those under his tattoo. They bunched and shifted beneath his skin as Joe moved across Scott's line of sight and knelt facing the headboard.

The mirror. Suddenly, Scott understood both its purpose and its position. Their eyes met in the reflection, just as they had in the sauna, but this time their positions were reversed.

Without even saying a word, Joe seemed to call Scott closer. By the time Joe had settled his hands comfortably on the thick black metal rail that ran across the top of his headboard, Scott had shuffled forward far enough to kneel between Joe's comfortably spread legs.

Unable to hold Joe's gaze a moment longer, Scott looked down. His cock was achingly hard. It rose away from his body pointing straight toward the cleft between Joe's buttocks. The condom was uncoloured, the flushed skin of his cock clearly visible through it.

He'd shaved before coming to meet Joe, and not just his face. As always, Scott's crotch was primed to be as vulnerable and sensitive as possible. From his hairless groin, Scott's attention moved to Joe's lubed-up hole.

Joe hadn't shaved. From the stubble on his jaw to the fine dark hairs that surrounded his hole, he was a perfect contrast to Scott.

No. Screw contrasts, Joe was just perfect.

Scott's hips thrust forward without consulting his brain. Luckily, their bodies were still separated by several inches of empty air. There was no way he could get his cock inside Joe from where he knelt, no matter how desperate he was. And that was good, because some things could never be attempted without a clear invitation, without an outright command, to ease their way.

Still, unable to keep his frustration to himself, Scott whimpered with need. His cock begged to be sheathed inside Joe, and part of Scott knew that the only way he could make that happen was to share his feelings with Joe. Scott tensed all his muscles. His hands formed into tight fists as he pulled at his cuffs.

Joe reached back with one hand and wrapped his fingers around Scott's cock. He didn't stroke, he didn't tease, but it was still all Scott could do to stop himself from coming from Joe's firm, confident touch.

Scott shuffled forward, as Joe guided him closer to his arse. The tip of Scott's cock brushed against Joe's hole. He groaned, desperate to thrust forward and bury himself inside Joe's body, but his submission won out and overruled every kind of physical need. Scott didn't make any kind of movement that wasn't suggested by Joe's touch.

"Look in the mirror."

Their gazes locked the moment Scott looked up, and Scott found himself unable to turn away.

Joe tugged him forward another fraction of an inch. Scott longed to look down, but he didn't dare do that without Joe's permission. Hell, he barely dared to breathe without a clear order.

Little by little, Joe drew Scott closer until the tip of Scott's cock pushed against the firm ring of muscle around his hole. Then, without Scott making any movement of his own volition, he suddenly found the first inch of his cock buried inside Joe's hole — inside his master's arse.

Scott arched his back. Every muscle in his body trembled. Joe was tight and hot and perfect, and maybe even more than that — the dominance shining in Joe's eyes didn't waver for a second. Scott gasped, desperately trying to remain still; although he had no idea if that was in consideration of Joe, who might well appreciate a moment to adjust and relax around him, or in simple obedience of his master.

Yet, at the same time, he knew that if Joe ordered him to move, good manners would go out the window. Staring into Joe's eyes, Scott could only submit to Joe's decisions and trust that he'd make the right ones for them both.

"That's right, Scottie," Joe praised. His voice was rough and pleasure hung from every syllable. "You're doing fine."

A wave of relief mixed with bliss swept through Scott's body, and almost prompted him to move. He resisted until Joe nodded, just once.

Scott didn't need to ask what permission Joe was granting him with the gesture. Still staring into Joe's eyes, Scott pushed forward. Inch by inch he slid his erection deeper into Joe's body. It felt like centuries since he'd felt that tight, hot, sensation wrap around his shaft, and there was nothing like it in the world.

As his hips came to rest against Joe's buttocks, Scott had no choice but to still, barely able to catch his breath.

Part of him wished there was some sort of chastity device he could ask to wear. Even if he hadn't already given Joe his solemn word that he wouldn't come without permission, Scott knew an accidental orgasm simply wasn't an option tonight. An early climax when Joe was topping might have annoyed Joe, but it probably wouldn't have completely ruined things for him.

Coming too soon when he was actually

topping... Scott whimpered. The consequences didn't bear thinking about.

He took another deep breath, only to let it out as a heartfelt moan, when Joe clenched and relaxed his muscles around him. It felt so good, but he couldn't allow himself to dwell on that, couldn't permit himself to really feel the offered ecstasy.

In the mirror's reflection, Joe nodded again.

Concentrating very carefully, Scott pulled back. Cold air caressed skin that had quickly grown to love the body heat that had encircled it. Every cell in Scott's body screamed that he needed to get his cock back inside Joe.

He lurched clumsily forward. Joe's gaze never wavered. Several jerky thrusts later, Scott saw Joe's expression change.

"Stop."

Scott froze. Even his heart failed to beat and panic bubbled up inside him.

Joe shifted his position, making his internal muscles do wonderful things around Scott's erection. Moving his right hand away from the headboard, Joe reached back. For a horrible moment, Scott thought Joe intended to push him away, but Joe's hand came to rest on Scott's side.

"Just follow me."

With the slightest pressure of his hand, Joe guided Scott's whole body forward, then back again. Scott made three thrusts that were no better than those that had gone before. Closing his eyes, he concentrated upon Joe's hand with every scrap of energy at his disposal.

Slowly, as if there were some strange and

primitive magic at work, he felt his muscles relax. As the tension left him, it became far easier for him to follow Joe's lead. His thrusts gradually became smooth, almost graceful.

"That's right."

Joe sounded just as in control of the world as ever, just as dominant as any man could ever be.

"That's exactly what I want from you."

And, somehow, those last few words made everything come into focus inside Scott's head. This wasn't about him and his cock, any more than it was about his tongue or his mouth when he sucked Joe off.

He wasn't topping, not really. He was simply using a part of his body to make his master happy and nothing could be more natural or right than that. All he had to do was concentrate on pleasing Joe, and everything would be fine.

Scott opened his eyes. He barely noticed when Joe dropped his hand away from his side a minute later. His attention was all on Joe's face as he fought to work out what sort of movements would please Joe best.

"Perfect," Joe whispered.

Scott's soul sung out in ecstasy at the praise and he thrust into Joe again.

* * * * *

Joe bit back a groan. He managed to keep his head up and his attention focused on Scott's reflection, but even that little modicum of self-control took more and more effort to maintain by the moment.

Scott had found his rhythm now. Apparently, he'd found his confidence too. His thrusts were strong and determined — and every damn one of them connected with Joe's prostate.

Joe had already let his hand drop away from Scott's side. Scott didn't need that kind of help anymore. But Joe would have been more willing to cut off his hand than return it to the bed frame.

Joe wrapped his fist around his cock and roughly stroked himself in counterpoint to Scott's well-paced thrusts. The joy pounding through his veins doubled over and over again. He hadn't indulged in this particular side of the game for so long, hadn't felt the need to, hadn't found anyone he wanted to do it with.

Scott moaned, a sound crammed full of both frustration and desire. Joe lifted his gaze back to the reflection. Scott was once more staring obediently into the mirror. Such a good submissive…

His desire to serve his dom and put his own pleasure last hadn't changed just because he was topping rather than bottoming. If anything, it seemed to have made that instinct even stronger. Joe's certainty that he had made the right decision when he planned out their scene for that night grew stronger than ever.

He saw in Scott's gaze that Scott hadn't missed the fact that Joe was allowed to jack himself off while he was being topped. Joe didn't need anyone's permission to do that. He didn't need to wait until someone else offered him a hand or an order. Joe was free to come whenever he wanted and by whatever means he chose.

The fact that everything they did that night was something happening for Joe's pleasure rather than because he wanted to give Scott a special treat seemed to sink a little more deeply into Scott's mind. His peaceful acceptance of that lit the last little firework of bliss that Joe needed to push him over the edge.

Joe yelled out as he came, his hand working his cock more and more rapidly as he spilled across the sheet beneath him. It was so easy to forget just how different it felt to be topped, when it had been so long since the depth of someone's submission inspired his desire to feel another man's cock inside him.

The spikes of ecstasy that strummed through Joe's veins hit different notes, the pitch it sung at was higher, the waves and vibrations of bliss that coursed through his body were far more rapid.

Joe tried to catch hold of the melody and work out exactly how it differed from the joys of topping another man, but it danced away from him, leaving him gasping, his grip on both his cock and his headboard white-knuckled.

Head bowed, Joe forced great gulps of air into his lungs. A full minute passed before he straightened up and could look in the mirror. Scott's eyes were closed very tightly, his face a picture of concentration as he bit down hard on his bottom lip.

Joe licked his own lips. He had no doubt Scott had broken his skin in his effort to control himself and not to come. Even though there was no earthly way he could twist around and bring their mouths together, Joe swore he tasted Scott's blood.

"Scott." His voice was gruff with satisfaction; the word was damn near barked out. "Look up."

Scott did as he was told. His eyes opened very wide, his terror of coming without permission shining brightly for anyone to see.

It was an easy fear to cure.

"Come." Joe held Scott's gaze as he said it.

Relief. Gratitude. Then, every single emotion was wiped away as pure rapture took their place.

Scott's hips bucked. He thrust his cock deep into Joe's arse several times in quick succession. He tossed his head back, screamed, and came. There was no way Scott could reach out and steady either of them. With his hands still cuffed behind his back, he was no more in control of anything than he had been on any of the times Joe topped him.

Joe was the one who kept them steady. He took everything Scott could give him without showing any reaction, and didn't move a single inch until Scott eventually fell still.

Keeping a careful check on Scott each step of the way, Joe separated their bodies. Scott's only contribution involved slumping back to sit on his heels in the middle of the mattress.

Joe left the bed and tidied himself up. When he turned back to the bed, Scott still hadn't moved.

Sitting on the mattress next to him, and refusing to squirm like a man who'd just been very well screwed, Joe ruffled Scott's hair — that made him look up.

"Hi."

Joe smiled. "Hi yourself," he murmured.

Without another word he removed the used

condom from Scott's cock. Scott didn't say a thing as Joe cleaned him up. When Joe guided him to lie down on the bed, Scott followed his every hint with his usual clumsy willingness, but his brain really didn't seem to be taking any part in the proceedings.

It was only when they lay together that Joe finally undid Scott's cuffs and released his hands.

Moving with obvious caution, Scott brought both his arms in front of his body and warily worked the blood-flow back through them. Within a minute, one hand came to rest against Joe's chest as he curled in closer to him.

Topping really hadn't made him the least bit toppy, but it had given him a strange kind of confidence. Joe was sure Scott would never have dared to snuggle that way at the end of any of their previous scenes – not without a clear order.

Joe happily welcomed Scott into his embrace and, content that all was well with the world, quickly began to doze.

* * * * *

Joe had been fast asleep for almost an hour now.

Scott knew that, if he had any sense, he'd have been as quick to follow Joe's lead in that as he was in everything else. It was already stupid o'clock in the morning. Most of Scott was perfectly willing to curl up and simply forget about anything and everything.

Afterglow danced in his veins; pride at being able to hold back and resist the temptation to come despite very, *very* severe provocation, took up a large portion of his brain.

He'd never imagined anything as erotic as the events of that night. He'd never felt lust like it.

Lust.

Scott sighed to himself.

After pounding so hard that he'd thought it might explode from his chest, Scott's heart had now settled into a slow steady rhythm; not entirely unlike the beat beneath his palm where it rested on Joe's chest.

Hearts.

If only the difference between his heart and Joe's had been to do with something so simple as beat or blood flow. If it had been something like that, perhaps it would have been easier to fix.

Surgeons could do wonderful things these days. Scott had read in the paper only the other day that —

No.

Scott closed his eyes very tightly, but that didn't make the matter any easier to hide from. There was no point avoiding the truth anymore. Denial had been increasingly difficult to maintain the last few weeks. He didn't need a cardiologist. If there were any specialist who could help him, it would be a psychiatrist.

Determined not to wake Joe up, Scott took as deep a breath as he dared and let it out as slowly and as calmly as he knew how.

He couldn't write it off as lust anymore.

Scott was in love with Joe Stuart.

There. He'd said it; only silently and within the confines of his own mind, but still, it had been said.

Scott might have been aware for a long time that he probably liked Joe far more than he should. Lust; he'd been in that with Joe since the first moment he'd set eyes on him. He'd desired him, fantasised about him, longed for him. Scott had done a hell of a lot of things that revolved around the sight, sound, and even scent of Joe.

He just hadn't been willing to fully admit to himself that he was stupid enough to have fallen head over heels for a man like Joe. Even now that he knew he had crash-landed into it, it was impossible for him to pinpoint the specific moment he'd given in to such a foolhardy emotion.

Not just tonight, that was for sure. The last time they'd met up? No, long before that, too. Scott shook his head slightly, causing his cheek to rub against Joe's shoulder.

The one thing Scott was sure of was that the moment he was given the chance to write his next note to Joe couldn't come soon enough.

He knew what he had to write in it. Now, he just had to keep his nerve when he put pen to paper.

Part Thirteen: Post Haste

Halfway through pouring a beer for one of the regulars at the club, Joe glanced up. Scott was standing just two yards down the bar. Joe smiled. He could always tell when Scott had arrived. A sixth sense, that he'd never been aware of possessing before he met Scott, drew his attention to him every damn time.

Joe mentally shook his head at himself. A sixth sense? He wasn't even out of his twenties and he was already getting soppy in his old age!

It was probably just the nervous energy that swirled around Scott like an emotional typhoon that pulled Joe's attention, no matter how many drunks and flirts stood between them.

As Joe served drinks, turned down propositions, and brought sloshed customers quickly into line, most of his attention remained on Scott. He seemed even more nervous than usual today. Whatever he'd written in his note had to be a real doozey.

Joe's cock strained against the inside of his fly in anticipation. What would Scott consider extreme?

It was impossible to be certain. There were times when Scott seemed to take the kinkiest of things in his stride and almost managed to act like the kind of subs Joe was used to. But on other occasions, even a chaste little kiss could have Scott blushing and stammering like an inexperienced teenager.

Joe kept doing his job, but he was working

370

almost entirely on automatic pilot now. He'd never in his life been more grateful to be on the early shift. He glanced impatiently at the clock placed discretely under the bar. Finally!

Catching the eye of the other bartender working that night, Joe pointed at his wrist. He wasn't actually wearing a watch, but the guy got the idea and waved goodbye in return.

Joe moved quickly to the other side of the bar. Within moments, he stood right in front of Scott.

Tilting back his head, Scott looked up at him. "Hello, s-sir."

Joe grinned at the honorific. Yeah, Scott was definitely in the mood to get kinky.

Taking Scott by the wrist, Joe headed for a quieter part of the club, so he could read Scott's note and hear what he had to say without the pounding beat from the speakers drowning out every other stuttered word.

Three rooms later, Joe finally found two seats in a cosy little corner that wasn't already occupied by guys making out and scrabbling at each other's flies.

Two high stools stood alongside a bar-height table. Joe hopped up onto a seat and held out his hand.

Scott took his right hand out of his pocket in response, but kept his fist tightly clenched around the envelope he held. He made no attempt to hand it over.

"Scott?"

Scott continued to stare at his hand and the envelope as if completely transfixed by how white his knuckles were and how creased the paper was getting.

"Scott?" Joe repeated.

Nothing. Scott didn't even blink.

Joe frowned. He reached out, intending to grab Scott's shoulder and shake him out of whatever daydream he was lost in.

Scott jerked his head up. His hand disappeared behind his back, taking the envelope with it and hiding it from Joe like a kid who was afraid that the school bully might steal his favourite toy.

"What the hell's got into you tonight?" Joe demanded.

Scott dropped his gaze. Bringing his hand back in front of him, he smoothed the crumpled envelope out against his knee. But Joe didn't miss the fact that Scott's grip on the corner of the letter remained as firm as ever.

Joe's heart raced faster and faster as he tried to work out what was wrong and what had suddenly changed between them. It soon felt like his chest might explode from the sheer pressure behind his pulse.

Joe stopped trying to hide his annoyance. "Scott, start talking," he ordered. "Now."

"Can I ask you f-for a f-f-favour, s-sir?" Scott rushed out.

Was that all? That's what he was so nervous about? "Ask."

Scott swallowed several times in quick succession. "C-c-can we do whatever you w-want tonight instead?"

Joe glanced down at the envelope. "Couldn't make up your mind what to write?" he guessed.

"No. I...I d-did write s-s-something. I j-just..." Scott paused for a deep breath. "I'd r-rather you didn't read it until the end of our d-d-date, if you don't m-mind, sir."

Joe studied Scott for a moment. He was damned if he could work out why, but the thing seemed to be important to Scott. And, for better or worse, that made it important to Joe too.

"Fine." Joe stood up, glad that was all sorted out and dealt with so they could move on to the more enjoyable part of their evening. "You can give it to me at the end of the scene."

"No!" Scott grabbed hold of Joe's arm.

Joe raised an eyebrow at him. "No?"

"I have to g-give it to you now, sir." Desperation filled every syllable. "But, I'd really r-rather you didn't read it s-s-straight away."

Joe held out his hand once more. Scott stared at his empty palm for several seconds before he finally placed the envelope there. The hairs on the back of Joe's neck prickled with unease. He quickly tore open the letter.

Scott's eyes opened very wide, but he made no complaint. He just sat on his stool with a look of pure horror on his face.

Unicorn.

That was it. Just that one word — Scott's safe word. Joe broke it down into syllables, then into single letters, but there was no way to avoid what the word was, to avoid what it meant.

Very slowly, Joe tore his gaze away from the

mangled piece of paper. Scott had gone from one extreme to another. He now had his eyes closed so tightly deep creases appeared at the sides of his face.

"Scott?" Joe thought he sounded very calm, all things considered.

Scott opened his eyes and moved to the edge of his seat. "I'll...B-before I go, can I just s-s-say how much I've enj-j-joyed...how g-g-grateful I am for everything you've—"

"Wait." Joe held up a hand. "Where do you think you're going?"

Scott blinked. "H-home, I—"

"The only place you're going is back to my place with me," Joe cut in.

Scott frowned. "But—"

"But nothing. I'll respect your safe word, Scott. But I'll be damned if I'll let you walk away without a hell of a sight more than this as explanation!" Joe pushed the envelope into his pocket. "Come on."

He took hold of Scott's hand and led him out of the club. Scott made no protest. He didn't even try to hang back. He left his hand in Joe's and meekly followed him through the crowd. He'd never projected a more submissive persona in all the time Joe had known him.

Joe's steps sped up as he noticed other men run their eyes over Scott as he walked passed them. Did one of them have something to do with this? If Scott thought he could wander off just because another dom had propositioned him, just because he thought someone bastard had made some sort of "better offer", then he was going to find out he was very wrong.

374

Joe didn't give up what was his without a fight. And Scott was his. Joe increased his grip on Scott's hand and frantically tried to quell the army of screaming banshees that raced through his head telling him that his relationship with Scott was under threat, that he could lose him.

Joe shook his head.

No. That wasn't going to happen.

Scott was his, and Scott was going to stay his.

* * * * *

As Joe slammed the door to his flat behind them, Scott pushed his hands into his pockets and shuffled his feet. He had no idea what to do next, no idea what Joe expected from him. He didn't even have an order to follow.

The silence was unbearable. "I'm s-sor—"

"No."

Scott met Joe's eyes for a moment, then looked quickly away, hating the anger he saw there, hating himself for being the focus of it.

"Don't apologise for using your safe word," Joe corrected. "It's not something a sub *ever* needs to apologise for. That's not the way things work." Joe pushed his hand through his hair. He paced along the corridor before retracing his steps back to Scott's side.

Joe nodded then, as if he'd made a decision. He took hold of Scott's hand and led him into the bedroom without saying a word.

When nudged to do so, Scott sat on the edge of the bed. Joe pulled a chair across the room and sat down facing him. Barely a foot of empty air lingered between their knees, but Scott had never felt further away from Joe.

"We're going to talk. That's all we're going to do," Joe said. "There's nothing to be afraid of."

"I'm not s-scared of you—"

Joe held up a hand. "We're going to talk. And the first thing you're going to tell me is why you wrote your safe word on the note you gave me."

When Joe fell silent, Scott knew that was his cue to start talking.

This. This was the reason why he'd written it down, because all he wanted to say when he sat face to face with Joe was "yes, sir". Scott closed his eyes. Joe wanted an answer from him. He couldn't keep him waiting forever. He had to say something.

"You t-told me that saying my s-safe word would stop everything that was h-h-happening between us."

"And that's what you want?" Joe asked, his tone of voice just slightly off. "For everything to stop?"

"I th-think it would be best," Scott said, unable to manage anything more than a whisper.

"That's not what I asked. Forget about what's best. Is it what you *want*?"

Scott opened his eyes. Joe was leaning forward, his elbows resting on his knees, one fist wrapped around the other. Scott stared down at Joe's hands.

"I w-want…"

A complete hush reigned for what felt like hours. Scott had never realised Joe had so much patience. He'd never realised he could hold his own breath for so long either.

"I'm n-not like you," Scott blurted out, when suffocation was his only option other than some sort of speech.

"Oh?" Joe prompted.

"I've never been able to move from one g-guy to the next without g-g-giving a damn about anyone I s-screw," Scott stammered.

"Good." Joe said it so simply, as if everything was that easy.

"But it's not g-good!"

"It isn't?"

Finally, Scott met Joe's gaze. "N-no. Because...b-because you're y-you and...and I'm m-me, and..."

Joe stared back at Scott, his forehead furrowing. He really didn't seem to get why those two facts alone meant that Scott needed to run for a set of hills as big as the Alps.

Scott ran his hands over his face as he groaned with frustration.

I have to go because I'm falling in love with a man who I know can't possibly love me in return. It was the obvious thing to say, and at the same time, the one thing he couldn't possibly say.

"I n-need to go," Scott muttered, and promptly sealed his lips before any further words could escape.

He pulled himself to his feet and tried to step past Joe, desperate to get out of there before his mouth won out over his brain and he ended up even more humiliated than he already was.

Suddenly, Joe's hands encircled both Scott's wrists. He'd moved so quickly the air must have blurred. He remained in his seat while Scott stood over him. But that didn't make his grip any weaker; it didn't alter his innate dominance either.

"You promised to do whatever I want tonight," Joe said.

Scott frowned down at him in confusion. "W-What?"

"Earlier this evening, you offered to do whatever I want tonight."

Scott blinked. "You said you'd w-wait and open the envelope at the end of the n-n-night." It was impossible to keep the accusation out of his tone. Scott had come so close to having one more perfect evening with him...

"No. You *asked* me to keep the letter for later. You made a request. I just didn't choose to grant it." Joe was silent for a few seconds, as if to let those facts sink into Scott's mind.

Scott nodded his acceptance. Everything Joe had said was accurate after all. Scott had always known that Joe had the final say in anything and everything they did together.

"You also made me an offer, which I accepted," Joe reminded him.

"Anything you w-want tonight," Scott whispered.

"Yes."

Scott nodded again, a little more jerkily this time. They were going to have breakup sex. That was good. He could do this. It would be everything that he had hoped would happen. It would just take place in a different order.

He was still going to get to be with Joe one last time — that was the important thing.

Scott nodded for a third time.

Then, as if it had been waiting in the wings, hopping from foot to foot in its eagerness to make its entrance, the peaceful feeling that Scott had only ever experienced when Joe took control of him raced onto the stage and stepped into the limelight. Scott had done his research. The internet called the feeling subspace. Scott called it paradise.

The whole world took a step back, leaving just Scott and Joe. There were no decisions to be made now; no choices to agonise over. It was just him and Joe. And, if the occasional choice did crop up, Scott knew someone who would be more than happy to take it off his hands.

"Tell me what you w-want me to do, s-sir?" Scott asked.

Joe leaned back in his seat and smiled up at him — so calm, so confident. Releasing Scott's wrists, Joe rested his hands on his thighs. Joe wasn't hard. Scott looked down to double-check and be sure. For almost the first time, other than when they'd just had sex, Joe wasn't turned on.

That situation had to be remedied; preferably before panic completely overtook Scott's psyche. Luckily, Scott knew just what to do to bring the world back to where it should be. There was one thing that Joe had always enjoyed receiving from him, right from that first time Scott had climbed behind the bar at the club.

Scott dropped to his knees and hurriedly reached for Joe's fly.

Joe didn't stop him. He let Scott undo his jeans and free his cock from behind the well-worn denim.

Scott had never been more grateful that Joe always went commando. Nothing else could get in his way. Dipping his head, Scott touched his lips to the tip of Joe's shaft and worked his tongue beneath the foreskin to tease the glans as he steadied the length with his hands.

Almost immediately, Scott felt Joe's shaft begin to swell and harden within his grip. Relief rushed through him. Everything would be okay now. Somehow, while Joe still got off on the way Scott went down on him, the world would keep turning on its axis and the seasons would pass just as they always had.

Closing his eyes, Scott pushed away any thought of what would happen to him after he left Joe's flat at the end of the night. This was his last chance to enjoy himself with Joe. He wasn't going to waste it worrying.

* * * * *

Joe stared down at the top of Scott's head. *Scott doesn't want to submit to me anymore.* The thought scrolled around and around in his mind. *Scott doesn't want to submit to me anymore.*

Joe frowned as confusion clouded in around the thought and made it blur. Scott certainly wasn't going down on him like a man who was even the slightest bit unenthusiastic about his task.

Just at that moment, Scott let out a whimper filled with pleasure and longing. As far as Joe could tell, Scott still thrived on being on his knees in front of him. Joe had always trusted his instincts regarding a man's desire to submit to him before, but now...

Reaching out, Joe ran his fingers through Scott's hair. He tugged firmly at the strands, encouraging Scott to tilt back his head and open his eyes, without taking his mouth from around Joe's shaft. Right on cue, Scott blinked up at him; big blue eyes sparkling with need and lust. Looking at him, any man would think nothing had changed between them; that everything was right and as it should be with the universe.

But, whoever thought that, they'd be wrong. Joe knew that nothing was right anywhere, anymore.

"God, you're beautiful." Joe hadn't intended to let those words out. They escaped from between his lips without his permission; his lack of control over the situation apparently ruining his control over his own voice box as well.

Scott glanced down for a moment.

Was that the problem? Joe's mind raced faster and faster as he scrambled to work it out. Was he being too soft, too romantic with him? Maybe Scott didn't think it was right for a dom to act that way with his sub. Maybe he just wanted straight forward sex and orders from him. Maybe he should never have let Scott top him. Did Scott think that an occasional desire to bottom to another guy made him less of a dom, less of a "real man"?

Joe stared into Scott's eyes as Scott looked back up at him. The pleasure Scott coaxed into him with every dip of his head didn't make it any easier for Joe to think clearly.

Scott's tongue flicked rapidly against the tip of Joe's cock, making him groan and tighten his grip on

Scott's hair.

Tell me what you want.

Somehow, Joe regained enough control over his voice box to keep the words inside his head. He'd always known that Scott wasn't the kind of man who'd be able to tell him what he wanted directly. He could hardly blame Scott for being the same man he'd always been.

No, Scott hadn't changed; Joe was the one who suddenly found himself acting in ways he never would have believed possible just a few months ago. Soppy dates. Snuggling. Spending the night. Admitting to occasionally enjoying catching as well as pitching...

Joe took a deep breath.

Scott didn't need to fix whatever had gone wrong between them. Joe was the dom; he had to be the one to sort it out. He had to find a way to make sure Scott wanted nothing more than to belong to him for the rest of his life.

Scott lowered his head, taking Joe's erection almost all the way to the base. As he pulled back, he caressed Joe's cock with his tongue, right up to the tip. On any other day, after a long shift at the bar dealing with idiots, Joe knew he'd have been quite content to lean back and simply enjoy watching the way Scott knelt and damn near worshiped his cock.

It wasn't any other day.

Action was required. Joe wasn't sure what sort of action; but that had never stopped him throwing himself into the first idea that arrived in his head before. Now was no time to be either sensible or cautious.

"That's enough." Joe pulled at Scott's hair, just to reinforce the order.

Scott glanced up at him through his lashes but, instead of lifting his head, he tried to keep it over Joe's lap and continue to work his mouth around his shaft. Joe glared down at him. Scott had kept his hands resting neatly on Joe's legs from the moment Joe's erection had stiffened enough not to need support. Now, Scott's grip on his thighs tightened, as if he actually intended to wrestle with him.

That was a bad idea. Joe knew that grappling with a man whose teeth were in such close proximity to his cock was bound to end badly. Yet, even primitive self-interest couldn't compete with Joe's need to take control, with his desire for Scott to know that he was in control.

He tugged harder on Scott's hair. "Do as you're told!"

Scott suddenly quit struggling. He brought his mouth up off Joe's cock and rose to crouch rather than kneel before him.

His surrender was too sudden. Joe didn't realise he'd won the battle quickly enough. He kept trying to drag Scott backward.

Scott tumbled off his feet. Springing from his chair, Joe caught hold of Scott's arms and tried to hold him up.

Momentum conspired with gravity. They landed with a thud so loud the downstairs neighbours were bound to complain about it next time Joe saw them.

Quickly recovering from his shock, Scott rolled and twisted around, trying to get out from underneath Joe's heavier bulk.

"Are you hurt?" Joe demanded.

"N-no, I just—"

"Then stay still."

Scott's brow furrowed. He parted his lips to question Joe's authority again.

Yes, that was the problem. Joe had been far too easy going with him. There had been too many attempts at romance and not enough statements of dominance. Well, at least that was something Joe knew how to correct.

He brought his mouth down against Scott's lips in a kiss that had nothing to do with gentleness and didn't give a damn about nice polite little social forms.

A primal urge to stake his claim rushed to the fore. He pressed down harder against Scott, crushing his body against the floor.

Scott whimpered. Joe tensed. He almost pulled back, just a fraction; just far enough to growl a question at him, to make sure he was okay and was able to keep up.

But without any warning, any need to check in with Scott disappeared. Scott grabbed hold of Joe's biceps and tugged at them, trying to pull him down even harder against him, as if there was some way they could get closer together without obliterating all the laws of physics, and quite a few laws of biology too.

Lube rested in Joe's bedside cabinet. There were condoms in good supply throughout his flat. However, things like that required control and coordination. They needed a dom to be able to focus and take time and care while preparing his sub.

Joe didn't want to be careful. He didn't have it in him to waste another second. He caught hold of one of Scott's wrists with one hand and pinned it to the floor alongside the base of his bed. At the same time, Joe slid his other hand between their bodies and fumbled with Scott's fly.

Years passed before he finally managed to free Scott's erection from both his jeans and his boxers. The fact he was still turned on was reassuring, but Joe only registered that for a fleeting second.

Finally, he was able to get what he wanted. He let out a moan, filled with both triumph and pleasure, as he wrapped his fingers around both their erections and held them tightly together.

* * * * *

Pure electrical heat shot through Scott as Joe thrust his cock against the underside of his erection. Pre-cum slicked their movements, but it did little to counteract the strength of Joe's grip. There was nothing soft and gentle about him now.

Scott tried to arch up off the floor, but there was barely room for him to breathe, let alone move. Joe had him pinned down more effectively than any wrestler playing about on a mat ever could have — possibly because the hold he had on his cock would have been illegal in even the most liberal of gyms.

Whimpering with need, Scott gave up trying to keep pace with Joe's kiss. He simply let Joe do whatever he pleased with every part of his body, acknowledging that Joe owned him completely. An extra jolt of endorphins shook Scott's world. This, this was what he needed; it was what made him whole.

Scott closed his eyes very tightly as the knowledge of how quickly he was going to lose it all almost made him miss out on enjoying what little time he had left. He clawed at Joe's shoulder with his free hand. In some far off place, fabric ripped, but it was hard to care about that while Joe was stroking their cocks even faster.

Coming too soon would ruin everything. Scott pressed his head painfully back against the floor in an effort to take his mind off his helpless need to come. It was no good. Scott squirmed, unsure if Joe would be more angry with him for pulling away, or for giving in to the pure perfection that tempted him to orgasm without permission.

Joe gasped into the kiss. He thrust down against Scott. Semen landed against Scott's skin, a droplet hit the head of his cock. Restraint became impossible. Scott came, just a moment after Joe.

Adrenaline rushed through him like a tidal wave. He clung on to Joe's shoulder even tighter, as if Joe might somehow be able to keep him afloat through the tsunami. Scott moaned, gasping for breath, as his lungs cried out for air, but pleasure continued to cascade through him and there was no escape.

Finally, he collapsed back against the floor, completely spent, unable to move a single muscle, as the tide receded. Just one part of him remained tensed — his right hand still gripped Joe's shoulder as if his life depended upon it. Scott was as incapable of unfurling his fingers as he was of doing anything else.

Joe was so much stronger than him; he was so much better a man than Scott could ever hope to be. Scott already knew that, but Joe proved it again when he recovered the ability to control his limbs long before Scott could even open his eyes.

Joe didn't release his grip on Scott's wrist, but he rolled off him and made it easier for Scott to breathe. Joe took his hand away from their cocks. Scott closed his eyes tighter, sure Joe's next movement would involve standing up and leaving him collapsed on the floor forever.

Something moved against Scott's stomach. He frowned, unable to immediately recognise what it was or what it might mean for his remaining time with Joe.

Fingers. A hand pressing against him. Circles. Cum?

"S-sir?" Scott managed to whisper.

"What?" Joe sounded completely composed and in control of his voice.

It was all Scott could do to make his words vaguely audible. "Are you r-rubbing your c-cum into me?" he rasped out.

"Yes."

"Why?" Scott finally asked, when it became obvious that no further information would be forthcoming unless he anted up and requested it.

"Why not?"

It was a childish question, but it was also one that Scott found difficult to answer. *Because I'm not going to belong to you once this scene ends.* There was no way he'd ever be able to say those words out loud.

Scott swallowed. Conscious that he was

probably wasting a very beautiful sight, he forced his eyes open. For several seconds, his vision remained hazy. When Scott finally focused, his eyes fell upon Joe's forearm.

Scott dragged his gaze up. He reached the edge of Joe's T-shirt sleeve. The fabric was black, just like almost every item Joe seemed to own. It was also torn.

Scott jerked and tried to sit up, only to stop short when Joe completely failed to release his wrist. Unable to become double-jointed at a whim, Scott halted just short of dislocating his shoulder and collapsed back against the floor.

Joe tightened his grip on Scott's wrist. "What the hell do you think you — ?"

"S-sir, your arm!" Scott cut in.

Joe frowned, but Scott couldn't focus on Joe's expression for long. His attention was drawn inexorably back to Joe's shoulder. Out of the corner of his eye, Scott saw Joe turn his head to inspect the area for himself.

Four long scratches broke the skin, travelling from his shoulder to the top of his arm. Joe was bleeding.

Scott had done that to him. He looked down at the nails on his right hand. There was blood beneath them. He'd done that to his master.

Scott's head spun. All the air seemed to race out of the room.

"Whoa there!"

Joe's grip on Scott's wrist disappeared. He'd let him go. Scott couldn't blame him. What kind of submissive would — ?

"Scott!"

Joe's hands moved against Scott's body as he twisted him around and pulled him into another position. Scott didn't struggle against it. All the fight had gone out of him.

The next thing Scott knew, he was partially reclined with his back against Joe's chest while Joe leaned against the side of his bed, his legs extended on either side of Scott's body.

"If you have that much trouble with the sight of even a tiny drop of blood, it's a good idea to warn a guy," Joe said.

Scott tried to turn to face him but Joe held him in place, refusing to allow him to move more than an inch in any direction. One of his arms looped around Scott's waist. Joe put his other hand on Scott's forehead, pulling his head back until it was trapped against his good shoulder.

"Still feeling dizzy?" Joe asked

Scott squinted up at the ceiling in confusion. "I'm f-fine."

"Then you might want to tell that to the skin on your face because you went as white as a sheet the moment you saw blood."

Scott tried to shake his head but Joe wouldn't allow it. "It w-wasn't that. I'm j-just...I know you d-d-don't like to hear me apologise, but it isn't for nothing this time, sir. I'm really s-s-sorry. I don't know w-what I was thinking. I mean, I couldn't have been th-thinking at all. I—"

"Scott, it's just a couple of scratches."

Scott fell silent.

"It's no big deal. Hell, you're making it sound like you broke my cock off or something," Joe said.

"Now, if you did *that*, I probably would be angry."

Scott couldn't help but smile.

"Good boy," Joe said, his voice softer now, almost tender. "That's better."

It was a lovely way to sit, now that Scott knew he hadn't really screwed up. He relaxed back against Joe's chest. It all seemed so peaceful, so glorious.

Then, Joe sighed. The sound cut through Scott's heart as if it had been purposely crafted to do that job. Nothing so wonderful could last forever, but that didn't stop Scott grieving because it came to an end.

* * * * *

"S-sir?"

The sudden uncertainty in Scott's voice only confirmed Joe's suspicions. He held back the urge to sigh again. It was bloody typical that him finding a man he actually wanted to be nice to on occasion, had to coincide with stumbling upon the only sub he'd ever met who didn't want a dom that ever treated him with any sort of tenderness.

Damn, but all those internet stories that hailed complete jerks as the best doms ever, had a lot to answer for! Or the guys in the club who boasted about their conquests — maybe they were to blame. Both gave subs the most stupid ideas.

Joe gritted his teeth and reminded himself that it had to be something like that. Some sort of outside influence had to have corrupted part of Scott's psyche long before they met, because Joe knew he hadn't given Scott any reason to feel as he did.

"Give me a minute or two, and I'll screw you or spank you or something," Joe bit out. "Until then, you're just going to have to sit here and deal with the fact I'm not interested in being a full-on sadist all the time." *And that's no reason for you to say your safe word!*

"W-what?"

"Doms are allowed to take some down-time between rounds," Joe said. "And while I do that, I enjoy keeping track of where you are. So I'm going to hold onto you until we're both ready to kink things up again. It's not snuggling. It's not soppy. It might not be sadistic, but it is dominant, and it's practical!" Joe hoped like hell it sounded less like begging to Scott's ears than his own.

"I d-don't..." Scott frowned over his shoulder at Joe, then shook his head. "I didn't s-say my safe word because I d-don't think you're a good d-d-dom."

"Save it, Scott. I don't need you to pat me on the head and humour me, you just—"

"I'm w-walking away now because I know there is no way in h-h-hell I can c-convince a man like you to keep me around f-forever," Scott cut in.

Joe twisted around, trying to get a better look at Scott's expression. "What?"

"I'm in l-love with you!" The last word was barely out before Scott slapped his hand over his mouth.

Joe stared down at him. "You're dumping me because you're in love with me," he said, carefully enunciating each word to make sure there was no misunderstanding.

Scott nodded, his hand still covering his lips.

Joe had obviously been wrong before. There were ideas that were even more bizarre than the fantasies people posted on the internet. "That makes no sense whatsoever."

"It m-makes perfect sense," Scott said as he lowered his hand. His words came out fast and frantic. "I have to l-l-leave now, while I still h-have the chance."

"The chance?" Joe repeated.

Scott squirmed, as if he intended to make a run for it before he'd even zipped up his fly. "There's no w-way it could work out, s-so—"

"What makes you so damn sure of that?" Joe demanded.

Scott dropped his gaze.

"Well?"

"You're you, s-sir," Scott said.

"And I'm what—incapable of giving a damn about anyone because I'm a dom?" Joe's head ached with trying to change mental tracks and flip the problem he'd thought he was dealing with onto its end.

"No, I d-didn't mean that," Scott rushed to explain. "But you're g-g-gorgeous, and you're always g-going to have a million d-d-different guys throwing themselves at you."

"So, I'm incapable of keeping my fly zipped?" Joe shook his head. "Is that what you think?" He tightened his grip on Scott's torso as his frustration with his inability to track down the true source of Scott's fear threatened to get the better of him.

"I didn't m-mean—" this time Scott cut himself short. He closed his eyes and took a deep breath.

"This isn't anything to d-do with me th-thinking that you're n-not good enough. I know you're the best m-m-man I'll ever lay eyes on, let alone get to spend so m-much time alone with."

He was so rarely that fluent. Joe found that he didn't have the heart to break Scott's flow.

"But, me—I'm not one of those g-guys, sir. I don't know why you've let me play with you so many times, but I know that I'm not really in your l-league." He looked down. "If I let myself fall any f-further than I already have, then I might get my heart broken so b-badly I won't ever be able to put the pieces back together again. And," Scott's voice trembled. "And I c-c-can't risk that, sir. I'm not s-s-strong enough."

He fell silent.

"Done?" Joe checked.

Scott nodded.

"I don't suppose it's ever occurred to you that I might be falling in love with you in return?" Joe asked, with forced calm. A few hours ago, he'd have laughed at the idea of making that confession tonight. Now, it was obvious that keeping it to himself would have been the ultimate cruelty.

Scott frowned. The possibility obviously hadn't even entered his head.

"If you were a dom, you'd get what's so bloody brilliant about you," Joe informed him. "You'd see why I keep coming back for more—why I intend to keep doing that for a hell of a long time to come."

Catching hold of Scott's arm, Joe dragged him around so Scott sat facing him.

"Do you believe me?"

Scott blinked at him. He obviously didn't know what to believe. Joe wasn't the only one who found it hard to turn his perceptions on their heads at a moment's notice. For a few seconds, Joe kept staring at him, as if that would somehow convince Scott to not only say he understood, but to really mean it.

It didn't work.

Joe dropped his hands back to his sides. "I'm not going to insist that you change your mind about anything right now." He paused and considered that statement. He ran his hands through his hair. "I'm not going to insist that you change your mind about anything *at any point*." Yes, that sounded better.

Scott didn't speak up to fill in the silence that followed. Joe couldn't bring himself to be surprised.

"All I'm going to say," Joe eventually went on. "Is that it's my turn to send a note to you, and I fully intend to do that. Understand?"

Very slowly, Scott nodded.

"Good," Joe said. "That's good." He wasn't sure which of them he was trying to convince. It didn't feel good to him. It just felt very slightly less awful than it had before. At least there seemed to be a chance that this wasn't the absolute end.

Joe took a deep breath. Scott sat on the floor in front of him, apparently waiting for Joe to make the next move, as if he fully expected Joe to know what that should be.

Shifting his position, Joe straightened his spine. It wasn't in him to let Scott down by admitting just how lost and clueless he felt.

"Get dressed," he ordered.

Scott pulled himself to his feet and began to

rearrange his clothes. Joe joined him, levering himself up off the floor, pulling up his jeans and tucking himself away.

Cum was smeared against Joe's skin beneath his jeans and T-shirt, but that wasn't something he was inclined to worry about. In fact, it was just the kind of tangible proof of how good things were between them that Joe was desperate to hold onto. It gave him hope that things could go on being good; that there would be a great many more shared orgasms in their futures.

Mere seconds seemed to pass before Scott was ready to leave. In the hallway, Joe forced himself to pick up his jacket.

"You're g-going out?" Scott asked, but he quickly dropped his gaze. "N-n-not that it's any of my b-b-business. S-sorry."

"I'm taking you home."

"You d-don't have to d-do that," Scott rushed out. "I'm f-f-fine and it's r-really—"

"It's not up for debate, Scott," Joe cut in. "I'm taking you home."

Scott seemed about to say something. Possibly, *you no longer have any right to give me orders.* Luckily for Joe, Scott seemed far too polite to actually utter those words.

Joe watched Scott like a hawk all the way from his flat down to the ground floor. It wasn't as if he thought Scott would make a run for it or be beamed up by aliens, but he still couldn't shake off the feeling that everything was at risk. The protective instinct he'd always felt toward Scott went into overdrive.

In the street outside the block of flats, Joe

considered his options. Bike. Car. Bike. Car.

He wanted to cosset and shield Scott from everything and everyone. Car.

But the desire to have Scott pressed tightly against him, for what might still turn out to be the last time…

Joe strode across to his bike. Scott made no complaint about their mode of transport, or about the way Joe brushed aside his hands and insisted on doing up every fastening on Scott's borrowed gear himself.

With both of them properly attired, Joe straddled his bike and nodded to Scott.

As obedient as ever, Scott got on behind him. Just a second later, he slid his arms around Joe's body. Joe let out a silent sigh of relief. He'd always known there was a good reason why he'd never taught Scott to use the grip behind the pillion seat.

Scott's hold on him was as strong as it had ever been, and damn, but it felt good.

Joe pulled away from the kerb and into the light stream of traffic.

There was another good thing about the bike. It made conversation impossible. It meant Joe couldn't say anything stupid on the journey to Scott's place. All he had to do was ride, and enjoy the way every burst of speed caused Scott to cling even more tightly to him.

Joe wasn't sure if Scott's responses signalled fear or excitement, or a mixture of both. Joe only knew how he felt himself. There hadn't been many times in his life when a good ride hadn't been able to put him in a much better mood, but it didn't work tonight. By the time they stopped outside the building where Scott rented a room, Joe was even more pissed off than when they left his flat.

Scott dismounted. When Joe did the same, Scott opened his mouth as if to say something, perhaps to protest. When he saw Joe's expression, he seemed to decide that continued silence was probably a much better option.

Gear removed and stowed away, they walked up to Scott's room side by side. Outside his bedroom door, they stopped and turned to face each other as if they were performing a complex piece of choreography that they'd been practicing for an entire lifetime.

Scott stared at the floor for a long time, but Joe waited him out. Finally, Scott looked up. Their eyes met. Scott looked more lost than Joe had ever seen him; more vulnerable and fragile than Joe would have believed possible.

Joe lifted a hand. He half-expected Scott to flinch away from him, but he remained still as Joe rested his hand upon his cheek before sliding it back to thread his fingers through Scott's hair.

Joe dipped his head. Scott's only reaction was to close his eyes. Joe brushed their lips together. Scott didn't hesitate to part his lips and encourage Joe to deepen the kiss. Tightening his grip on Scott's hair, Joe held him in place and kept the kiss slow and controlled.

He explored Scott's mouth as if he might have to sit an exam on the subject—one he was determined to pass with all colours flying. Their lips lingered together. It took Joe a long time to convince himself to lift his head and break the kiss. When he did, Scott's eyes remained closed.

Joe stood very still, his hand lingering in Scott's hair. The moment Scott opened his eyes and was, in theory at least, able to take care of himself, Joe dropped his hand back to his side, turned on his heel, and walked away.

Down the corridor, out of the shared house, and all the way to his bike, Joe had to force himself not to spin around and retrace his steps up to Scott's room.

Scott would let him in. Scott would let him screw him too; Joe had no doubt about that. It would be so easy for him to ride roughshod over Scott's wishes. Joe started his bike.

Scott wasn't watching him go. Even if he'd wanted to, his room was at the back of the house. But Joe still felt like he could feel Scott's eyes on him as he rode away.

Joe revved up and leaned into a corner. There was a good reason why he hadn't said goodbye when he left Scott at his door. Goodbye meant the end, but this wasn't over, not by a long shot.

Part Fourteen: Yours Faithfully

"Bloody stupid thing to write! Makes me sound like an idiot!" Joe crumpled up a sheet of notepaper and tossed it on the floor alongside his bed. He'd long since given up aiming for the rubbish bin; the damn thing was already overflowing with failed attempts. Crushed rejects littered the bed too— standing out, stark and white against the black cotton sheets.

Joe slumped back against the pillows he'd propped up against his headboard. Closing his eyes, he rubbed at the bridge of his nose with his thumb and forefinger. He'd come up with some pretty inventive ways to torture willing masochists over the years. Almost all of his methods had involved either some kind of leather or a substantial amount of clattering metal chains.

Now, Joe knew that he'd missed a trick. There was apparently no limit to the amount of pain, frustration, or temporary psychosis that could be achieved by giving a man a pen and a piece of blank paper. Even the most experienced pain-slut could be brought to his knees by this.

Joe took a deep breath and let it out very slowly before he realised that he was now copying Scott's method for trying to stave off a panic attack. He immediately straightened up and squared his shoulders.

That was no way for a dom to behave. A sub was allowed to have doubts and let on when he was nervous. A dom had to keep it together. Who could expect anyone to hand over control of his life to a man who couldn't even write a damn letter?

Joe knew what he wanted to say. He knew all the things he had to explain to Scott, and what Scott needed to understand. So why was it so sodding difficult to put those things into words on a page?

More importantly, how the hell was he ever going to talk Scott down off the ledge and convince him to give their…their relationship another shot if he couldn't even put this first part of his plan into action?

Joe shook his head and picked up his notepad one more time.

* * * * *

"H-hello." To Scott's surprise, his voice didn't come out in an embarrassingly squeaky soprano. He almost sounded sane.

Joe turned away from whatever it was he'd been doing behind the bar. The club was closed. Not a single customer stood in front of the long, dark counter. There was no music, no commotion. The silence was eerie. A shiver ran down Scott's spine.

Their eyes met. Joe appeared so serious it would have been scary if he hadn't still looked as hot as hell. Scott swallowed rapidly. Somehow, Joe managed to make a simple black T-shirt and jeans seem like a statement of his ability to do a whole host of very interesting things with leather.

Scott cleared his throat. "Your t-text said you w-w-wanted to see me." And he hadn't been capable of disobeying a summons from Joe. Forget all his careful plans to avoid Joe until his heart had recovered and his cock had learnt how to respond to less intimidating guys. The moment he'd realised who the text was from, Scott had been Joe's to command.

"Sit down." Joe pointed to the far side of the room.

Almost all of the chairs and barstools were up on top of the tables, presumably so the floor could be cleaned more easily. Only one chair remained down; it had obviously been placed there for Scott's use.

Pain stabbed through Scott's mind. Joe couldn't have chosen a seat further away from the bar if he'd tried. To be called close only to be banished to what felt like miles away the very next second—it was hardly the joyous reunion Scott had subconsciously prayed for.

Regardless of the confusion racing through his mind, Scott walked across the room and lowered himself onto the seat. It stood alongside an empty table. Scott rested his hands on it and tried not to fidget. Without saying a word, Joe rounded the bar and headed toward him. Scott's heart rate doubled.

He rose to his feet. "Shall I g-g-get another chair d-down for you?"

"No."

Scott's backside hit the chair again.

Joe came closer still, until he stood directly opposite Scott, on the other side of the small table.

Scott had to tilt back his head to stare up at Joe's face. He looked good, perfect, just as he always did. So calm, so confident, so exactly what Scott wanted and needed in his life...

Reaching into his back pocket, Joe took out an envelope and placed it on the table.

"I—"

"No." Joe held up a hand. "Don't talk. Just read it." He turned on his heel and marched back to his place behind the bar. Even after he'd rounded the long wooden barrier, he kept his back to Scott.

For half a minute, all Scott could do was look from the nape of Joe's neck, to the envelope on the table, and back again. Finally, his gaze settled on the letter and stayed there.

Scott.

The word was scrawled across the front of the envelope, just like most of the other notes Joe had given to him while they'd been playing that silly little game, passing messages back and forth like teenagers in class.

"Don't just sit there, Scott. I told you to read it."

Scott jerked his head up. He looked toward the bar, but Joe still had his back to him. If Joe had snuck a glance in his direction, Scott had missed it.

This time, Joe's order sunk deeper into Scott's mind. He picked up the envelope, opened it, and took the single piece of paper from inside. Closing his eyes, Scott took one more deep breath before forcing himself to obey Joe's command. Read.

He was used to seeing just a few words scattered across the page. Joe wasn't one to waste syllables. He'd never used one word more than was required to get his orders across.

Come to that, during all their time together,

Scott had never noticed Joe paying any particular attention to things like making sure his handwriting was legible. The writing in this message was printed very carefully, as if to make sure there could be no mistaking its contents.

The changes unsettled Scott, but he gradually made himself look at each word in turn rather than the overall picture they created on the page.

Scott,

I'm not big on words. You know that already. I'm not a huge fan of buggering about either. So, here are the facts.

I'm a good dom. Not perfect, but good. I'll set my skills in the playroom against anyone's.

I like being in control. You like being told what to do. We're good together.

You're a great sub. You don't have much confidence, but you have damn fine instincts – and a lot more balls than you give yourself credit for. You've learnt a lot about kink over the last few months, too.

I want you to belong to me. I've wanted that for weeks. If I'd known you thought this was a casual thing for me, I'd have told you that you're a fool a long time ago. I'd have to be an idiot to want to walk away from something as good as we could have together, and I'm no idiot.

If the idea that I wasn't committed to this was the only reason you ran away, great. We're sorted.

I'm not shy about putting on a show, but I'm not the kind of dom who likes to share, so you don't need to worry about me lending you to other guys or any of that bull. And I don't screw around behind my sub's back either; I haven't played with anyone else since we did our first scene.

If there's another reason you're not happy, if there's something else you want, you need to tell me so I can sort it out for you. If there's something you're scared of, spit it out.

So, yeah. Think about it, and tell me what you need.
Yours faithfully,
Joe.

Scott set the letter carefully down on the table.
Yours "faithfully".

It would have sounded weird and formal if Scott hadn't been so sure that Joe meant the word the way it was used everywhere except at the bottom of a letter. Faithful—Joe was promising to be faithful to him.

Scott tried to take a deep breath, but his lungs seemed to shake within his ribcage. The idea of having no relationship with Joe, of never exchanging anything more than a casual hello with Joe, was frightening. Taking a risk and trying to get a real relationship with him was more akin to terrifying.

He ran his fingers over the letter, not re-reading any part of it; just reassuring himself that it was real. Joe had really said all those things to him. This was truly happening, whether he was ready for it or not.

"Well?

Scott jerked to his feet.

Damn, but Joe could walk quietly when he wanted to. He now stood directly opposite Scott, casually drying his hands on one of the cloths he used to wipe down the bar.

When his fingers were dry enough for his satisfaction, Joe slipped the thing through one of the belt loops on his trousers and folded his arms across his chest in that pose Scott loved so much. And Scott just stood there like an idiot.

"Are you going to run away?" Joe demanded.

Scott shook his head.

"Then sit down."

He hadn't been given permission to stand up. Scott's knees buckled the moment he realised that.

"Do you have anything to say?" Joe asked.

Scott cleared his throat and ran his fingers over the letter again as he flattened it out a little more. The envelope had obviously been stored in Joe's pocket for quite some time. The creases were pretty much ironed into it.

"Are you g-going to sit d-d-down?" he blurted out.

Joe glared at Scott for a few seconds before lifting a chair off one of the neighbouring tables, turning it around and straddling it. "Now, talk."

Scott didn't know why he'd thought Joe would be less intimidating while sitting. Joe really didn't need to loom to make Scott as nervous as hell. Between Joe's presence and the contents of the letter, Scott wasn't sure he'd make it through any sort of conversation without having a nervous breakdown.

"Th-thank you, sir," Scott finally blurted out. "For the l-l-letter, I mean." He stared at it for a few moments.

Leaning forward, Joe reached around the back of his chair and set his forearms on the table. "Tell me what you want, Scott. What is it that you need from me in order to stick around and see if we can make this work?"

"I..." Scott closed his eyes. "I d-don't know." He managed to pry his eyes open with great difficulty. "I'm n-not trying to be awkward, s-sir. I don't know w-w-what I need."

Joe stared at him for several long seconds. Scott held his breath as he waited to hear his verdict. When Joe finally spoke, his words were slow and deliberate. "Then, tell me what you want—not for the rest of your life, just for tonight. Tell me what you want at this exact moment."

"You." Scott had never known a question that was easier to answer. He wanted Joe, just as he always had.

"Specifics," Joe ordered. "You want us to have a drink together? You want us to have sex?"

"Anything I c-can—"

"No." Joe slammed his fist down on the table. "What *you* want. Not what you think you deserve, or what you think I want you to want. Just..." He paused for a moment, apparently to pull himself together. "Just tell me what you want us to do together; right here, right now."

"Kiss me." Scott's grip on the edge of the table was so tight his fingers cramped. "I w-want you to k-kiss me. Then I want us to have s-s-sex. I don't care about the d-details. I just want to f-f-feel you against me, to feel you inside m-me. And I want to pretend it d-doesn't matter what happens in the future. Just for one n-n-night, I want to forget to be scared and just b-b-be with you."

He had no idea if he made any sort of sense, or if his rambling would be the straw that broke the camel's back. All he could do was sit there and hope like hell Joe would forgive him for any and all sins he'd committed and decide to screw him anyway.

* * * * *

Joe stood up. The legs of his chair scraped against the freshly mopped floor. Even to his own ears, the sound was loud and harsh. Scott damn near jumped out of his skin.

"Come on. We're going back to your place."

"M-my place?" Scott repeated, blankly.

"Yeah. Your place." Joe walked around the table and pulled Scott's chair out while Scott still sat on it. "Get up." If Scott hadn't obeyed, Joe knew he was capable of picking up the chair and tossing him out of the damn thing, but Scott pulled himself to his feet in time.

Joe guided Scott out of the club and to his car with a firm grip on his elbow. For the first half of the journey toward the house in which Scott rented a room, silence filled the car. Joe tapped his fingers against the steering wheel as he stopped at a set of traffic lights.

"I am *s-s-so* s-s-sorry," Scott suddenly said.

Joe glanced across at him. "For what?"

"I d-don't have any m-more toys than I h-h-had before," Scott rushed out. "If I'd known w-w-we'd be coming back to my place, I c-c-could have—"

"Toys aren't necessary." Joe pulled away from the junction.

"Maybe we c-c-could stop somewhere and I could—"

"Scott," Joe snapped. He took a deep breath

407

and made a point of gentling his voice when he saw how Scott tensed. "It's okay. I've got everything under control."

He stole another glance at Scott just in time to see Scott nod his head. His lips moved as if he was silently repeating those words to himself.

"Everything's going to be fine," Joe told him, with far more confidence than he felt.

"Yes, s-sir."

He sounded so much happier now than he had while trying to explain his relatively toy-less status. Joe smiled to himself—he was the one who'd made Scott feel that way. Pride at that simple accomplishment gave Joe a moment of pleasure, but it didn't last long. As they arrived on Scott's street, Joe had no choice but to focus his entire mind on making this evening go well.

A lucky parking space meant they only had to walk a short distance, but Joe didn't take his eyes off Scott for a second. He only managed to stop short of grabbing hold of Scott's wrist and marching him down the street like a criminal who'd just been arrested, because he knew he didn't have the right to manhandle him right then.

By the time they got to Scott's room, Joe's patience was at breaking point. The memory of the first time he'd visited Scott there took over. The door barely clicked shut before Joe had Scott pressed back against it.

Scott tensed and Joe immediately stilled, dreading that Scott intended to tell him to get out, that he'd changed his mind about them getting together that night.

Another second passed; neither of them even dared to breathe. Then, very slowly, Scott relaxed against the door. He dropped his head back against the peeling paintwork.

He blinked, almost sleepily. He smiled.

Joe smiled back at him, relief making his mind spin. "Until I leave this room, you're mine."

Scott nodded his perfect willingness to go along with that idea.

Lifting one hand, Joe ran his fingers through Scott's hair, pushing it back from his face. He didn't try to make his touch artificially gentle. There didn't seem to be any point, not when Scott instantly tried to force himself up onto his toes and rub his scalp against Joe's fingers all the more firmly.

He seemed to need an even firmer hold than usual that night. Joe tightened his grip on Scott's hair as he dipped his head and brought their lips together.

Fierce or gentle? Warring factions battled inside Joe as he tried to work out the best way forward. Were things ever what they seemed with Scott? Was what Scott wanted the same as what he needed?

Pulling back after the briefest kiss they'd ever shared, Joe stared down at Scott. "How thin are your walls?" he demanded.

"My w-what?" Scott said, frowning as he leaned forward in an attempt to recapture the kiss.

"The walls," Joe repeated, leaning back to make sure there was no way for Scott to get that kiss until he allowed it. Letting go of Scott's hair, Joe slammed his hand against the plasterwork alongside the door. "How thin are they?"

"Quite th-th-thin, I g-guess…" His eyes pleaded with Joe to tell him that was okay; that he wasn't displeased with him for someone else's choice of building materials over a century ago.

"How much do you care about someone overhearing us doing a scene?" Joe asked next. He studied Scott's eyes very carefully.

"I d-don't care at all, s-s-sir. We can d-do anything you w-want." Scott licked his lips. His eyes confirmed that everything his mouth had uttered was true.

There was no need for Joe to ask any other questions. "Naked, on your bed, now."

"Yes, s-sir."

Scott scrambled out from the small space between Joe's body and the door. For several seconds, Joe remained exactly where he was, one hand still pressed against the wall. The thing might be relatively thin, but it wasn't some flimsy bit of plasterboard. It was Victorian brick. Joe glanced at the wall. He hadn't damaged the plasterwork, but he'd made his entire fist throb.

Behind him, Joe heard Scott rushing around. Then came silence. Joe turned. Scott sat naked on the very edge of the bed, his cock erect, his eyes uncertain.

"On your hands and knees, face the headboard."

Scott twisted around, so eager to please, so responsive to Joe's every order. Joe stopped alongside the bed and stripped off his own clothes. Never taking his eyes off Scott, he tossed everything he wore onto the floor around him.

Scott was so bloody beautiful. Even after all the scenes they'd played together, he still took Joe's breath away and stole a part of his mind every time they were together.

Joe knelt on the bed, facing Scott's side. As he sat back on his heels and made himself comfortable, he saw Scott risk a glance in his direction.

"S-sir?"

Joe placed his hand, very lightly, on Scott's arse. The skin was so pale it was hard to believe it had ever been spanked, but Joe knew better.

The sound, the warmth that had spread through his palm, Scott's reactions — every detail about Scott's first spanking was deeply embedded within Joe's mind. He was almost ready to swear he could feel Scott's body moving back and forth across his lap as he lost himself in the memory.

"Please, s-sir," Scott whispered.

Joe met Scott's eyes. Maybe Scott had been telling the truth when he'd said he didn't know what he needed in order to feel safe and secure under Joe's protection for the rest of his life. But, right then and there, Joe knew exactly what they both needed, and he saw the same knowledge reflected in Scott's gaze.

Joe began to move his palm in circles over Scott's arse; around and around, letting the skin warm gradually under his increasingly firm caresses.

Scott whimpered. As he sank deeper into his submission, he dropped his gaze. Barely a moment later, he bowed his head toward the blanket beneath him. Joe didn't alter anything about his own actions in response. That was important. Scott had to know he could react however he needed to, and it wouldn't change a damn thing about Joe's plans for him.

All the pressure to make choices and influence the world around him—that all belonged to Joe now, and he relished every bit of it. Scott's universe was his to bend and shape. Everything Scott felt, everything he sensed, was under Joe's control now.

Moving his hand to Scott's other buttock, Joe rubbed his hand over the skin there too. Again and again, as if time didn't mean anything and they were the kind of guys who didn't have to get up the next day and work to pay the rent.

Joe frowned. Was that part of it? Was Scott worried that Joe wouldn't be able to provide for him, that he wouldn't be able to look after him financially if he needed to? Joe's mind raced as he flicked through a mental scrapbook of the time they'd spent together. It was possible that Scott thought Joe was barely able to care for himself financially, let alone another man.

Never betraying anything about his thoughts, Joe turned accountant and raced through a whole host of calculations he'd never bothered with before. Wages. Overtime. Rent. Bills. Joe hadn't done that much mental arithmetic since he was in school.

* * * * *

"My toy collection is complete."

Scott snapped out of his near Zen-like state with a jerk. He'd known deep down that Joe would be disappointed to find that he hadn't even added an extra fly swat to his toy collection since his last visit. Scott had been to Joe's place often enough to know how important having the right equipment was to him. Hell, Joe didn't even seem to own anything that wasn't kinky. "I'm s-sorry. I d-didn't—"

"I'm not complaining," Joe cut in. "I'm perfectly happy with my hand. I'm just...mentioning it."

"Yes, s-sir." Scott peered blindly down at the blanket beneath him, trying to work out what the hell Joe was trying to tell him.

"So, I don't need to spend any more money on toys," Joe went on.

"Yes, s-sir," Scott said again. It seemed like the only safe thing to say while he remained completely baffled.

"The club and the sauna both pay well," Joe announced. "So do the other places I work occasional shifts. And a lot of my income will be freed up now I don't need to buy any more leather and stuff."

"Yes, s-sir." Finally, something inside Scott's brain joined the dots. An image of the real conversation taking place appeared before his eyes. "N-No, sir!" Scott twisted around and tried to look over his shoulder.

Joe's hand came to rest on the back of his neck and stopped him short. "Stay where you are."

"I d-don't want your money," Scott blurted out.

Joe's grip on his neck didn't ease in the slightest.

"It's n-not about that." Scott closed his eyes. The obvious thing to follow up that statement with was what this *was* about. He drew a complete blank and dipped his head toward the bed sheet in defeat.

He really wouldn't have blamed Joe if he walked away from him in disgust that very second.

As soon as Scott stopped trying to look over his shoulder, Joe eased the pressure on his neck. He went back to rubbing his palm across his buttocks.

Scott tried to breathe deeply and slowly, but he was only moderately successful.

Joe's hand disappeared.

Scott tensed, waiting for Joe to take another guess at the root cause of his idiocy. Instead, Joe's hand came back, connecting sharply with Scott's right arse cheek.

With a yelp that had everything to do with shock and nothing to do with pain, Scott shot forward on the bed.

Apparently, Joe hadn't expected that. He made no move to try to stop him. Scott automatically turned to look at him. This time he succeeded. Joe blinked at him, obviously too surprised to hide his first reaction.

A moment later, Joe's lips twitched and his expression cracked into a grin.

Blushing brightly, Scott moved himself carefully back onto his hands and knees, presenting his arse to Joe again.

Joe didn't punish him for his mistake or make him beg. He immediately settled his fingers back against Scott's arse. A few circles later, Joe lifted his hand. The palm came down on Scott's left buttock this time.

Now that he knew what to expect, Scott didn't flinch. He remained exactly where he was and took the firm smack with pleasure. Heat radiated out through his body until it reached the tip of each finger and toe.

He clawed at the blanket and tried to hold onto his wits as the spanking began in earnest, but no grip on mere cotton had any chance of helping him keep his sanity.

Joe stole his mind as easily as he ever had.

"Please, s-sir." Scott had no idea what he begged for; only that he needed something, and Joe was the only one who could provide it.

His hand fell on Scott's arse again and again.

Crying out as both his intellect and his emotions spiralled and whirled out of control, Scott kicked out against the sheet. His limbs were no longer his to control and —

"Scott!"

The word cut through all the madness and confusion in Scott's head. It sliced straight toward that part of him that was the most ancient and primitive. The syllables didn't matter; the tone made Scott freeze.

Dominance, authority, confidence. Whatever it was that filled Joe's voice, it swept away all Scott's uncertainty and brought him back to the here and now. Scott cautiously stole a glance over his shoulder.

His gaze met Joe's.

Joe stared back at him very seriously for several moments and Scott found himself incapable of looking away. Then, Joe smiled. He lifted his hand closest to Scott's face and rested it tenderly against his cheek.

He kept his other hand on Scott's arse. He didn't caress or stroke. He didn't need to. Every bit of Scott's skin that Joe touched still trembled with bliss.

"That's right," Joe said, his voice dripping with gentle reassurance. "You're fine, aren't you?"

Scott nodded.

Joe moved his hand over Scott's spanked arse very slowly, making him whimper. "Painful?"

Scott shook his head.

"Sore?"

Scott shook his head again. He probably should have been sore, but pleasure overruled the possibility of any negative sensation entering his body right then. "Just h-h-hot, sir," he managed to whisper.

"Hot's good," Joe said. "I've always thought you were the hottest sub I've ever met, but when you're like this, it's the icing on the kinky cake."

Several minutes passed before Joe moved his hand up and rubbed his palm over Scott's freshly spanked arse once more. This time, he dipped the tips of his fingers between Scott's cheeks and caressed his hole.

* * * * *

Joe didn't just admire Scott's arse as he teased the cleft between his buttocks. He studied every line and muscle in Scott's body. There was no hint of fear or pain in him. He was all acceptance, all submission. If there had just been a little more certainty of his own worth mixed in with it, he'd have been undeniably perfect.

Joe's need to reassure collided with the desire to bury his cock deep within Scott's arse and make everything very simple and straightforward between

416

them.

His erection ached, but so did something deep inside his brain.

"Lay down."

Joe didn't expect to issue that order, or *any* order. One second he was busy trying to decide what to do next; the next moment, his instincts had taken over and the decision had already been made.

With no possible way of knowing how much confusion reigned in Joe's head, Scott obeyed him without any hesitation. He lay down on his stomach, turning his head to the side so he could see Joe and track his movements.

Nothing complicated. Joe had no doubt he'd be able to find plenty of pervertable things among Scott's belongings if he wanted to tie him up, or do any of a dozen other kinky things with him. But this wasn't the time for any kind of elaborate set up. Joe grabbed lube and a condom from his jeans, then tossed the crumpled denim back onto the floor. It only took him a moment to sheathe his cock with latex. Scott made no comment, although he watched it all.

Slicking his fingers, Joe wasted no more time before finding Scott's hole and starting to prepare him. His buttocks were scorching hot after the spanking. The heat seeped into Joe's palm as he steadied Scott while he worked the fingers of his other hand deeper inside his body.

Joe knew Scott's body better than he'd ever known another lover's. And even if he hadn't, he didn't need to look at a guy's arse to know what he was doing. Joe was free to look at Scott's face, and he eagerly watched each emotion and reaction spread across his features.

God, but he was gorgeous.

Scott's whimpers and moans filled the air. He sounded as incredible as he looked. Joe had never heard anything so beautiful.

If the walls weren't soundproof, whoever lived in the rooms on either side of Scott would have no doubts about just how much their neighbour was enjoying himself—no doubt that Scott's boyfriend was very capable of keeping him satisfied. They'd have to have been idiots to think he needed anyone else in his life.

Joe wished he could believe that Scott was as happy and content as he sounded. Perhaps he couldn't know that for sure until he read whatever was in Scott's next note to him and fixed whatever was broken between them. But, if nothing else, Joe was soon certain that Scott's hole was as ready for him as it could ever be.

Moving one hand to Scott's waist, Joe tugged at his torso until Scott got the hint and rolled onto his side with his back toward Joe. Scott shuffled around the bed very carefully, obviously doing his best to follow Joe's silent orders without making a single mistake.

Soon, Scott was spooned in front of him.

"That's right," Joe whispered, as he lay down behind him. The moment their bodies lined up, he had his cock nestled snugly between Scott's super-heated cheeks. "So good."

Scott murmured his agreement and rolled his hips, encouraging Joe to thrust deep inside him. Placing one hand on Scott's hip and holding him still,

Joe pushed forward. He only allowed the head of his cock to enter Scott's hole; then he stopped.

Scott took a shaky breath and squirmed beneath Joe's grip on him. Joe refused to offer Scott any hint of freedom, or permission to move. Keeping everything very slow, very controlled, Joe pushed his cock just a little deeper, before retreating. Barely an inch of his shaft slid into and out of Scott's arse with each movement of Joe's hips.

Scott clutched at the blankets on the other side of his body. His whimpers had ceased while Joe rearranged them. Now they came back, and their volume had doubled. Joe thrived on every sound Scott made. He teased Scott with the possibility of being completely filled, and their bodies finally coming together, but he refused to actually let that happen.

Joe remained in complete control of every detail through sheer force of will. Scott had to know that Joe wasn't all impulses and quick stolen little moments. Joe could play his part in another man's life for the long haul. He was trustworthy, dependable, patient. He was all the things he probably didn't appear to be at first, or even second glance.

In that particular moment, Joe was also a man who really needed to come. The spanking seemed to have made Scott's hole hotter and tighter than ever. Joe growled, low down in the back of his throat and tightened his hold on Scott's hip. If Scott moved now, Joe couldn't guarantee he'd be able to reign himself in and outlast him.

"Mine," Joe whispered into Scott's ear.

Scott tensed.

"Right here. Right now. Mine." If nothing else, if never again, Scott at least had to allow him that.

Scott moaned with an even deeper brand of pleasure and nodded his head.

That deserved a reward. Joe thrust into Scott's body, sheathing his cock to the hilt. His crotch came to rest against Scott's freshly spanked buttocks. The heat radiating out from his skin was astonishing. Joe slid his hand around Scott's body and placed it low down on his stomach, just above his erection; both holding him in place, and demanding he remain perfectly still.

Time passed, but it had little meaning for Joe. Pressed against Scott's back, he sensed every breath Scott took and every beat of his heart. They were as close as any two men could get, and Joe didn't want to let that go.

He loved Scott.

He'd been trying to avoid acknowledging just how deeply in love with him he'd been for weeks. But suddenly, it became impossible to hide behind vague ideas of "I *might* be falling in love with him". As if his body wanted to distract him from the admission, he lost any ability to remain motionless.

Joe's hips began to rock and he was helpless to stop them. Soon, the movements turned into powerful thrusts. He could hardly pound into Scott while they spooned together, but within a few minutes, both of them were writhing on the bed and gasping for breath.

Joe moved his hand down a few inches and wrapped his fingers around Scott's erection. He must have been just as desperate to come as Joe was. A few strokes and a word of permission had Scott spilling across the blanket in thick, creamy ropes. He yelled as he came.

There was no improvised gag to help him this time, and Joe made no attempt to quell the sound. The whole building probably heard him. Scott thrashed and kicked out, pushing his arse back against Joe's cock until his orgasm gradually faded away.

Joe had enjoyed every moment of Scott's orgasm. Now, he permitted himself his own moment of bliss. One deep thrust, then another, and Joe came. For a few blessed moments, he had no doubts about anything. It was all very simple and just as it should be.

Scott was in his arms, pleasure rushed through his veins, and Joe's world was perfect. Even after the ecstasy ebbed away, Joe kept his eyes closed and clung to that feeling.

* * * * *

Scott didn't dare move. It felt suspiciously as if Joe had fallen asleep behind him; their bodies still joined together, their limbs entwined. Moving meant risking waking Joe. Scott wasn't willing to do that; not even when the position which had brought him so much ecstasy offered only aching muscles and soreness in some very intimate places.

Breathing carefully so as not to jostle Joe, Scott looked for something neutral to think about; something which could distract him from the way his buttocks burned with the combination of Joe's hand falling on them earlier, and Joe's crotch pressed against them now.

It was no use, whatever he thought of brought either pain or sadness with it. Almost everything about Joe and the time they'd spent together went straight to Scott's cock, and his shaft wasn't ready to harden again without making its displeasure known through his entire nervous system.

As for sadness, thinking about the future hurt his mind just as much as memories of the past hurt his body. It was too soon to think about those things.

Scott frowned. He'd been so lost in his own thoughts he hadn't noticed how tense Joe had become. Every muscle in Joe's body had turned rock-hard behind him.

"S-sir?" The plea for reassurance was impossible to keep back.

"Have you given any thought to what you want to write in your next letter to me?"

Scott's frown deepened until his forehead threatened to cramp. Was that what had made Joe so stressed out? Was Joe worried that he'd ask for too much, or maybe not enough? Did he think that he'd lie, or just that he wouldn't like the truth when he read it?

"I..." Scott had no idea what to say.

Joe pulled away, separating their bodies. Scott closed his eyes but he didn't sense Joe leave the bed. Joe merely rearranged himself before bringing their bodies close together again.

"It's okay if you haven't made any decisions yet."

Scott relaxed slightly, but only slightly. He had the distinct impression that Joe didn't really mean that. As unlikely as it was that a man as exacting as Joe would lie to try to spare someone's feelings, Scott couldn't believe that his words had any other purpose.

Joe probably wrote his note to him in just a few seconds. There would have been no worrying or hesitating. Joe was far more sensible than that. Scott was the only one who was so stupid he couldn't even string together a few words well enough to explain the most important thoughts that would ever exist inside his head.

"Here's what's going to happen," Joe suddenly announced, lifting himself up to lean on one elbow and look down at Scott.

Scott turned slightly and gazed back up at him in return, holding his breath as he waited to hear what his future would hold.

"Pass my jeans to me."

Scott obediently leaned over the side of the mattress and pulled Joe's jeans up onto the bed.

Joe reached over him, dug into one of the back pockets, and pulled out an envelope. "You're going to put some thought into exactly what it is you want from me, from your life, whatever. Then, you're going to write it down. Then, you're going to call me and tell me you're ready for us to meet up. Any questions?"

Scott stared at the envelope as if it already held the answers to those questions. "How l-long do I have, s-sir?"

"As long as it takes." Joe even sounded like he meant it. "Here."

Scott took the proffered envelope, but he had

no idea what to do with it at that particular moment. He held it very carefully, although it was impossible to believe that any more creases could fit onto the crumpled surface.

Scott ran his fingers over a deep fold in the paper. Joe was always hard on envelopes. They rarely arrived in particularly good condition, but the contents were always fantastic.

"Any other questions?" Joe prompted.

Scott shook his head.

"If there's anything you need in the meantime, you're to call me immediately."

"Yes, s-sir." There could be no doubt that Joe was trying to make him feel better now, and Scott knew it was probably his duty to repay that kindness by actually cheering up, but he couldn't do it.

He still felt as if someone had cut a piece out of him. It was too late, he realised, in that very moment. It was pointless for him to worry about what would happen if he fell too far in love with Joe and ended up getting his heart broken beyond repair.

He'd already done the falling. It felt like his heart was already halfway through the breaking part, too. He was in love with Joe. If their, their whatever it was they could have together, ended now or in a year's time, it was going to hurt like hell.

His choice wasn't about how much pain; it was just about when he'd feel it. If he was sensible about it, Scott knew he'd end it now. Joe might be able to tempt him, but he couldn't insist they become some sort of item. He was bossy, but Scott had always known that Joe would take no for an answer if it came down to that.

If Scott walked away now, the ending would be safe, predictable. Scott liked safe and predictable; always had, always would.

"Scott?" Joe prompted.

"Do you have to leave s-s-straight away, sir?" Scott blurted out.

"No. I have time," Joe said.

"Maybe you could r-rest for a while before you l-l-leave?" Scott asked, as emotionlessly as possible.

"Yeah, I can do that," Joe said, as if it were no big deal.

Scott closed his eyes. It was a huge deal. As Joe lay down and wrapped his arms more firmly around Scott, it was the most humongous deal ever.

Scott dipped his head and pressed a kiss against Joe's arm, just in case he wouldn't get the chance to do it again. Opening his eyes, he looked down at the envelope Joe had given him to fill.

You have far more balls than you give yourself credit for…

There was just a small chance that Joe had been right when he wrote that. Scott took a deep breath. As crazy as the possibility sounded to him, maybe he did have it in him to be brave and take a risk. Maybe this really wouldn't be the last time he'd share a bed with Joe.

Part Fifteen: Dear Sir

Dear Sir…

It was the obvious way to start a letter, especially when addressing a man that Scott was growing ever more attached to calling sir.

For several seconds, Scott stared down at the piece of paper. If only the rest of the letter would come to him as naturally as those first two words had. He closed his eyes, but there was no hiding from what he needed to say. There was no way he could be careful and consider each word either. He'd drive himself mad if he tried to make the letter as perfect as the one Joe deserved to receive.

When Scott opened his eyes, the blank page glared back at him, as if daring him to place his pen on the surface. The dark wooden top of the old fashioned dresser in the corner of Scott's bedroom surrounded the white paper.

There was a mirror was attached to the back of the dresser. Scott really wished he'd been able to move that as easily as he'd pushed aside all the junk that lived on the dresser's surface. When Scott looked up from the paper, it was impossible for him to avoid his reflection.

As he met his own gaze, every taunt that small-minded bullies had thrown at him over the years hit its target all over again.

What the hell did he think he had to offer a man like Joe?

Maybe Joe had proved that Scott could find a guy in a sauna who wouldn't kick him out of bed for eating crackers, but that didn't mean he was good enough for Joe. He was scrawny and stupid, ugly and clumsy; a stuttering little fool who no one like Joe would ever want to touch, let alone love.

"No." Scott said the word so loudly, he shocked himself into looking away from his reflection. He looked down at the paper once more.

This time, he didn't even allow himself time to take a deep breath. He started writing. The pen moved over the notepaper more rapidly than it had in any exam he'd sat while he was in school.

Barely permitting himself to think with the conscious part of his brain, Scott just wrote as quickly as he could move his pen. The letters that appeared on the page weren't neatly formed, the sentences weren't properly structured; but none of that mattered. Scott doubted Joe would give a damn if he wrote in Shakespearian verse or text-speak.

Joe just wanted to know what was in his head—honest and unedited. That was what he'd asked for, and that was what he was going to get.

Scott kept writing. Turning over the page, he kept going. His fingers cramped. His knuckles turned white as he tightened his grip on his pen, but Scott didn't falter.

Finally, he lifted his hand away from the second double-sided page. Grabbing the envelope, Scott pushed the letter inside before he could change his mind or lose his courage. He licked the envelope, sealed it, and turned it over.

Smoothing out the pale surface, Scott did his

best to ensure it would look as immaculate as possible when it arrived in Joe's hands. He didn't look up or glance in the mirror; that would have been far too big a risk to take.

Staring down at the envelope, Scott finally gave himself a moment to pull himself together. His lungs moved breaths into and out of his body as if nothing momentous had just happened. Even though Scott wasn't entirely sure what he'd babbled out in total, he had no doubt it had the power to make or break the rest of his life.

There was no way he could deliver it in person. The alternative was obvious. Picking up his pen once more, Scott wrote a little more calmly this time. Taking intense care with each letter, he wrote out Joe's address, applied a stamp to the top corner of the envelope, and walked to the door leading out of his rented room.

Not stopping to pick up a coat, or even his wallet, he left the building with nothing more than his room key and his letter. The nearest post box he knew of was over half a mile away. Scott marched himself to it without allowing any time for doubts to creep in. He soon stood alongside the bright red pillar-box.

He pressed a hasty kiss to the letter and pushed it through the slot.

Letting out a deep breath, Scott smiled slightly as he turned to walk back to his room. The wind was bitter. He was damn near freezing. He also knew that, even if Joe tore up the letter and disappeared off the face of the earth without ever saying another word to him, he'd always carry something of Joe inside him.

If nothing else, Scott was well aware that the

man he'd been when he first met Joe would never
have had the courage to post that letter.

* * * * *

Joe stopped in the main hallway of the block of
flats where he lived and unlocked the little mailbox
marked with his flat number. He was running late,
again. That was probably what came from not being
able to sleep for more than twenty minutes at a time.

Scott was driving him insane. Worse of all, he
was managing to do it long distance. Joe didn't even
have the opportunity to enjoy the sight of him, let
alone touch him, or kiss him, or pin him down, or…

Joe growled irritably under his breath as he
stuffed his mail into his leather jacket for safekeeping
and marched out to his bike. He didn't spare a
thought for his post until he took off his jacket when
he reached the club, three minutes after his shift
should have started.

The place was practically empty. Even though
it was open, there wouldn't be many customers for at
least another twenty minutes. Hanging up his jacket,
Joe dropped his mail on the rickety table in the staff
room at the back of the club.

Slumping heavily onto the wooden chair next
to the table, Joe picked up the first envelope and
tossed it straight in the rubbish bin. Junk mail. More
adverts and fliers followed the same path.

Then, right at the bottom of the pile, a real
letter, addressed to him both by name and by hand.

Scott.

Joe tore open the envelope and unfolded the

paper.

Someone walked into the staff room. Whoever it was said something. They were probably talking to him, but Joe didn't answer. He didn't even take in what they said.

Frowning, Joe ran his eyes over line after line of words.

There were too many of them. As much as Joe loved Scott, he also knew that he wasn't the kind of guy who found it easy to get to the damn point and just tell a man what he really wanted.

Turning over the paper, Joe turned his attention to the very last paragraph.

Thank you, sir. If you still want me to belong to you, I really want that too.

Joe bowed his head over the letter. Whatever Scott's requests or demands were, whatever the earlier portions of the letter contained, Joe knew now that everything would be fine.

"Joe, are you actually intending to do any work today?"

Looking up, Joe saw Mark, the shift boss, standing in the doorway doing his stern and pissed off act.

"Bloody hell, are you okay?" Mark asked. His eyes opened very wide as any attempt to act like a hard-arse failed him. "You look like shit."

"I'm..." Joe glanced down at the letter. "I'm going to take a sick day today."

He must have looked authentically ill because Mark didn't even make a token protest. With more than ninety percent of Scott's letter still unread, Joe headed for the exit. If he'd had his car, he could have driven around the corner, pulled over and read it properly. On his bike, and with the rain pattering against his leathers, that wasn't an option.

Joe revved up his bike and turned it toward Scott's place. By the time he reached it, torrential rain poured down around him. He took the stairs up to Scott's room two at a time, dripping rainwater with every step, and hammered on the door.

Water pooled around his boots as he glared at the woodwork and waited impatiently for Scott to answer. It was the middle of the night. If Scott wasn't there, Joe damn well wanted to know where he was, what he was doing, and, perhaps most importantly of all, who the hell Scott was doing it with.

Nothing.

Joe pounded on the door again.

"The guy's at work."

Joe glanced down the corridor. The man who rented the neighbouring room stood in his open doorway, sleep mussed and unshaven, wearing nothing but his boxers.

"What did you say?" Joe demanded.

"The guy from that room — he's at work. And if you two are going to have the headboard banging against the wall again, or be screaming blue-murder when you get off, find a room somewhere else. Some of us work regular hours." He slammed his door behind him as he retreated into his room.

A frown still creasing his forehead, Joe pulled his phone out of his pocket and called up Scott's number.

It rang once, twice, a third time.

"Hello—"

"Where the hell are you?" Joe demanded.

"S-sorry, sir. I-I'm at work. D-did you get my l-l-let—?"

"Where?" Joe bit out.

Scott only hesitated for a moment before he gave Joe the address of a factory estate on the edge of town.

"I'll be there in fifteen minutes." Joe hung up before giving Scott time to comment on that plan. It wasn't up for debate.

Storming back down the stairs and out of the house, Joe didn't have room in his head for any thoughts that didn't revolve around getting to Scott as quickly as possible. Even an inch of space existing between them at a time like this was completely unnatural.

Joe had behaved himself and he'd played nicely. He hadn't rushed Scott. He hadn't contacted him once since he promised to give him whatever time he needed in which to write his letter.

Now wasn't the time for that kind of politeness.

Scott wanted to belong to him. Scott was his. Scott had no right to be any place other than by his side. Or, even better, Scott should be trapped beneath Joe's body while Joe pounded into him.

The building Scott had directed him to was in near darkness. Only four lights were on. One was beneath a sign proclaiming it to be the security office. Two shone through the windows of what appeared to be some sort of office area. The final light was set outside and illuminated what Joe guessed to be the entrance leading to those lit-up offices.

Under that last light stood what was easily the most beautiful sight Joe had ever seen. Scott. He was in his shirtsleeves. The rain had plastered the thin white fabric against his skin. His trousers were equally damp. His hair was slicked down to his scalp, and he was gorgeous.

Joe stopped his bike directly in front of Scott. He jumped off almost before the tires ceased spinning. "Does anyone who works here think you're straight?" he demanded the moment he'd pulled off his helmet.

Scott frowned. It was hard to imagine any more anxiety being able to fit onto his face, but he made room somehow. He shook his head. "I-I'm c-c-completely out, s-s-sir."

Joe didn't give him the chance to say anything else.

Two strides put him in Scott's personal space. Another three had Scott's back pressed against the wall alongside the entrance.

Scott gasped against Joe's mouth, allowing Joe to deepen the kiss without even needing to ask for access, let alone demand it. Just like so many times before, Scott relaxed and moulded himself against Joe's body the moment he knew that Joe had taken control of his world.

He kissed Joe back as if he'd never been happier for his mouth to meet another man's lips. The rest of his body quickly decided it was quite pleased to see Joe too—especially Scott's cock. Joe grinned into the kiss as he felt Scott's shaft harden. By the time

Joe broke the kiss, Scott's erection was straining against his fly.

"You got my l-l-letter?" Scott asked, although it was obvious he already knew the answer.

"Are you going to get in trouble for me being here?" Joe countered.

Scott shook his head. "It's only m-me here. Well, and Stan on s-security, but I rang him and t-t-told him someone would b-be joining me. He doesn't care. He's watching s-s-some sports thing anyway."

Joe took hold of Scott's hand and led him into the building. One of the internal lights turned out to be set in a corridor. It guided the way to the only lit office.

"Why are you working in the middle of the night?" Joe demanded, as he closed the door and sealed them in the office.

Scott swallowed rapidly. "Y-you tend to work l-late at the club a lot. Whenever we've met up, it's always been l-l-late. I asked my b-boss if I could work the s-s-same kind of s-s-shift pattern you do. He said he didn't mind what t-t-time I did my work, as long as it got d-done. So I..." Scott shrugged.

He'd rearranged his work hours to suit Joe's lifestyle. Even if he was trying to avoid saying it outright, it was the obvious truth. Joe mostly worked nights, so now Scott mostly worked nights too.

Until that moment, it hadn't occurred to Joe to wonder if it was convenient for Scott to meet him at what the majority of the population would probably consider to be really odd and sleep depriving times.

"I sh-should have asked for your p-permission, r-r-right?" Scott asked with a strange mixture of shyness, anxiety, and pleasure.

"What do you mean?" Joe stripped off his leather gloves and jacket and set them aside.

"I'm not sure how it works wh-when one man b-b-belongs to another man... sir."

Joe stopped. He stopped moving. He stopped breathing. He stopped rushing around like an idiot. And, he finally started thinking about what Scott needed rather than what he wanted for himself.

Decisions made, Joe nodded to himself.

The handle of the door leading back into the corridor was fitted with a lock. Joe turned the key and made sure it was secure. The windows were covered with blinds. No one could see in.

"Strip."

Scott blinked.

"I'm not being kinky, darling. You're dripping wet and ten minutes away from freezing to death. Take off your clothes. Put them on the radiator so they can dry while we talk."

As Scott reached for his shirt buttons, Joe sat down on the room's only chair. Taking the letter out of his pocket, he placed it on the desk in front of him. It was time to get serious.

*****

Scott froze when he saw his letter on the table.

For some reason, he hadn't expected Joe to bring it with him. Once the letter had left his possession, Scott hadn't anticipated ever seeing it again. Its appearance made his throat turn dry. He tried to swallow and almost choked on the attempt.

"Forgotten something?"

Scott's attention snapped back to Joe, who looked pointedly at Scott's underwear.

There was no practical need to remove his boxers, the rain hadn't actually soaked through his trousers enough to make them soggy; but Joe commanded, and Scott obeyed. If Joe wanted him naked in his office, that's what he'd get.

"Good boy."

Those two little words made the chilly air worth every shiver.

Suddenly, Joe stood up and took his jacket off the back of the chair.

"You're l-l-leaving?" No! Joe couldn't just walk out. Scott instinctively stepped in front of the door, even though he knew in his heart that it wouldn't do any good. A single order would easily clear Joe's path.

Completely ignoring the door, Joe walked over to the radiator where Scott had draped his clothes, and dropped his jacket on the floor at its base. "Kneel there. You'll be warmer."

Returning to the desk, Joe picked up the chair and carried it over to the same corner of the room. The moment he sat down, Scott rushed over to kneel at his feet.

Joe's jacket was padded to offer protection on his bike. It was also well worn. Scott ran his fingers over the edge as he shifted his weight and sat back on his heels. One day he was going to be in Joe's life for that long—for the kind of time it took to become moulded to someone's shape and be completely comfortable for him.

Scott's thoughts scattered when Joe reached out and ran his fingers through his wet hair.

"If I thought you could get through it without a panic attack, I'd order you to read this to me," Joe said, tapping the envelope on his knee. His smile let Scott know he was only teasing.

At that point, Scott felt his body take over and push aside all the nice sensible things his mind had to say on the matter. He reached out and took hold of the letter.

"Let me r-read it, sir?"

If Joe wanted it read aloud, Scott would do his very best to make that happen. It was only a formality anyway; Joe had obviously read it before coming there. Scott wouldn't be telling him anything he didn't already know. There was no reason to be scared.

Joe seemed to have to think about it for an unexpectedly long time before he finally handed the letter over. "Word for word," Joe ordered.

Scott nodded. Of course he knew he'd babbled a lot, but truth be told, he needed to know the specifics of what he'd written just as much as he needed to please Joe by reading it out loud. He'd been in no condition to create a concrete memory of its contents when he wrote it.

Scott took a deep breath and let it out slowly. Naked at Joe's feet, he ran his eyes over the first few lines of the letter. Then, he started to read...

Dear Sir,
Thank you. I have to say that first. I have to say thank you for everything that's happened between us over

the last few months. I've enjoyed every moment we've spent together. I never imagined when I first met you that I'd ever be lucky enough to get a date with you, let alone that we'd get to know each other so well...so intimately.

You asked me before if money is important to me. It's not.

You also mentioned other men. I don't know how to explain to you just how relieved I was to hear you say that you wouldn't want either of us to be involved with other guys. But, if I'm going to be as honest as I promised myself I would be while writing this letter, I'd have accepted having to share you with other men. If that's what it took to remain part of your life, it would have been worth it. I'd have hated having to let other men use me, but I'd probably have gone along with that, too.

Anything that kept me in your life would have been worth it.

Scott paused, but he couldn't bring himself to look up to see the expression on Joe's face. He'd felt a burning need to be accepted by Joe for almost as long as he could remember; now, it was a raging inferno. If he laid himself open and vulnerable, and Joe laughed at him and told him he was an idiot, then —

Scott gulped in some air and hurriedly resumed reading, before he completely lost his courage.

I guess I don't have to tell you what I'm really afraid of now. It's probably obvious. It's not being broke, or being cheated on. I'm terrified of letting you all the way into my life because, if you walked away, I don't know how I'd ever fill the gap you left in your wake.

I love you, sir. I'd never told a man that before I met

you. It's not a Hollywood kind of love, where everything is candlelight and roses and sparkles. It's not the happy ever after kind, either. I'm not that naive. I don't expect that from you.

What I feel is the kind of love where two men live alongside each other and grumble about having to get up to go to work each day. It's the kind where I do anything and everything I can to make your life easier and more pleasurable, not because I want anything in exchange, but because I can't think of any other way I'd prefer to spend my life than in being of service to you.

I love you, sir.

Scott paused again. He had to swallow rapidly before he could go on — not because he was choked up with emotion, but, because his throat was so dry with nerves, his stuttering words had become raspy and thin.

I love you, and I would love to belong to you and submit to you for the rest of my life.

You asked what I wanted from you in order to be able to offer you my submission without hesitation. I'm not a romantic, sir. I'm not asking for false promises. I know that most relationships don't last forever. So I'm asking that, even if we don't remain together, you'll consider promising me that you'll never cut me out of your life completely.

Whatever form it took — friendship, the occasional text — please let me know that I'll always have some sort of contact with you. That's the only thing I'll ask you for.

No matter what your decision, once more, thank you, sir — from the very bottom of my heart.

If you still want me to belong to you, I really want

that too.

Yours, Scott.

Scott dropped his hand holding the letter down onto his lap. He lowered his gaze, too. He was so nervous he wasn't even vaguely hard any more; his softened shaft rested meekly against his thigh.

As the words from the letter ricocheted through Scott's mind, all he could do was kneel there, completely vulnerable, and try like hell to work out what he could have been high on to have said so many stupid things.

"Look up."

Scott obeyed.

Joe stared down at him, his expression completely unreadable. He reached out and threaded his fingers through Scott's hair, down by the nape of his neck. A tug pulled him forward so he no longer sat back on his heels.

Scott opened his eyes wide in surprise. His lips parted. A second later, their mouths met. Caught as off guard as ever, Scott rushed to catch up.

He still held the letter in one hand. Technically, the moment he'd posted it, the piece of paper had become Joe's property. It seemed impolite to either crumple it in his fist or drop it on the floor. Scott kept both his hands at his sides, half to keep the letter safe, half because, after everything he'd said, it felt wrong to reach out to touch Joe without some sort of official permission.

Scott had bared his soul. Taking any additional risks was out of the question.

"Yes." Joe growled the word into the kiss.

The next thing Scott knew, he'd been pulled up onto his feet; but that state of affairs didn't last long. Joe quickly toppled him back onto his desk.

Scott hurriedly set aside the letter, placing it safely on top of the printer cabinet to his left. As soon as his hand was free, he grappled for some sort of purchase on the desk beneath him. Whoever designed it hadn't been farsighted enough to put any sort of useful handholds on this particular range of office furniture. Scott's breath caught in his throat as he realised he was unable to manoeuvre himself in any sort of helpful way.

"Freeze." Joe pulled back, positioning his hands on the desk either side of Scott's prone body and straightening his elbows.

"Did I do s-s-something wrong?" Scott asked.

Joe shook his head. "I just want to look at you."

Scott automatically looked down his body to see what Joe's view of him might be. He lay on his back across his desk. His cock had quickly recovered from its nervousness. His erection flourished. He was shaved just as Joe ordered him to be.

He wasn't perfect. But Joe had always seemed to approve of the way he looked. There was no reason to believe that would have changed in the last few minutes, but Scott still couldn't quite convince himself not to hold his breath as he waited for Joe's verdict.

* * * * *

"You're gorgeous," Joe said, eager to remind Scott that he had nothing to worry about in that department. He was perfection. If the rest of the world didn't see that, they were idiots.

After a few moments, Joe forced himself to stop admiring Scott's body and turned his attention to his eyes instead. "And, yes, I can promise you that you will always have a place in my life. Forever."

Scott swallowed rapidly. Emotion swirled in his eyes, threatening to get the better of him.

"Do you have lube in your desk drawer? Any condoms?" Joe asked.

Whatever emotions Scott felt immediately rushed away to make room for panic. "No, I'm s-s-sorry, I—"

"Good," Joe cut in. "If you did, it would mean you were screwing around at work, and that's not acceptable."

Scott let out a little burst of laughter, all his tension disappearing as if it had never existed.

Joe grinned triumphantly. Yes, that was how he wanted Scott—relaxed and happy. "Luckily, I always stay prepared," he said. "Just in case I have to ride across the city to screw you at short notice." He reached into his back pocket and pulled out his wallet. He tossed aside everything except what he needed for the task at hand.

Scott didn't try to move; he lay there, completely content to let Joe do whatever he wanted with him. Catching hold of Scott's legs, Joe guided them back toward his body. Scott quickly grabbed his knees and held them in place. Unless Joe was very much mistaken, Scott was just as desperate as he was.

Joe hurriedly undid his fly and sheathed his cock in latex before slicking his fingers. Scott was calmer than Joe had ever known him to be. It didn't just show on his face. Scott was relaxed and ready to take him in moments.

There was no place for teasing in their activities that night. More than happy for everything to move as fast as physically possible, Joe caught hold of Scott's calves and lifted his legs so that Scott's ankles could rest upon Joe's shoulders.

"You have permission to come."

One thrust and Joe had his cock sheathed inside Scott's body to the hilt. Scott arched, pressing his head back against the desk as he moaned with pleasure. Joe held himself perfectly still, simply taking the moment to admire Scott and enjoy the hot tightness encasing his shaft.

Scott was magnificent. Blinking open his eyes, he looked up at Joe; his expression a strange combination of peace and lust.

Joe held Scott's gaze as he pulled back and thrust into him once more. Again and again. Neither of them looked away. Their breaths grew more rapid. Joe's heart raced faster and faster, but it had little to do with the cardio workout he was getting.

A midnight hook-up in a deserted office shouldn't have been able to feel romantic. Pounding, desperate sex shouldn't have felt as if it meant anything more than two men who were frantic to come. But, roses, candles, and diamonds couldn't have inspired any of the sentiments that raced through Joe's veins when Scott caught his gaze and held it that way.

Suddenly, Scott cried out. He jerked with pleasure; his hole tightened around Joe's cock. Scott's eyes dropped closed as his head tipped back.

Joe wasn't sure if Scott's orgasm triggered his own; or, if it was simply that something inside his own psyche had held him back, unwilling to let him come when it might have meant dropping his gaze first.

Whatever the cause, Joe came just a moment after Scott began to spill across his own stomach and chest.

Joe didn't yell out. He didn't even breathe. All he could do was enjoy the moment of unadulterated bliss that filled his body, right down to the tips of his fingernails and the end of every strand of hair on his head.

Months might have passed before Joe was able to collect up his scattered brain cells and open his eyes. He had no way of judging time. It wasn't important anyway. Scott was all that mattered.

Carefully separating their bodies, Joe looked around the office, taking in a few extra details this time. A clock hung on the wall. Its tick was the only thing that broke the silence.

Joe fixed his clothes and pushed his hand through his hair as he shoved afterglow aside and forced himself to be practical when he really wasn't in the mood.

Scott had been working. Joe had interrupted him. Scott probably needed to put in a few more hours before he was done and could go home. As much as Joe wanted to whisk him away on his bike that very second, and as certain as he was that Scott would let him do that without a word of protest, Joe had a concrete responsibility toward Scott now, and

444

he was damned if he'd neglect it.

It was time he started acting like the kind of master Scott deserved.

* * * * *

"Is s-s-something wrong?" Scott gingerly levered himself into a sitting position on the edge of the desk and looked across the office at Joe.

He wasn't sure what he'd expected to happen after they'd come, but it hadn't involved Joe just standing in the middle of the office staring at the clock.

"No, everything is perfect." Joe smiled and held out a hand to help Scott off the desk.

Scott automatically accepted the assistance even though it wasn't needed.

"You should clean yourself up and get back to work."

Scott chuckled.

Joe didn't. Apparently, he hadn't been joking...

Scott stood naked before Joe. Courage. Joe had said that he believed him to be far braver than he thought he was. Scott hoped like hell that he'd been right. He looked up at Joe and met his gaze. "I think my c-c-concentration might be shot for the night, s-sir."

Joe frowned.

Scott didn't look away; he didn't even allow himself to blink.

"I should have thought of that," Joe muttered, apparently more to himself than to Scott.

Putting a hand on Joe's arm, Scott pulled his

attention back to him. "It's not a p-problem."

"You have the right to get your work done," Joe informed him, seriously.

Scott gave in and looked down, but he had the feeling he was starting to understand the problem. "You were supposed to b-b-be working tonight t-t-too."

"I called in sick."

It was what Scott had guessed. "Maybe, just this once, I could do the s-s-same, s-sir? There's n-n-nothing I can't c-catch up on tomorrow."

"Just for tonight," Joe allowed, after a second's consideration. He nodded, it was all settled. "Get dressed."

Scott pulled his clothes on as fast as humanly possible. They were warm, but still damp and not at all comfortable. Now, he was getting cum-stains on them too, but Scott doubted he'd be wearing them for long anyway. His clothes always had a way of disappearing whenever he entered Joe's flat.

A quick check around the room to make sure they hadn't left any evidence of their activities; a call to the security guard to tell him he'd be leaving earlier than usual, and Scott was ready to go.

Within a few minutes, Joe had kitted Scott out for the ride and they were on his bike, whizzing their way to Joe's place. Scott wrapped his arms tightly around Joe's body and closed his eyes, relishing both the closeness and the vibrations being Joe's pillion passenger provided. The journey rushed past in what felt like moments.

Almost before he was ready for it, Scott found himself standing just inside Joe's flat. Just as he'd mentally predicted, Joe's order arrived barely a moment after he'd clicked the flat's front door closed behind them.

"Strip."

Scott did as he was told. The rain might have stopped when they were busy in his office, but his skin was damp from the wet clothes and his hair had yet to dry out properly. The cold was starting to sink into his bones. Without a word, Joe disappeared deeper into the flat. He issued no command for Scott to join him.

Unsure what else to do, Scott remained by the front door. A shiver ran down his spine. He shuffled his feet as subtly as possible, in an attempt to make himself warmer.

"Here." Joe appeared, bearing a large navy-blue towel and wrapped it around Scott's shoulders. It was warm and fluffy. It felt marvellous against Scott's chilled frame. A few minutes later, a much drier Scott found himself bundled into Joe's bed. The even more marvellous heat of Joe's naked body replaced the warmth of the towel.

Scott was in something close to nirvana as he gloried in Joe's embrace. Minutes slipped past. Scott felt his eyes drift closed, but he quickly re-opened them.

Joe chuckled behind him, sending tremors of pleasure through Scott's whole body. "Get some sleep."

Scott shook his head. "I'm f-fine, sir. I—"

Joe clamped his hand over Scott's mouth. "Do as you're told. Get some sleep. I'll still be here when you wake up."

Scott nodded against Joe's shoulder.

Joe took his hand away, but he didn't let even a breath of air creep between their bodies. Unless Scott was very much mistaken, Joe was trying to fuss over him, in his own leathery kind of way. Scott smiled as he closed his eyes. Leathery was good; knowing Joe cared about him was amazing.

* * * * *

Joe was gone.

Scott gasped as he jerked completely awake and sat up in the middle of the bed. He looked in every direction, but there was no way to avoid the fact that Joe was gone. Panic fountained up inside Scott. When he'd fallen asleep, Joe was there and now —

And now, Joe was coming out of the bathroom. He was nude, his hair was sleep ruffled, his chin coated in stubble, and he was as gorgeous as ever.

Joe rubbed his face and yawned. He blinked as their eyes met, any trace of sleepiness vanishing from him. "Did you have a bad dream?"

Scott cleared his throat, aware that Joe had sensed his panic, but not sure what to say to excuse it. "Would you l-l-like a blowjob, sir?"

Joe frowned.

Scott mentally cursed, but he couldn't think of anything more distracting to say.

"Did you think I'd left while you were asleep?" Joe said, making his way across the room.

Scott fidgeted with the edge of the blanket. "Um, m-maybe, just for a m-m-moment, sir."

448

Joe sat next to Scott on the bed. "One." He pointed to the index finger of his right hand. "I don't walk out on guys when they're asleep. I may have been a bastard to a lot of men, but I've never been a coward." He moved onto his middle finger. "Two. I told you earlier that you mean a hell of a lot to me, that I'm serious about you. So, I'm not going to run off; not when you're awake, or asleep, or anything else."

Scott sat in silence as Joe pointed to the next finger along. "Three. This is my flat. Where the hell would I go? I'd have to come back at some point, wouldn't I?"

Scott felt the blood drain from his face. He'd screwed it all up. They'd barely been officially together a minute and he'd made a mess of it all and—

"Four." Joe indicated his little finger. "So, about that blowjob…"

Scott frowned.

Joe grinned as he gave up counting Scott's errors in favour of sliding his fingers through Scott's hair and settling his hand on the back of his neck.

"I'm not going to be side-tracked out of keeping an eye on you and explaining why there's no need for you to be scared," Joe said. "But that doesn't mean I won't take you up on any offers you make whenever you're trying to wriggle out of a lecture."

Scott smiled. His terror drained away, leaving him light-headed with relief. "Yes, s-sir."

Joe pulled his feet up onto the bed and made himself comfortable against the headboard. Scott didn't need to be ordered to go down on him. He couldn't even bring himself to wait for a more formal invitation.

"We'll talk about how everything will work between us and what each of us should expect soon," Joe promised, as Scott climbed over one of Joe's legs to take his place between his knees. "You'll feel more at ease when everything is sorted out and you know exactly where each of us stands."

"Yes, s-sir."

"For now, I want you to put your hands behind your back," Joe said.

Scott obeyed, catching his left wrist within the grip of his right hand.

"Keep them there until I give you permission to move them."

"Yes, s-sir."

Joe rested one hand on the nape of Scott's neck, as if to reinforce the fact that his hands were free to do as they pleased.

"Until we're both ready for that conversation, this will be the perfect way to pass the time. I've missed your mouth while you were working things out."

Scott blushed. He couldn't have asked for a better compliment.

"Take it nice and slow," Joe ordered.

"Yes, s-sir." Scott's head was already bent so low, he was effectively whispering to Joe's cock.

"We have all the time in the world."

It was a reassuring sentiment. Scott caught hold of it and wrapped it around him. "Th-Thank you, sir." On the last word, he touched his lips to Joe's shaft in an almost chaste first salute.

There was something supremely comforting about going down on Joe. During sex, Scott inevitably became far too distracted by his own desires. Even giving Joe a blowjob turned him on so strongly he could barely keep his thoughts in order, but at least he was able to focus a little more on doing his very best to ensure Joe enjoyed himself.

Taking the tip into his mouth, Scott slid his lips down Joe's cock, slow and deliberate. As he reached the base, he relaxed his throat. This time, luck was on his side. His gag reflexes failed to kick in. His throat welcomed Joe and let him slide in even deeper into his body.

Pulling back very gradually, Scott let Joe's cock slip from between his lips.

Slow.

That tiny bit of deep action was merely a promise of what would come later. For now, Scott forced himself to change tactics and not give Joe his throat right away. He lapped very gently at the head of Joe's cock several times before working his way down the length with tender little licks and kisses.

Each touch of his lips to the velvety soft skin sent a wave of delight through Scott as well as Joe. Scott murmured around Joe's balls as he took each one into his mouth in turn and laved them with his tongue.

Joe stroked the back of Scott's neck, calmly petting him and reassuring him that he was satisfied with his actions, but Scott's own hands remained behind his back, unable to touch either Joe or himself. A whimper escaped the back of his throat as he prayed that Joe would be truly happy with his efforts to please him.

* * * * *

Joe stared down at the top of Scott's head. Scott had developed some seriously impressive oral skills over the time they'd known each other. More than that, his talents were so obviously very specific. He'd learnt exactly what Joe liked and how to provide it. He didn't waste his time giving him what he thought he should enjoy, or what some nameless, faceless ex had enjoyed.

Joe stroked his fingers through Scott's hair. The opportunity to please his new master seemed to have calmed Scott's fears for the moment, but it hadn't magicked them away. The damn things were still there, like shadows, creeping behind them; never far off and always ready to leap out whenever a bright light shone down upon them.

Shifting positions slightly, Joe only allowed part of his mind to enjoy the wonderful sensations Scott's mouth offered him. The other part of his psyche was put to work on finding a way to quell Scott's fears forever.

Joe had never had a sub he expected to love for the rest of his life. Something inside him tensed as the full weight of that responsibility came to rest upon his shoulders. He had to get this right. He had to find something that would give Scott complete confidence in his abilities as a submissive, and in his master's love for him.

Despite his best efforts, the part of Joe's brain which was able to maintain any kind of rational thought process grew smaller and smaller, until ecstasy completely overtook him. He shouted out his pleasure, more than happy for Scott to hear how much bliss he'd given him as well as for Scott to taste it as Joe spilled across his tongue.

Forcing his eyes to remain open as he came, Joe stared down at Scott. He swallowed everything Joe had left to give him without hesitation, but he didn't look up. Scott was completely focused on his task. Even when Joe relaxed back against the pillow, Scott seemed unwilling to even peek up toward him.

Scott gently suckled around Joe's cock until he was completely soft. Pulling back then, he lapped gently against his shaft, licking away any residue that might linger there.

"There's one envelope left in the packet," Joe said, his voice more gruff than he intended, his vocal cords still recovering from that yell of joy and triumph.

Scott froze. A few seconds slipped past before he finally turned his attention to Joe's face.

"We're going to rest here for a little while. But later, you're going to go back to your place."

"Yes, s-sir." Scott obviously did his best to hide his feelings of rejection, but he didn't quite succeed.

"I'm going to send you a note through the mail," Joe went on, determinedly. "It will take a day or two to arrive. I want you to use that time to pack everything in your room into boxes. If you need to give notice to your landlord, I want you to tell him you're leaving. Understand?"

Scott nodded. He didn't say anything, but his eyes were full of questions.

Joe smiled as he pushed a few stray strands of hair back off Scott's face. "You'll be moving in here soon, but that's not something you need to worry about. When you get my letter, just do exactly as it says — exactly as it says," he stressed, as the last of his plan came together in his mind. "I'll take care of everything else."

"Yes, sir."

A tug on Scott's hair ordered him to move up the bed and lay beside Joe. Joe wasn't sure if it was expectation or nerves but, even after Joe gave him permission to take his hands from behind his back, it took a little while for Scott to relax properly against him.

That wasn't important, though, because tonight was just one night of many. Joe had complete confidence that everything would be much easier for Scott very soon.

Joe was now Scott's master; making everything okay was his job, and he intended to be damn good at it, right from the start.

Part Sixteen: With Love

The orders in Joe's letter were very simple. He'd even laid them out in a nice little to-do list. If he'd been willing to deface Joe's message, Scott could have crossed off each item as he completed it. As it was, Scott contented himself with reading the list over one more time to reassure himself that he'd done everything just as Joe had commanded.

Pack everything you own into boxes — no exceptions other than the clothes on your back and what's in your pockets.

Settle any outstanding rent with your landlord.

Go to the back door of The Prince's Oak on Canal Street at ten o'clock Friday night.

Ask for Frank. Do as he says.

Yes. Scott nodded to himself as he carefully put the letter back in his pocket. He was exactly where he was supposed to be. Everything was as Joe wanted it and, even if he did look as scary as hell, at least Frank hadn't ordered him to do anything but sit in a bleak little room at the back of the club.

Everything was fine, Scott reminded himself again. He belonged to Joe now, and —

"Hello."

Scott jerked to his feet. The metal legs of his chair scraped loudly against the rough concrete floor before it toppled over and clattered to the floor.

If he'd been able to tear his gaze away from

Joe, Scott would have checked if Frank, or the other security guy who was enjoying a quiet smoke with him at the back door of the club, had turned to glare at him. But it was no use. Joe held Scott enthralled the moment he saw him. No one else existed in his world.

"Have you been doing what you're told?" Joe asked.

"Yes, s-sir."

Joe indicated that Scott should pick up his chair and sit down. Joe pulled up another seat and sat down opposite him. There was no other furniture in the room. It looked more like a storeroom than anything else, except perhaps a prison cell. Since it was tucked away at the back of a leather club, the odds on which it actually was were probably close to even.

"You l-look great, sir," Scott blurted out. It was nothing less than the truth, but that didn't mean that Scott had the right to say it. He was reasonably sure that this was the type of club where a sub didn't have any rights at all.

Damn, he should never have spoken without permission. Scott's pulse doubled.

"One," Joe pointed to a fingertip, the same way he had the last time they met up. "Don't worry about fitting in—I've brought something for you to change into." He moved on to the next finger. "Two, there's no one here you need to be afraid of. Most of the guys look psychotic, but I can tell you something about every man here that would make you see him in a whole new light."

Scott hadn't intended to look sceptical, but maybe his face had a different idea, because Joe raised an eyebrow as if accepting a challenge.

"See that guy talking to Frank, the one with the flame tattoo running up the side of his neck?"

Scott nodded. The guy was certainly memorable.

"His name's Tony. His favourite hobby is crochet—I think that's a kind of knitting, or something. He makes these weird little animal, monster things and sells them on the 'net. Apparently, they make good money."

Scott blinked and checked the guy out as discretely as possible, just in case there was something un-terrifying about him that he'd missed earlier on.

"And Frank—he's seriously into breeding Persian cats—you know, the ones Bond villains like to stroke when they're plotting to take over the world. He has far more cat toys in his place than he has cat-o-nine-tails, and that's saying something."

Scott smiled slightly as he tried to picture Frank petting a fluffy little kitten and failed.

"They're just ordinary guys who happen to like playing with handcuffs—just like you and me. You're as good as any man in this place, Scottie, and you've got as much right to be here as anyone else. Understand?"

Scott nodded. He certainly knew what each of Joe's individual words meant. Believing what they amounted to when joined together, that was more difficult, but Scott took a deep breath and gave it his best shot.

When the silence became uncomfortable, Scott cleared his throat. "Am I allowed to ask w-w-why we're here, s-sir?"

"Because, as much as I'd like to keep you to myself forever, we need to be seen together in public properly before you develop some stupid idea about me being ashamed of you or some other bull like that."

Scott shook his head.

"We're not going to stay long, but we are going into the club," Joe said firmly. "We're going to have a drink. I'll introduce you to a few people. Everyone will see us together. Then, when I'm sure that you really *believe* I'm happy for the whole world to know we're together, we'll go back to my place and have hot, rough, amazing sex. Sound good?"

Scott nodded. He really liked the last part of the plan, if nothing else.

"Any questions?" Joe asked.

"If I said that I b-b-believe you're not ashamed of me, can we skip forward to the b-bit where we go back to your place and — ?"

"No." The word wasn't snapped or shouted. Joe said it perfectly pleasantly, but also with the sure knowledge that he had the last say in the matter — in *every* matter. "But there's one more thing we have to sort out before we go into the club," Joe added.

For the first time, Scott took an interest in the sports bag that Joe had brought into the room with him. It lay on the floor at Joe's feet. As Scott watched, Joe bent forward and unzipped a compartment.

"I have to get ch-ch-changed," Scott remembered. His heart sank as he saw Joe had only opened a very small partition at the far end of the bag. Whatever costume he considered appropriate for

Scott to wear, it couldn't be much bigger than the cock ring he'd worn at the boots only night.

"No, before that, too," Joe corrected.

"Oh." Scott smiled in relief.

Joe straightened up, a length of silver chain in his hand.

"That's a c-c-collar."

"Clever boy," Joe murmured, but his focus was all on the clasp he was undoing. "Come here."

Scott hesitated for a moment, glancing toward the security guys at the back door, but no, what Joe thought of him was far more important than anyone else's opinion could ever be. Scott lowered himself onto his knees in front of Joe's chair; presenting his neck at what he hoped would be the most appropriate way.

Joe hadn't suggested Scott should wear a collar. He hadn't asked Scott's opinion. Scott was well aware that Joe had made the decision long before either of them had reached the club that night. It probably hadn't even occurred to Joe that Scott should be consulted.

Scott smiled to himself. Joe's read on the situation couldn't have been better. Being presented with the final decision suited Scott right down to the ground and added an extra layer of perfection to the situation.

The collar clicked into place at the back of Scott's neck. "Done."

Joe tucked a knuckle under Scott's chin and encouraged him to look up. With his other hand, Joe caught hold of the collar. Was that what the collar was all about, Scott wondered, an easy way for Joe to hold onto him and control his movements? Some of the porn stars Scott had seen online had used collars that way, but —

"It means you belong to me," Joe said, as their eyes met.

Scott stared up at him, shocked by how deadly serious Joe looked. It was obviously far more than a convenient handle to him.

"It means you're my submissive and I'm your dominant. It means you're answerable to me, and that, in a slightly different way, I'm answerable to you, too."

"Yes, s-sir." Scott couldn't think of anything else to say.

"I own you, and I'm responsible for you. Your job is to obey me, and mine is to make sure I issue the right orders."

Scott swallowed. "Yes, s-sir."

"Whatever happens, from this moment on, this collar doesn't leave your neck for any reason." He frowned slightly, as if something had just occurred to him to make him think that wasn't as wonderful a statement as Scott thought it was.

Scott held his breath as he waited for Joe's final verdict.

"If you have to have an x-ray, or something, I'll get you a temporary replacement that's not metal." Joe nodded, as if very pleased to have solved that problem. "Either way, you're going to wear some version of my collar for the rest of your life — and I'll be right there to make sure you do."

Scott wished there was something suitable for him to say in response, but the only words in his head were those Joe had just said to him. They swirled through his mind, filling every part of his psyche. There was no room for other thoughts or for words that were Scott's own.

"Yes, s-sir," was all he managed to say.

"I won't insist that everyone in your life knows you're kinky," Joe said, his voice and his expression as serious as ever. "It can just be a silver necklace as far as the vanilla people are concerned. But, any man who knows about leather will know what it is. He'll know that you've been claimed, that he has no right to even smile at you without my permission; and I'll never consider that to be anything other than a good thing."

"Yes, s-sir."

Scott's words were little more than whispers now, but Joe continued confidently.

"You're mine. Never doubt that."

Scott nodded again. "Yes, s-sir."

Joe's seriousness slowly drained away to be replaced with a grin. "Good boy." He bowed his head and brought their lips together.

Scott didn't hesitate to close his eyes and give himself up to the kiss. He had the strangest feeling that, in a dingy room in the back of a leather bar, with only two nicotine-addicted bouncers as witnesses, he'd just got married to Joe.

You'll wear this collar for the rest of your life.

Until death do us part.

A wedding ring by any other name…

Scott whimpered into the kiss and tried to make himself a little taller so he was more easily accessible. Joe tugged at Scott's collar in response, encouraging him to strive up into the kiss even while he remained on his knees.

It felt so perfect, so right. For the first time, it actually seemed possible to Scott that what they had could last forever; that Joe could want him for an entire lifetime.

The kiss ended, but neither Scott nor Joe pulled away. Their lips remained just a breath apart. Joe tilted his head and brought his temple to rest against Scott's forehead.

"I love you. I may not be the kind of guy who remembers to say it as often as I should; but every time you touch this collar, every time it moves against your skin or you feel its weight around your neck, that's what it means."

Scott closed his eyes very tightly. Without being conscious of it, he lifted his hand and hooked two fingers through the collar right alongside Joe's fingers.

I love you, too. Except Scott was certain that Joe wasn't saying anything to him just to hear it echoed back at him.

"Thank you, s-sir." That seemed like a far more appropriate response.

* * * * *

Joe smiled down at Scott.

Was there a different light in his eyes when Scott looked up at him in return? It would be wonderful to think so, but it would probably be equally unrealistic to expect a collar to act like a magic wand.

"Come on, before I get carried away and screw you right here on the floor."

Scott parted his lips.

"Not an option," Joe cut in, before Scott had a chance to tell him just how fine he would be with that scenario.

Scott put his lips back together.

"Time for you to get changed," Joe said. "Give me your coat."

Scott gave up the garment without a word.

Glancing across to the club's rear entrance, Joe saw that Frank and Tony were nearly done with their smoke break. "Hey, you two." They turned to face him. "Bugger off."

Both men laughed and good-naturedly made their way past the makeshift sitting area and on into the club. As Frank passed, Joe reached out and shook hands with him; Scott didn't seem to think there was anything strange about that.

Satisfied that all was going to plan, Joe waited until the other two men were out of sight. Sitting back in his seat, he nodded to the bag. "Your new club clothes are in the centre section."

Scott opened the bag with obvious caution. Joe watched him pull out the pair of leather trousers he'd bought for him, then the simple white sleeveless T-shirt. Right at the bottom were the traditional military style boots, complete with some thick socks.

Joe was reasonably sure he knew Scott's body perfectly. He'd run his hands over every inch of him often enough. He smiled to himself as Scott bashfully stripped off, then proved him correct in every estimated measurement. The trousers fitted Scott like a second skin. Catching hold of Scott's hips, Joe pulled him forward to stand directly in front of his seat.

"Perfect."

Even in the muted storeroom lights, the silver collar shone beautifully. Joe adjusted it so the little tag attached to it lay neatly against the notch between Scott's collarbones.

It really was so bloody tempting to just take Scott home. Only the fact that it would bugger-up all the timings he'd worked out, kept Joe from doing exactly that.

Joe stood up. Standing around in the queue out front would make Scott nervous. Sod that. Nothing was allowed to ruin their night. Taking Scott by the hand, Joe led him into the club the back way.

As they entered the public areas, Joe kept walking, refusing to give Scott a moment to build his nerves up to monumental proportions. Within a minute, they stood alongside the bar. For once, having worked in damn near every leather flavoured club and pub in the city worked in Joe's favour.

"Two barman specials," he said to a familiar face, handing over his cash.

Two beer bottles were duly passed across the stained wooden surface with a friendly nod of recognition. Joe handed one bottle to Scott before moving to stand behind him so he could wrap his arms comfortably around Scott. The gesture was only partially about making Scott feel safe. He was also marking his territory in front of the other doms present.

Pinning Scott's back against his chest, Joe

spread out his fingers and covered Scott's abs with as much of his hand as possible.

"Don't just cradle your drink," he ordered. "Take a swig. It will cool your nerves."

Scott did as he was told, just as Joe had come to expect, but one sip had Scott frowning at the bottle.

Dipping his head, Joe whispered in Scott's ear. "In a certain kind of club, it doesn't look good to have everyone behind the bar drinking lemonade all night. That doesn't mean the staff are allowed to get sloshed on the job."

Scott nodded his understanding and took another sip of his carefully disguised soft drink.

"Good boy," Joe whispered into his ear. "I want you clear-headed for what will come later. If you're good, that just might involve you coming."

* * * * *

Scott took a deep breath and closed his eyes. It was so easy for Joe to say that the drink would cool his nerves, but there was no way the chilled lemonade could compete with the way Joe's muscular frame was pressed tightly against his back.

Scott took another swig of his beer-bottle-lemonade. Its fizziness did nothing to stop his erection straining painfully against the inside of the crazily tight leather trousers Joe had given him. Nothing would ever be cold enough to stop Joe being able to make Scott feel hot and bothered whenever he wanted.

"What do you think of the club?" Joe asked.

"It's int-t-teresting, sir," Scott said. He dipped

his voice on the last word.

"There's no need to be discrete, sweetheart," Joe told him with a chuckle. "Everyone here understands why one man calls another sir. Everyone respects it."

Slowly lifting his gaze from his drink, Scott took his first real look at the club. No one paid them the least bit of attention. Men stood around, chatting and getting friendly with each other. Most of them wore a certain amount of leather. Some wore collars, too—submissives of all shapes, sizes, and ages.

Gay. Kinky. Both were par for the course. There was nothing special about his relationship with Joe—nothing an outsider would be able to see, at least.

Scott tilted his head slightly to one side.

"They all understand what it means to be a sub or a dom," Joe went on.

In the background, music played. The beat pounded through the air. Joe's hard-on rubbed against Scott's arse every time Joe moved his hips in time with the beat. It made it damn difficult for Scott to think.

"It's safe for you to be yourself here, and your collar means no one will lay a hand on you," Joe pressed a kiss against Scott's neck. "Except me, of course."

"Yes, s-sir." Scott made a point of not whispering his response. He over-compensated. It came out far louder than he intended. Damn! Scott dipped his head as heat rushed to his checks.

"Say it as loud as you like. Shout it at the top of your voice. That's fine, too," Joe promised.

Scott took a hasty sip of his drink.

"What are you supposed to do if you feel nervous?" Joe asked, speaking his words softly against Scott's earlobe.

The collar. Scott lifted his hand and hooked his fingers around the silver links. They brushed against something that he hadn't noticed before. Some sort of tag?

Craning his neck, Scott tried to peer down and see what it was.

"You can look at it in the mirror when we get home."

When we get home.

It was a simple thing for a Joe to say, but such a wonderful thing for Scott to hear. He had a home now, and it was with Joe. Scott closed his eyes and leaned more comfortably into Joe's embrace. There was no actual need for them to go to Joe's flat; Joe was home to him.

All thought of the tag on his collar slipped from Scott's mind. He floated through the next hour, high on how wonderful life could be. Joe spoke to other men, each one seemingly more pierced and tattooed than the last. He introduced Scott to them as well.

Apparently, Scott wasn't required to do anything other than nod and smile. That was fine with him. A few of the guys wearing collars shook hands with him, but even then, Scott wasn't required to step away from the comfort and safety of Joe's embrace. Joe's arms remained wrapped around him; his presence completely enveloping Scott in a safe cocoon.

"You're a good sub, and a good man. I'm proud as hell to have you in my life, and I have no hesitation in showing you off to anyone." Joe dipped his head toward Scott's ear again. "Any doubts about any of that?"

"No, sir," Scott said. "No d-d-doubts." To his own surprise, he realised that was actually the truth.

"Good, because if we hang around here any longer, there's no way in hell I'll be able to wait until we get home. I'll end up jumping you in the car." Joe put his bottle down on the bar. Taking Scott's drink from him, Joe set that aside, too.

For damn near the first time that night, Joe took his arms from around Scott's torso. Immediately feeling vulnerable and exposed without top to toe physical contact with Joe, Scott dropped his gaze.

A second later, Scott found his hand going to his new collar. Joe was still wrapped all the way around him. Scott's heart rate slowed. It became easier for him to breathe. The whole world was, in fact, a much better place.

Joe smiled, caught hold of Scott's free hand, and led him from the club. Scott followed, somewhat in awe of his own newfound confidence. In Joe's car, he relaxed back in his seat. He'd made his decision. Joe had accepted his decision. He belonged to Joe. And now, they were going back to Joe's place. He closed his eyes and leaned his head against the rest behind him.

The only part of Scott not one hundred percent happy with events was his cock; and that was only because he really wanted to come and his erection saw no reason why he should have to wait until they reached Joe's flat.

But, even though his shaft pressed more painfully against the front of those overly tight leather trousers by the minute, Scott found that he was neither disappointed nor relieved when Joe failed to pull over and jump him at any point on their journey across the city.

It was Joe's choice. Everything was Joe's choice now. Scott smiled to himself. He only opened his eyes and lifted his head when the noise from the engine suddenly disappeared. They were outside the block of flats where Joe lived. Scott blinked and tried to push his brain into something like a sensible thought process, but it wasn't easy. He was drunk on relief.

Joe undid both their belts, exited the car, and walked around to open Scott's door.

"Th-thank you, sir."

Joe wrapped his arm around Scott's shoulders and guided every step he took, all the way up to his flat. Without even a drop of alcohol in his system, Scott was as incapable of looking out for himself as any sloshed partygoer had ever been.

Three yards from their destination, Scott tensed, all his happy sleepiness vanishing. He came to a complete stop just a few feet away from Joe's front door, bringing Joe to a halt alongside him.

The lights in the public hallway were dimmed in deference to the late hour, and Joe hadn't bothered to power them up when he obviously knew every step of their journey off by heart. A thin strip of brighter light was visible beneath the base of Joe's door.

"D-d-did you leave the l-l-light on when you lleft, s-sir?" Scott asked. His voice sounded hollow, even to his own ears.

Joe gave him a strange look. "Why would I?"

Exactly, Scott thought. He never remembered there being a light on in Joe's flat when he was out.

Why tonight? The question rolled around in Scott's mind, but no answer came with it.

Scott's blood grew colder, until it was barely fluid enough to flow through his veins. "I th-think…" he finally managed to say. "I th-think you might have been r-r-robbed while we were at the c-club, s-sir."

* * * * *

Joe stared down at Scott for several seconds, wondering where the hell that had come from. He'd known for months that Scott was the type to worry about anything and everything in the universe. But really, panicking about the possibly inadequate security in a flat that he hadn't even moved into yet was…

Joe thoughts died a very slow painful death as he traced Scott's line of sight and spotted the light shining beneath the front door. For the first time in his life, he didn't know enough swear words to fit the situation.

"Everything's fine," Joe said first, in an instinctive effort to comfort Scott.

Scott's shoulders remained tensed. Even in the dim hallway light, it was easy to see the worry in his eyes.

Joe reached out and rattled the door handle. "See, it's still locked. I must have just forgotten to switch off the light when I left. No big deal."

Scott followed him into the flat without a word, but his gaze darted into every corner; checking for missing items, or perhaps for lingering intruders.

Joe led the way straight to the bedroom, determined to get the sequence of events he'd planned out back on track as soon as possible. Scott's footsteps followed Joe's for a little way, but suddenly fell silent halfway to the bedroom. Joe turned just in time to see Scott reach for the handle on the living room door.

"No!"

Scott froze, his hand hovering mid-air. He looked toward Joe, but quickly dropped his gaze. "May I just ch-check very quickly, s-sir?" he asked.

Joe kept his face expressionless through sheer force of will. "There's no need."

Scott didn't move his hand toward the door, but he didn't snatch it away either.

"What do you think I've got that's worth stealing, anyway?" Joe asked. He aimed for a light-hearted tone, but he wasn't sure he succeeded. Tonight was important, damn it, and he had a plan.

Scott made no reply. He'd back down if Joe ordered him to—Joe was certain of it. And, at the same time, Scott would learn that he'd been wrong to trust his master with a request that was obviously important to him.

Shit!

"S-s-something feels off, s-sir," Scott said, softly. "I know I'm probably j-j-just being silly, b-but..." *But will you humour me anyway, sir. Please. I wouldn't ask if it wasn't really important to me.*

It was what Scott didn't say, that he wasn't yet sure enough of Joe's love to say, that convinced Joe to abandon all his carefully laid out plans.

He joined Scott by the living room door. Rather than give him permission, Joe opened the door for him. Reaching inside, he switched on the light. Even when the room was fully illuminated, Joe didn't look inside. His attention rested squarely on Scott.

Scott's expression didn't change as his eyes travelled slowly from one point within the room to another. Finally, his gaze stilled and he peered down at the floor just in front of his feet as if it were the most fascinating thing he'd ever seen.

"Scott?" Joe prompted.

"You b-bought a sofa, s-sir."

"Yes."

Scott nibbled lightly at his bottom lip. "It's n-n-nice."

Joe studied him more ferociously than ever. The sofa was a battered old leather thing, twenty years out of style but still as comfy as hell. He didn't give a damn if Scott thought it was nice or not. "Notice anything else that's different in there?"

Scott's teeth bit down harder this time. When he released his lip, he took a deep breath. It obviously wasn't the sofa that was freaking him out. "There are quite a f-few b-b-boxes in there, s-sir."

"Boxes?" Joe asked.

"All the b-boxes from my p-p-place," Scott finally specified.

"Yes." Joe didn't dare blink in case he failed to spot some flicker of emotion from Scott—he couldn't afford to miss any clues.

"You b-b-brought them here, s-sir."

"Yes," Joe said again.

There was still no way to tell if Scott was about to completely freak out or not. Joe watched. He waited. There was nothing else he could do. Dominance didn't mean a damn thing in that situation. Everything rested with Scott.

"W-when?" Scott eventually asked.

"I lifted your key from your coat pocket when you got changed. Frank and Tony went to your place to get them while we were at the club. They're good guys. I'd trust them with my life."

Scott nodded, very slightly.

"Your things wouldn't have been safer with a police escort."

Another nod.

Joe resisted the urge to yell out at the top of his lungs through pure frustration; or, to demand Scott give him any sort of verdict before he was ready.

Scott reached up and hooked his fingers through his collar. He whispered something under his breath. The only word Joe caught was "real."

"What did you say?" he demanded, unable to make the question sound anything like a polite enquiry.

Scott blinked. He turned to look up at Joe. "This is r-real, isn't it, s-sir?" he said. "It's really h-h-happening. You really want me to m-move in with you. You r-really g-gave me a c-c-collar."

"Yes."

Scott didn't say anything, but he no longer needed to. His smile told Joe everything he needed to know. Joe let out the breath he'd held for damn near the whole conversation.

"You're really mine," Joe confirmed, his confidence once more sky high.

Scott turned to face Joe properly. He took a step toward him. There was no nervousness in him, no sign that he wasn't completely sure of Joe's acceptance of him.

Another half step forward, and Scott was in Joe's arms. It would have been perfect if there hadn't been a stupid amount of fabric between them. Leather was all well and good, but it shouldn't have been allowed to separate skin from skin.

Capturing Scott's lips in a kiss that demanded nothing less than complete submission, Joe walked Scott backward into the living room. Scott reached up and wrapped his arms around Joe's neck, accepting every decision Joe made as if nothing could ever feel more natural to him.

Sofa. Skin. Sex.

Joe had done everything he could to make Scott feel wanted and safe. Now, it was time to get on with the rest of the night's activities. Joe had to direct them to the sofa, get rid of their clothes, and find the skin beneath. Then, finally, *blessedly*, they'd be allowed to screw each other without any concerns or uncertainties hanging over their heads.

Joe had only taken a few steps when he realised that he should have specified that the guys should stack the boxes on the other side of the room. A whole obstacle course now existed between where they stood and the sofa.

Breaking the kiss for a moment, Joe looked over his shoulder toward the bedroom; his nice, familiar bedroom with all his toys within easy reach, and with a completely clear access route.

No. That space was still all about him; it would take time to change that. The sofa was going to be about them right from the start, and they were bloody well going to have sex on it tonight.

"S-sir?" Scott asked. The *why the hell have you stopped kissing me* part of the question remained unsaid, but it hung in the air nevertheless.

"Do you trust me?" Joe asked Scott.

"Yes, sir." He didn't even stutter on the S.

"Good. Hold on to that thought."

* * * * *

Without anything that Scott was willing to consider sufficient warning, Joe picked him up, lifted him over the high back of the sofa, and dropped him. Well-padded cushions softened his landing, but they did nothing to absorb his shock.

Scott squirmed, desperately trying to pull himself up into a sitting position, but his journey over to that side of the sofa had stolen both his coordination and his balance. He flailed like a recently landed fish, and only just sat up in time to see Joe throw himself over the sofa back to join him.

It was impossible for Scott to remain shocked for long, mostly because Joe pounced on him the second he'd recovered from his own less than graceful landing, and pinned him down.

Joe's lips covered Scott's mouth. His hands tugged at Scott's clothes.

"You're allowed to help get us both naked,"

Joe mumbled into the kiss.

From any other man, it would have sounded sarcastic. From Joe, it sounded like a perfectly sensible decision.

A moment ago, Scott didn't have permission to do anything, so it was fine that he'd lay there and merely accepted whatever Joe wanted to do with him. Now that he had permission, lying there idly was no longer an option. It would have been a crime to waste that kind of opportunity.

Scott scrabbled at Joe's T-shirt, pushing it up, desperately trying to get at the skin beneath. Every inch of Joe deserved to be worshiped; and now, Scott knew he was going to have time to do the task justice. He wriggled beneath Joe's body in a concerted effort to touch every bit of him while at the same time desperately trying to get his own trousers off.

Scott had just reached for the tab on his fly — and was sending up thanks that he was finally going to be able to get out of his far too tight trousers — when Joe caught hold of first Scott's right wrist, then his left. With both of his arms suddenly pinned to the sofa seat on either side of his shoulders, Scott was trapped, his fly as firmly fastened as ever.

Joe moved his legs apart to straddle Scott's hips and lifted himself up, parting their bodies so he could stare down at him.

"Mine."

Scott nodded as he fought to catch his breath. "Y-yes. Y-yours," he agreed.

Joe grinned. At some point, his T-shirt had been tossed aside, so had Scott's.

Scott glanced down between their bodies. Joe's

cock was no longer hidden away behind painfully tight layers of fabric. His erection stood proudly away from his body, curving up toward his stomach, hard and glorious. Scott's fingers twitched, but there was no way he could get free.

His permission to touch Joe had been taken away as easily as it had been granted.

"P-please?" Scott asked.

Joe raised an eyebrow. "Please what?"

"Sir," Scott quickly corrected. "Please, s-s-sir."

Joe smiled, but he shook his head. He hadn't been hinting about the honorific. "Tell me what you want."

Scott swallowed. He licked his lips. "Your c-cock." He was surprised just how easy it was to say; to admit that he wanted anything more than whatever scraps of affection Joe might offer him of his own volition. "I w-w-want your cock, sir."

Joe stared down with something that looked very much like success shining in his eyes. "Where?"

Scott didn't drop his gaze from Joe's face for a moment. He looked him straight in the eye. "My m-m-mouth, sir."

It had to be his mouth. Scott wasn't sure he'd be able to stay sane for long enough to get out of those leather trousers. He needed Joe *now*.

* * * * *

"Stay exactly where you are," Joe ordered.

Scott bobbed his head very slightly, as if he'd been about to nod; but remembered just in time that he wasn't supposed to move — not for any reason.

Joe grinned. "You can move your lips and your tongue," he allowed. "It wouldn't be much fun for either of us if you couldn't do that, would it?"

"I understand, s-sir." Scott licked his lips.

Joe released Scott's wrists and straightened up, settling a little more of his weight against Scott's crotch.

There was something wonderfully erotic about binding Scott in place with nothing but an order. Leather could never have entwined itself around Scott's limbs more securely than five simple words from his master.

Stay exactly where you are. There wouldn't be any digging through drawers looking for the key to that particular lock afterwards.

"Good boy," Joe murmured, as he ran his gaze over Scott's half-exposed body. Without really giving it too much thought, Joe wrapped his fist around his own erection.

Scott's cock was trapped inside those very pretty trousers, but Joe had easy access to his own shaft. He'd jacked off to a mental image of Scott so often, masturbating to the sight of the real thing was almost second nature.

Scott whimpered.

Joe didn't need to stare at his own cock to know what it looked like. It was far more fun to watch Scott squirm mentally, knowing he wasn't allowed to wriggle physically.

Scott was so obviously desperate to reach out and touch Joe. Leather cuffs would have been a blessing for him. If bonds had held him in place, it would have been easy.

Joe watched as a frustrated frown deepened across Scott's forehead. He'd have bet everything he had in the world that something less challenging wouldn't have proved to be anywhere near as much fun for Scott in the long run.

There was something in Scott that loved striving to please. Succeeding in obeying his dom against all the odds, would just make his eventual orgasm all the better. Joe smiled. Watching the show wasn't going to do his own climax any harm either. Their kinks fitted together just as perfectly as their bodies always had.

With his hand still working his shaft, Joe lifted his weight forward onto his knees. Scott instantly opened his mouth, as if he might somehow be able to reach the tip of Joe's cock from there.

Joe's grin never faltered. Carefully manoeuvring his way up the sofa, he brought his cock closer to Scott's mouth, just an inch or two at a time.

Scott whimpered. He nipped at his bottom lip. A moment later, his tongue moistened the skin he'd just come so close to splitting. He moaned low down in the back of his throat and swallowed rapidly.

But, as he watched, Joe was well aware that there were a far greater number of things that Scott *didn't* do. He didn't move his wrists from where Joe had pinned them against the sofa. He didn't try to reach out. He didn't complain. He didn't attempt to hurry the process along at all.

Scott took the tiny bit of freedom that Joe had given him — his lips and tongue — and he made the most of it, but he didn't ask for anything more. He didn't try to take anything for himself.

Inching forward, Joe finally had his knees spread to either side of Scott's shoulders. The arm of the sofa was behind Scott's neck, lifting his head and tilting it forward. His position offered his mouth up at a beautiful angle for Joe's cock. It was almost as if the sofa had been designed just for that.

Joe stroked himself again, still denying Scott a taste. Scott once more opened his mouth in readiness. Looking up, he met Joe's eyes. No demand. No request. Just complete acceptance and, quite possibly, a whole lot of hope.

Joe guided his cock to rest against Scott's bottom lip. Pre-cum leaked from the tip and Joe carefully painted both of Scott's lips with it, marking him out as belonging to him in yet another way.

Scott groaned with an extra dose of frustration, but he kept his mouth open and remained motionless while Joe completed his task.

Joe waited for several extra seconds to pass before he nodded. Scott quickly licked his lips, lapping up every trace of pre-cum that lingered there, and swallowing it down with obvious enjoyment.

Scott opened his mouth again, in a silent plea for more. This time, Joe relented. He offered his cock into Scott's mouth so he could taste him properly.

As pretty as it looked, their positions would never enable him to thrust more deeply. Joe didn't try. He only rocked his hips a fraction, more than happy to simply enjoy sliding the head of his cock back and forth across Scott's tongue.

Scott's eyes dropped closed in pleasure; but Joe wasn't going to let anything steal away the sight that lay before him, not even for a second. Joe kept his eyes open and took in every detail.

"Good boy."

Scott blinked his eyes open when he heard the praise, just as Joe thought he would. Their eyes locked. Joe smiled down at him and thrust his hips just a little more quickly, moving the tip of his cock more rapidly against Scott's tongue.

It would have been so easy to get off on the way Scott's mouth felt, but Joe wanted more. He remained where he was as long as he could without risking an unintended orgasm, teasing himself as much as he did Scott; but eventually, he had to fall still.

"I want your arse," he announced, gritting his teeth to hold himself back from coming.

Scott murmured what sounded very much like an acknowledgement that it was a bloody wonderful idea.

Joe tortured himself with just a few more shallow thrusts before he pulled away. "You're allowed to do absolutely anything that will speed us up," he said as he dragged himself up onto his feet.

Scott launched himself upright, already scrambling at his own fly.

Joe grabbed a condom and lube out of the back pocket of his jeans, then tossed them onto the sofa. He turned his attention to helping Scott undo his jammed fly. Apparently deciding that Joe would be a lot quicker dealing with the zip on his own, Scott snatched up the condom, opened it, and reached out to Joe in return.

Every movement Scott made was strong and confident. He had permission, and he evidently wasn't going to question it. He wrapped his fingers around Joe's shaft, steadying his cock as he rolled the condom down with his other hand.

Joe finally managed to tug Scott's fly down. Turning him around, Joe pushed him down onto the sofa. Scott reacted in plenty of time to break his fall, and he willingly crawled across the cushions to brace himself on the far arm to make room for Joe to kneel behind him.

Scott's trousers were so tight, it would have taken far more patience than Joe possessed to wait for him to squirm out of them entirely. He only pushed the leather down as far as was absolutely necessary before he slicked his fingers and slid them against Scott's hole.

Working quickly, he soon had Scott ready for him. Steadying Scott with his hands on his hips, Joe lined up behind him. Pushing forward, he lodged himself deep within Scott's body. It had never been harder for him to stop himself coming on the first thrust.

* * * * *

Scott frantically tightened his grip on the sofa arm; trying to both maintain his balance, and to control himself so he didn't come without permission.

It was almost impossible to process all the pleasure that rushed through him as Joe's cock rubbed against his prostate again and again. As if determined to drive Scott mad with need, Joe ploughed even deeper inside him, setting a relentless pace from the first moment their bodies came together.

"You're allowed to come whenever you want to."

Scott was completely incapable of answering. Whimpering, he tried to spread his knees further apart, but it was no use. His trousers wrapped around his thighs just as tightly as they'd ever imprisoned his cock, making it impossible for him to spread his legs for Joe.

Looking for another option, Scott lowered his head toward the sofa arm. Arching his back, he offered his arse up as high as he could. He wasn't sure what it did for Joe, but the slight change in angle caused pretty white lights to dance and spiral behind Scott's eyelids.

He cried out, and it was all over. Any thoughts of lasting long enough to make it a marathon session died; so did quite a few of Scott's more pleasure-prone brain cells.

Gasping for breath, he tried to pull himself together well enough to apologise for coming so soon, but there was no time. Joe's grip on his hips tightened until Scott knew there would be pretty marks left there for quite some time.

Joe's thrusts sped up. He yelled out less than a minute after Scott. He'd lasted just long enough for Scott to recover in time to enjoy feeling Joe come too.

He collapsed over Scott's back as his hips eventually stilled. A few nudges later, Scott realised that Joe was telling him to straighten his legs and lay down properly. Once he understood the order, Scott was more than happy to obey. He quickly wriggled around until he laid full length on the sofa with his head on the low, cushioned arm.

Joe separated their bodies, but he didn't try to change the way he lay over Scott. His body covered Scott from top to toe; almost all of his weight pressing down on him.

"Too heavy?" Joe asked.

Scott smiled. "No, s-sir. Feels g-g-good."

Joe made a vague noise that let Scott know he'd heard. It vibrated through Joe's chest and into Scott's torso. The space between Joe's skin and the sofa cushions was snug and warm. Scott turned his head slightly in an effort to make his position one hundred percent comfortable.

His collar shifted around his neck, as if on purpose, just to remind him of its presence.

"You okay with everything?" Joe checked after a while.

"Yes, s-sir." Scott only hesitated for a second before he shyly spoke up again. "Thank you for having all my s-s-stuff brought here."

"No problem," Joe said, his voice still thick with a mixture of deep relaxation and a strong inclination toward sleep.

"Is there a r-reason why you never g-g-got a sofa before, sir?" Scott said, just as sleepy as Joe, but knowing he'd forget to ask if he gave in to slumber with the intention of posing the question later.

"Never had a sub I wanted to sit and relax with as well as screw around with," Joe said. He pressed a kiss against Scott's neck, and shifted his weight so he lay more alongside Scott than directly on top of him.

It didn't put any extra distance between them;

it just made their positions ones they could maintain comfortably for far longer.

Scott smiled. Yes, that made sense. Belonging to Joe wasn't a fleeting, temporary thing. Guys had to be comfortable if they were going to stay together forever.

Scott turned more serious. Even though he knew what he wanted to say, he wasn't entirely sure how to utter the words, or if the time was right. He cleared his throat. "Are you going to think I'm s-s-soppy if I tell you I l-love you, s-sir?"

Joe gave a deep chuckle. "I'm not that much of a hypocrite that I could object to you saying it any time."

Scott frowned. "S-sir?"

"What do you think it says on the tag on your collar?"

Scott found the tag with his fingers, but he realised that he still didn't know what any engraving on it might say.

"On one side it says: *Property of Joe Stuart*," Joe whispered in his ear. "And on the other side it says: *Given to Scott Evans, With Love.*

Scott smiled. He didn't say anything else before they both drifted off to sleep. He didn't need to. There wasn't anything left to say.

About the Author

Kim is a bisexual submissive from Wales (UK). First published in 2008, she has since released 100 BDSM erotic romance titles ranging from short stories to full-length novels. Having worked with a host of fantastic e-publishers, she has just moved into self-publishing.

While she has occasionally ventured towards other pairings, Kim's first love is still, and probably always will be, Male/Male stories. But, no matter what the pairing, from paranormal to contemporary, and from the sweet to the intense, everything she writes will always feature three things - Kink, Love and a Happy Ending.

You can find out more about Kim's books on her website kimdare.com.

Series

Werewolves & Dragons
The Avian Shifters
Kinky Cupid
FIT Guys
Thrown to the Lions
Rawlings Men
Sex Sells
Sun, Sea and Submission
The Whole A-Z
Pack Discipline
G-A-Y Lust Bites
Perfect Timing
Collared
Pushing the Envelope
Kinky Quickies

Kim has also written several free short stories.
You can also find links to them on her website.

www.ingramcontent.com/pod-product-compliance
Lightning Source LLC
Chambersburg PA
CBHW020824030726
47496CB00001B/79